Best wishes –
Barbara Anne King

The California Immigrant

A Novel

Barbara Anne King

First Edition

Cypress Point Press

ISBN: 978-1-7335369-0-5

Book Cover Design by Jenny Q, Historical Fiction Book Covers

Disclaimer

This is a work of fiction. Howwever, the author tried to stay true to known historical facts but may have taken a few creative liberties with them in order to better serve the story. Names, characters, business, events and incidents are either the products of the author's imagination or are used in a fictional way.

To my family and friends who made Watsonville their home. And to my children whose ancestors lived this story.

Author's Note

I was working on another project when I came across some very interesting material about the early history of Watsonville which I knew little about. It inspired me to write a book set in the first part of the Twentieth Century which would allow me to play out the events in real time. Coincidentally, I was planning my first trip to Croatia from where my paternal grandparents immigrated to America. Ancestry research led to some interesting facts about my grandfather that helped inform the book. I have read many books about World War II but none that are set in a small American town where so many momentous events took place, especially those related to the war in the Pacific. I only wish I had known more about this history growing up. And so, I wrote a fictional story as a record of life in Watsonville during an extraordinary period of time. I hope you get as much out of reading this book as I did writing it.

Chapter 1

August 1904

Martin Petrovich walked out of the apartment, carrying an old suitcase bound with twine, shutting the door behind him. He wound his way through the narrow alleys, up and down stairs, past pillars and posts, until he got to the main road running through Old Town Dubrovnik. He thought he would at least come across one friend who would bid him goodbye, who would wish him Godspeed, who would tell him he'd be missed. But Dubrovnik at this hour was a ghost town, the sun not yet making its presence known. He felt abandoned to the fates, friendless and forgotten. Where was Marika selling vegetables from her cart? Where was Father Novak scattering feed for the pigeons? Where was Tony readying his shop for the fresh catch of the day? None of them were there to say goodbye.

Martin wanted to look back for them one more time, but he knew the Bible warned against that—always counseling to move forward—so that is what he did. But he couldn't help but feel sad he would never see his home again. Martin walked up the ramps to where the city gate stood open and went through its Renaissance arch for the last time. It was all he could do to resist looking back at the city's patron, St. Blaise, presiding in a niche above the arch. Martin crossed the drawbridge and glanced to his left across the Adriatic Sea, which dawn still had in its grip—a gray veil of mist hiding the azure blue waters. This is what loneliness feels like. It is the color gray—neither black nor white—just a dull feeling of emptiness.

Then directly ahead, he spotted the wagon with his father, mother, and sisters already aboard. His older and younger brothers, Peter and John, stood holding the reins. Peter stepped forward. "What's taken you so long?" He grabbed the suitcase and tossed it into the wagon. Martin was about to climb aboard when an argument broke out between a man and woman on the street across from them. It caused him to hesitate while he turned toward the source of the yelling. "It's only a man trying to shoo the Serbian woman away," said Peter. "She should know by now that she is not welcome to sell her wares here." At that, there was nothing left for Martin to do but climb aboard.

His father made a clucking sound while shaking the reins to signal the horses to move ahead and pull their load. It was only a short distance to the port of Gruz where the ship to Trieste would be waiting, but the bumps and ruts made it slow going. Martin hoped they wouldn't break a wheel spoke which would be nothing short of a disaster on this day when he was holding a ticket on the only ship available for weeks. But luck was with him and they arrived with time to spare.

Martin jumped off the wagon and paused to catch his suitcase, which John had hurled overboard. Then he helped his sisters, Veronika and Zara, down. Peter had already gone around to the other side to help his mother off her seat. His father managed on his own and handed the reins to John when he alighted.

Martin took one look at his family and wanted to cry. Their faces wore sad looks; his mother looked frightened. He could tell tears were welling up in her eyes and soon would be streaming down her face. If he didn't leave now, he never would. He kissed his sisters and shook hands with his brothers, giving them hugs as well. Then he shook hands with his father and hugged and kissed his mother several times. Her tears were flowing and soon his sisters were crying, too. His father and brothers tried to be stoic, even though water welled up in their eyes.

At sixteen years old, Martin now had the responsibility of a man on his shoulders. He was tall, almost six feet, and strong as well as handsome, with dark wavy hair and gray-green eyes. He was wearing wool trousers, a fisherman's sweater, knit hat, and boots. Over his arm he carried a leather jacket, which he would need for additional warmth.

He had to succeed in the New World so he could help his family who stayed behind in Croatia. Fortunately, his Uncle Anton promised him a job at his restaurant in San Francisco. It would be a good start if he could just get there. Being alone, poor and not speaking a word of English, it would be a miracle if he made it. But Slavs are a tough breed—they don't give up—not easily, not ever. He had fortitude running through his blood. Little did he know how much he would need it.

Martin boarded the small sailing boat that would take him along the Adriatic to Trieste where he would board the steam ship for America. He stood on deck, looking out at his family who was waving and now seemed happy for him. Then he couldn't help himself from turning to get one last glimpse of Dubrovnik, the fortified city that had stood since the 10th century, despite enemy attacks, and would probably remain standing until the end time. The ramparts, rising to great heights, were a masterful work of engineering that could be reached by stairs and walked upon circling the town below. But it was the view from that vantage point that Martin regretted abandoning. He would gaze over the clear, blue sea past islands close to shore to watch for merchant ships returning with their wares. The Croatians were great seamen and ship builders having once ruled the Mediterranean not to conquer but to trade. Their ships flew a white flag with the single Latin word *Libertad,* meaning freedom, to alert foreign peoples they came in peace. As soon as a ship landed, Martin was on the dock, helping to unload in an effort to learn what the cargo contained.

Martin was awakened from his reverie by the sound of sails unfurling, their flapping a sign the wind would be strong. It was not long until the crew threw off the lines and the captain steered his ship into the sea where they would make their way through Croatia's archipelago, second to Greece's in the Mediterranean, with over seven hundred islands. Nearby Korcula, a favorite of Martin's, would be one of the first they passed. He often stopped there when fishing with his father to relax on the beach before returning to Ston, where most of their fishing fleet was moored. Korcula claims to be the birthplace of Marco Polo. It is famous for the two swords dance known as the Moreska but even more notable for being the first place in the world to end slavery in 1214.

The sailboat tacked its way through the archipelago past the islands of Brac and Hvar, nearby Split, the town built inside Diocletian's palace. Then up the coast aiming toward Zadar, maneuvering around the Istrian peninsula past the towns of Pula, Rovinj, and Porec until finally reaching Trieste for embarkation. Once the ship was tied up at the dock, all the passengers disembarked, making their way toward to office of emigration.

Martin took his place in line but grew impatient with the wait. It seemed many of the people ahead of him, especially families, did not have all their paperwork in order, which held up the entire process for everyone. He could feel his impatience rising. Martin wished he could just take a number and comeback when it was his turn so he could explore Trieste, an Italian city with an abundance of Austrian influence most notable in its architecture. He would especially like to stroll around the main square, Piazza Unita d'Italia, which he spied across from the port featuring a number of cafes. He'd love to sit down at one of them and have a coffee right now. Martin did not know much about Trieste other than the talk he'd heard about an attempt here to assassinate the Emperor Franz Joseph. Croatians disliked living under the emperor's rule, but even if he had died, there would have been another emperor to take his place so they would have been no better off.

Finally, Martin's papers were processed and he was issued an Austrian passport. He went back to the port in search of the steamship *Carpathia*, which would take him to America. Once he found it, he went up the gangplank and was directed to steerage several layers below deck in the bowels of the ship. Single men had one side and families the other. He entered the quarters already smelling of body odor and was lucky to find a lower berth still available. Not only would it be easier to get in and out, but sleeping low would ensure he would not be tossed about as much especially during rough seas. As soon as Martin struck his claim to the bunk, he headed back upstairs to stand on deck for the departure.

Soon he could hear the engines starting and saw the gangplank pulled up. The steamship slowly pulled out of the port and entered the Adriatic. Martin would get a chance to see the Dalmatian coast again before heading toward the Atlantic. In much less time than it took to sail, the ship had reached Dubrovnik. Even at a distance it was an awesome sight that made him proud of what his ancestors had accomplished. The ship turned to enter the Mediterranean, skirting the boot of Italy as it headed toward the strait of Gibraltar before entering the Atlantic. Now Martin was in unfamiliar territory, and knew he was really on his way to America, a voyage that would take nearly two weeks. He hoped the seas would be calm since the steam ship did not need wind to move. The first day he was blessed and even spotted some dolphins following the boat. He knew they would bring good luck.

CHAPTER 2

About the third day, the sky drew dark and thunder blared, sending out one boom after another. The sea responded with swells that developed into huge waves beating against the sides of the ship and tossing it around like a flimsy toy. Martin had heard stories of ships being so battered they came apart, scattering their cargo and passengers in the ocean where they either drowned or were devoured by sharks.

Just the thought of sharks sent a shiver through Martin, causing him to touch the crucifix he wore around his neck as if it were a talisman warding off evil. Martin clung to his cot to wait out the storm as its fierceness grew and it lashed out in fury. The night had been a long one. What little sleep he got was filled with nightmares of sharks and sea monsters. But when day dawned, the sun was shining and the seas had returned to calm.

Martin got dressed and went back up on deck to look around. He spotted another boy about his age whom he had seen in his bunkroom. They began to chat about their voyage—where they were from, where they were going. Michael Latskovich was from Split. He was taller than Martin and had blond hair that was cropped short. His eyes were a clear blue, like the Adriatic, features even except for his nose, which was somewhat bulbous like many Croatians. "I heard some families are sick," Michael told Martin.

"Oh no. I hope it's not the plague. Best we stay away from them." Michael nodded in agreement. "And stay out here in the fresh air as much as possible. Breathing in the stench down below can't be healthy." Again, Michael nodded.

The next few days, the seas stayed calm and on occasion, Martin would spot a whale blowing water through its spout at a distance. He scanned the sea for more creatures, but they eluded him—even the dolphins, which he hoped would return to guide them. Martin took a deep breath of the fresh, clean ocean air with its fishy fragrance. He felt a cold coming on and didn't want to be sick when he arrived at Ellis Island. He had heard too many stories of people getting turned away or at the very least having to wait until a doctor cleared them. He did not want that to happen to him, to have anything jeopardize his entrance into America, the home of the free.

Freedom—that's what he most yearned for. Living under the oppressive Habsburg regime did not offer an opportunity for a better life. His parents did all they could do to cobble together the bare necessities. If the sea did not offer up its riches, they would be too poor to survive. Martin took in a few more inhales while noticing the clouds forming in the west and knew that meant another period of rough seas.

He went back down below, covering his mouth and nose with a handkerchief to filter the odors and germs. It was going to be a long night. But first he would have some dinner to hold him over. Martin grabbed his silverware and plate and headed to the kitchen where a mystery stew awaited, served from kettles. He found it difficult to make out what was in it. At least a home, his mother always provided a good meal with the main course, fish, always being recognizable. Thank goodness there would be an end to his journey in a few days but how long he wasn't sure.

Martin's stomach was rumbling by the time he got back to his bunk. He certainly did not want to add to the disgusting smells already hanging in the air by vomiting. He opened a canteen to take a sip of water and took deep breaths through his mouth. That seemed to settle his stomach. Now he just had to try to fall asleep, but the swells were mounting and he feared what was yet to come. In the middle of the night, he awoke to the sounds of screams and waves crashing against the ship, making horrific sounds as if the end of the world was upon them. There was nothing he could do but wait it out and hope. He fingered his crucifix while saying a prayer.

At times like these, one needs faith. He fell asleep murmuring the Our Father and Hail Mary prayers. When he awoke, all was calm again.

Martin pulled on his pants and grabbed his jacket as he headed back up the stairs to stand on deck. Michael was already there, looking a bit peaked. "How did you fare last night?"

"Not good but I'm still here as you can see."

"Have you spotted anything out at sea?" And just as the words came out, a pod of dolphins appeared alongside the ship. "My prayers have been answered."

The two boys hung out on the deck for several hours. Michael offered Martin a cigarette and they both lit up. "I rolled these myself. I only have a few smokes left, which need to last me the rest of the trip. But it's always nice to share one with a friend." After taking a few drags, Martin told Michael about growing up in Dubrovnik and fishing with his father. "The first time I was only eight years old and we went out into the sea at night fishing for anchovies and sardines."

Michael told Martin about his life in Split, the medieval city built inside Diocletian's Roman palace. "My father has a small grocery store. Now I miss all the fruits and vegetables we had so abundantly at our table. I hope I will have them again in America. My uncle is a farmer near San Francisco and that's where I'm going."

"San Francisco. That's where I'm going, too, but to work in my uncle's restaurant. I only know a little about cooking from my mother but I'm going to learn to be a chef. People always need to eat. So, feeding them should ensure I can always put bread on my own table."

"Do you want to own a restaurant one day?"

"Yes, that's my dream…be a businessman…my own boss…make money for my family."

CHAPTER 3

The rest of the journey was smooth sailing for the passengers aboard the *Carpathia*. The captain had the crew pass the word that they were nearing New York Harbor where the immigrants could catch their first glimpse of the Statue of Liberty. She came into view amid gasps of awe that could be heard throughout the ship. As they drew near, Martin saw the colossus up close, holding out her arms and lighting the way.

Upon docking, the first and second-class passengers were let off first since they did not have to go through Ellis Island. Each steerage passenger was given a tag to wear with a manifest number then, like animals, they were herded onto barges to make the short journey to Ellis Island. Martin and Michael stayed together so they had each other for support. Once they debarked, an interpreter came up to them, speaking Croatian. This was an unexpected surprise but not out of the ordinary since interpreters spoke at least six languages and sometimes twice that number.

Now it was time for the medical inspections. Martin knew he would pass since he didn't limp or have any health issues. But regardless, he would have his eyes checked for trachoma, a terrible disease that could blind and deny a person entrance to America. The buttonhook exams put fear into even the bravest when the doctor took the hook to invert the upper eyelid to check for signs.

Once that was over, Martin moved to the area where inspectors were asking a series of questions of immigrants. He passed with flying colors and was admitted. He looked around for Michael but did not see him in the crowd so he proceeded to the moneychanger. Martin had just enough money for the train ride to San Francisco with a little to spare for food. He took the change and put it into his money belt and asked directions to the ferry terminal where he could buy his train ticket.

To his surprise, Michael was already there in line. Martin called out to him and they waved. "I'll wait for you inside," Michael said. But when it was Martin's turn at the ticket window, he found he was short train fare. *That moneychanger must have cheated me.* And it was not uncommon for that to happen to new clueless arrivals who were an easy mark. Now what?

As he left the ferry terminal, a man in a dark suit approached him, speaking Italian, which he could understand a little since many Italians lived in Dubrovnik. "Do you need work?" Martin nodded yes. "Then follow me." *What choice do I have*? *I need to make enough money to get to California*. So, he followed the man in the navy, pinstripe suit with the swarthy face and narrow eyes to an area known as the seaport located on the East River near the Brooklyn Bridge. Little did Martin know that this area was the domain of river pirates and mobsters. But he may have suspected something was amiss in the neighborhood populated with whorehouses, dog-fighting pits, and drug addicts. However, as they got closer, he could smell fish. And finally he saw it. More fish than he had ever seen before in his life and more varieties—in fact, millions of fish a day went through here. This was the Fulton Fish Market and Martin was about to become a fishmonger.

The man in the pinstripe suit guided him into the fish market, which was already done for the day. Work started at the wee hours of the morning and ended well before noon. The man approached a group of workers and began speaking in a language Martin assumed was Italian. Then the man, whom the others had called Vito, said, "Come with me." Martin followed him through the fish market littered with fish heads and entrails until Vito came upon another Italian man in a bloody white apron. The two men talked while Martin waited. Then the fishmonger, named Luigi, handed Martin an apron and broom. "Clean," he said. Not knowing what to do, Martin looked around and noticed others sweeping up the debris, scooping it up and putting it in a garbage bin. Martin began imitating what he saw while Luigi wiped down tables, shoving more blood and guts onto the floor.

This was not the American dream Martin had had in mind when he left home and endured a miserable sea voyage. But he didn't know what else he could do to get the money he needed for the train fare. He worked for a couple of hours and was told to return at two in the morning. He had no watch so he wondered how he would be able to tell the time. Martin left and walked aimlessly around lower Manhattan until he came upon Battery Park, which had benches scattered about. Some were already occupied by sleeping bums, or were they actually immigrants, like him, exhausted from a day's work with no place to call home? Fortunately, he found an empty bench and laid himself down to rest but fell into a deep sleep.

When he awoke it was still dark. He hurried back to the fish market, which was just beginning to set up again with trucks full of fish to be off-loaded. Martin wove his way through the confusion until he came upon Luigi. "You are late," he said, pointing to his watch. Martin shrugged. Luigi shook his head and then took Martin to a truck where he grumbled something. Martin understood that he wanted him to bring the crates of fish to his table. He picked the first one up. It was heavy but full of the fresh fish aroma he loved that reminded him a bit of home. When all the crates had been moved, Luigi showed Martin how to open them. Then while Martin removed the fish, Luigi began cleaning them and cutting them into filets.

The work was going smoothly, and Martin began to feel at ease in a place that had some familiarity. Then he heard Luigi let out a cry, and turning his head, he saw blood gushing from one of Luigi's hands. Martin quickly grabbed a towel for Luigi to hold to stem the flow. Between winces of pain, Luigi cursed and cursed over and over again. Martin noticed he had barely fileted half the fish so he flew into action, taking a fish, slicing off its head and tail, slicing it down the middle, removing its entrails and bones. Luigi stood by astonished. He had never seen anyone with such skill. "Where did you learn to do this?" he asked.

Martin shrugged and said, "Home…father."

"You have saved the day for me," Luigi said as he gave Martin a pat on the back.

Martin continued to filet fish for the customers until closing time arrived. Then he went back to cleanup—first wiping tables down and then sweeping up the floor. He left feeling a sense of pride in a job well done. But he had not yet been paid. Tomorrow he would ask about the money, but for now he was content that he had proved his worth.

The rest of the week Luigi had Martin filet the fish since his hand was in no shape to do it. On Friday, he finally received his pay. Martin counted enough for the train but not enough for food to carry him through the journey. He would have to work another week to have what he needed.

As he left the fish market, he saw Vito standing nearby wearing a bowler hat and smoking a cigar. "Come here, kid," he said. Martin walked over to where he stood. "Do you want to make some money, big money?" he asked.

Martin only understood that he was offering him a job so he said, "Yes."

"Good. Now take this satchel to the address on this paper and when you have delivered it, come back for your pay."

Martin was naïve to the ways of the world, so he did as he was told. When he got to the address on the lower east side after asking directions several times, he knocked on the door and a man, another Italian, answered. Martin was about to hand him the satchel when a fellow brandishing a gun ran up the steps, grabbed it, and began shooting. Martin jumped off the stoop and starting running, and he didn't stop until he got to the ferry terminal. He went right up to the ticket window and said, "San Francisco," while opening his money belt and laying out its entire contents. He was surprised that the attendant left him a few coins to spare.

It wasn't long before the ferry arrived to take him to Jersey City where he would catch the Trans Continental train. He was glad to be away from lower Manhattan and especially Vito. He now realized he was a bad man but not until much later would he realize he had been involved with a precursor to the Mafia.

The Transcontinental Express was waiting on the tracks. Martin walked down the line of cars to find third class. He passed the luxury first-class coaches, which would take passengers less than four days to reach the West Coast. But third-class passengers were not as lucky. When Martin finally reached his boarding place, it was a freight car attached to the back of the passenger coaches. He climbed aboard and found the car filled with people who appeared to be immigrants sitting shoulder to shoulder on hard wooden benches, eyes downcast, faces resigned. Someone told Martin the trip could take them up to ten days since freight cars were often forestalled to allow passenger trains to pass. Ten days was a long time to go without food and water. Thank goodness he had had the presence of mind to fill up his canteen. And he still had the hard tack and dried apricots his mother had packed. Somehow he would have to stretch them.

When the train pulled out of the station and he got his last look at New York City, he was not the least bit sad to leave it behind. Nothing much good had happened there except his entrance into the US and the sight of The Statue of Liberty when he arrived, a hopeful greeting for an immigrant searching for freedom. But he had learned freedom also has its downside. As far as he knew, Croatia didn't have hoodlums perpetrating crime on people. But now he was aware that America did, and he would keep his guard up.

CHAPTER 4

The train trip was worse than Martin imagined it would be. The car was cramped, noisy, smelly—as putrid as steerage on the ship. Babies cried almost nonstop, husbands and wives argued, and men came to blows over the cramped conditions. Not to mention everyone was hungry. Martin wished he had enough food to share, but he had to save everything for himself and he had to be secretive about it. He would wait until it was dark before he pulled out a bit of hard tack or dried apricots so others would not try to steal it, and then he would hold the piece in his mouth allowing it to soften so the food could slide down his throat without chewing so as not attract unwanted attention.

The days dragged on and on and on. Martin wished he were back on the ship for all its drawbacks. At least he could breathe fresh air on the deck, sleep in a warm bed and get a hot meal even if it was only a bit of gruel. He felt like a prisoner doing penance, the train accommodations sheer torture.

The only saving grace was that when the car stopped, they could open the door to allow fresh air to circulate and could get out to walk around. At the next opportunity, Martin climbed out of the car and spent time walking around in the sunshine. He had counted the sunrises so this must have been his sixth day on the train, but he had heard they still had to cross the Sierra Nevada Mountains, which he had not yet seen.

When he got back to his seat, he was hungry and decided to have a little hard tack to stem the stomach pangs. He reached into his knapsack and felt for the secret pocket at the bottom but nothing was there. Then he put the knapsack on his lap where he could peer into it, but the hard tack and fruit seemed to have vanished. In a panic, he dumped the contents of his knapsack on his lap to search through everything. Still he came up empty-handed. That was when he heard the snickering and turned to see two men across from him with smirks on their faces. Then he knew he had been robbed and would have no more food to sustain him for the rest of the journey.

Each day seemed like an eternity until the mountains came into view that separated them from the West Coast. At last there was an end in sight. Martin was close to starving with only a few drops of water left to quench his thirst. He tried to sleep so time would pass more swiftly but found his anxiety kept him wide-awake. After what seemed like an eternity, the train finally made it past the mountain range and roared onto its final destination—San Francisco, California.

When the train finally came to a stop, Martin was among the first to touch his feet down on the West Coast. Both tired and elated, he moved through the train station to the street bustling with activity. He stopped for a minute to orient himself, and that's when the magnificent San Francisco Bay made its appearance. He blinked several times to make sure it wasn't a mirage or that he wasn't dreaming of the Adriatic. But it was real and he knew he had reached his new home, which reminded him of the one he had left behind with the beautiful sea and hills paired in surreal splendor.

Martin stood still, gazing at the view for some time before a more pressing matter came to mind. He needed to find his uncle. Martin had put the address of his uncle's restaurant in his money belt that he now removed. The address was written in both Croatian and English—522 Sacramento Street. He had no idea how to get there but would find someone to ask. At first he tried to stop people on the street, but they always seemed to be in a hurry if not afraid of the young man looking like a beggar and speaking a language they had never heard. Then it occurred to him to go back into the train station to ask a clerk. At least he could show him the address written in English.

Luck was finally with Martin as he found a friendly, helpful clerk who went to the trouble to draw a map for him to follow. He sent him off, pointing him in the right direction. Martin was not used to reading maps, other than nautical charts, but this one was fairly simple and it appeared the restaurant was not far. After some twists and turns and a few retraced steps, he finally arrived at 522 Sacramento Street with a sign out front announcing Adriatic Coast Cafe.

Before entering, Martin buttoned his coat and ran his fingers through his wavy hair to spruce up his appearance. He didn't want his uncle's first impression of him to be a bad one. Then he put his hand on the door handle to open it but it wouldn't budge…it was locked. Now what was he supposed to do? He peered in the windows but no one seemed to be around. Martin had no idea what time it was, but he guessed it was too early for the restaurant to open. They'd have to show up sooner or later, he thought. So he sat down on the stoop, leaned against the doorway, and fell asleep from pure exhaustion.

The door finally opened causing, Martin to wake up and nearly fall onto the floor. A man, dressed like a waiter, started yelling at him, taking him for a bum. Martin had no idea what he was saying but tried to respond politely in Croatian. "My name is Martin Petrovich. I am looking for my uncle who is the chef here."

The waiter raised his eyebrows in surprise and then responded in Croatian. "He has been expecting you. Come this way." Martin followed him through the small restaurant making his way around the rustic wood tables already set for lunch. The waiter introduced Martin to a vital-looking man who resembled his mother. He was shorter than Martin and somewhat portly with short blond hair, blue eyes, and the Croatian trademark: a bulbous nose. As soon as he saw Martin, he wrapped his strong arms around him in a bear hug and said, "Welcome to America. We are so glad you are finally here. But you don't look well…too skinny and pale. The first thing you need is a good meal. Sit down at the table here and I will make you something to eat. Vlad, bring Martin some water and milk while he waits."

Uncle Anton set a plate of seafood risotto down in front of Martin, along with a green salad, bread and butter. Not only was this a feast but also it reminded Martin of home and his mother's cooking. How did Uncle Anton know that seafood risotto was his favorite dish in the whole wide world?

"Now, the last lunch has been served and eaten and the last patron is out the door, fully satisfied, at least that is my hope. Let's sit and talk." He motioned to Vlad to join them.

Martin was too exhausted when he entered the restaurant but now he noticed it had a typical Croatian décor—white stucco walls, beamed ceiling and framed pictures of Dubrovnik on all the walls. It felt like an oasis in the desert. Martin sat down on a wooden chair to join his Uncle and Vlad at the table.

"Martin," Uncle Anton began, "this is your cousin Vladimir." Vlad was tall and thin with dark hair, almost black, a Roman nose and brown eyes topped with thick black eyebrows. Martin opened his eyes wide in surprise. His mother hadn't mentioned cousins. Then he gave a wide smile and extended his arm to shake hands as he took his measure.

"Martin, we expected you a couple of weeks ago. What happened that you did not arrive on time?"

"Oh, it's a long story. First, I was short changed by the clerk at Ellis Island and needed to make more money to afford the train. A man got me a job at the Fulton Fish Market."

"Fulton Fish Market. I've heard of it. It is a big operation and they process lots of fish."

"Yes, I have never seen so many fish in one place in my life, except maybe for a school of sardines in the Adriatic. Anyway, I finally had the money to travel third class by train but those cars take much longer than the first and second coaches. But at last I made it."

"Now"—Uncle Anton became serious—"you have come here to work and earn money so you can prosper and help your family back home, especially my poor sister Marija, oh how I miss her. But now back to the job. You will come here every day with me and not leave until I do. If you want to learn how to run a restaurant and be a chef, you have to start at the bottom—washing dishes. That will allow you to be in the kitchen to observe what everyone is doing and basically learn how a restaurant operation works. Does that sound good to you?"

"Yes, Uncle, I would like to learn everything you know about cooking and running a business. I want to have my own restaurant one day."

"That's the American way, Martin, start your own business, be your own boss, get rich in the process. And one more thing. You will start English lessons right away. You have to know the language to get ahead."

Martin was having trouble keeping his eyes open and let out a big yawn. Uncle Anton and Vlad looked at each other and nodded. "Martin, I can see you're very tired and know you have been through quite an ordeal. Vlad will take you home where your Aunt Mirna will make you comfortable. She already has a room waiting for you."

CHAPTER 5

Martin grabbed his suitcase and followed Vlad out of the restaurant. At that moment, he heard a clanking like some sort of bell and the sound of metal on metal. Vlad put out his arm to hold Martin back while a vehicle passed by with a swish of wind. "What is that monstrosity?" Martin asked.

"It's called a cable car. They're a great way to get up and down the hills of San Francisco if you can afford the fare. They've been around the city as long as I can remember."

"Everything is so new to me here. We have nothing like it in Dubrovnik. People either walk or ride in carts pulled by animals."

"You'll also see some rich people driving themselves in automobiles. They're the latest invention."

"First, there's a train that goes all across the country, then there's cable cars traveling up and down hills, and now you're telling me there are motorized carts that people drive themselves. This country is amazing."

"That's true. People are always inventing something new to make our lives better. But unfortunately, not all of us can afford the new gadgets. Anyway, we have arrived home. Follow me up the steps."

Martin stood for a moment on the sidewalk, looking up at the townhouse in front of him. It was a narrow building with a bay window and an elegant oak door with a brass knocker in the shape of an anchor.

"Come on," Vlad called. "What are you waiting for?" Martin climbed up the steep steps entering into a hall with a high ceiling and crystal chandelier. As soon as she heard their voices, Aunt Mirna appeared to welcome

Martin to their home, kissing him on both cheeks in the European-style. Aunt Mirna was full of zest. She had a round body, dark eyes, and black hair streaked with gray, worn in a bun.

"I have tea and cookies for you in the kitchen. Then I will show you to your room where you can rest until dinner."

Martin set down his suitcase in the hallway and followed Aunt Mirna into the kitchen. It was modern compared to his mother's with a tile floor, wooden cabinets, and a large black stove. In the middle, a table covered with a floral oil cloth was already set for tea. Aunt Mirna asked Martin to take a seat while she poured tea and set out the cookies—kolache filled with apricot jam.

Vlad took his leave to head back to the restaurant. Then Aunt Mirna turned to Martin and asked, "How was your journey?"

"About as expected." He did not want to go into all the problems he had encountered with his aunt.

"And how is your family? I have not seen them in many years."

"They are fine but life is hard. Thank goodness the sea always provides."

"Well, finish your tea and then I will take you to your room. You look like you could use a nap."

Martin followed Aunt Mirna back into the hallway where he grabbed his suitcase and then went up the stairs. She opened the door to a small room with two twin beds. "This is my older son's room. Marko's away at the university now but will be home for Christmas when you will have to share the room. But until then you have it to yourself." She then proceeded to show him where he could store his clothes and other items. But when she left, he didn't unpack. He lay down on the bed and fell into a deep, deep sleep.

Two days later, just as Uncle Anton had said, Martin started work at the restaurant. First, he helped unload trucks filled with supplies and groceries, and then he helped put the perishables in a cool place—the icebox for items needing the coolest temperatures. Then he stood by watching his uncle and his helper prepare the food for the various dishes that would be served.

At one point, Uncle Anton tossed him a rag saying, "Go wipe down the tables, then help Vlad set them." Martin did what he was told and in no time the restaurant was ready for customers. At 11:30 a.m., Vlad unlocked the front door, letting in customers already standing in line. Then Martin went back into the kitchen to find out what he needed to do next.

Uncle Anton handed him a couple of dishpans and told him to fill them with water adding soap to one. It wasn't long before Vlad put in the first orders and Uncle Anton and his sous chef prepared the first dishes. Most customers ordered fish—fried sardines, fish stew, pasta with clams and, of course, seafood risotto. When the dirty dishes were brought back by Vlad, Martin was told to scrape the leftovers into the garbage and then wash, rinse, and dry each dish and piece of silverware before setting it on the rack to dry.

There was a system to dishwashing, which Martin learned quickly and his Uncle noticed with approval. Finally, the lunch hour was over and a thorough cleanup began while preparations were made for dinner. There wasn't much of a break between the two but the staff all sat down to share a meal together and talk.

Uncle Anton was the first to speak between bites. "Martin, you learn fast. I was impressed with how efficiently you washed the dishes. You are going to be a great restaurateur one day."

"Thank you, Uncle. I tried my best."

"It certainly showed. Now, starting next week you will get up early and go to English class before coming to work at the restaurant. You need to learn the language if you want to go far in this country."

Martin nodded as he thought about what his uncle had just said. There was so much to learn before he could make his own way. He only hoped he could do it.

Saturday was a big day in the restaurant. It seemed there was never an empty table from lunch through dinner. Martin washed dishes nonstop for hours until finally the *closed* sign was put on the door. Now to wipe down tables, sweep floors, and perform other necessary duties to get the restaurant ready for the next day. When he was done, he looked around and felt pride in the work he had done for his uncle.

When they got home, Aunt Mirna was waiting up with a tea service set on the table. Uncle Anton, Vlad, and Martin sat down, filled their cups with tea, and took a few savories and sweets, which Aunt Mirna had made. Once Uncle Anton had finished his first cup of tea he said, "Martin, tomorrow is Sunday, a day of rest, a family day. The cafe will be closed so we can enjoy some leisure time. First, we will go to church, our own Slavic church, The Nativity of Our Lord, which we Slavs funded with hard-earned donations. You just missed the dedication—such a big celebration of what we can do when we work together. Then we will go to the Slavonic Mutual and Benevolent Society for a little conversation and entertainment. And then we will be home for a lovely dinner prepared by Mirna. She cooks so I can truly have a day off."

CHAPTER 6

On Sunday morning, Martin woke up looking forward to the day ahead. He wanted to take a walk around the city to get himself acclimated and see the sights. Vlad was already having breakfast when he came downstairs so he mentioned his interest in taking a walking tour. "I'd be happy to show you around after church," Vlad said. Martin beamed a wide smile at him, showing his pleasure.

When church was over, Vlad and Martin set out, telling Uncle Anton and Aunt Mirna they would see them later at the Slavonic Society. "First, I want to take you to Nob Hill where you will see how the rich people live." They climbed the hills of California Street being passed by several trolleys along the way. Finally, they reached the top. "These are the mansions of the big four—the men who built the Central Pacific Railroad."

The first one they came to belonged to Leland Stanford. It was a huge structure with many ornamental details and bow windows on the sides. "This is the largest single-family residence in California." The next ones they came to were the homes of Mark Hopkins, Charles Crocker, and Collis Huntington. Martin was awestruck both by these monstrosities the millionaires called home but also by the enormous wealth they represented. Martin stood and looked at the view from the top; for some, America is paved with gold.

Then Vlad led Martin back down the hills until they came to the waterfront, the bay gleaming in the sunlight. "You will notice that many of these businesses are owned by Croatians." Martin looked at the signs on coffee houses, restaurants, saloons, and groceries and recognized many that bore Croatian words. This was the neighborhood where the Slavonic Society was located. Upon entering, Martin immediately heard the sounds of an accordion and felt transported back home.

The room was filled with families—men having drinks while discussing politics, always a popular pastime even in Croatia, women swapping recipes and a bit of gossip, and young people filling the floor to dance the kolo, the traditional circle dance. Martin had no idea so many Croatians lived in San Francisco. Of course, some of them patronized his uncle's restaurant but many Italians did as well as other nationalities he did not easily recognize. Vlad grabbed Martin by the arm and led him over to a group of people their age and introduced him around. Some of them shook his hands, some gave him hugs, and a few girls even kissed him on the cheeks. What a way to get a welcome. I wonder what else is in store for me in this new land.

Martin and Vlad got back to the townhouse just before dinner. "Go wash up," Aunt Mirna said. "Katarina and her husband will soon be here and maybe Marko, too." Martin knew about Marko but Katarina he had not yet heard about. She must be the daughter.

When Martin got back downstairs, Katarina and her husband had just arrived. Uncle Anton made the introductions. "If you had come a year earlier, you would have been invited to the big wedding party and met a lot of pretty Croatian girls."

Katarina at twenty-two was the eldest of the Kovach's three children. She was a pretty blonde with clear blue eyes—the color of the Adriatic Sea. Her high cheekbones, a Slavic trait, gave her a sophisticated look beyond her years and marked her as a real beauty. Her husband, Paul, had straight dark hair, chiseled features, and blue eyes with a hint of green. He was about the same height as Martin, six feet, but had a much slimmer build. He was friendly and offered his hand to Martin.

"Paul owns one of the grocery stores you passed along the waterfront," said Uncle Anton. Martin was impressed—so young and already in business.

"Katarina and I work long hours," said Paul, "but we are making a good living and even save money for a house we hope to buy soon."

"I would like to visit your store one day to learn how a grocery store is run."

"We are closed on Sunday, your only free day, but perhaps you can stop by after English class before you go to work at the restaurant if my father-in-law doesn't mind you coming in a little later."

"We can work it out. Now, please sit down at the table. Mirna has fixed a lovely dinner in honor of Martin's arrival in America."

Right on cue, Mirna brought out the first course, seafood risotto, which she had learned was a favorite of Martin's. Just as they were finishing the course, the door opened and Marko appeared. "Hello, everyone. Sorry I'm late but I encountered difficulties getting here."

"No apology needed," said Mirna. "We are all glad you could join us to celebrate Martin's safe arrival." Then she went back into the kitchen and brought out a heaping plate of risotto for Marko. While he ate, she cleared the table.

Marko clearly had a hearty appetite, making quick work of the first course. He was blond with blue eyes and thin lips that curled up at the ends as if in a perpetual smile. He was about the same height as Vlad but had wide shoulders and a muscular build.

"Marko is going to be an engineer," said Uncle Anton proudly. "He is studying at the university—Stanford in Palo Alto."

Again, Martin was impressed. One cousin was a businessman. The other was studying to enter a respected profession. He wondered about

Vlad. Was he learning the restaurant business or would he go on to college? He would have to wait to find out.

"The state is on the move," said Marko, "and I want to be part of it. Roads, bridges, buildings are all going to need to be constructed. There will be more work than can last a lifetime."

"You probably have building in your blood," said Martin. "If you had ever seen old town Dubrovnik, you would realize what an engineering marvel it is. No matter how many enemies have tried to destroy it, the walls still stand protecting the city."

"I'd like to see it sometime. It's important to study well-built structures to learn the secrets of their construction."

"Yes, and did you know that when they built the fortress in anticipation of the Venetian invasion, they put a wall on the right of the stairs leading up to it so the enemy could not draw their swords. But there is no wall on the other side so those going downstairs, our compatriots, could dispatch the enemy quickly."

"And don't forget," said Uncle Anton, "that they made the wall thinner on the side facing the city so if need be they could send a cannonball that would shatter it trapping the enemy inside."

"I guess I could learn a lot from my ancestors," said Marko.

"Yes," said his father, "in their case necessity was the father of invention. They were surrounded by so many enemies they had to be very clever to survive."

"Not to change the subject," said Marko, "but how was the afternoon at the Slavonic Society?"

"It was much as usual," Vlad said, "but Martin really enjoyed it, didn't you?"

"Yes, I felt right at home. But I am curious about the society. I know they help immigrants and that is where I will be taking English class but what other sort of help do they offer?"

At that moment, Mirna appeared with a roast leg of lamb smelling of garlic and rosemary, surrounded by a variety of roast vegetables—potatoes, eggplant, zucchini, peppers, and onions. Martin thought he had died and gone to heaven. And when he tasted his first bite, it was so tender and succulent.

"Martin," Paul said, "all the vegetables on the table are from our store. We are fortunate that there are many farming communities nearby where we can get our supplies. And you must have some salad—the greens are so fresh and tender and the tomatoes, flavorful and juicy."

After Uncle Anton helped himself, he passed the platter around. When he saw that everyone had filled their plate, he said, "Martin, you asked about the Slavonic Society and what help they offer. Let me tell you they are a godsend to our poor relatives arriving here with nothing but the clothes on their back. The society provides financial aid, helps immigrants obtain a post office box so they can receive mail, and offers insurance."

Insurance. He had never heard of it before so he just had to ask. "What is insurance?"

"Insurance is a kind of protection. Let's say there is a flood and Paul's store fills with water. He can get money to clean up and replace whatever is damaged. I have insurance on both this house and the restaurant. Fires seem to pop up all the time, leaving destruction in their wake. Insurance helps people start over."

Martin nodded his head, which felt like it was about to burst with all the new information about life in America. It would take time to process it all, and he would have to ask many, many more questions.

At that moment, Mirna and Katarina rose to clear the table. Then Mirna appeared with a silver tea service followed by Katarina with a tray of baked goods. "The one good thing about being under the Austrian Empire was we all learned to bake," said Mirna as she passed around the tray filled with an assortment of pastries, cakes, and the all-time favorite, apple strudel.

The guests soon departed and Martin was sad to see the day end. Tomorrow would be another week of drudgery. He only hoped he could move ahead quickly in this new world.

CHAPTER 7

On Monday morning, Martin got up early to start English classes before work at the restaurant. Aunt Mirna was already in the kitchen, apron tied around her thick waist, making breakfast. Bread and butter was on the table along with a variety of fruit jams—strawberry, peach, apricot. In another minute, Mirna put a plate in front of Martin. It was filled with the American tradition, eggs and potatoes, and prosciutto and cheese, the typical Croatian breakfast. Then she brought a mug filled to the brim with rich, dark coffee, something he would need to begin his long day. "Thank you for the wonderful food," Martin said. "Now I will be on my way."

Martin wasn't exactly sure how to get to the Slavonic Society, but he knew he would hit the wharf where it was located if he just headed downhill. It wasn't long until the San Francisco Bay, glittering in the morning sunlight, came into view. Once he got to the waterfront, instinct told him to turn left and within five minutes, he was at his destination. People were starting to stream into the building so Martin just followed the leader, assuming he knew where he was going. And he did.

Martin signed his name on a sheet on the teacher's desk and then took his place near the rear. He was hoping to go unnoticed so he would not be called upon. Martin looked around the classroom, taking stock of the other students, the vast majority of them young men like himself. Up in the front row his attention was drawn to a young girl with long chestnut hair full of curls but whose face he could not see. *I guess I will have to wait until we leave and be surprised.* Martin began counting the minutes for class to end.

The teacher was a severe-looking, middle-aged woman, thin as a rail, wearing a long dress in the dullest color of blue he had ever seen. By the look of her, this class was not going to be very enjoyable and again his instincts had been right. When she stood up to begin the class, Mrs. Vukovich put the fear of God in her students. "Please rise," she said, "and face the flag. Now, repeat after me. 'I pledge allegiance to the flag…'" Clearly, Mrs. Vukovich put discipline and order above all else. But when class ended, Martin realized he had learned something and that Mrs. Vukovich's methods had been effective.

Martin hurried out of his seat and tried to catch up with the girl in the front row. She was walking with a couple of other students so he did not think he would have a chance to meet her today. But when he passed, he took a look at her face and he was momentarily stunned. She was a real beauty. Her high cheekbones set off her deep blue eyes and gave her face a sculpted look, which was so prized. Her bow-like lips were full, and she had just the hint of a dimple in her chin. Martin kept the picture of her face in his mind all the way to the restaurant.

The dreamlike state he was in came to a grinding halt when he entered the restaurant about to open for lunch and heard all the commotion going on. He quickly hung his hat and jacket on the hooks by the door and went to his station in the kitchen. It appeared that the assistant had not shown up, and Uncle Anton was in a frenzy as he tried to prep the food. "Martin, come here, I need help." Then he handed him a chef's knife and pointed at the onions lying on the carving block. "Chop those," he said. Martin did not know the proper way to chop onions but he had watched his mother chop them a thousand times. So he started to do what just came naturally. Uncle Anton looked over and said, "Not bad for a novice. But when we have a break I will show you the chef's way to do it, and you can practice until you become a master." Martin's eyes were starting to tear up from all the fumes the onions gave off but he persisted until he had finished the task.

"Now," Uncle Anton said, "I want you to chop carrots, then celery. Those two vegetables along with onions make what the French call mirepoix used to create flavoring for sauces, stews and the like. A dish will be flat without it."

Martin was beginning to feel like a real chef as he chopped and learned the secrets of the culinary tradition. But once dirty dishes began to arrive, it was back to dishwashing for him. That task was certainly a grind, one he had already mastered and would like to put behind him.

When lunch was over, Uncle Anton called him over. "Martin, you did a good job chopping vegetables today but I want to show you the right way. Watch me. If you practice, you will have knife skills which are so important in a kitchen. And, before you start, always sharpen your knife like this on a stone. A sharp knife is your best tool but a dull one is dangerous."

"Why is that?" He always thought a too-sharp knife was risky.

"Because it can slip and then you will injure yourself possibly badly."

Martin heeded his uncle's advice and continued to practice the chopping technique.

The next day, the assistant again was missing. "I don't know what happened to him, but I need you to help me again today."

After Martin had made quick work of the vegetables, Uncle Anton poured some olive oil into a pan and added some of the mirepoix. "Now come over here, Martin. You are going to learn how to sauté." Again, Martin had watched his mother do this from the time he was young so he tried to imitate what he had observed while listening to Uncle Anton's directions.

After dinner was over, Uncle Anton pulled Martin aside. "I am giving you a promotion which you have earned. Tomorrow you will be a line cook."

This took Martin by surprise since he thought it was too soon to have that responsibility. "What about the dishes? Who will wash them?"

"It's always easy to find a dishwasher since there are new immigrants seeking employment. I'll put out the word at the Slavonic Society and by tomorrow evening I feel certain the job will be filled."

And the next day Stanislav showed up, a boy Martin recognized from his language class, one who was walking with the girl with the chestnut hair. What a coincidence. It must be fate that brought him here. Now I'll be able to find out more about her and meet her, too. His heartbeat quickened just thinking about her lovely face framed by the chestnut curls.

Stanislav was Nevenka's brother, it turned out. He, too, had chestnut-colored hair, though straight as a stick, and blue eyes overlooking a Roman nose. He was shorter than Martin and had a wiry but well-toned body. The family was fresh off the boat from Korcula along with their parents and three other siblings. Their father, too, had been a fisherman and had found work at the waterfront on one of the fishing boats.

The next day in class, Martin sat near Nevenka in the second row where he could admire her hair and get an occasional glimpse of her face if only in profile. When class ended, he caught up with Stanislav and his sister to get an introduction. Nevenka's smile lit up her face, making her appear radiant when she said, "It is a pleasure to make your acquaintance."

Martin was momentarily tongue-tied and then found his words to say, "Hello." They walked in silence for a short time and then Martin and Stanislav had to change direction for the restaurant. On the way, Martin asked Stanislav if his family would be going to the Slavonic Society on Sunday.

"I suppose we will. I heard my father and mother making plans so they can meet more Croatians and become part of the community."

"I'll be there, too. My uncle's family goes every week to have a bit of social life."

Now, Martin could hardly wait for Sunday. That was all he thought about all week, even though he stared at Nevenka's beautiful chestnut locks all throughout class. It was a wonder that he was picking up any English at all but, in fact, he was learning the language quickly. Even Mrs. Vukovich in her severe way complimented him on his progress. It certainly helped to spend all day in a restaurant where he often heard English spoken even if he did not speak it himself.

On Sunday, it would be the usual routine—church, the Slavonic Society, and a family dinner. After church services were over, Martin hurried ahead of the family to get to the Slavonic Society as soon as possible. He spotted Stanislav right away and made a beeline for him. Nevenka was standing nearby and offered a wide, welcoming smile. She introduced him to her parents and siblings just as the band struck up a kolo and partners moved to join the dance. Martin held out his hand to Nevenka and she took it, following him to the dance floor. They joined the circle, holding hands while their feet moved to the lively rhythm of the native sounds from the accordion, tamborica, and frula. Some of the dancers made very intricate and often syncopated steps, their feet wearing opanci, shoes made of pig skin that were molded to the feet. Martin was working up a sweat and thought the music would never end as he tried to keep up the pace. When they finally left the dance floor, Nevenka looked as fresh as ever while Martin's heart was beating rapidly as he gulped air to recover. Maybe it wasn't the dance. Maybe it was being so close to Nevenka, touching her, that brought on his overly excited condition.

Martin and Nevenka sat down at a table to talk, but the band was still playing so loudly they could barely hear each other's voices. Finally, Martin asked if she would like to take a walk, and after getting her parents' permission, he led her out of the hall. "Do you know your way around the city, yet?" asked Martin.

"Not yet. Mostly I go from home to school and to a few shops nearby to do errands."

"Let's walk along the waterfront. It's such beautiful day." Martin pointed out the grocery store Paul and Katarina owned and told Nevenka what a good businessman Paul was and that he would be rich one day. "Many of the restaurants and coffee shops along here are owned by Croatians. They will all be rich one day, too."

They walked another block or two and then Martin said, "Let's get a coffee." So, they entered a coffee house in the Austrian style with dark paneling, brass chandeliers, and paintings of Croatian sights on the walls. They took a table in a corner away from the piano, which was being played to the delight of most patrons. While the sounds of Mozart filled the room, Martin and Nevenka shared some stories about themselves. Both of them knew each other's cities so they had that in common. By the time he finished his last sip of coffee, Martin was starting to fall in love. "Next week, I'd like to show you some of the sights around the city that my uncle has told me about. Would you like to do that?"

"Of course, but I have to ask my parents' permission first."

"Well, let's go back to the Slavonic Society and ask them now so I have time to make plans."

When Martin and Nevenka, arrived her family was about to leave. Mrs. Dukich said, "I'm glad you're back. We were worried."

"We only went for a coffee down the street," Nevenka said, "so we could talk and hear each other. But Martin wants to ask you a question."

"Mrs. Dukich, would it be possible for Nevenka to accompany me to the Golden Gate Park next Sunday. My uncle says it has beautiful flowers and even a Japanese Tea House where we could have tea."

"If Nevenka would like to go with you she has my permission," Mrs. Dukich said. "But you need to meet her here and bring her back here so you are not out too long."

"That I will do. Thank you."

Martin noticed his family had already left so he walked out with Nevenka and hers. Then he hurried uptown for the family dinner, looking forward to sharing his excitement about next Sunday.

Once they were all gathered around the table, plates filled with roast pork, fresh vegetables, and candied sweet potatoes, Uncle Anton opened the conversation, looking directly at Martin. "So, you appear to have a girlfriend. She's quite pretty and knows how to dance the kolo well even without the benefit of opanci."

Martin took a hard swallow, trying to clear his mouth so he could answer. "She's Stanislav's sister. Her name is Nevenka Dukich. She's in my English class so that's how I met her."

"Well, she looked to be a very nice girl. You'll have to bring her to dinner one Sunday."

"Thank you for the offer, uncle. But next Sunday we are going to the Golden Gate Park you have talked so much about."

"Oh, it should be so beautiful with so many flowers still in bloom," Mirna said. "I haven't been there in a long time. We used to take the children there for picnics, remember Anton?"

"How could I ever forget. Some of our best family times together were spent in Golden Gate Park."

"I remember when Paul took me to Golden Gate Park the first time," Katarina said. "It was so romantic—just the two of us having a lovely picnic surrounded by so much natural beauty. I think that's when I fell in love with you, Paul."

Martin glanced at Paul and saw a flush come over his face. He, too, would have felt embarrassed by this revelation in front of his in-laws. Then his gaze shifted, capturing Vlad just as he was rolling his eyes.

Chapter 8

The week began to fall into a routine—first English class, then the restaurant, and finally Sunday, a day of rest and entertainment, a day full of surprises. Martin was progressing quickly at the restaurant. "In a few of weeks," Uncle Anton said, "you will be a sous chef. Do you know what that is?"

"Not exactly," Martin said.

"Anton turned to face Martin, holding up his large chef knife as he spoke. "It is the under chef—the second in command in the kitchen. If you apply everything I teach you, that's what you will become sooner rather than later. A great accomplishment."

Martin was almost speechless; he could only nod agreement. Once he found his voice he said, "I want to honor the faith you have in me."

When Sunday arrived, only the thought of spending the day with Nevenka revived him. After church, he went to the Slavonic Society where he met her and greeted her family. They stayed a short time to visit and dance a kolo before heading out. Since the distance to Golden Gate Park was more than four miles, about an hour and a half to cover on foot, Martin decided it would be best to take a trolley part of the way so they would have enough time to enjoy the park. When they finally arrived, they still had plenty of energy left to meander through the pathways, passing gardens and lakes and even men playing horseshoes. There were so many trees that the atmosphere never lacked birdsong, although spotting them was much more difficult as they hid themselves high above in the foliage. After walking for the better part of an hour, Martin and Nevenka came upon a sign pointing to the Japanese Tea Garden. Once they had crossed the stone path and bridge, Martin noticed a definite change in the garden—the way plants were arranged and shaped in such an artistic way but different from what he had ever seen. When they came to a pond, Nevenka pointed, "Look, there's fish in it."

"My uncle told me about them. They're call koi, a type of carp considered good luck."

"Maybe they will bring us luck."

Up ahead they could see the Japanese Tea House, a small bamboo structure with open sides that had been built in 1894 for the international exposition. The only room of the tea house was nearly filled with people sipping tea and snacking on a variety of Japanese treats. But Martin and Nevenka had luck and were shown to a table overlooking a pond by a Japanese girl dressed in a kimono who took tiny steps, slowly moving across the floor. After they were seated, she handed them a menu and left. Martin took one look at the menu and felt his face flush with embarrassment—he couldn't read a word. Nevenka looked up from her menu at Martin and laughed. She, too, had no idea what the menu had to offer. "Look," she said pointing, "part in English, part in Japanese characters. It's all Greek to me." Those words relieved the tension for Martin so when the waitress returned he used international language—pointing and signs.

They were relieved when she returned with tea and snacks but were confused when she didn't immediately pour the tea into cups. The waitress instead cleaned the tools to be used before preparing the tea. Then she poured the tea into a bowl to be passed and shared. Martin watched Nevenka as her lips touched the bowl before taking a sip. He so wanted his lips to touch hers, to feel their warmth and her breath. When the bowl was passed, he put his lips where hers had been and looking up into her eyes, took a sip. It was wonderful, this day was wonderful, Nevenka was why it was so wonderful. The waitress passed a plate of cookies, saying in broken English, "Fortune cookie. First made here. Bring good luck." So much good luck in this place of exquisite beauty.

Martin would reflect on this over and over again throughout his life. The carp in the Dragon Gate story his uncle told had defeated all odds by swimming upstream in a swift current to leap over the falls and be turned into a dragon, the most auspicious creature. The carp symbolizes strength and perseverance, two important qualities that his uncle told him he would need for success.

After tea, both Martin and Nevenka had to hurry back to the Slavonic Society to meet their families for dinner. He held Nevenka's hand the whole way on the trolley but longed to kiss her, although he knew it was too soon. Instead, before they departed with their families, they gave each other the European-style kiss on each cheek and then turned to head in opposite directions.

Once they had finished dinner and were waiting for dessert, Uncle Anton said to Martin, "So, how was your afternoon with Nevenka in Golden Gate Park?"

It was an open-ended question leaving Martin to answer how he chose. Thinking about their lips meeting on the tea bowl, Martin said, "The tea ceremony was almost as beautiful as the gardens even though it was an unfamiliar ritual."

Uncle Anton nodded. "Yes, so much about the Japanese is unfamiliar—they live here in a society that is closed to the rest of us. That's one reason the tea house was built by a Japanese man—to let us have a glimpse of the culture we don't see."

Paul added, "The Chinese live in a more open way. Even though both are Asian, they take a very different approach to life here in America."

So much to learn, Martin thought. America has so many different types of people from cultures he never encountered back home. In New York someone told him hundreds of dialects are spoken. How can people speaking so many different languages ever understand each other, ever learn to function together, ever share the same American dream? Or, on the other hand is there strength in diversity? He did not know. Right now, all he could do was ask questions.

Chapter 9

On Monday, Martin awoke early to get to English class and then to the restaurant for a full day of work. Aunt Mirna had breakfast waiting, which saved Martin some time. Then he flew out the door, headed toward the waterfront. Today fog had moved in to cover the bay, and it was creeping up toward the city, covering it in a thick blanket of gray.

But once he was in the classroom, Nevenka's smile brightened Martin's day. He took the seat next to her but didn't have a chance to even exchange a word since Mrs. Vukovich had arrived, giving the class a stern look before turning to the blackboard to write some vocabulary. Martin was thankful he was learning English, but he was not enjoying one minute of it with this humorless teacher. When class was over, Martin walked out with Nevenka but again they didn't have much time to talk since he had to break away to get to the restaurant with Stanislav whom he now called Stan, a shorter and more American name.

Uncle Anton was already busy prepping food for the day. Martin washed his hands and put on an apron before starting the chopping ritual for mirepoix. His knife skills were getting better the more he practiced, and he actually found he enjoyed the work. Today Uncle Anton gave him a fish to clean. "I assume you know how to do it since you worked at the Fulton Fish Market."

"Yes, I do. But it was my father who taught me the technique. He knew how to do it better than anyone at the Fulton Market." Then Martin proceeded to demonstrate his skill to his uncle, finishing the job in record time.

"You are a master and here is your reward." With that, Uncle Anton set a basket full of fish at Martin's feet for him to filet. Some reward. But he took pride in his skill and found the work satisfying. Then a thought occurred to him. "Uncle, do you think they could use my skill down at the wharf?"

"They certainly could but when would you have the time? And besides, they start early in the morning."

"Maybe I could go before English class."

Uncle Anton let out a deep belly laugh that jiggled his double chin. "What and smell like a fish in school?"

Martin realized his mistake. Not only would Mrs. Vukovich not permit him in her classroom but he'd risk Nevenka never speaking to him again. "I guess there's no time in the day right now. But maybe when I finish my classes I could do it to earn money quicker."

"You're ambitious, Martin, and not afraid of work. You will succeed. Just be patient."

Martin lived for Sundays and now another one had arrived. Today he wanted to take Nevenka to the Chinatown he had heard about. But when he first arrived at the Slavonic Society, he did not see her anywhere. He went outside to look for her but did not see her coming so he went back inside to spend time with his family. When the band struck up a kolo, Martin was feeling low but his cousins insisted he join the dance. Then unexpectedly someone cut in next to him—it was Nevenka. Martin raised his eyebrows in surprise as his eyes lit up his entire face and he held her hand tenderly in his. By the time the dance ended, Martin's heart was beating so fast he barely had breath to ask Nevenka's father if he could take her for an excursion.

Once the pair passed under Chinatown's gate, they knew they were in a different world—men with long pigtails scurried about in wide-legged pants, women with bound feet took tiny quick steps as they went about their errands, young children dressed in native costumes pranced in the streets and lurked around corners. Martin and Nevenka felt out of place as they passed stores with strange-looking fruit, whole chickens hanging by the neck, and other unfamiliar foods that smelled as bad as they looked.

"Let's find a place for tea," Martin said. Nevenka nodded in agreement and within the minute, they found themselves seated at the Lotus Blossom Tea Room with a waitress, in a red silk dress, ready to take their order. "We have dim sum today," she said with a lilted accent. Martin and Nevenka looked at each other, neither understanding what she meant. The waitress caught their looks and said, "Small bites." Then she pointed at the next table of guests who had just been served dumplings.

Martin exchanged a glance with Nevenka. "Just dumplings, please."

The waitress disappeared and then returned with a steaming pot of jasmine green tea, which she poured into two cups. Martin and Nevenka had to blow on the surface to cool it before taking a sip. They looked up at each other and smiled. But Martin liked the Japanese way better of passing the bowl. He'd have to find another way for their lips to meet.

Soon the waitress was back with dumplings—one filled with pork, the other with shrimp. They fumbled with their chopsticks as they tried to pick up a dumpling but failed over and over again until they gave up and used their fingers. The waitress hesitated, not knowing whether to offer them a fork or not. She didn't want to insult them, so instead she went into the kitchen, giggling, to share her story of the ignorant foreigners.

When Martin was presented with the check, he was pleasantly surprised to see two fortune cookies accompanying it and gave one to Nevenka while he kept the other for himself. They opened their fortune cookies but since they could read neither English nor Chinese, they put the fortunes away for safekeeping. "We could ask Mrs. Vukovich to translate," said Nevenka, not knowing Martin's opinion of the teacher.

"Better to ask my uncle. Give me yours and I'll have him translate it, too."

Martin looked up at the wall clock and saw it was getting very close to four o'clock, the time they needed to head back to the Slavonic Society to meet their families. He hurried Nevenka out of the tea room and through the town until at last they had passed back under the gate. The tea had revived them so they were able to keep up a brisk pace all the way back. They arrived just in time for the final kolo, which they both danced with joy.

CHAPTER 10

The year 1904 was drawing to a close. The season of brotherhood and good cheer had begun as halls were decked, candles set in windows, and shoppers hustled along the streets, ducking in and out of stores in search of special gifts for loved ones. And Martin was no different. He wanted to give Nevenka a gift that revealed his heart, but not too much. He thought about asking his aunt for advice and then dismissed the idea. But when he saw Katarina at Sunday dinner, he decided to approach her since she was still young and in love. "Paul gave me a locket in the shape of a heart with his picture in it. That said more to me than a thousand words could have." So, now Martin had the idea but he had to find the perfect one.

The following Sunday on the third Sunday of Advent, the Slavonic Society was holding its annual Christmas Party, which included the usual social time and dancing but also a potluck dinner. Before he left for the festivities, Martin slipped a little package wrapped in gold with a red satin bow into his pocket. It contained a gold locket in the shape of a heart with the letter N engraved in a Copperplate script. Martin thought it was an elegant piece of jewelry and only hoped Nevenka would appreciate the thought that went into it. He needed to find the right moment to present it to her at the party this afternoon.

The Slavonic Society hall was filled with families when they arrived. The men had on their best suits, a starched dress shirt with cuff links, and a necktie held in place with a jeweled tie clasp, drawing attention to the kravata invented by Croats and introduced to Western Europe by Croatian mercenaries. The women were attired in fancy long dresses, if not silk then a shimmery fabric with intricate hand-beaded designs on the bodice. At first glance, one would think this was a regal gathering in a European salon. Even though Croatians were poor and oppressed, they were cultured, which was so evident in their dress.

Martin was humbled amongst these people in his only suit of poor quality and ill fit. But once the music started up, he forgot all about himself and began the search for Nevenka. She was standing in a corner surrounded by family and friends, but when she saw him she came forward in a stunning deep-blue dress with a sweetheart neckline. Martin thought he had never seen a lovelier looking young woman in his life. And the pendant would be the perfect finishing touch on the exposed white skin that shimmered in the light even without the addition of jewels. Martin extended his hand to lead Nevenka to the dance floor where a kolo had already begun.

The warmth of so many bodies in the room made Martin feel feverish as he moved in a circle while his feet tapped out the rhythm. When the music ended, Martin led Nevenka to the punch bowl and offered her a cool drink. Once they had quenched their thirst he took her by the elbow to move her away from the crowd and said, "I have a Christmas present for you." Nevenka's blue eyes widened as she blushed. Then he presented her with the package, which she carefully unwrapped. And with a gasp of pleasure, she gently removed the necklace, unclasped it, and put it on. "It's so beautiful Martin. I only wish I had a mirror to see how it looks on. But it feels so right."

"I can tell you how you look. Lovelier than ever. Between the regal-style dress and the pendant, you look like a real princess." Nevenka blushed again. "At least to me," he said. Now Martin wanted to kiss her but he didn't dare in this room full of eyes. Instead, he lifted her hand and pressed his lips tenderly upon her palm, feeling the heat of passion.

The arrival of the Christmas tree, a balsam evergreen, heralded the Twelve Days of Christmas beginning on Christmas Eve. The tree was placed in the living room in front of the bow window, which would showcase its decorated splendor, beaming with candlelight. Aunt Mirna and Katarina decorated the tree with many old-world ornaments brought from Croatia, various beaded garlands of pearl, gold, and silver, and candles that would be lit in celebration. The nativity scene was carefully set upon the mantle, surrounded by greens and red holly berries. No one was allowed to enter the room until it was time for the celebration to begin. Meantime, Aunt Mirna had the bakalar en brodo stew on the stove simmering, homemade bread in the oven baking, fritule dough on the counter rising. A variety of salads and vegetables awaited their time in the dark, cool pantry.

Dinner would be served late as the restaurant was open tonight, although it would be closing at 8:00 p.m. instead of 9:00 p.m. Uncle Anton liked to keep the restaurant open on this holiest of nights for the poor souls that had no one to be with or had to work not allowing them to spend the time with their families. It was often policemen, firemen, and nurses who filled his tables on Christmas Eve, and he always tried to make it a special meal for them.

Of course, he would have bakalar en brodo on the menu but he also had other favorites such as salmon, duck, and even rack of lamb. Anton knew this meal might be serving as the Christmas dinner as well. He always had special desserts on the menu and passed out Christmas cookies as his way of showing appreciation to his customers who made his living possible. Besides, hospitality was a serious practice in Croatia and considered a Christian virtue. Anton embraced hospitality with a loving heart—one reason customers returned to his restaurant over and over again. People could get a meal anywhere, but one made with love had the ingredient that sustained not just the body but also the soul.

Martin would remember his first Christmas in America the rest of his life. From the elegant Christmas Eve dinner to the Christmas tree aglow with lights and jewels with presents piled beneath, wrapped in butcher paper and tied with ribbon, but enchanting no less. The Church of the Holy Nativity came alive Christmas morning with the voices of a hundred or more children singing hymns in the choir. Afterward, the Slavic community gathered in the hall for coffee and cakes since there would be no event at the Slavonic Society this day. Instead everyone would depart for home to spend time with their families.

Aunt Mirna cooked most of the Christmas dinner herself. The piece de resistance was suckling pig, her specialty. The cavity was filled with a rice, apricot, and walnut stuffing which imparted an aromatic flavor to the pork and added a sweet flavor to the drippings for gravy. When the meal was over, the family gathered around the Christmas tree while Katarina played traditional carols on the piano, leading everyone in song. In the wee hours of the morning, everyone headed upstairs to bed and no one could have been happier than Martin.

The week went by quickly until it was time for New Year's Eve and the party at the Slavonic Society. Martin had not seen Nevenka during the holidays and looked forward to spending the evening with her. She was not in the room when Martin arrived but entered shortly afterward, wearing a shimmery gold gown and the locket, shining like a beacon under the lights. Martin immediately went up to greet her and her family. He felt a bit awkward, not knowing what to say to her parents, and was saved by the band, which struck up a kolo. Martin took Nevenka by the hand, leading her to the dance floor.

Shortly before midnight, waitresses passed glasses of champagne around and Martin took two, handing one to Nevenka. Martin had been anticipating this moment all week, and when the clock rang in the New Year, cheers went up and, seeing couples kissing all around him, Martin pulled Nevenka toward him and brought his lips to hers in a tender caress. He could feel the passion rise in him, wanting more. But he knew the time was not right. It was too soon. Besides, there were too many eyes on them, especially those of her parents. He didn't want to risk losing her because he had appeared too forward. Nevenka was too special. She was going to be a big part of his future.

CHAPTER 11

One morning, Martin entered the kitchen to find a copy of the *San Francisco Caller* on the table with the bold print headline: "Mrs. Stanford is Dead at Honolulu." That came as a shock to Martin just like it did to most people living in the City by the Bay, not so much because Mrs. Stanford was dead but because foul play was suspected—arsenic poisoning. Martin could not read the whole story since he did not yet know English well, so he looked forward to getting the scuttlebutt at the restaurant.

Stan had not heard about the suspected murder so there was not much more to learn on the walk to the restaurant. However, Vlad was full of rumors and theories: some think it was the maid, others the Chinese cook, still others the president of Stanford University who was often at odds with Mrs. Stanford. Uncle Anton said, "This is such a dramatic story that no news could be found today on the Russo-Japan War. Incredible."

Day after day sensational stories appeared about the investigation with far-flung facts and outright lie. Public opinion, which had been anti-Chinese since the city's early days, sought to demonize the Chinese cook even after he was cleared as a suspect. Martin could not believe what he had heard. His visit to Chinatown not long ago with Nevenka had been a pleasant experience, especially at the teahouse where he had been welcomed so warmly. He did not understand what could cause this kind of hatred. But he would try to find out.

After church on Sunday, Martin told his family he would meet them at the Slavonic Society later in the afternoon. They asked no questions so he did not volunteer that he was going to Nob Hill to take another look at the Stanford Mansion. On the way, Nabobs in newfangled automobiles passed him on the street. When he got there, he noticed guards had been posted around the entrances to the house. *I guess the estate lawyers fear looting.* As he stared at the massive structure so opulent and ornate, he could only think how sad it was that wealth had not protected Mrs. Stanford from one of the worst fates known to man—death by the hand of a trusted associate, in this case mostly likely a maid. Martin had learned that a few weeks earlier, Mrs. Stanford had suspected poisoning and let a maid go who had not been with her long. But now the finger pointed at someone who had been in her employ for many years, someone she relied upon and trusted. Martin wondered what would happen to this mansion since the Stanfords' only child had died young. Money, he thought, does not shield a person from the grim realities of life. His parents had always taught him to follow moderation as the proper way to live one's life. The Stanfords were an example of those who achieved great success in the world but in the end were left with nothing except a monument to their excess. Martin took one last look at the mansion, shook his head, turned, and hurried in the direction of the Slavonic Society. He wanted to see Nevenka and enjoy the day. That was his idea of riches.

CHAPTER 12

One Sunday in late fall the family was gathered for dinner and had just finished dessert while waiting for Mirna to bring in the coffee service. Once she arrived with it, Paul stood up and said, "I'd like to make an announcement." A hush fell over the room. This had never happened before so no one knew what to expect. "Katarina and I are expecting our first child this summer." Mirna broke into tears hugging Katarina who sat next to her. Then Uncle Anton stood up. "This calls for a toast. Vlad, please go to the basement and get a bottle of Mumm's and while you're at it, bring up the sljivovica, too."

Vlad wasted no time with his errand. When he returned with the bottles, crystal champagne and liquor glasses had already been set at everyone's place. Anton nodded to Vlad who opened the champagne expertly with a pop, not allowing even a drop to escape. He went around the table filling glasses—first his father, then his mother, next Paul, Martin, and himself. Then he looked to his mother for advice on Katarina's portion. "A little won't hurt."

Once Vlad sat down, Anton rose from his place at the head of the table and raised his glass. "To the next generation. May Paul and Katarina receive the blessing of many children."

"You must write Marko and tell him the news," Mirna said to Katarina. "He will be so happy for you just as we all are."

Martin could hardly wait to tell Nevenka about the baby. After class he pulled her aside and said, "Guess what?" She gave him a perplexed look. "Katarina is in the family way."

Nevenka looked at Martin with her big blue eyes and smiled. "I love children. I hope I'm lucky enough to have a dozen."

It was then Martin knew Nevenka was ready for marriage and would accept his proposal when asked.

Marko was home for Christmas and it was even more special this year with the anticipation of the first grandchild. Mirna had been knitting every spare moment to create little sweaters, hats, booties, and blankets for the layette. She also had plans to make a special homecoming outfit that would suit either a boy or girl. She had already purchased a soft yellow yarn and mother of pearl buttons for the one-piece romper that would have a white jacquard pattern across the front.

Katarina had arrived early on Christmas Eve morning to help prepare food and then decorate the tree. Mirna was already in the kitchen. "Put on an apron and join me. This will give us time to plan the nursery and a date for the baby shower." Katarina gave a smug smile. She was secretly happy for all the attention her pregnancy had brought her.

"Did I tell you I have your old bassinette stored in the attic? It is white wicker and just needs a new cover for the cushion. It's the perfect size for a newborn baby and can serve as a bed for several months. So you can wait to purchase a crib."

"Mother, I have started making a list of everything we'll need at first. After the holidays are over, I'll share it with you and you can add the benefit of your wisdom."

"I shall look forward to that. A baby is such a wondrous creature full of mystery, just wanting to be loved. I can hardly wait to hold him in my arms."

"Him, you say. It could be a girl you know. Remember, I was your firstborn so that may be the family pattern."

"I didn't mean to imply I prefer a boy. Of course, a little girl would steal my heart just like you did."

"Oh, Mother…you're so sentimental."

"And practical, too. Now here are some onions for you to chop."

By the time the men returned from the restaurant, Mirna and Katarina had the meal prepared, the table set, and the tree decorated with presents surrounding it. "What a dinner hour we had tonight," said Anton. "Tables were filled all evening while I cooked nonstop, trying to get the meals to the customers. Even Marko had to help out to keep up with the demand."

"Well, now you can finally relax. Go and get ready for dinner. You have plenty of time before I ring the dinner bell to gather around the table."

The traditional dish, bakalar en brodo, was the main course of the feast. Cod, a simple if not humble fish, saved millions from starvation and changed the world as people learned to preserve it by various methods including salt like the Croatians do. Before everyone was ready to dig in, Anton said, "May we always remember the humble cod and understand that following the simple path can have a big impact on our lives."

Martin was reminded of the Stanfords who did not live simply. The meek shall inherit the earth.

CHAPTER 13

When the holidays were over, Uncle Anton pulled Martin aside and said, "Let's talk." A thousand thoughts ran through Martin's head, imagining what his uncle wanted to talk about. But he followed Uncle Anton into the living room where they could speak privately without other members of the family intruding.

"Martin," Anton began, "you have learned your lessons well. There is not much more that I can teach you. At this point, you are ready to become a head chef but, unfortunately, I have only one position at the restaurant, which I fulfill and will be doing so for many years to come, God willing."

Again, thoughts began running through Martin's mind. *Is he going to let me go? Does he want me to find another job? How am I going to make money to save for my future, for Nevenka?*

Anton saw the look of shock on Martin's face so he continued to relieve his anxiety. "I think you are ready to start your own restaurant, with my help, of course."

"But uncle, I don't think I have enough money saved to do that."

"Don't worry about the money. There are ways to get it, believe me. But the way to achieve your dreams is not working for minimum wage but to be a business owner. And I know you have it in you to do it."

Martin took a deep breath, relieved he still had a job and would not have to start out on his own. "What do I need to do to start a restaurant?"

"First, you have to find a good location and I already have several picked out that would be suitable. You need to take a look yourself, and then we can go after the money you need to sign the lease."

The next day, Martin contacted the leasing agents to set appointments to view the spaces available. The one he liked best had been a restaurant before, so there would be little renovation needed. It was also in a good location near a shopping area where he knew he could get prospective customers passing by. He wondered why the other restaurant had given up the space. When he asked the agent, he learned the restaurant had moved to a new, larger space in a more affluent part of town. This news boded well for him, he thought, so he brought Uncle Anton by to see it early one weekday before work at the restaurant began.

"This is perfect, Martin. And the size is just right. You don't want to take on too much when you are starting out. Let's ask about the lease and then figure out the financing." By the end of March, he had signed the lease and was on his way to becoming a restaurateur.

Martin could hardly wait to share the news with Nevenka. He was establishing himself and planned to make her his wife by the new year if all went well. To celebrate, he brought Nevenka home to Sunday dinner with the family. Once they were all gathered around the table, Uncle Anton asked everyone to raise their glasses and said, "To Martin, may his restaurant be as successful as mine has been." Martin clinked glasses first with Nevenka as he smiled and mouthed the words, "I love you."

Martin was overwhelmed with all the tasks that needed to be accomplished to open the restaurant by May 1. While there was a stove and cooler already there, he had to order cooking equipment, dishes, silverware, glassware, linens, and the list just went on and on and on. Not to mention, he had to decorate the restaurant and come up with a name. I think I'll call it the Dubrovnik Diner. Uncle Anton was always helpful with advice without which he never would have been able to get the business underway. Nevenka took an interest in decorating. She had pictures of Dubrovnik framed to hang on the walls, and she picked out red and white checked material to be made into curtains, the colors of the Kingdom of Croatia. Martin could tell Nevenka had a talent for the domestic arts and would create the type of home he only dreamed of. He could hardly wait to propose and planned to ask for her hand before Christmas so he could present her with an engagement ring on the holiday.

In 1906 both he and Nevenka would turn eighteen, a prime age to marry. And Martin did not want to wait a moment longer to make Nevenka his wife. To him, she was the most beautiful, sweetest woman he had ever known or would ever know. Together, their love could only flourish.

CHAPTER 14

On the morning of April 18, 1906 at 5:12 a.m., Martin was nearly catapulted out of bed by a strong jolt. While he was contemplating what it could have been, severe tremors began causing him to grab onto the sides of his bed in an effort to hang on while the shaking continued, growing in intensity, causing windows to shatter and beams to crack and plaster to fall. When the shaking finally stopped, shock overcame him as his body shivered with fear. It was then that Martin realized he had survived a major earthquake that released its fierce power over forty-two seconds of savage fury. When it ended, Martin was paralyzed by panic and the possibility another round of terror would be unleashed. But then he heard Uncle Anton burst out of his room yelling to Vlad, "Are you safe?" When Vlad reassured him that he was, he ran down to Martin's room and repeated, "Are you safe?"

They all gathered in the hallway, still shaking from the near brush with death. "Let's go downstairs where we can gather our wits," said Uncle Anton. They all sat around the kitchen table while Mirna put out orange juice, milk, bread, butter, and jam. Anton had warned her not to use the stove since gas lines might be broken or disturbed in some way. But other residents were not so wise and their poor judgment started fires that spread across city. "We need to get out of here before we're all consumed," Uncle Anton said. "And I don't know how long it will be before we can come back so take basic necessities with you."

It took only a few minutes for everyone to reassemble to leave, and as they stepped out the door they could see fires spreading across the rooftops just minutes away from where they stood. "Let's head down to the waterfront," said Uncle Anton. But Martin decided to head to Nevenka's to check on her first. When he arrived, her family was standing outside their building. He didn't see Nevenka, but he spotted Stan and went up to him to find out where she was. "Oh, Martin," said Stan, "I don't know how to tell you this. Nevenka is dead."

It took a while for Martin to fully process what Stan had said. "No," Martin said. "That cannot be. I'm going to go inside and find her."

Stan grabbed a hold of Martin's jacket. "No," he said. "You don't want to remember her like that. She was crushed by a beam that fell from the ceiling." Stan put his arms around Martin as he let out loud sobs and called out Nevenka over and over and over again, hoping she would hear him and appear. "I love you, Nevenka." *Without you, without love, I am nothing.*

Still in shock, Martin followed the crowd down to the waterfront where he planned to meet up with his family. When he arrived, it was so crowded he did not know how he would find them. He made his way to the grocery store and immediately spotted Uncle Anton standing out front with Katarina in his arms and Mirna kissing her. Vlad had seen him coming and intercepted Martin before he entered the scene. "Paul died."

Martin felt his face go white with shock upon hearing more devastating news. "First Nevenka and now Paul," he said.

"Not Nevenka, too." Vlad and Martin stood together while tears flowed all about them. Then Vlad grabbed Martin's hand and led him over to the family. He heard Katarina say, "Paul gave his life for me and the baby." He had lain on top of her to protect her from falling debris, his body shielding her when the ceiling collapsed, absorbing its brunt force.

People were setting up makeshift shelters while they watched the city burn until ninety percent of it had been destroyed, including the Nob Hill mansions, and the lives of three thousand people, the cherished loved ones of survivors. No one had been left untouched by the tragedy.

CHAPTER 15

As soon as he could, Anton took his family across the bay to live with relatives. No one knew how long that would be, but Marko had already gotten a job with an engineering company that planned to start rebuilding the city right away. He would start as soon as he graduated in May.

Uncle Anton told Martin it was good that they had insurance, but it would be a long wait before their claims would be settled. Nevertheless, they had to put them in so they eventually had resources to start over.

Martin did not know if he wanted to start over. His American dream had shattered into such miniscule fragments that he would not be able to put them together again. Above all, he could never bring Nevenka back—how his heart ached, how his zest for life had been snatched in a flash of time. One minute his life looked so full of promise. The next it seemed hopeless. Now he only had his faith in God to sustain him and his uncle's family who shared his grief.

Martin knew he couldn't live off the generosity of relatives forever. He had to make a decision—to stay here or go home where Dubrovnik had stood for centuries always strong and secure. But he had little money and he was in California so he had to find work here. He overheard some men talking about the need for laborers to pick fruit in the Central Valley. Apricots were almost in season—the pay would be good and housing would be provided. He asked Uncle Anton about what he had heard and he told him that as a young, able-bodied man he should go since nothing was holding him there. Martin left with a group of men, all survivors of the earthquake, telling his family, "I will be back before Christmas to see you and the new baby."

The men were trucked downed to Bakersfield where they were left off at farms. The orchard had trees full of fruit ready to be picked. Martin grabbed a basket, climbed a ladder, and gently removed the fruit from its stem, and with even more gentleness, placed it in the basket careful not to bruise it. Bruising was always one of the biggest risks to the harvest since it would cause the fruit to discolor and rot quickly. After filling a basket, Martin climbed back down the ladder to arrange the fruit in crates that were stacked in the rows between trees. The work was hard especially in the hot afternoon sun but it paid well, simple meals were provided, and at the end of the day, he had a place to lay his head in the bunkroom. Most of the men he shared space with were refugees like him and immigrants, too—some from Croatia, others from Italy and even Chinese whose town was completely destroyed.

Martin made his way through the Central Valley, following the harvest. When apricot season came to a close, he began harvesting apples, which drew him out of the Central Valley to a town on the coast named Watsonville, the Apple Capital of the World. Martin was surprised to learn that Croatians were some of the rich apple growers in the area. He found himself on a farm owned by one of his countrymen and quickly established a reputation as one of the best pickers not only because he was fast and efficient but also because he was careful not to bruise the fruit. Just like apricots, bruising could lead to a rotten end. Martin was paid by the crate so it was an incentive to fill as many crates as he could in one day. While the work was hard, requiring climbing up and down ladders, the weather was much more moderate and as fall set in, not even a chill could be felt in the air.

One day when he was packing a crate, Martin looked up and thought he saw a familiar face—they locked eyes in astonishment. Martin said, "Aren't you Michael from the boat?" Michael had told him he was going to work for his uncle at his apple farm near San Francisco but he had forgotten all about him until now.

"It's me," said Michael. "I can't believe we have run into each other after almost two years of separation. What brings you here?"

"I'm sure you've heard about the earthquake in San Francisco. We lost everything. I was about to open my own restaurant and had even signed a lease. Then I was going to propose to my sweetheart." Tears began to fill Martin's eyes as he choked out the words, "But she died."

Michael was shocked and didn't know how to respond. So he just stood there with a sympathetic look on his face, saying nothing until he saw Martin back under control. "You look like you could use a cigarette," Michael said, offering Martin one and taking one for himself. They stood together in silence, smoking until the butt was too short to be held any longer. Then they dropped them, grinding them into the ground. "Well, let's talk more this evening. I want to introduce you to my uncle and his family—I have told them all about you. I'll come by your bunkhouse after dinner."

Martin managed a smile. Fate had at least done him this good turn by putting Michael in his path. Friends are always a blessing and a help in times of need. Michael couldn't have come back into his life at a better time. Maybe things will start looking up, he thought. He touched his crucifix medal and put his faith in God.

On Sunday, Michael took Martin out to meet his uncle and the rest of the family. It was a day when everyone was home relaxing before dinner. "This is my Uncle Luka," Michael said. "And this is my aunt Nicola."

"Pleased to meet you," said Martin. "I couldn't help but notice all the apple trees you have. It must be a lot of work getting the apples to market."

Luka laughed. "Well, it is difficult but made possible with the help of many farm hands."

"It seems there are so many Croatians living here and most seem to be in the apple business."

"Yes, we have a talent with farming. My father came here around 1850 and worked as a farmhand until he could save enough money to buy his own orchard. He started small and with God's blessing he was able to buy more land and plant more trees until we have what you see."

"Michael told me that Watsonville is the Apple Capital of the World. How can it be that such a small area grows enough apples for the whole world?"

Luka laughed again this time from his belly, which jiggled with each chuckle as his blue eyes twinkled in the light. "We are blessed with very fertile soil and we always try to improve by learning new methods that will increase the yield. Why are you so interested? Do you want to be a farmer, too?"

"I don't know. I was training to be a chef and even took out a lease to open my own restaurant right before the earthquake struck."

Michael didn't want his uncle to ask too many questions that would bring up bad memories for Martin. So, he tried to change the subject. "We're going to look around town to see if there is a good location for the type of restaurant Martin wants to have."

"If it is a Croatian one, there will be no problem getting customers," said Luka. "Best look near Main Street since that is easily accessible from both town and farms."

"Thank you for the tip," said Martin. "So far, I like what I've seen from this town and would like to stay. It will be a long time before San Francisco is rebuilt."

The next Sunday after church, Michael took Martin around town to scout out locations for his new restaurant. They saw a couple of sites that looked like they would meet the specifications Luka had mentioned. Afterward, they went to the Slavonic Society to socialize. Martin danced the kola with a couple of young girls but neither of them appealed to him like Nevenka had. Michael told him it was too soon. He needed more time to heal and to put Nevenka's memory in a special place concealed in his past.

Martin picked apples all the way up until December and now he had quite a bit of money saved. During the months he had lived in Watsonville, he had grown accustomed to the town and almost felt like it was home. He would go to San Francisco for the holidays to see the family and especially Katarina's baby. But he would be back in time to work the fields in the spring.

CHAPTER 16

Martin got a ride to Oakland in an apple truck from Luka's farm. He only had a short walk to where the family was living from the place he was dropped off. Martin had almost forgotten the house until he climbed the steps and knocked on the door. Mirna was the one who answered it with a scream. "It's Martin. He's back. Come everyone and say hello."

Martin gave Mirna a long hug while they waited for the others to arrive. Anton was next, followed by Vlad and finally Katarina with a baby in her arms. "I especially wanted to see your baby," he said.

Katarina drew him near Martin and opened the blanket so he could see the baby's pink face and dark hair, almost black. He let out a cry when he felt the cool breeze on his skin. "He's a boy. Of course, I named him Paul but we call him Pauli. I think he is going to look like his father. Certainly, I hope so."

Martin peered at the bundle in Katarina's arms. Paul, he thought, was the treasure his father guarded so closely that he gave up his life for him. "He does resemble his father," Martin said, even though he didn't really think a baby could possibly have the form of an adult so soon.

In the time leading up to Christmas, Martin and the family spent time at a makeshift Slavonic Society in an empty building near where the family was living. Many of the people Martin had met in San Francisco were there including Nevenka's family. It was hard to face them without her. As much as possible, Martin kept his distance and even avoided Stan until he was confronted by him. "I do not understand why you are no longer friendly to us."

Tears welled up in Martin's eyes. "You bring back too many memories. I know I should put Nevenka behind me but I can't."

"Nor will we ever. But to deny our friendship is like another death."

Martin knew Stan was right but could not bring himself to look him in the eye. Instead of facing his feelings, he had run away from them so he wouldn't feel the pain. But being back had brought all his old feelings to the surface in a raw form that hurt like hell . Maybe I won't be able to move on unless I grieve. Then he turned to Stan. "You have been a good friend. I want us to stay that way. Let's walk over to your family so I can extend my greetings."

Christmas 1906 was very different from the one before when there was so much joy, so much to look forward to, so many dreams. No matter how Mirna and Katarina tried, the place they were living in just wasn't up to the festive atmosphere that had been created at the townhouse. There was a Christmas tree, of course, but the old world ornaments had been left behind in storage and were probably destroyed. Instead, they had strung garlands of popcorn and tied bows made out of red satin ribbon that had a sheen to it when the light hit on the branches. They also hung fruit and candy to add some color. But the tree looked a bit sad, like all of them, as if it were meant for orphans.

Certainly, nothing about this Christmas was anything like the last one except for the food. It was the only familiar thing that could be transported. And, Martin thought, that was what made food so wonderful, what inspired him to become a chef. No matter what, food could always fill the emptiness if it was made with love. Mirna brought out the bakalar en brodo and Anton gave the blessing. "This cod that has saved bodies will also save our souls. It is a tradition that binds us through the generations." Martin looked around the table and caught tears in everyone's eyes.

Uncle Anton waited until after New Year's to take Martin across the bay to San Francisco. The purpose of the trip was to meet with the insurance representative to find out when claims would be settled. The insurance company had set up on the waterfront near the Slavonic Society and Croatian businesses. When they arrived, others were already in line so they had to wait their turn. Finally, when they had a chance to meet with a representative, he said, "Be patient. We are working on it and will be in contact with you when we have some news."

Uncle Anton and Martin made their departure but Anton was peeved. "What does he think we've been doing? It's been over eight months. If the insurance doesn't pay soon, we will end up in the poorhouse."

Anton led Martin on a walk through the city. It had an eerie feeling as if the spirits of all those who died now inhabited it, turning it into a ghost town. "It doesn't look like the same place, does it?" Martin shook his head and thought it didn't feel like the same place either now that Nevenka was gone.

They walked a few blocks and came upon Anton's restaurant, which appeared almost untouched. "I was lucky. As soon as the insurance money comes through, Marko is going to help me with repairs and then I'll be back in business. People are always hungry and need to be fed. A good meal will go a long way to sooth the soul."

Next they came upon the townhouse. "Look how well this held up. It's made of solid brick not like those fancy houses on Nob Hill that were made of wood. Once the neighborhood gets cleaned up, we might be able to move back in."

"I hope that's the case. You are one of the lucky ones for sure."

"Not just luck, Martin. Good decisions, too, about what type of home to buy. Marko has taken a walk around town and everywhere construction had been cheap or frivolous it was disaster. A home needs to last."

Everywhere they walked they saw disaster but they also saw people cleaning up and even starting to rebuild. Martin was amazed at the strength of the human spirit and its refusal to give in to despair. And he knew he had that spirit in him, too. In fact, most Croatians did. They always had to struggle to survive, never, never giving up.

CHAPTER 17

Martin certainly understood Caruso's sentiments when he said he would never again sing at San Francisco's Opera House after being caught in the earthquake. Martin wanted a fresh start, too, so he went back to Watsonville in the spring to help with the crops. Michael had promised him a job so that's where he headed as soon as he hit town. "I'm glad to see you back," said Michael. "How was San Francisco?"

Martin shrugged his shoulders as tears welled up in his eyes. "San Francisco was depressing. But things will get better. And little Pauli will help get the family through as they see hope for the future."

"Okay, then. I'll show you to your bunkhouse where you can stash your gear, then you can follow me around today to learn what we do to bring in a good harvest."

Martin began learning what it took to be an apple man. He spent much of his time tilling the soil so the trees could get moisture. It was hard, back-breaking work but when he saw the trees beginning to leaf and flower he felt rewarded as the sound of buzzing filled the orchards while bees did their important work of pollination. In mid-summer fruit appeared, signaling it would soon be time for harvest. Martin was already an experienced apple picker. He felt completely at ease on a ladder high up in a tree, but the best apples were picked a little lower where they were not exposed to so much sun and rain.

Martin picked alongside Chinese and Filipinos who came to town for the harvest. Usually, farmers had a system for getting the fruit picked so they would ensure none of the harvest went to waste. They helped each other and everyone prospered. When the apples were packed in boxes they were taken to the foothills where red wood stands shaded the fruit, keeping it cool until it was ready for market. The pay wasn't much but Martin was able to save a little, and when his insurance money came through, he would have enough to open a restaurant.

He and Michael scouted locations near Main Street and had a couple sites picked out. But then in 1907, there was another stock market panic that put fear into every businessman including apple growers. Fortunately, the panic only lasted a year, but it demonstrated the clear need for a national bank.

Martin didn't know if he had made a mistake coming to the United States. It seemed there was one crisis after another, not allowing for his American dream to even gain a foothold. But he had witnessed his uncle's success and now in Watsonville he saw how many of his countrymen were making a fortune in agriculture. The dream was possible but not easy. He would just have to persevere until he achieved it.

In the summer of 1908, as the stock market recovered, Martin received word from his uncle to come to San Francisco to collect his insurance check. It was more money than Martin had expected, and he went back to Watsonville to sign a lease on space for his restaurant. He had been able to recover some of the Dubrovnik pictures Nevenka had purchased for his San Francisco diner. And he remembered the red and white checked cloth she had made curtains out of and wanted to replicate those. But he needed help to get the restaurant ready for its opening so he asked Michael if he knew someone.

It amazed Martin how quickly word got around. After the harvest was over, a couple Croatian women showed up to measure the window for curtains and show Martin samples of the cloth they could use. Croatian handymen appeared, too, all prepared to do whatever task Martin needed—painting, building tables and chairs, laying tile for the floor.

For anything he needed, all he had to do was ask and the help was there. *I finally feel I have a new home.* Everything is perfect…well almost. Tears came to his eyes as he thought of Nevenka. Would he ever find love again? Maybe in this town he would. The thought gave him hope and brought a little smile to his lips. *I'm already twenty years old. It's about time I found a wife.*

Chapter 18

The Dalmatian Coast Cafe opened after the harvest on a Tuesday, which is usually slow in the restaurant business. Martin used Dalmatia in the name because so many Dalmatians lived in town that even the writer Jack London called it New Dalmatia. Martin hired Liu and Hong, Chinese men whom he had met apple picking, for the positions of sous chef and waiter. Liu was tall for a Chinese man and thin with graceful hands that were an asset in the kitchen. Hong was short and stocky and always looked as if he were about to laugh, a quality that endeared him to customers. They were both from San Francisco's Chinatown which had been completely destroyed in the earthquake and they had restaurant experience.

Martin knew they were going to open their own restaurant as soon as they had saved enough money to do so. But he couldn't believe his luck finding two helpers who already knew the business. And when they moved on, he had been assured they would find their replacements who would be just as good if not better. But, of course Martin knew, they would take the best ones for themselves.

As expected, opening day there were few patrons, but Michael had been one of them, and he brought along his uncle's family, which helped to fill a couple of tables. They all ordered fish, even though there were a variety of meats on the menu because, not only was fish a favorite food, but it would be a true test of Martin's skill as a chef. As the orders came in, Martin noted seafood risotto, bakalar en brodo, pan fried sand dabs, a local catch, and Dalmatian stew, a delicious combination of lobster, scallops, clams, jumbo prawns, and white fish of some sort in a light seafood broth accompanied by garlic bread for dipping. *These customers are certainly throwing a challenge down, but I know I'm up to it.*

Martin had what all good chefs needed, and that was timing. Since the diners were one family who wanted to enjoy their meal together, it was important all their entrees arrived at the table at nearly the same time. But until they did, Martin provided them with some little appetizers of tiny fried shrimp and calamari that Croatians are usually crazy about. He knew that would buy him some time while the customers indulged themselves. Most of the meals that were ordered required quick last-minute cooking with the exception of the bakalar, which had been simmering for hours just like Aunt Mirna's on Christmas Eve. So it wasn't long until Martin called Hong to deliver the dishes to the table. Then Martin thanked Liu for his assistance and stood listening to what the family had to say about their meals. From what he could tell, they were enjoying themselves since there was much eating and little talking. Finally, Michael shouted out, "Martin, come over here. We want to compliment you." Martin took off his chef's hat and apron and wiped his hand on a rag before coming out of the kitchen to meet his guests.

Michael's uncle stood up, "I want to salute you. I have never tasted better fish even in my own mother's home who came from Croatia and should have known all the secrets to cooking it in a most succulent way. But you have far surpassed her. Let's all raises our glasses in a toast to Martin and his success, which seems almost certain."

Martin felt his face grow warm and knew he must be blushing. But, nevertheless, he was proud of his accomplishment on this first night of his own restaurant. "Thank you, Luka, for the kind words about my cooking. But even more, I thank you and Michael for giving me a job that allowed me to make the money I needed to open this business. And to show my gratitude, I have a special dessert for you on the house." He hoped Liu had the oil heating so the dessert would go quickly…again timing. He didn't want his guests to lose interest before dessert arrived.

But Liu and Hong had teamed up to start the process, and fritule were already rising to the surface, and as they did Martin captured them in a slotted spoon and set them on paper to dry. Then he sugared them lightly before bringing them out.

"Fritule," everyone shouted in a harmony of joyous tones. These donuts were usually only served before Lent so it was a sign of a special occasion that they were being served tonight.

"Not only do these donuts have raisins in them but sljivovica, too." Martin knew the plum brandy from his homeland paired well with raisins and would be especially appreciated by his countrymen.

"Martin," said Luka, "bring the rest of the bottle here. We need to make another toast." Hong had heard the request and was already bringing the bottle to the table along with small liquor glasses, which he set at everyone's place. "To the Dalmatian Coast Cafe. May she always be a gathering place for Croatians in search of a home-style meal." At that, Luka tossed the liquor back in his throat and swallowed. And may St. Blaise always bless you."

The next couple of days, apple men starting coming in from the fields for lunch. Michael and his uncle must have passed the word along, thought Martin. These men all had hardy appetites so instead of fish they focused on meats—leg of lamb, grilled marinated skirt steaks and tripe stew, a nutritious dish, simmered for hours to achieve tenderness, which many wives refused to make due to the smell and preparation involved. Martin liked to use the honeycomb tripe which is superior to the others and not only involves multiple washings but also brushing to remove dirt between crevices. He cut the tripe in strips and placed it in a pot with tomato puree, carrots, onions, green peppers, and paprika, a popular spice introduced to Croatians by Hungarians. By the looks of their clean plates, the apple men had enjoyed their meals, tipping Hong well for his service.

In between meal times Martin, Liu, and Hong cleaned up and prepared for the next one. After lunch was over, they usually took a break and ate. This was a good opportunity to get to know each other and smoke a cigarette. "How long have you been in America?" Martin asked the pair.

"Our ancestors came for the Gold Rush and to build the railroad over and through the Sierra Nevada Mountains," said Liu. "We did very difficult labor that no one else wanted to do."

Martin did not know anything about this so he asked, "Did only men come or families, too?"

"Many men came alone. Then later sent for their families. But eventually the United States government passed the Chinese Exclusion Act, which didn't allow any more Chinese to immigrate."

"What was the reason?"

"They were afraid of us. They called us the yellow peril. But we multiply fast and were able to build a Chinatown."

"So, I know that your Chinatown was destroyed in the earthquake. Now what will you do?"

"Rebuild, of course, on the same spot since our ancestors are buried there."

"I'm sorry to hear all these sad experiences you have had since coming here."

"Not all has been bad," said Hong. "The earthquake destroyed documents so many of us have been able to claim citizenship through residency. Families are already arriving to join their relatives." Hong and Liu caught the stunned look on Martin's face. "We Chinese are very clever and take advantage of every opportunity."

"I could certainly learn a lot from you."

CHAPTER 19

On Friday, Martin was expecting a crowd of Croatians at the restaurant since it was a day of fasting for Catholics. Sure enough, at lunchtime the tables were filled with farmers and then at dinnertime families began to arrive. Martin noticed one in particular—a single young girl with a couple who appeared to be her parents. Unfortunately, the girl sat with her back to the kitchen so he could only see her long blond hair glistening in the candlelight. She looks like an angel.

Hong stepped up to their table, and Martin noticed the father seemed to do most of the ordering, starting with a variety of fried appetizers and Crab Louie's. That was followed by a round of clam chowder and salad and then the main course. Since abalone was on the menu tonight, that was requested along with sand dabs and sardines. This is a family of seafood lovers, Martin thought. As he cooked, he looked up from time to time hoping to get more of a glimpse of the girl. Finally, when they had finished their meal and before dessert was ordered, there was a lull in the restaurant that allowed Martin the opportunity to go around greeting and thanking guests.

When he got to the girl's table, she turned toward him and her face almost took his breath away. She really was an angel. She had big crystalline blue eyes fringed with dark lashes that were in stark contrast to her pale, almost white skin. Her high cheekbones, Greek nose, and bow lips all contributed to her extraordinary beauty. Martin couldn't take his eyes off her. Finally, the father interrupted to introduce himself. "I am Karlo

Bakovich, and this is my wife, Pauline, and my daughter Lena. You really know how to cook fish, and I should know because I'm a fisherman."

"Thank you for the compliment. And what a coincidence. My father, too, is a fisherman."

"Then why are you not fishing?" Karlo asked. He was a big, forceful-looking man, with wavy, gray hair and dark brown eyes that bore down on whoever he had his sight on.

"My Uncle Anton had a restaurant in San Francisco where I learned to cook so I could open my own restaurant and be my own boss."

"Well, you certainly know fish. You can be assured that I will be here often and spread the word. Finally, we have a good Croatian restaurant in town."

Martin wished he could speak with Lena, but her father just kept talking on and on and on. Even the mother stayed silent. Finally, Martin excused himself to go back to the kitchen, but at least he now knew her name. He would ask Michael about her. He'd be sure to have information.

The next day, Michael came by for lunch. After he was served, Martin stopped by his table to ask about Lena. "Yes, I know her. She has three sisters, all married to apple men. If you come to the Slavonic Society tomorrow, they are sure to be there, and I'll introduce you properly."

Martin could think of little else while he cooked endless dinners on Saturday night. He was amazed that he didn't make one mistake since he had trouble concentrating on his cooking. When the dinner hour was over, he was exhausted and couldn't wait to put his head down to sleep. Meantime, while he and Liu cleaned up and prepared for next week, Hong got out his abacus and added up the receipts for the night. Martin was astounded when he gave him the results. "You made a good profit tonight as well as for the entire week. It won't be long before you are looking for a bigger restaurant. At this rate, you are going to get rich quick."

Martin smiled. It was a good way to end the week of hard labor. *But an even better end will be tomorrow when I have a chance to see Lena again.*

Then he locked up the restaurant and went home to rest and dream of his future.

Chapter 20

On Sunday morning, Martin got up and dressed for church, putting on the only suit he had, the ill-fitting one he had brought with him from the old country. He took one look at himself in the mirror and vowed to buy a new suit with the profits he had just made. But for now he had to make do so he just wouldn't think about it. He'd think about Lena instead.

Martin was renting a room at a boarding house on Main Street, which was only a couple of blocks from St. Patrick's Catholic Church. The fog had started to clear, allowing a bit of sunshine to peek through, filling the day with its warmth. St. Patrick's, an English Gothic-style church, had been built only a few years before in 1902. Its crowning glory was the spire rising over a hundred feet above the roof, topped with a bronze cross. That Christian symbol could be seen for miles on a clear day. Unfortunately, today was not one of those days but since Martin was only a short distance away, he had a good view of the cross to guide him.

Martin entered the church through its front doors, climbing numerous steps to do so. Stairs did not daunt him after growing up in Dubrovnik where several hundred steps would be climbed just going about your business in a day. The congregants were just beginning to fills the pews so Martin had his pick of a place and chose to sit on the aisle near the back where he could watch everything and perhaps spot Lena. Right before Mass began, he saw Lena and her parents enter by the side door and take a seat up front. They were all dressed for the occasion. Karlo wore a dark suit and tie, Lena had her shoulders covered in a white shawl and a small pill box hat on her head, Pauline, who could almost match Karlo in girth, wore a wide-brimmed straw hat that shaded her handsome face but not her smile.

After Mass was over, Martin lingered on the steps hoping for a chance to greet the Bakovichs. But they must have made a quick exit through the side door. He had no other choice then to head to the Slavonic Society and hope they showed up.

Michael was already there when he arrived, looking very dapper in a sharkskin suit and a brightly colored paisley tie. Martin felt shabby standing next to him and hoped this would not hurt his chances with Lena, remembering Mark Twain's words: "Clothes make the man." Purchasing a new suit would be his next priority. "Have the Bakovichs come in yet?" Martin asked Michael.

"If you're asking me if Lena has arrived, the answer is no. But I have seen a couple of her sisters with their husbands."

"Can you point them out so I know who they are?"

"That's them in the far corner. One is wearing a green dress; the other has on purple. Both are blondes like Lena as well as the fourth sister."

"Are they as pretty as Lena is?"

"I don't know—you can judge for yourself."

At that moment, Lena walked into the room with her parents. She was wearing a blue dress that made her eyes flash even bluer. Even her hair looked blonder. "Come with me, Michael, to say hello."

The pair walked over to the far corner of the room where Lena had already joined her sisters. Michael introduced Martin to everyone. Karlo said to his family, "He is the best fish cooker I have ever known."

"You'll have to bring some of your fresh catch to him to cook for you," said Danica, one of the daughters, also a blue-eyed blonde, taller than Lena but not as pretty.

"I'd like to cook one for you under a bed of salt. That's the best way to ensure the fish is fresh and succulent."

"Next time I get a sea bass, I'll bring it right to you. What a feast it will be."

Martin knew from previous experience that Karlo was a talker. He didn't want to get caught in his web all afternoon. Just as that thought occurred to him, a kolo started up so Martin extended his hand to Lena to join him. She was a good dancer—light on her feet—and when she danced she radiated pure joy. Martin had not danced a kolo with anyone since Nevenka. But now he could feel the old pleasure return as the last vestiges of his grief were released and replaced by this new love.

Martin continued to make the Slavonic Society his Sunday ritual. And he was always rewarded by Lena's presence there with her family. After watching his daughter and Martin together for several weeks, Karlo said, "Next Sunday I would like to invite you to dinner. But I have one condition…you cook seafood risotto…I will supply the fish."

So, the next Sunday Martin found himself in Pauline's kitchen, which had everything he needed to prepare his course. As he added the fish—shrimp, mussels, cod, squid and sardines—he took a whiff of the fresh smell of the sea. He missed going out on the fishing boat with his father and gathering the sea's bounty in the net, which would not only put food on their table but make money from the surplus that could be sold to Tony's shop. One day, he would ask Karlo if he could go out on his boat. He would like to witness what type of skill he had as a fisherman and what techniques were used in the new world. More importantly, he would love to spend the day on the sea again. Marino was his given name—it means man of the sea. He changed his name to Martin when he immigrated to sound more American. But in his heart, he would always be Marino.

The family was all gathered around the big oak table when Martin brought out his first course. The serving bowl was hot so he held it with kitchen towels while he went around the table offering it to each one.

He served himself last before placing the remaining risotto on the table near the center where it could easily be reached by all. Martin waited for everyone to take a spoonful before he began. As he hoped, words of praise began to be heard from every corner of the table. Karlo's words were especially meaningful. "My fish have never tasted better. Martin, you are a master. Truly you work wonders with seafood." Then he reached for the serving bowl and took another heaping spoonful. "Would anyone like more?" But the family knew Karlo's big appetite was expecting to finish what remained.

When the second course arrived, a leg of lamb surrounded by roast vegetables, talk turned to apples since the three sons-in-law were present. Filip, a big, brawny Dalmatian from the isle of Brac was married to the eldest sister Danica. He and his family had immigrated to Watsonville in the late 1880s, and after working as a farmhand, his father had purchased acreage to start his own apple orchard. They grew the Bellflower and Newtown Pippin varieties, which were most commonly grown in Watsonville. "We had two and a half million boxes of apples this year," Filip said. "And shipped more apples than anyone else in the world."

"That's right," said Henrik, Morana's husband, another Dalmatian. "We think it's time to have a celebration—our own Apple Annual like Spokane has."

"When do you plan to hold it?" asked Pauline.

"Next October, before the harvest is finished. It is going to be a big event with entertainment and even a parade," said Henrik.

"It is going to attract a huge crowd since we'll be promoting the Apple Annual at the state fair and in San Francisco at the Ferry Building," said Josip, Nikola's husband.

Not to be left entirely out of the conversation, Martin added, "Promoting the event in San Francisco is a good idea. There are so many Croatians living there that they are sure to come to share in the success of their countrymen. I will personally extend some invitations, especially to my Uncle Anton and his family."

As Martin prepared to leave, the men made a point to shake his hand and the women gave him kisses on both cheeks. But when Lena kissed his cheeks, he could feel a blush rising to his forehead. Looking down into her face, he saw a similar flush covering her cheeks, and knew she had strong feelings for him.

On his way home, Martin reflected back on the evening and thought it went well. Certainly, everyone liked his seafood risotto. And he enjoyed getting to know Lena's family better. Her brothers-in-law were certainly hard working businessmen who were gaining much success. He wondered if he would ever be able to compete with them. Lena may not want to be the poor relative. Nor would her parents want her to be.

These thoughts worried him. Maybe I should sell my restaurant and go into the apple business where the big money seems to be right now. But he knew his heart was in being what he was—a chef. It was both creative and rewarding when he saw how his cooking could please people. Not to mention, he was a man of the sea. If not fishing, than cooking fish was his destiny. He could think of no better way to spend his time making a living. Uncle Anton obtained great joy out of his profession as a chef. And he also appreciated the opportunity to extend hospitality to his guests, some of whom had no one to share a meal with. During the holiday season, especially, he brought good cheer to those who could not be with their own families to celebrate. I want to follow in his footsteps.

The Slavonic Society was becoming a ritual where Martin met up with Lena and her family. He now knew she was the girl for him, and he thought she felt the same about him, although words to that effect had not yet been exchanged. Before he proposed to her, Martin wanted to make sure he was in the best possible position to be accepted. He was already a restaurant owner but did not yet make as substantial a living as he imagined Lena's brothers-in-law did from their apple crops. He needed to do something more.

Then an idea occurred to him. The town needed a grocery store like the one Paul had started in the city, now being managed by Vlad and Katarina. The town had places to buy vegetables and fish and meat and even a small variety grocery store but nothing on the level of Paul's. The more he thought about opening a grocery store the better he liked the idea. It was a natural pairing with a restaurant, which might even give him better margins on the food he purchased for it. And he knew he could get help from Vlad and Katarina especially since he would not be a competitor. They might even be able to go in on purchases together, helping to improve profits.

Martin was very excited as he pondered this new venture. Soon it would be Christmas when he would close the restaurant and spend the week with the family in San Francisco. That would give him an opportunity to run the idea by Uncle Anton and Vlad as well as thoroughly research their grocery operation. Maybe he would even spend a few days helping out so he could really learn the ins and outs of the grocery business.

The Sunday before Christmas, Martin spent the day with Lena at her home and stayed for dinner. It was too early for the house to be decorated for Christmas, but Pauline was preparing a special holiday dinner in his honor since he would be away between Christmas and New Year's. She had made a suckling pig, which instead of having a stuffing was surrounded by apples, sweet potatoes, Brussels sprouts, and a variety of other vegetables. After dinner was over Karlo called for the sljivovica and made a toast. "To a happy holiday season. May you receive all of our Lord's blessings." Then he tipped his glass and swallowed the liquor in one gulp, letting out a satisfying sigh. The brothers-in-laws followed suit, cueing Martin to do the same. He was now fortified for the walk home.

On Christmas Eve, Martin looked up and was surprised to see Lena's entire family entering the restaurant. Filip, Henrik, and Josip took turns with their families and this year it was the Bakovichs' turn. No one had ever spent a holiday in a restaurant before so this was a new experience but Karlo was insistent that they do it this year. Martin had the restaurant decorated in a festive way with a tree in one corner and candles surrounded by greens and holly on the tables. After they were all seated, Hong came over to hand them menus but Karlo waved him off. "I'll do all the ordering. Let's start with the fried fish appetizers and make sure you have enough bakalar en brodo to go around."

Hong went right back to the kitchen to have a word with Martin. He took one look at the cod stew simmering on the stove and said to Hong, "Don't sell any more. I'm not sure even this will stretch for their appetites."

"Let's go heavy on the appetizers," said Liu. "And, of course, let's not spare the bread."

"Perhaps, we should also make a couple of extra special tasting dishes to help fill them up."

"A big salad would help, too."

"Liu, as soon as you have a minute I want you to start preparing the batter for fritule. This dinner must end on the right note."

Lena and her family lingered, waiting for the other diners to clear out. When Martin came over to wish everyone a Merry Christmas, Karlo signaled him to sit down and then pulled out a bottle of sljivovica from under the table. Hong did not need to be asked to bring out the liquor glasses since he had them on the table almost as soon as the top was off the liquor bottle. "Let's toast to the New Year," said Karlo. "May it bring all of us much happiness." He glanced from Martin to Lena before taking his shot. The liquor brought a smile to his face as Liu appeared with the fritule. He had made a double batch of batter but could not keep up with the demand of the sweet tooth's the family had that evening.

Martin bid everyone goodbye, saving two kisses on the cheeks for Lena. As he did so, he whispered in her ear, "Let's make a date for New Year's Eve. I will be back and have a surprise for you."

CHAPTER 21

On Christmas morning, Martin took the early train to San Francisco since he had attended the midnight Mass that covered his Holy Day obligation. When he got off the train, he was near the wharf and decided to walk by Paul's grocery store so he could peer in the window to get another look at how everything was organized. He was impressed. Under Vlad and Katarina's management, the store layout was better than ever. He especially liked the produce section, which had a market feel to it, with wide aisles and an oval counter in the center, featuring the best of everything. Martin closed his eyes, imagining the store he would open soon, patterned after this one.

He continued to walk to the townhouse the family had moved back into a few months ago and noticed the city was being rebuilt even quicker than he had expected. But there were still large swaths of empty lots filled with rubble and debris. Martin's path took him by his uncle's restaurant, The Adriatic Coast Cafe, which had been completely restored. He put his face up to the window and looked in. Everything had been returned to its former arrangement. But then it hadn't been damaged too badly.

Finally, Martin reached the townhouse and climbed the steps, knocking on the door with the brass anchor. He heard quick steps in the entrance hall, and then Aunt Mirna stood before him, welcoming him in with kisses. Uncle Anton appeared even before Martin set foot in the entrance hall. "We are so happy you could join us for the holidays. It wouldn't be the same without you."

Anton and Mirna escorted Martin into the living room where the others were waiting. The Christmas tree stood in its traditional place in front of the bay window, blazing with candlelight and showcasing the old-world ornaments that survived the earthquake. While he was taking in this heartwarming scene, he heard a little squeal and turned—it was Pauli squirming out of Katarina's lap. When his feet touched the ground, he ran toward Martin and hugged his knees. Pauli was about two and a half years old now, walking and also talking, although Martin found it difficult to understand what he was saying.

"Sit down, Martin. Make yourself comfortable," said Uncle Anton. "Dinner is not yet ready so we will have cocktails first." But before he sat down, he went back to his suitcase to retrieve the gifts he had brought. Then he went around to everyone and gave them a present as he wished them Merry Christmas. He saved the best for last. Pauli could barely contain himself as he tore into the wrapping, opened the box, and pulled out a toy train with a little track. "Let me show you how this works," said Martin as he set up the track and then pulled the tiny train around on it.

"Me, me," said Pauli as he grabbed for the train. Martin surrendered as Pauli took control, completely enthralled with the moving vehicle.

"So," Martin said, "I see the town is coming back to life."

"Yes," said Marko. "We have placed the emphasis on building fast while building steel–framed, A-class buildings that can better withstand an earthquake, which we know we will get again even if it takes more than a century."

"Believe it or not," Vlad said, "within three years we will have built twenty thousand new buildings. There's talk of a big party to celebrate."

"Marko certainly chose the right profession," said Uncle Anton. "But he hasn't had a moment's rest and may not get one for a long time."

"Actually, I'm thinking of starting my own engineering firm with a couple of partners—guys I went to school with. We've gained so much expertise in such a short time that we feel we will have no shortage of business."

Martin looked around the room. So much had happened in such a short time. Paul is gone. Pauli is here. The city was destroyed and now was rebuilding in record time. And Marko planned to start an engineering firm. But what about Chinatown?

"Tell me what's happening with Chinatown? I have two Chinese who work for me at the restaurant who will be curious."

"Well," Uncle Anton said, rubbing his chin, "there was a big battle over that. Many wanted it moved, but the Chinese wanted to stay put. They threatened a trade boycott, which destroyed the opposition. The new Chinatown has pagoda roofs, which even its detractors find charming."

"There was a big scandal here," said Vlad. "Politicians were looking for under-the-table bribes for city services and licenses."

"Graft and corruption will always be with us," Uncle Anton said. "Someone trying to make a buck out of another's misery."

Aunt Mirna and Katarina had left the room and were now calling for everyone to join them around the table. Katarina scooped up Pauli and set him in his high chair between Aunt Mirna and herself so they could help feed him. Then Mirna appeared with a large bowl of seafood risotto and began passing it around. She had remembered that it was Martin's favorite dish.

The day after Christmas, Martin set out to walk the streets of San Francisco so he could see all the new buildings that had breathed life back into the city. But first he planned to head to the Church of St. Francis of Assisi. Marko had said that all the walls and tower had survived even as the inside was being consumed by fire. And once he reached the 600 block of Vallejo Street, the tower came into view. Those walls had been made from adobe bricks, which can last a long time in dry climates but are especially susceptible to an earthquake. It was a miracle, Martin thought, that the church survived. St. Francis was watching over both his church and his city that day and continues to bless it. Nothing else could account for the stupendous comeback.

As he contemplated the miracle of the church, Martin realized it was a metaphor for himself. His body had remained strong through the earthquake but his insides—his heart—had nearly been destroyed. But like the church, he would be rebuilt and Lena was the one to do it. When Martin came back to his senses, he noticed a Tau cross had been planted next to the church—the cross of St. Francis. Now he knew what he would bring back for Lena—a Tau cross—a reminder of the miracle of the church and also of himself.

It was not long until Martin stumbled upon a jewelry store. He didn't see a Tau cross in the window so he went into ask. The clerk showed him two—one in gold, the other in silver. Both were small—just the right size for Lena. He bought the one in gold since the city, whose patron saint is Francis of Assisi, was incorporated in 1850 at the height of the Gold Rush. Ironically, the day was April 18—the same day as the earthquake fifty-six years later. Lena had lived in San Francisco for several years after immigrating with her family. The cross and its symbolism would mean a great deal to her. At least, Martin hoped it would.

Martin's final stop on his self-guided tour was the grocery store, which he always thought of as Paul's grocery store. But now he saw it had a sign—Jurich's Grocery—no mention of Paul. Martin pushed the door open and walked in, a bell announcing his entrance. Vlad looked up from his perch at the back, letting out a big welcome. Then he hurried to the front of the store to show Martin around. "We tried to create a bit of a feeling of an old-world market," said Vlad. "Notice how the oval counter in the center just lends itself to showcasing all of our produce along with some of the cheeses and other specialty items."

"It puts me in the cooking mood," said Martin.

"Exactly. This is what we call marketing," Vlad laughed. "It gets people in the mood to buy and spend."

"How is your strategy working?"

"Very well—much better than before. But, of course we don't have much competition right now. So it's still too early to be sure."

"One reason I wanted to see your store is that I'm thinking about opening a grocery myself in Watsonville. There isn't anything like the one you have there."

"Well, if I can help you by sharing my knowledge that would please me very much. In fact, I would like to help you get set up but only if Katarina thinks she can manage alone. Maybe we could even go into business together."

"That was what I had been thinking, too. Between the restaurant and two grocery stores, we might be able to purchase in bigger lots and save money. Then there would be more profits all around."

"It didn't take you long to learn, did it? Profits are the name of the game in America. The more the better."

Vlad's comment made Martin remember his time picking fruit. Workers, too, need to share more in the profits. After all, they're the ones who make the profits possible. He hoped he would never be so successful that he forgot what it was to be poor—to be a man working for little wages, living hand to mouth.

CHAPTER 22

Martin got back home in time for the New Year's Eve party at the Slavonic Society. He hoped Lena would not forget their date, because this was going to be an important event for him. Remembering that clothes make the man, he had hunted all over San Francisco for the right suit to wear this evening. Michael was the first person to spot him at the party. "I almost didn't recognize you." Martin was wearing a dark, wool suit in a twill weave tailored to fit with a blue paisley tie. He had pomaded his wavy hair to slick it back, which made his jade-colored eyes even more prominent. His new black leather shoes were polished to perfection. "What happened? You are transformed."

"I visited San Francisco for the holidays so I took advantage of their after-Christmas sales."

"Well, I'd say you did more than that. No one is going to believe you are the same person."

So, it must be true, clothes do make the man. No sooner had that thought crossed his mind, then he spotted Lena entering across the room. *And clothes make the woman, too.* Lena was wearing a white satin ball gown with a bodice embroidered with gold thread. The Tau cross will look perfect with it. As he approached her, a look of astonishment crossed her face. Before he could speak, she said, "Martin, you look so handsome tonight."

Karlo stepped up and slapped him on the back. "You now have the air of a successful businessman."

Martin did not know what to say in response to these compliments, so he turned to Lena. "You are the most beautiful woman in the room." She blushed as Martin took her hand to dance.

After they had finished the kolo, they sat down to talk. Time passed quickly until it was almost midnight, and champagne appeared on trays held by waiters wearing tuxes. Martin took a glass and handed it to Lena and then took one for himself. There was still time before the clock struck the New Year, so Martin took the small box wrapped in silver out of his pocket and presented it to Lena. "This is a small token of my love for you."

Lena unwrapped the box quickly and opened it with a gasp of pleasure. "Oh, Martin, I love it." She held the necklace out for him to fasten around her neck. "How does it look?"

"Not that you needed it, but it adds to your beauty. I'm sure you know it is a Tau cross."

"Yes, of course, the cross of St. Francis."

"Did you know his church survived the earthquake? He is a powerful saint. And one with wisdom to know what is important in life."

"He believes in the simple life. And I do, too. That's what I appreciate about you, Martin. You are a Franciscan in so many ways."

"And that's what I like about Watsonville. Here the simple life can be lived to the fullest." But even in cities, a person can still find the route.

Now the clock chimed midnight and everyone around them kissed. Martin had not yet kissed Lena on the lips, but tonight he would do just that. He took Lena in his arms and drew her into him. Looking down at her, he tilted her chin up until their eyes met, sparks flying between them. Then he drew closer until their lips met in a tender caress that deepened into a passionate connection both of them could feel. When they parted lips, they were both breathless and on fire. Martin was glad that Lena's family was on the other side of the room. But then he heard Karlo's booming voice. "Happy New Year." And he bent down to kiss Lena on the cheek as Martin gave Mrs. Bakovich a hug and peck on each cheek.

Chapter 23

The next day while the restaurant was closed, Martin went to visit Michael. He found him at his uncle's ranch. "I'd like to talk with you about my new idea for a business venture."

"Let's go inside and sit down." No one was in the parlor so Michael commandeered it for the meeting. "Now tell me what new idea you're cooking up."

"If by cooking up you think I'm going to open another restaurant, you're wrong. What I'd like to do is open a grocery store but not just any grocery store—one like my cousins have in San Francisco."

"Grocery store. We already have plenty of places to get supplies. What is so different about the one you want to open?"

"As you know, there is not one store that carries everything, although a couple make an effort to do it. But nothing like Jurich's Grocery. In addition, having a grocery store would enable me to get ingredients for my restaurant at a lower price. Vlad might even go in with me so we could both benefit and keep prices even lower."

"I guess you really are a businessman, Martin. You have it all thought out already. Do you have a location scouted out yet?"

"Not yet. I was hoping you'd have some ideas."

"Well, you want it accessible to housewives. They're always shopping on Main Street as well your restaurant is nearby, which would allow you to easily go back and forth."

Martin found a vacant space on Main Street that was near Ford's Department Store where so many housewives shopped. He had to keep the housewives in mind, not only for location but also for the look and feel of the store as well as items carried, since women did most of the shopping. He wanted to create an environment that would draw them in—an environment that would also provide a social opportunity like the markets he knew back home. Market Day was often the highlight of housewives' week in Croatia.

Martin knew he needed to get a woman's input. Lena was a bit too young, and she still lived at home where her mother ran the household. But she had three sisters who were all housewives. Maybe he could get one of them to help him if not all three. So, he talked it over with Lena and she agreed to ask them.

"Martin, Danica really wants to help you, and she would be the best one because she has been married the longest and is also a wonderful cook and hostess." So, between Danica and his cousin Katarina, Martin got more than enough input; in fact, at times he wondered if he had lost control.

Opening Day was a huge success. Housewives were lined up early to be first in the door. They loved the market setup as you walked in because they could easily spot who else was there and chase them down for a bit of gossip. But Martin noticed they were also impressed with the quality of the produce. He heard one say it was as good as a farm stand and maybe even better. Of course the produce was better because he only had the best quality. Katarina came down with Pauli to help, which made everything go so smoothly. Lena's family hosted them for the few days they were in town, which was a relief to Martin since he did not have extra funds to pay for a hotel nor could he put them up at the boarding house. It was also a good opportunity for the two families to get to know each other because Martin planned to ask Lena to marry him soon.

Both the restaurant and grocery business flourished as townspeople patronized both. The ladies looked forward to their shopping day at

Martin's Fresh Market and the farmers especially liked gathering at the Dalmatian Coast Cafe at lunch for a substantial meal and a chance to talk politics, something every Croatian man likes to do. After he finished cooking, Martin would always join the group and share whatever he had heard earlier in the week. Meantime, Liu and Chao, the new waiter, would prepare for dinner. Hong had been promoted to Assistant Grocery Store Manager since Martin needed someone he trusted to be there when he couldn't be. Chao was proving to be equally efficient. He had a smile for every customer paired with a hospitable manner that always left customers satisfied. Liu was happy to stay where he was since he wanted to learn all of Martin's secrets before opening his own restaurant, which he hoped would be soon.

CHAPTER 24

In October, San Francisco was holding a big five-day party to celebrate the rebuilding of the city called Portola Days, in honor of Gaspar de Portola who discovered the City by the Bay. Uncle Anton had written to invite Martin and Katarina had written to Lena's family to invite them, although they could not offer them hospitality other than meals. Nevertheless, Karlo wanted to go and take his family with him since San Francisco had been their first home in the United States, although they were lucky to have missed the earthquake. All three husbands of Lena's sisters also decided to attend since they had very little chance to spend time in the city and only knew small-town life. So, all ten boarded the train for what would be a real adventure—one they would always remember.

They arrived just in time to see Portola making his entrance via the bay amidst ships from the Pacific Fleet and other navies around the world. Portola was then paraded on horseback down Market Street, the first of several parades that would be among the numerous events signaling the world that San Francisco was back in business. All of California's cities had been invited to send a float. The two that stood out were from the Asian communities—a dragon float entered by Chinatown and a float featuring cherry blossom trees entered by Japanese residents.

The family group secured several cabs to take them to their hotel—the Fairmont on Nob Hill, which had just finished construction before the earthquake and withstood the shocks from its perch above the city, although the interior saw fire. Everyone gasped at the magnificence of the hotel as they drew up to the entrance. Once in their rooms, they had no time to relax as Martin urged them on. "Uncle Anton is expecting us at his restaurant for lunch." Martin was anxious to show Lena and her family where he got his start washing dishes. He wanted them to know how far he had come, how his ambition has propelled him forward and would continue to do so until he fully realized his American dream.

The sign on the Adriatic Coast Cafe's door read, *Closed for private party.* Martin was impressed that his uncle had made this thoughtful gesture to show his generous hospitality as well as his love for his nephew and the family he expected him to join in marriage.

Uncle Anton was at the door, waiting to greet everyone. When Martin walked in, he hardly recognized the cafe. The tables were pushed together to create one big square to accommodate everyone. And in keeping with the red and yellow Portola theme, a red cloth adorned the table with a large bouquet of yellow sunflowers as the centerpiece. Everyone gazed at the pictures of the Dalmatian Coast on the wall, with Karlo announcing, "That picture on the right is Split, our ancestral home, where we emigrated from. I'm starting to feel nostalgic."

"And I hope you do," said Anton. "That was my intention with the special menu I have put together for all of you to enjoy." Before he could elaborate, the door opened and Mirna walked in, carrying a tray of baked goods, which Anton relieved her of and took to the kitchen for later.

"Greetings, everyone," she said with a warm smile, her eyes twinkling in the light. "I have come to join you so we can all get acquainted. But I think I have met some of you before...perhaps many years ago at the Slavonic Society."

"I think you're right. But we were all so much younger then. We left a few years before the earthquake," Pauline said.

"The earthquake," said Anton. "That's how we tell time now. Something is either before or after the earthquake—no longer BC or AD—it's BE or AE." They all laughed. It helped break the tension, which is often so palpable during first encounters, especially when you're trying to make a good impression.

The meal started with an assortment of fried fish—oysters, calamari, and small shrimp—and then continued with Martin's favorite dish, seafood risotto, and finally finished with a sea bass baked in salt served with assorted roast vegetables. Anton chose the fish in salt to make an impression, and he elicited Martin's support to do it right—carefully cracking the salt casing, removing the skin and bones, and plating the succulent white fish with a drizzle of extra virgin olive oil imported from Italy and a squeeze of lemon. An assortment of colorful roasted vegetables completed the presentation as glasses were filled with a white wine chosen to compliment the dish.

There was little conversation around the table until the plates were cleared. While Mirna took charge of dessert and coffee, Anton held court. "On Friday, we are going to have a parade of over three thousand cars, which you will not want to miss. And at the Emporium there is a display of over one hundred sixty cars of 1910 vintage—the first of its kind in the world. I've already seen it and will have you know this alone will be worth your trip."

Karlo teased his sons-in-law. "Maybe we should go home in style in one of those cars." They looked at each other and shook their heads, knowing they could not yet afford a fancy driving machine.

On Saturday night, the last night of the festival, Martin had arranged a special dinner in the Fairmont dining room for just Lena and himself and had requested a table for two with banquette seating so they could sit side by side, a more romantic way to dine. They both had dressed in their best outfits—for Martin that was his new charcoal gray suit, and for Lena it was a gold satin dress with a princess neckline that was perfect for the Tau cross necklace. Afterward they planned to join the crowd on Market Street for the electric parade of floats with actors telling stories about San Francisco's early history from the founding of the Spanish missions to the Gold Rush.

Martin and Lena thoroughly enjoyed their dinner, and he waited until they were having dessert to pop the question. Martin had been trying to get up his nerve all evening and the wine certainly helped fortify him. But it was now or never. Martin said in his most sincere tone, "Lena, you know I love you. I want to spend the rest of my life with you." And before he said the last line, Martin pulled a small box from his pocket. "Will you be my wife?" he asked, as he opened the box to reveal an engagement ring—a small, round European-cut diamond in a six-pronged setting of yellow gold. Lena let out a little cry when she saw the ring. Martin reached across her and grasped her left hand, sliding the ring on her finger.

Lena looked at Martin with tears in her eyes and said, "Yes, yes, yes. I love you, too." Then Martin turned her head toward his and gave her a tender kiss in full view of the other patrons.

As if on cue, a waiter arrived with a tray holding two glasses of champagne. Martin handed one to Lena and took the other for himself. "Let's toast to our future. May God bless our union and grant us a long life together." At that, they clinked their glasses, taking a sip while looking deeply into each other's eyes.

They headed for Market Street arm in arm, making their way through the crowds as they took in the sights of the floats ablaze in colored lights. Bands and orchestras had struck up dance numbers while couples danced in the street. Martin took Lena into his arms while a polka played, bringing back memories of home in Dubrovnik. They continued to dance far into the night carried away on love.

After Mass at the Nativity of the Lord Church the next morning, the two families headed to the Slavonic Society for a buffet brunch put on by members of the community. When Karlo and Pauline walked in, they were greeted by friends they had not seen since they had moved away. Martin leaned toward Lena's ear and whispered, "Did you tell them yet?"

"Not yet."

"Well, take off your glove and surprise them."

Pauline had been watching the couple carefully. She suspected something was different between them and when Lena's finger was exposed she yelled, "Papa, another wedding."

Karlo looked her way in surprise. Ten he saw the ring and ran over to his youngest daughter to give her a hug and kiss. Martin had already asked for her hand, so it was not a big surprise. t's just that he didn't know when. The timing had been good, he thought, a joyous time filled with love. What better foundation could Martin and Lena have for their future lives together?

CHAPTER 25

The year 1910 dawned with so much promise. Martin and Lena were making wedding plans, and the town was preparing for its first Apple Annual to be held in the fall.

At dinner one Sunday in January, Pauline brought up the wedding. "A May wedding when the apple trees are in bloom would be lovely." Lena gave a hesitant smile while casting her eyes toward Martin.

"If we plan for the week after Christmas, my restaurant will be closed so we can take a honeymoon right away. Otherwise, we might have to delay it."

For once, Karlo kept his mouth shut, allowing his wife to take the lead. "Why don't you two discuss it, then when you've made a decision we can begin to plan," said Pauline.

After dinner, Martin and Lena were left in the parlor to themselves. Lena seemed to have a cold of some sort that was not unusual this time of the year, and she kept coughing as they talked. At one point, Martin thought he saw her give a little shiver, even though the temperature in the room was warm. "What do you think about the date?" he asked.

Holding her hand to her mouth to cough, Lena finally said, "I don't know. Whatever you think is best."

"The sooner I can make you my wife the better for me."

"Well then," Lena said weakly, "perhaps we should defer to my mother's preference and have a spring wedding."

When Martin left that evening, he had a bad feeling about Lena's health. A cough was never a good sign and often the first clue to a serious disease. But he told himself it was winter when the common cold was making its annual rounds and eased his mind thinking it was nothing more than that.

A few days later, Pauline went into Lena's room to retrieve a perfume she had borrowed. She noticed the bed was unmade so she decided to do Lena the favor of tidying up her room. When she pulled the sheets up, she noticed they were damp. Could Lena be having night sweats? As she stood there pondering, Lena appeared in the doorway.

"Mother, is something the matter?"

"No, I only came to get the perfume you had borrowed and while making the bed I noticed the sheets are a little wet. Are you sweating at night?" Lena nodded yes.

"Now I'm worried. First, you have a cough. Now night sweats. You also seem to have lost your appetite and are becoming fatigued. Is there anything else you want to tell me?"

Lena was evasive. She was afraid to admit the other symptom she was having but now felt she had to be truthful. "I'm coughing up blood."

Pauline ran to her and pulled her close in a hug. "We have to get you medical care right away. I'll call Dr. Rosen and make an appointment." Dr. Rosen had been their family physician for years and was trusted like a member of the family.

"What do you think is wrong?" Lena said. "Am I going to die?"

Pauline calmed herself before answering. "It's probably just a routine bug that has been going around. Of course, you're not going to die." But she was afraid for her daughter.

Dr. Rosen gave Lena a thorough examination, peering closely through his glasses, as well as a skin test and then called her into his office to talk. "I don't want to alarm you but I suspect you have a serious illness—we'll know for sure in a few days." Lena's face lost all its color and she began to tremble. Dr. Rosen continued, "Let's not get ahead of ourselves until we receive the test results. In the meantime, I want you to rest."

When Lena returned for her next appointment a few days later, Dr. Rosen said, "I regret to inform you that you are suffering from tuberculosis."

Lena almost fainted when she heard the diagnosis. "Tuberculosis… the white plague. I'm too young to die."

Dr. Rosen tried to keep his voice calm. "While tuberculosis is a serious disease, there are some simple treatments to get it under control, although you will never be completely cured and it could come back at another point in your life. Right now, you don't look too white, by that I mean anemic, so I think we caught the disease in its early stage."

"So, what is the treatment I must undergo?"

"You will need rest, plenty of fresh air, and nutritious food. Most people with the disease go to a sanatorium that is devoted to the right care. In fact, there is a new one in Marin County that is exclusively for women."

"Why is that? Do more women get the disease than men?"

"After the 1906 earthquake, many more women were stricken mostly because they worked indoors where they breathed in pathogens while the men were outside building in fresh air."

"How much will a stay at a sanatorium cost? I'm not sure we can afford it."

"I'll look into it. But you can start right away at home. Even though it's winter, our temperatures are mild, which will allow you plenty of time in the out of doors. I recommend you bundle up and spend time on your porch. A little sun will be good for you, too. Vitamin D is a wonder vitamin. Now, please take a seat in the reception room and send in your mother."

When Pauline arrived, Dr. Rosen broke Lena's diagnosis to her as gently as possible. Then he filled her in on his prescribed treatment as well as the recommendation of a sanatorium.

When Lena and Pauline left the doctor's office as white as ghosts. It's not only tuberculosis that causes the white plague, Lena thought, shock can do it, too.

Martin finished cooking early that night and left the rest to Liu so he could see Lena before she went to bed. When he heard the diagnosis he was mortified. He knew the disease had been around since ancient times, and many people in Dubrovnik had succumbed to it where they lived in close quarters. But he was determined that would not happen to Lena. "Starting tomorrow I will provide you with nutritious meals, the best that can be had here. Soup will be at the top of the list, prepared from homemade broth and packed with so many healthy foods that it will be a powerhouse of nutrition. And it will be made with love, the one ingredient sure to cure. In addition to love, the power of St. Blaise, a healer and patron saint of Dubrovnik, can help restore you to good health." Martin pulled a medal of the saint out of his pocket and clasped the chain around Lena's neck where it could begin its spiritual work.

Lena spent most of her days on the porch, passing the time with knitting and embroidery. Dr. Phillip Brown, the San Francisco doctor who founded the sanatorium Arequipa, meaning place of rest, also believed in no strenuous activity in addition to rest and nutrition. He felt by doing something such as a craft a person was taking control over their situation, which would help them to heal. Dr. Rosen highly recommended Lena not sit by idly but be active in some way.

In between the lunch and dinner hours, Martin always came by to visit and bring Lena soup as well as a nutritious meal. He would watch over her while she ate and not leave until she finished even if that meant a late start on dinner. But he could always count on Liu; in addition, he had devised better ways to prepare for the dinner hour in the event he was delayed.

The days and weeks passed slowly with Lena still an invalid. Dr. Rosen made regular house calls to check on her progress and seemed pleased that her color had returned. But he cautioned, "Full recovery takes time. Don't expect her to be dancing the kolo any time soon."

Despite the doctor's positive prognosis, Martin was worried. He had already lost one love, and he didn't think he'd be able to survive if he lost another. Lena had become his whole life. Everything he did now was for their future. He tried not to let his thoughts go dark, which they often did when he was alone at night in his room. He kept his Bible on a table next to his bed and would open it to read a passage whenever he felt despair overwhelming him and needed to be comforted.

While Lena continued to recover, the town fathers made plans for the first Apple Annual to showcase Watsonville as the apple capital it had become with over a million apple trees, forty packing sheds, and two and a half million crates of golden apples, mostly Bellflower and Newtown Pippin, shipped to customers around the world. The event was promoted at the state fair as an "Apple Show Where Apples Grow," which helped attract a crowd of thirty thousand, stretching Watsonville to its seams. The record apple fair attendees found lodging in private homes and nearby towns when the few hotels on Main Street no longer had rooms to rent. By the time the weeklong event opened on October 10, Lena was well enough to take part, although she had to pace herself with naps in the afternoon.

Martin had more restaurant business than he could handle, filling tables from lunch through dinner. But he made time to slip away to take part in the festivities. One afternoon there was an automobile parade so he made a point of getting there between meal times. The evening parade was going to be the highlight, and he wanted to take Lena to it. As the sun set over the town and darkness appeared, Martin and Lena took their places along the parade route on Main Street.

Everyone cheered as floats and bands went by. But when the lights of a thousand lanterns began to appear, a hush fell over the crowd. The lanterns were carried by Japanese, many of whom were responsible for the rich harvest. No one watching had ever seen Japanese in such numbers before since they lived in their own Japantown isolated on the outskirts of Watsonville. Japanese lantern bearers, beaming their pride as they marched side by side, were a sight no one would ever forget.

CHAPTER 26

Now that Lena was feeling better, Martin's thoughts turned to their wedding. Lena, too, had been thinking about it and was ready to plan. "I think we should wait until the spring," she said, "so we can have the wedding mother had envisioned."

"I don't want to wait that long. Besides, I will have the restaurant closed between Christmas and New Year's which will allow time for a little honeymoon."

"All right then. At dinner on Sunday, let's express our wishes to my parents and get their blessing."

When Pauline and Karlo heard the date for the nuptials, they both held themselves in reserve until they learned how anxious both Lena and Martin were to be joined in holy matrimony. What more could be said? They gave their blessing and Pauline started the wedding plans even before they had finished dessert. "Martin," she said, "I assume your family will come from San Francisco."

'That is my hope. Now that we have a date, I will let them know right away. Uncle Anton's restaurant will be closed so he and Aunt Mirna should have no problem attending. But Vlad, Katarina, and Marko may be another story."

Lena said, "I think we should keep the wedding small with only relatives and a few close friends."

"Even with just those people," Karlo said, "we will have a full house."

"Of course, you'll have a church wedding," said Pauline, "then we'll have the reception at home. And with all the holiday decorations still up, the atmosphere will be very festive."

"I can have the bridesmaids were red or green and carry bouquets made of evergreen and holly."

"Don't worry about flowers. We have so many flower growers around here that we should be able to put together lovely bouquets."

Two days after Christmas, the family gathered at St. Patrick's church for the wedding. All three of Lena's sisters served as bridesmaids, wearing emerald green gowns and carrying bouquets of white roses mixed with green foliage. Martin had chosen Michael as his best man and Vlad and Marko as his groomsmen. Danica, Lena's eldest sister, was to serve as matron of honor. Once it was known that Katarina would be attending, Lena asked her to be a bridesmaid, too, even though she was a widow. Now Martin needed another groomsman to balance the bridal party so he asked Filip, Danica's husband, who accepted the honor.

Only the front pews of the church were filled, but Lena started her walk from the traditional place at the back of the church. As the organist struck up Wagner's *Bridal Chorus*, Lena stepped out on her father's arm in a Victorian-style dress with a lace bodice and silk skirt, trailing a full-length tulle veil behind her. Martin, momentarily stunned by the first glimpse of his bride, remained stock still until she reached his awaiting arms. Tears were rolling down his cheeks when he turned toward her veil covered face and even though the fabric was blocking Lena's eyes, he saw she had tears, too, a release of emotions they had been holding back for months during her illness. Neither one of them thought they would ever reach this day. But their prayers had been answered and now they stood before God, family, and friends to profess their love and join themselves in an everlasting bond.

After their vows were exchanged, Martin pulled back Lena's veil and gave her such a passionate kiss it almost took her breath away. She felt so weak in the knees she almost couldn't process back down the aisle to

Mendelssohn's *Wedding March* but, with Martin's strong arm to support her, she was carried along until they reached the foyer of the church where they greeted family and friends.

After pictures, the group headed to the Bakovich home where Liu, Hong, and Chao had all the preparations ready. As guests entered, Chao was there to greet them with a glass of champagne while Hong took their coats. Lena and Martin had to blink several times to take in the scene. While the home was well decorated and still had a Christmas tree displayed, other touches had been added—garland on the stairway, sprays of flowers scattered about and swags on the French doors that stood open to the living room. And then there was the food. A three-tiered wedding cake decorated with fondant flowers and birds was the centerpiece, with the bride and groom cake topper presiding over the feast. Fish was the star of the day in all its forms—fried, baked, poached, grilled, and even raw as plump oysters on the half shell were opened expertly for guests to enjoy. Liu had made Chinese dumplings—one filled with shrimp, the other with pork. When Martin spotted them, he knew this was Liu's way of showing his love, sharing his joy in the celebration.

And what a celebration it was. Lena's brother-in-law, Henrik, had brought his accordion, which added to the festiveness of the occasion. A few strong men pushed furniture aside in the living room so the kola could be danced, and guests moved around the room in the traditional rhythm.

As the champagne flowed and the party wore on, Martin was feeling so good he stepped up and asked if Henrik knew "O Sole Mio." When he began to play, a hush fell over the crowd at the familiar tune. Then Martin's tenor voice filled the room along with whispers that he was another Caruso. When he was finished, applause resounded along with shouts of encore. Few present had known of Martin's singing talent, although the beaming Chinese trio had heard him almost nightly as they closed down the restaurant. Not being aware of Caruso, they had not known what an impressive talent Martin possessed.

Not long afterward, Martin and Lena left for the train that would take them to Monterey for their honeymoon. They would only have a few nights for their marital getaway so Martin had splurged on a reservation at the Hotel Del Monte, one of the finest resort hotels in the country, which was frequented by the wealthy as well as movie stars, presidents, and celebrities. Martin was keeping the hotel a secret because he wanted Lena to be surprised if not overwhelmed.

As their taxi turned up the long driveway, the large gothic wooden structure came into view, the horizon dominated by its grandeur. Lena was mesmerized as they continued their journey to the hotel's impressive entrance. As she alighted from the vehicle, Lena said to Martin, "I feel I have just entered heaven." Martin nodded while thinking, you'll know what ecstasy feels like before the night is over.

After they registered and were shown to their room with a garden view, Martin ordered a bottle of champagne to set the mood. Neither he nor Lena had had much to drink or even eat at their wedding reception since they were filled with excitement of the day and busy showing their guests hospitality. Shortly before the champagne arrived, Lena had slipped into the bathroom to change. After she heard the waiter leave, she emerged, wearing a chiffon negligee in a pale pink shade with matching robe, and stood before Martin. "You are a vision of loveliness," he said, while kissing her tenderly before handing her a glass of champagne. "To our future," he said, while intertwining his arm in hers so they could take their first sips from each other's glasses. Lena was a bit dizzy after the first sip. Seeing this, Martin took her hand and guided her to a nearby chair. But with the affect the liquor was having on her, Martin knew it wouldn't be long before they headed to bed to consummate their union. And he was right.

While Lena waited, serene and giddy, Martin stripped down to his shorts and then scooped Lena up in his arms, laying her gently down on the bed as he slid in beside her and began stroking her fine, long hair. Then the caressing began, first with her face and lips, and then her breasts, which were full and firm and soft like velvet. Lena let out low moans so he knew she was responsive to his touch. And even though neither of them had had much experience, their love guided them into the eternal mystery meant for both their bodies and souls. As they savored their passion, they clung to each other until they fell asleep in each other's arms.

At the break of dawn, Martin awoke and gently stroked Lena until her blue eyes opened and met his in a sincere look of adoration. Martin was overcome with emotion and just had to make love to her again but before he made the first move, Lena pulled her nightgown over her head, tossing it to the floor with a flick of her wrist. "This time," she said, "I want to feel your skin on mine and have our whole bodies meld into one." Martin stroked and caressed Lena's body all the way from her head to her toes, and when he entered her, they both discovered the ultimate pleasure marriage had promised.

Martin and Lena barely left their room during their honeymoon except for some walks in the gardens and a special tour in an automobile along 17-Mile Drive with its ocean views and lush forests and the Lone Cypress tree presiding over the Pacific from its granite throne. "In Croatia," Martin said, "we have Italian Cypress trees that are long and lean like spaghetti. Our Cypress trees exist in stands and don't branch out. But this tree here is demonstrating its independence, just like so many people in this country, as it battles the elements and survives, more than a century so far, to fight another day." As Martin continued to stare at the Lone Cypress, he thought, *It's a lot like me, fighting to survive alone in this country, but now I have Lena and together we'll weather life's storms.*

When Martin and Lena returned from their honeymoon, he moved his things out of the boarding house and into her family home where they planned to live until they could find a place of their own. Martin had been living independently for several years so it was going to be a big adjustment for him, especially since he knew Karlo would always be looking to bend his ear over every thought that popped into his head. Somehow he would just have to keep his distance so he didn't get pulled into his orbit too often. But it wasn't going to be easy to avoid him in his own home.

And he didn't want to work longer hours than necessary to do it because that would mean spending less time with Lena. They would just have to find a home of their own as soon as possible. *I will make that a priority.*

Martin put out the word to all his friends and customers that he was looking for a small house to rent and possibly buy, although he didn't think he could afford to do that right now. Hong came up with the lead from one of the grocery customers. The little, one-bedroom cottage sat behind a three-story Victorian just off of Main Street. It had been used as servant quarters, but after the owner died, the big house had been divided into apartments. Once Martin took a look and noted it was move-in ready, he brought Lena to see it. "This will be perfect for us. It just needs a few decorator touches—curtains, wallpaper, rugs—and it will be a cozy retreat for just the two of us." Martin got in touch with the leasing agent and signed the papers that afternoon. In a few days, they were moved in and Martin felt himself his own man again. Without independence, it is not possible to be a real man. And he felt Karlo was man enough to understand.

As often as he could manage it, Martin would go home to the little cottage, or their love nest as they called it, between the lunch and dinner hour so he and Lena could recapture the ecstasy they had discovered on their honeymoon. Lena was always waiting in a negligee that barely hid her voluptuous figure with hair streaming down her back and arms ready to embrace him. She had turned out to be an enthusiastic partner and Martin had discovered a passion he never knew existed in him as her lover. In the evening, after work, they would retire to their bedroom as soon as possible to again lie in each other arms and make love until the wee hours of the morning when they could no longer stay awake.

Of course, Liu and Chao noticed how tired Martin was when he arrived to cook lunch, and they would tease him about it. But Martin would never admit the real reason he was so tired, although it gave him an excuse to go home in the afternoon for naps. Within a few months, Lena announced she was in the family way. Martin was beaming as they shared the news with her parents. "I hope you have a son," said Karlo, who had four daughters and no son. "Someone to follow in your footsteps."

Pauline frowned at him. "But Karlo, our daughters have brought us wonderful sons through marriage. How can you not wish their child to be a girl?"

Karlo apologized. "As long as the baby is healthy, it will be a blessing upon you and our family."

The baby was due in December, exactly one year after their marriage. As luck would have it, the baby was a girl and they named her Clara, after St. Francis' disciple, St. Clare of Assisi. Now instead of spending midday at the cottage, Martin tried to avoid it at all costs. If the baby wasn't crying, then she was wetting her diaper, which Martin refused to change. That is women's work, he thought. And then there was Lena who had not yet regained her figure and seemed to have lost interest in his amorous advances and become moody. His brother-in-law Filip told him all this would pass and to be patient. The one good thing to come of all of this, Martin thought, was that there will not be another baby soon.

CHAPTER 27

On April 15, the Dalmatian Coast Cafe was all abuzz about the sinking of the *Titanic*. Martin said to Liu, "This is just incredible. I don't know how that could have happened with all the safeguards that had been put into the ship." But the ship had hit an iceberg and filled up with water, quickly despite compartments that could be sealed off. "That sea water must have been freezing," said Liu as he gave a little shiver. "It's a wonder anyone survived."

After lunch was long over, the door swung open wide and Michael appeared, anxious and out of breath. He had run the whole way from the farm where he was working. "Did you hear the news, Martin?"

"If you mean the news about the *Titanic*, yes I heard it. You know how fast bad news travels."

"Not only that…but about the rescue…the ship?"

"What about it?"

"It was the *Carpathia* that rescued the survivors. They're calling its captain a hero."

"*Carpathia*…you mean our ship…the one that brought us to America?"

"The one and the same. Our ship has just made history and just think we had once sailed on it."

"You could say it's a lucky ship. It brought us here safely, despite some of those storms…remember?"

"How could I forget?"

"And now it has been responsible for a heroic rescue. This calls for a celebration. Chao, please bring out the sljivovica."

Chao filled two tumblers and the pair tossed them back, swallowing the liquor in one gulp. "Another, please." And Chao complied.

This time, Martin and Michael sipped the sljivovica since they were already feeling the punch it packed. "I made this myself," Martin said proudly. "It's eighty-proof, more or less."

"I'd say more, the way I'm feeling. But it's a good feeling."

"Chao, you better put away the bottle, since we both have to go back to work this afternoon."

When Chao got into the kitchen out of sight, he poured a couple more tumblers for Liu and himself, and they slugged it just like they had seen Martin do.

"What do you think?" said Chao.

"Well, it's not rice wine, but it's good…very, very good," said Liu, as a smile grew wide across his face.

Chapter 28

At the end of June 1914, Martin's brothers-in-law, Filip, Henrik, and Josip, came into the restaurant to talk with him about the situation in the Balkans. In Sarajevo, a Bosnian Serb had murdered the heir to the Austria-Hungarian throne, Archduke Franz Joseph and his wife Duchess Sofie. The restaurant was already packed with Croatians, including Michael who came over to join them at their table.

"Michael," Filip said, "you haven't been gone long from the Balkans. What do you think is going to happen next?"

"I don't know but there's been bad blood between the Bosnians and the Crown ever since Austria-Hungary took them away from the Ottoman Empire."

"Do you think there'll be a war?" asked Henrik.

Martin had heard the question, wiping his hands on his apron he approached their table. "I bet money there will be some sort of fighting, which is not unusual in the Balkans, if only to punish the murderers and keep the rest of the Bosnians under control."

"That's right," Michael said, "Emperor Ferdinand was not only shocked over the assassination but angry as well. Anger only grows in my homeland until fighting breaks out and no man is left standing."

"Well, let's just hope it will stay a regional skirmish and not affect more of Europe. We have good apple markets over there, which may get disrupted."

"On the other hand," Filip said, "there is often money to be made off war and not just from weapons and their parts."

The four sitting at the table looked at each other and smiled. Martin watched as greed overcame them. He did not like the idea that some people would profit from war while others suffered and died deaths so horrible no one would ever speak of them. He was glad he made a good living that left him with peace of mind.

By the end of July, the dominos began to fall. Austria-Hungary declared war on Serbia; Russia declared war on Austria-Hungary; Germany declared war on Russia; and England declared war on Germany. Europe was now at war while the United States sat on the sidelines, President Wilson observing non-intervention. But in May of 1915, Germany sank the *Lusitania* passenger ship with 128 Americans aboard, outraging the country. In April 1917, Wilson could no longer avoid declaring war on Germany after its submarines had sunk seven US merchant ships, and Germany had sent what was known as the Zimmerman telegram to Mexico to form an allegiance in return for the states of Texas, Arizona, and New Mexico. It didn't take long for America to build its army, drafting 2.5 million of its men and granting citizenship to Puerto Rico so it could help fill the ranks.

Martin, too, wanted to join up. He came home from the restaurant the evening of April 6 and announced, "I'm going to the navy recruiting office tomorrow to help the war effort."

Lena was stunned. "What and leave me with two babies? And then who is going to run the restaurant and grocery store? We'll starve without the profits to put bread on our table."

"I have to do it. It's my duty. With a given name like Marino, man of the sea, I'm a natural sailor. I grew up on the sea; boats are second nature to me."

"You might not come back. Then where will we be?"

"Don't worry. Most of the battles will be fought on land. I want to help the merchant marine ships get supplies to the Mediterranean. I know those waters like the back of my hand."

"Well then. As soon as you join up, I'm moving back home. I can't stay in this cottage alone."

That night in bed was a cold one. Lena clung to her side, turning her back on Martin. He lay awake most of the night thinking about his decision. Of course, he was a family man and business owner. People were depending on him. But he was also an able-bodied man who had something to offer that most other American's didn't—knowledge of the Mediterranean and superb sailing skills. In his heart, he knew he was doing the right thing. The world needed to be saved from the aggressors—especially Germany and Austria-Hungary whom he despised. If men didn't do their part to fight for freedom, we'd all be no better off than dogs. Before Martin turned on his side to face away from Lena, he leaned over and gave her a kiss on the cheek. Under his breath he said, "I love you."

In the morning, Lena still had a frosty air about her. But Martin pretended not to notice. He put on his good suit and tie and pomaded his hair to give himself a youthful appearance. He had heard there was a navy recruiting station on Beach Road so that's where he headed. When he arrived, he had to stand in a long line before he was able to meet with the recruiter. The lieutenant in charge looked him over, asked him a few questions, and then passed him on with a smile. "Welcome to the navy." Martin still wasn't sure he'd done the right thing, remembering the submarines that showed up at Port Watsonville for the Apple Annual, one miscalculating and getting stuck in the mud. He couldn't help but wonder if he wasn't miscalculating as well.

CHAPTER 29

It was only two weeks until Martin was scheduled to leave. When he moved Lena into her parents' home with Clara and Frankie, named after Saint Francis, Karlo said, "Don't worry about them but you need to take care of yourself."

The next day, Karlo drove Martin to the train with Lena accompanying them. When it came time to board, Martin took Lena in his arms and held her close to him for several moments before moving in for a passionate kiss. She had been warm to him on his last night, and even though they were in her parents' home, they'd made love long into the night more tenderly than they ever had before, reaching climax after climax until they had completely exhausted themselves and feel asleep. Martin knew, that after their lovemaking, no matter what happened she would never forget him. And, he too, would have memories to carry him through whatever lay ahead.

The train took Martin to San Francisco where he hopped a transport to the new training facility at Mare Island. When he arrived, there was only accommodation for six hundred recruits in the barracks. But not long after that, Mare Island would be able to handle five thousand. It turned out that in 1916, even before entry into the war, the navy had begun a six-year expansion project that would make the US Navy one of the best in the world.

Martin's training was brief, the navy not wanting to delay sending men into battle after its late entry into the war. In San Francisco he bid good-bye to the City by the Bay and boarded the transcontinental for the trip to the East Coast where he would be assigned to a ship. This time, instead of traveling in the miserable third-class car, he rode second-class in a regular passenger car that was scheduled to arrive in four days—still a long trip but nothing compared to the one he endured coming out the first time. There was even a dining car where he could take his meals, although Lena had packed him enough food for the journey.

The train was mostly filled with servicemen bound for various military bases along the route. At each stop, a group of men loaded down with gear got off the train, and an equal number took their place for points farther east. After they crossed the Sierras, Martin struck up a conversation with a man sitting nearby. Somehow he felt he knew him from somewhere before… No…it couldn't be. "May I ask your name?"

"It's Stan…Stan Dukich."

Martin let out a gasp. "Stan…it's me Martin." Now they both looked at each other in astonishment. It had been almost ten years since they had last laid eyes on each other and a lot had changed. "I didn't recognize you until you began to speak. You're missing most of your hair."

"We'll you have aged a bit yourself but not as much as me. Men who lose their hair always look older than they are."

"I'm a family man now so that responsibility and worry has put on the years."

"Vlad told me you got married. I'm happy for you." They both took a moment of silence thinking about Nevenka, but neither one wanted to bring up her name and the old wounds that would open.

"Where are you headed?" Martin asked.

"To Boston. Then from there the Mediterranean, I hope."

"What a coincidence. That's my plan as well. Maybe the ship will pull into the port of Dubrovnik and I can see my family again."

"Or into Korcula where I can see mine."

"What do you mean? Your whole family is in San Francisco."

"Not everyone. I still have aunts, uncles, cousins, and grandparents in Korcula. At one time we were all very close."

"And do you have your own family as well in San Francisco?"

"Yes, of course, that is life's plan. I married a Croatian girl I met at the Slavonic Society and we have three children—two boys and a girl who is a dead ringer for Nevenka." After he said that, Stan realized it might upset Martin so he gave him a quick glance and caught his eyes opening wide in astonishment.

"Praise God. The circle of life continues even after death has intervened. I'd like to meet her and your entire family sometime."

"After this war is over, you certainly will and our friendship will never be broken again."

Darkness began to envelop the train, and Martin realized he hadn't eaten since breakfast. He opened his knapsack and pulled out the rations Lena had packed for him. Thank goodness there's no hard tack among them. Instead, there was a prosciutto and cheese sandwich on French bread, not quite fresh but not yet stale. When he sank his teeth into it and tore off a hunk, the flavors filled him with a taste of home. He looked over at Stan who also pulled food out of his knapsack. Instead of a sandwich, Stan had a slab of ham and cheese with pickles and potato salad on the side. "What a feast we're having," Martin said.

Stan's mouth was full so he only nodded until he swallowed. "So, I hear you finally got your restaurant."

"Yes, a little diner near downtown and a grocery store as well. Life is finally being good to me. And you, what work are you doing?"

"Like you, I'm a chef. Anton taught me well…so well, in fact, that I work in the Fairmont Hotel kitchen."

"Now I'm impressed and it's a bit of a coincidence, too. That's where I proposed to Lena in 1909 when we came for the celebration."

"No kidding. In my hotel."

"Not only your hotel but your restaurant. Maybe you brought me luck because she said yes."

CHAPTER 30

The time passed quickly as the train roared across the plains, over the Mississippi River and into the Eastern states. When Martin and Stan heard the conductor call out "Boston next stop" it almost caught them unawares. As the train pulled into Boston South station, they gathered up their luggage and debarked, catching a transport to the Boston Navy Yard. Martin had not expected such humid weather but the breeze off the harbor helped to cool the air a bit. Once he and Stan had checked in, Martin said, "I want to walk around the city awhile and see a couple of sights. My cousin Marko said to be sure to check out Harvard University's campus as well as the Massachusetts Institute of Technology, both the best in the world."

"That would be an experience," said Stan. "I've never been on a college campus."

"If it weren't for Marko's graduation from Stanford, I never would have been on one either. Stanford is built in a western style so it will be good to see a couple in an eastern style."

"I've heard this is the city where the American Revolution took place and that there are many historic sites."

"Of course, I learned about the American Revolution during my citizenship classes but I don't remember much about it."

"Don't you know that the Americans were fighting for their independence from England…for freedom from oppression."

"Maybe that's why it's not taught in schools back home. The authorities don't want us to get any ideas."

"But now that we're here, ideas are nothing to be afraid of."

It was not long until they came to Harvard Square where the university was located. They noticed students coming and going to class, carrying books, discussing what they learned. "If only we had had such an opportunity," said Martin, "we'd be on top of the world."

"We're not doing so badly. Now that we've seen what's out there, it's for the next generation to accomplish it."

"That's right. It was enough for us to just get here and find a way to make a living. We can't do everything in one lifetime."

By the time the pair returned to the Navy Yard, it was time for supper in the mess hall. Most of the tables were already filled by the time Martin and Stan had gone through the food line, but they managed to find a couple chairs when some men had gotten up to leave. Martin looked down at his tray full of food and smiled. "I guess the navy is going to feed us well."

"If this is their standard, we'll do all right."

"I've heard cod is very plentiful around here. Of course, we have it every year for Christmas Eve to remember how much power there is in humility."

"Dip your spoon into this clam chowder. I've never tasted anything like it."

"It's so rich and creamy but also has the strong taste of clams. We could learn something about cooking seafood here."

After that comment there was no more talking as they focused on eating and enjoying their meal…one of the last they'd have on land for quite a while.

The next morning, Martin and Stan got their ship assignment, the USS *Lydonia*, a private yacht that had been acquired by the navy, 180 feet long, equipped with four three-inch guns and two machines guns. That afternoon they sailed out of Boston Harbor toward the Caribbean where they would meet her. From there, it was on to the Mediterranean to their base in Gibraltar, a strategic British territory, which controlled passage in and out of the Mediterranean. The crew would be escorting convoys and supplies to their allies. They were also supposed to be on the lookout for German U-boats, but an encounter was deemed unlikely.

The Allies had the Adriatic blockaded as well as Constantinople, which gave their ships nearly conflict-free passage in the Mediterranean. U-boats, though, could slip under the blockade and still pose a threat. When Martin and Stan heard about the blockade, they both let out sighs. They knew their hopes of seeing family again had been squashed.

When the sun finally rose over the Mediterranean, both Martin and Stan cheered. The full-blooded American sailors just looked at them, not understanding their enthusiasm until Martin said, "It smells like home... the clean, salty, slightly fishy smell that I love." Stan let out another yell in agreement. They were both on home turf now where they felt so alive, pulses beating quickly, blood rushing through their veins.

The *Lydonia* pulled into port at Gibraltar where they would have a day's rest before taking on their assignment. When Martin and Stan got off the boat, they found themselves surrounded by monkeys looking for a handout. Not knowing what to do or if the animals posed any danger, they just stood still until someone shouted, "Don't feed them. Just move on." Still it was hard to do, since there were so many in every direction, even hanging over the path from tree branches. This was definitely not something that was covered in training, Martin mused. As they continued along the road into town, they noticed a body of land across the strait. "Africa," they heard someone say. They turned to give each other looks. They had not known how close they would be to the African continent, but the strait was a mere eight miles wide at this point. This was truly another world.

The next day Martin and Stan boarded the USS *Lydonia* to begin their mission. The ship had already been loaded with supplies bound for Italy and France. The days were long and monotonous. but Martin thrived on life at sea. With Stan it was a different story. While he had grown up on the Adriatic, he had not spent as much time on a boat, so his bunk often provided a retreat from seasickness.

Soon it was the end of the year and holiday time. They had a chance to celebrate with their crew and others as they feasted on local delicacies and sang carols into the night. But then it was back to the work a day grind.

By 1918, it seemed there were so many battles and wars going on it was difficult to keep track. Once in a while they would get reports of the action and were especially concerned to learn there was a revolution going on in Russia. "I wonder what that will mean to our families in the old country?" asked Stan.

"I don't know but it could set off the Serbs and that would be bad for the rest of the Balkans."

In February, the *Lydonia* shot at two German U-boats but missed. "It's too bad we were in the stern when we finally got some action," Stan said. And Martin agreed. They were getting a bit bored just shuttling back and forth with supplies and wanted to experience the thrill of war. Even though they were family men, they were still young and had that need to prove themselves. On May 8, they got their chance. This time Martin and Stan were on the bridge where they could be part of the action when a German submarine sank a merchant ship they were escorting. The *Lydonia* teamed up with a British destroyer opening fire. Before they could confirm the hit, they had to return to the merchant ship's location to rescue survivors. But later they learned they had been successful.

"While I'm glad we saw some action, I don't know if I'm up for this on a regular basis," said Stan.

"Let's just pray this war will end soon so we don't have another day like this one. Once was enough for me to get the taste of war, and I have to say it left a bad flavor in my mouth."

In mid-July when Martin returned to Gibraltar after another mission, he encountered British sailors toasting the RMS *Carpathia* in a local bar.

He said to one of them, "I thought enough time had passed since the *Titanic* rescue. Why are you still raising your glasses to the ship?"

The sailor gave him a sad look. "I guess you haven't heard, a German U-boat sunk it off the coast of Ireland. It took three torpedoes to bring it down. Fortunately, most of the crew survived."

"The *Carpathia* was the ship that brought me to America."

"Well, that Cunard ship has had quite an impressive history from transporting immigrants to the New World, to rescuing *Titanic* survivors and finally to its wartime service to the Crown, transferring American and Canadian forces to Europe."

"And to think I had the honor to be aboard her." But for some reason, the news depressed Martin more than ever, leaving him to count the days until he could return home.

Chapter 31

At the 11th hour on the 11th day in the 11th month of 1918, World War I came to an end and with it the Austria-Hungarian regime. Nine million soldiers died and twenty-one million were left wounded. Another five million civilians died from starvation, disease, and exposure. But Martin and Stan had survived its trail of death…but not quite, as a deadly menace lurked nearby—the pandemic known as the Spanish flu.

The flu had taken its toll amongst soldiers who lived in close quarters or were cramped together in trenches along the Western Front. The virus had swept through US training camps, and troops took it with them to the battlefront in Europe. Martin, Stan, and their shipmates feared the Spanish flu even more than they feared German U-boats. And since Gibraltar was on Spain's Iberian Peninsula, there was much cause for concern.

Martin noticed that Stan began to spend even more time in his bunk and appeared lethargic whenever he saw him. He worried that Stan had put himself at risk for infection by spending so much time inside in close quarters. Meantime, Martin tried to spend as much time as possible on the deck in fresh air, one of the best means to stay healthy. He recalled that Lena had been prescribed fresh air when she was trying to overcome tuberculosis and it had worked. The *Lydonia* was not even half way back across the Atlantic when a flu outbreak struck. It was not a surprise that Stan was among its victims.

Martin was worried about his friend. He heard how the virus could strike a healthy man in the morning, leaving him dead by nightfall. He did not want Stan to meet that fate. But what could he do to help?

Everyday Martin went below deck to the bunkroom to check on Stan but not before covering his mouth and nose with a clean handkerchief. Somehow Stan was holding his own against the virus, but Martin did not know how long he would be able to keep up the fight. As the ship drew closer to the US coastline, life grew grimmer aboard as man after man succumbed to the illness. But so far, Stan had not been among the dead.

The captain made an announcement that the *Lydonia* would be pulling into port at Baltimore where the crew would debark and be transported to the Naval hospital in Bethesda for quarantine, observation and treatment, if necessary. Martin was relieved as he noticed more and more of the crew developing dark spots on their cheeks and turning blue as a result of a lack of oxygen in the lungs. It was anybody's guess who would be struck next.

Stan made a fine recovery at the naval hospital and Martin's quarantine kept him from getting it. Now the pair made their way to Washington's Union Station to catch the transcontinental train back to San Francisco. With their war experience behind them, the return journey was more subdued as they thought of reuniting with their loved ones back home in time for Christmas. They slept most of the way, no longer interested in the scenery as they had already seen enough to last a lifetime.

When the train pulled into Union Depot, a Beaux Arts building akin to Washington's Union Station, their families were waiting for them. Martin and Stan spotted them right away but got separated from each other as they moved through the crowd. When Martin laid his eyes on Lena, he picked her up in his arms and twirled her around before hugging her close to give her a sensual kiss. He wanted her to know what she could anticipate as soon as they got home. Before he could even embrace his two children, Lena said, "You left me with more than memories." Then she turned to point to a baby in Karlo's arms. "I named him after you."

Martin looked at the swaddled bundle nearly seven months old. "Why didn't you write to tell me?"

"I did. But my letter was returned a month ago so I thought I would just wait and surprise you."

As he released her from his embrace he said, "Well, you certainly did that. Any more surprises that I should know about before getting home?"

"None that you need to know about right now. Your safe return is the most important thing at the moment."

"If I can find him, I want to introduce you to Stan and his family." Martin looked around him but didn't see Stan anywhere. He felt sad that they had departed without even a goodbye.

But once they had exited, Martin saw Stan lingering on the sidewalk surrounded by his family. They exchanged addresses with a promise to get together and then headed off through the crowds with their families in tow.

Martin had been gone from home for sixteen months. He knew he had changed, and he wondered how home had changed—if there would be any more surprises.

He had not noticed Pauline's absence at his arrival, but once they walked into her home and she was not there to greet them, he thought it strange. "Where is your mother?" he asked Lena.

"She is not well, Martin. We have been keeping her in her room. It could be the flu. So many families have lost loved ones while you were away that no one was untouched."

Martin's face became red as he tried to hold back his fury. "You mean she is lying there in a sick bed and you and the children are living under the same roof. You could all end up dead if the disease spreads."

Tears rolled down Lena's cheeks. "We are doing our best. But someone has to take care of Mama so I've been elected since we're living here."

Martin tried to calm himself before speaking again. He did not want his homecoming to be fraught with conflict. That would be no way to begin the next phase of their lives. "I'm sure you did your best under the circumstances. But now we might have to think about another solution."

That turned out to be unnecessary. The next morning when Lena went in to check on her mother, she ran out screaming. "She's cold as ice. No breath. Her eyes are glazed over like a corpse."

Karlo hurried into the room to confirm Lena's findings and let out a bellowing primal cry. "My love has been snatched from me by the Angel of Death." As he pulled up the blanket to cover her face, Karlo murmured, "May your soul rest in peace."

Once the undertaker removed Pauline's body from the home, the task of sanitizing the room as well as the whole house began. Even though it was December, every window was thrown open to allow fresh air to circulate to help rid the house of airborne pathogens. "You need help," Martin said to Lena. He put out the word and soon Mexican laborers who were still in town after the harvest showed up, glad for the work. They were willing to do any job no matter how risky to earn money to live and provide for their families. The house had to be readied quickly to receive mourners since the funeral was only two days away.

When mourners arrived, filling the house with a sea of black, Martin noted the stark contrast to his wedding reception when the house was filled with guests dressed in colorful finery, wearing smiles on their faces. Liu, Chao, and Hong had come early to prepare for the reception, a simple lunch of ham, turkey, and salads in keeping with the occasion. The only dessert was dried fruit and nuts. But liquor flowed freely as it always did at wakes and funerals, including sljivovica, which Martin had included from his own collection. The liquor could be counted on to soothe wounds no matter how deep.

CHAPTER 32

Karlo told Lena she was now the lady of the house. And the three sisters emphasized that she needed to be responsible for their father since she was living with him. Martin was not fond of the new setup. He liked his independence and still found Karlo a bit much to take at times. But it appeared he had no choice in the matter. "One day this house will be yours," Karlo said to him. "But until then I am still the master of it." Under the circumstances, Martin had to put up with the situation but he was determined to find another solution.

Christmas was only a few days away. There were three children in the house expecting Santa Claus to visit but there was no Christmas tree, no stockings hung by the chimney with care, only a wreath with black ribbon hung on the door. Calla lilies, brought by mourners, adorned every room, and the adults in the house wore black garments and a stoic look on their faces, trying to hold back tears of grief. "What are we going to do for the children this holiday?" Martin asked Lena.

"I don't think father will want any celebrations. It's too soon after mother's passing."

"But Christmas comes but once a year. Children do not understand mourning rituals; they live for the moment. Can't we just have a few presents under a small tree for them?"

"I'll have to speak to father about it." Martin did not like her tone. Nor did he like that her father had to approve everything about their lives. Karlo could skip out on Christmas if he wanted to, but Martin did not want his young children missing out on their high point of the year. Besides Christmas was not only about Santa Claus but about Christ's birth, which is a holy day on the Church calendar. If Pauline could speak from her grave, Martin felt certain she would tell them to go ahead, "Let the children have their happiness while they can."

Martin reflected back onto Christmas 1906 that he and Uncle Anton's family shared in Oakland. They were still mourning Paul's death but Pauli had been born bringing joy and renewed hope. That Christmas had been a melancholy one and even the Christmas tree reflected their mood with its branches, spindly and sagging, bearing the weight of homemade ornaments. But the family was together, with the exception of Paul. And when they'd gathered around the table to partake in the traditional Christmas Eve meal, they felt an almost sacramental blessing in each other's presence. *Yes, we have to take every moment of happiness when we can. I'm even looking forward to Santa's visit.*

The holiday season passed slowly for Martin with his restaurant closed for the week and finding himself at home with Karlo without a means of escape in the evenings. During the day, he spent as much time as possible at the grocery store, observing the operation and going over the books. The women seemed to be happy shoppers and when they picked up a piece of produce to inspect it, the item usually found its way into their baskets. That told him they were pleased with the quality and the price was right.

When the workweek started up, Martin returned to his restaurant where he would spend long hours most days. Liu and Chao had noticed how he dawdled at closing time and wondered about the reason, but they never wanted to intrude by asking him outright. Even they knew, while there could be multiple women in a household sharing the duties, there could only be one man of the house.

A couple months later, Martin came home one evening to find Lena at the table, crying. He had never seen Lena like this and became alarmed. Putting his arm around her, he said, "It can't be all that bad. Tell me what's wrong."

"Oh, Martin, I'm in the family way again. And I don't know how we'll manage this time without mother. She took such good care of me and also the children."

Martin dropped the arm around Lena and stood back in surprise. "The family way? How can that be? With your father around keeping me up late talking, we haven't had much time for romance."

"It only takes one time. I think it happened the night of my mother's funeral when you had had so much sljivovica and I needed comforting. I remember falling into your arms and you being so tender and loving that we got totally swept up in our passion."

Martin smiled. "I remember that night, too. When I came home from the war, you had been in no state to give me a hero's welcome, and I didn't expect it. So, my welcome had been delayed until that night. I will never forget it." Then he moved toward Lena and gave her a kiss on the cheek. Extending his hand, he helped her up, drew her into his arms, and kissed her like he had never kissed her before, causing her to swoon. It was then that he heard Karlo call out, "Everything all right in there?"

Still holding Lena in his arms, Martin grimaced. "There's nothing for you to worry about." At that, he scooped Lena up in his arms and carried her off to bed, hoping Karlo would stay in his room and leave them undisturbed.

CHAPTER 33

Lena gave birth to another baby boy in August, christened Tomis Paul—Tomis after Tomislav, the first King of Croatia, and Paul, after Pauline whose death had brought forth his life. The celebration was a typically joyous affair with plenty of food and champagne flowing freely. Unbeknownst to guests and hosts alike, it would be one of the last times for a long time that alcohol would be part of such a celebration.

On October 28, 1919, Congress passed the Volstead Act, the National Prohibition Law, and by mid-January the country would be dry, although farmers could make wine for personal use. Meantime, grape growers had found a new market, rushing to produce grape concentrates for the demand. With so many farmers in Watsonville as well as easy access to nearby vineyards, the townsfolk could continue imbibing in the privacy of their own homes.

However, Martin had a problem and he needed to find a solution. His restaurant patrons were accustomed to having wine with dinner and then following with shots of sljivovica and other liquors. Where he came from, wine was part of the meal and even children enjoyed it, albeit a little watered down. Moreover, there was a bigger profit to be made from liquor sales, so without them he might risk his restaurant going under.

While farmers could make their own wine, the sale and transportation of it was prohibited. Perhaps, he could make the wine at the restaurant and not overtly charge for it. Patrons would be made to understand their entrees would end up costing a bit more if wine was served.

The first few Saturday dinner hours after the country went dry, most tables remained empty until closing time. Martin didn't know what to make of it at first until Michael stopped in for lunch one day and he asked him about it. "Don't you know people are going up to San Francisco to the speakeasies." Now it all made sense.

Martin had heard that many fine-dining restaurants were struggling to survive, giving rise to fast-food-type establishments such as lunch counters in department stores. If Ford's decides to do that, it would be all he'd needed to shutter his restaurant. But Martin's instinct was to fight—he dug his heels in, refusing to give in and accept defeat.

At first, everything went to plan. He was able to obtain wine bricks from vintners, which contained the instructions to dissolve the brick in a gallon of water to make fruit juice. But each brick also carried a warning not to put it in a cool cupboard for twenty-one days since it would turn to wine under those conditions. Of course, Martin took the warning as further instructions, as they were secretly meant to be, and within a few weeks had wine to serve his customers, and many returned for the Saturday dinner hour rather than travel the distance to a speakeasy.

It wasn't long before the authorities caught on, and Martin received a visit from a policeman at closing time. "Are you serving liquor?"

While Liu and Chao made themselves busy cleaning up the kitchen, Martin met the officer in the dining room to answer his question. "You know that is illegal now," he said, trying to evade a direct answer.

"I'm glad you're not going to plead ignorance. But you didn't exactly answer my question, so I'm going to have to take a look around." The policeman moved toward the kitchen.

Liu and Chao continued to work until Martin said, "Step out here so the officer can see we have nothing to hide."

Liu and Chao followed instructions, since they had had plenty of time to clean up and put everything away for safe storage. The policeman looked around and took a couple of deep inhales to determine if he noted any familiar odors. Even though all the dishes had already been washed, he took a glass in his hands to give it a sniff. Then he opened all the cupboards and searched for contraband but came up empty-handed.

The policeman came out of the kitchen and went up to Martin. "I didn't find anything this time, but don't think you're off the hook. I'll be back."

"We live in difficult times, officer. You're welcome back anytime, but I doubt you will find anything more than you did today."

When the officer left, Martin returned to the kitchen where Liu and Chao had been listening. "Thanks for cleaning up. But we may have to be even more careful in the future."

That night when Martin returned home, he told Lena the story of his near miss with the law. Lena opened her eyes wide, and Martin thought he saw a ripple of fear cross her face. "Martin, please don't do anything to get yourself in trouble, to risk our future."

"By now you should know, Lena, that everything I do is for our future. Of course, I won't do anything to harm our family."

Lena began to sob. "It's just that everything is so difficult now, especially with mother gone. I just couldn't bear it if you went off to jail. How would we even survive?"

"Don't worry about me. I've survived worse…much, much worse. Don't forget I survived a long, rough sea voyage, the earthquake, and the war. This is nothing in comparison." Martin put his arms around Lena and just held her tightly. She continued to cry for a time and then they headed off to bed.

A few weeks later, Officer Soldati came by again, but this time he did not wait until closing time. When he showed his face, customers were still at the tables, enjoying the last drops of their liquors. He made a beeline for Martin in the kitchen. "So, I see you are violating the law. I should not only arrest you, but all of your customers, too."

Martin motioned for the officer to enter the kitchen where they could speak privately. In addition, this would give time for Chao to hurry the customers out before they were caught up in the net.

When Officer Soldati came into the kitchen, he said, "Turn around," clamping handcuffs on Martin. "Now you're coming down to the station with me."

Martin looked in the direction of Liu and Chao who were trying not to listen and had turned their backs on the situation. "I want to make a phone call before I go."

"You can do that after you're booked. But right now you're coming with me." Then he forced Martin out of the restaurant, pushed him into the back seat of his car, and took off. Martin was aghast at the indignity of it all. They took a mug shot and fingerprinted him before letting him make a call. Afterward, they put him behind bars like a common criminal. Martin had called his brother-in-law Filip who met him at the police station.

"Martin, I think you should get an attorney. You don't want to complicate matters for yourself by not having good legal advice."

"Of course, you're right. If you know someone, can you call him for me?"

"Yes, I can do that. But now you have to realize you have two choices."

"What's that?"

"You can stop serving liquor or you can pay protection money."

"Protection money?" Then he remembered Vito at the Fullerton Fish Market and didn't want to have anything to do with the underworld. "That's not for me."

"Well, then that means you have chosen to stop making and selling liquor. Now you've doomed your restaurant." Martin took a deep breath. He knew he couldn't let the restaurant fail. "If you want to be a businessman in America, you have to learn how things work and how to get things done."

"Maybe I've just been naïve. How do I go about arranging protection?"

Officer Soldati continued to make visits, but now he only wanted to collect his envelope containing the money required to protect Martin and his business from the law. Business went smoothly and even continued to prosper, so Martin felt it was money well spent. But it still didn't sit well that he had given in to Vito's evil twin.

CHAPTER 34

Now the battle on the home front continued to escalate. One night, when he arrived home after cooking all day, Lena confronted him. "Father spends all day yelling. If it isn't at the boys, then it's at me. I don't think I can stand to live like this much longer." Martin knew he was able to avoid the worst of the home life while at work. He had not intended to live under Karlo's roof as long as they had, but it had enabled him to save money to reinvest in his businesses and build a nest egg for the future. Maybe the future is now.

"I know something has to give. We all can't continue to live together. Old men and boys just don't mix. Not to mention, an old buck and young buck are apt to lock horns and fight to the death, so to speak."

Lena nodded, although Martin thought she didn't quite understand his meaning. "What is the solution then?"

"Isn't it obvious? We have to have our own home."

"Oh, Martin, this is our home." Now Lena began to cry and Martin realized the situation would not have an easy answer.

"The other solution is for your father to move out, but this is his home so I don't think we can expect him to do that."

At that moment, Karlo came into the kitchen. "I thought I heard my name mentioned. What seems to be the problem?"

Martin did not want to address him directly, and he certainly did not want to cause a problem between Lena and her father. "We were just discussing how active the boys have become and the fact that they are wreaking havoc in the house."

"You can say that again. Now that we're on the subject, you need to get those boys under control, after all you're they're father. You can't expect Lena to do the job for you."

Now Martin was mad but he knew better than to blow his top, even though he could feel his blood pressure rising and pulse quickening. He looked away and took a couple of deep breaths. Thankfully, Lena stepped into the breach.

"Father, you know Martin is working hard for the family. But his schedule just doesn't give him much time for the children. He's doing his best to be a good father."

"Well, best is not good enough. Before you know it, those boys will be juvenile delinquents. Thank God Clara has you as a role model."

"Karlo, it seems we all can no longer tolerate each other. Do you have a solution besides my finding a new career and giving up my business to spend more time at home?"

"All I know is I'm too old for all this racket I have to put up with. And don't think Clara is so innocent. She screams while the boys fight and carry on. Maybe I should help you down at the restaurant so I can get away, too."

That's all I need. "Look, it's getting late and tomorrow is a school day so the kids will be up early. Let's think things over and talk about this again another time."

The first person in the door for lunch was Karlo. He took the table nearest the kitchen so he could talk with Martin during breaks between customers. Liu noticed him first and pointed. "Martin, look who's here."

Martin stopped what he was doing to take a glance in the direction of Liu's pointer finger. "What in the world is he doing here?" Martin looked down to continue his cooking tasks and pretended that he had not seen Karlo. But since no other customers had yet arrived, Karlo had no hesitation in going into the kitchen to speak directly to Martin.

"I didn't want to wait until some unspecified future time to discuss the home front. We need to come to some sort of resolution."

"Well, your timing is off. Can't you see I'm getting ready for the lunch hour and am in no frame of mind to brainstorm solutions with you?"

"Okay. I'll wait until lunch is over. Then you should have time to focus on the issue. Meanwhile, I might as well eat. What is the fish of the day?"

"Sit down. I will send Chao over with the menu, and he can answer any questions you might have." Karlo shuffled back to the table. This was the first time Martin noticed his gait. He didn't pick up his feet and his stride was off. He's starting to get old—that's what's wrong with him. Young and old just don't mix.

Once lunch was over, Martin pulled up a chair to sit down at Karlo's table. "You had the catch of the day. How did you like it?"

"Sand dabs are one of my favorite fish. It was always a good payday when I pulled them up in my net. And you cooked them to perfection."

"You have so many good memories of fishing, maybe you should go back to it." Even as he humored Karlo, he knew he was getting too old for the type of physical work commercial fishing required, especially in the Pacific Ocean where seas could be rough, unlike the Adriatic which was always smooth sailing.

Karlo shook his head. "You know as well as I do that my fishing days are over. But now let's talk about what's going on at home when I'm there and you're not."

"Go ahead and tell me what's on your mind." Martin did not want to volunteer to move his family out of the house because he did not have the money yet to replace the home they were living in.

"I know nothing can happen right away. So, I propose you give me a job so I have something to do away from the house. Maybe I could work at the grocery store."

Martin thought a minute before answering. This may turn out better than he thought, at least it would bide him time until he could find a solution to their living arrangements. "Karlo, give me a minute to take off this apron and put on my jacket and let's go over to the grocery where we can talk about what you might like to do."

Karlo had only been in the store once before since Lena did the shopping, so he was completely taken by surprise by what he saw. The store was packed with women shopping and gossiping and having coffee together. It was so lively, totally different from what he had been used to or expected.

Martin escorted Karlo through the store, giving him the grand tour, stopping from time to time, while women asked Karlo about himself and the family. Finally, Martin got to the last stop on the tour. "What do you think of our fish counter?"

"Well, give me a chance to study it." Karlo looked carefully at each fish selection before answering. "From this side, I think some improvements can be made to make the fish more appealing such as a different arrangement. But what I really want to study, especially with my nose, is the other side of the case. Fish has to smell fresh to sell it."

"Okay. Let's go around the corner so you can inspect the fish from the fishmonger's point of view."

Karlo took a whiff. "Oh, how I love the smell of the sea. Fresh fish should smell of the sea." Then he went down the line of fish, taking an olfactory sample as he moved along. "That one—the cod—is not fresh. My advice is not to sell it. Throw it out. The neighborhood cats will thank you."

"Are you crazy. I'm not throwing it out. First, I'll try to cure it with salt. And then if it's still not good when I try it months later, then I'll get rid of it." But all this talking about fish gave Martin an idea. "Karlo, how would you like to become a fishmonger? You know so much about fish already, and I bet you know how to filet them, too. You'd be a natural salesman behind the counter, giving tips to housewives on what to buy and how to prepare it. What do you say?"

"I don't know. I'll have to think it over. You'll have my answer tonight." Martin caught a smug smile cross his lips and knew he liked the idea. This might be good for both of us.

CHAPTER 35

When Martin arrived home that evening, Karlo was waiting for him. "I've made my decision. I'll become a fishmonger."

"That's good news. You can start tomorrow."

"Tomorrow won't be soon enough for me."

"Be ready by seven a.m., and we 'll go together so I can get you started and introduce you to Hong who will show you what you need to know."

The next morning Karlo was waiting for Martin in the kitchen over a cup of coffee. He looked more energetic than he had in a long time. This was going to give him a new lease on life, Martin mused. "Let me join you in a cup of coffee. Then we'll find something for breakfast at the store."

Martin and Karlo arrived at the grocery store just as Hong was opening the door. Martin introduced Karlo and asked Hong to join them at the fish counter as soon as he finished his opening duties. In the meantime, Martin gave Karlo an apron and a tour of the fish area. When Hong appeared, they showed Karlo how to set up the fish counter for the day with ice and the wide variety of fish stored in the cooler. Karlo had his own ideas, which he suggested they try for the display. With the three of them all pitching in, they had the counter ready in no time. It wasn't long before a customer arrived. Karlo stepped right up to help her. Martin and Hong stood back watching, amused and impressed. The woman left with several pounds of fish, some of which she had never tried before, but had been convinced to purchase.

Martin smiled all the way to the restaurant, thinking about how cleverly he had solved the home front problem. But his smile did not last long. At dinnertime, the first person through the door was Karlo. Martin looked up in surprise. "What are you doing here?"

"I finished my shift at the grocery and now I'm here for dinner. The last thing I want to do after a long, hard day as a fishmonger is to enter that noisy house with children carrying on and Lena screaming at them."

Martin frowned. When Karlo took a seat at a table, he went back to preparing for the dinner hour but he couldn't keep his mind from thoughts of Karlo's presence and what that meant for the future. But he was soon to find out.

Karlo didn't stay in his seat for long. Since there were no customers yet in the restaurant, he went into the kitchen to watch Martin and shoot the bull with him. "My plan is to have dinner here every evening after work. Maybe you can give me a task or two here as well."

Martin scowled but he did not want to get in an argument. "We can talk about that later. Did Chao tell you the specials of the day?"

"Not yet so why don't you."

"We have some fresh abalone. I'm going to dredge it in flour, then sauté it and nap it with a beurre blanc. Risotto and asparagus will round out the plate."

"You've sold me. Maybe you should become a fishmonger, too. Did I tell you that most of the customers bought more than they had intended. Hong was impressed."

After Karlo finished his dinner, he continued to hang around, talking to friends and barging his way into the kitchen whenever business slowed down. Martin was beside himself. This cannot continue.

Martin didn't know whether Karlo had gotten the message his body language was sending or not. Or if he wanted instead to eat his dinner at home, even though Martin could out-cook Lena even on a bad day. But he was happy Karlo wasn't showing up night after night and didn't give it another thought until a few weeks later.

"How's it going with Karlo home again in the evenings?"

Lena raised an eyebrow. "He's not spending his time here. I thought he was with you down at the restaurant."

Martin gave a sly smile. "I guess we have a mystery to solve."

"I doubt there is anything sinister going on. Let's just ask him when we see him next."

As Martin and Lena prepared to head off to bed, they heard the lock on the door and Karlo lumbered in, humming to himself. They looked at each other, quizzical expressions on their faces. Before they could utter a word, Karlo appeared in the living room.

"What…are you two waiting up for me? Am I not old enough to make my own curfew?"

"Now that you bring up the subject, we would like to know what's been keeping you out late."

"If you must know, I have a lady friend. We met at the fish counter so it's as if we were properly introduced." Lena's mouth opened wide as if in shock. Martin had a difficult time suppressing a chuckle.

"Don't look at me like that, you two. Anna finds me a very attractive man, even if I'm only a shadow of my former self."

Lena regained her poise. "Anna…what is her last name?"

"Kolonich. Her late husband was Matteo Kolonich. He started one of the packing plants in town. Now Anna's two sons run the business."

"Well, now that we know you have a lady friend, when are we going to meet her?" said Martin.

"When she gives me an answer."

Lena was almost afraid to ask. "What answer?"

"The answer to my proposal. I want to marry her," Karlo said with a mark of pride on his face.

Lena and Martin looked at each other, not knowing what to say. Then Martin took the initiative. "So, when she accepts, we will have a celebration with the family."

"It might be a wedding reception. At my age, I don't want a long engagement."

It wasn't long until Karlo announced that Anna had agreed to marry him. He told Lena and Martin, "Her sons seem to have some reservations about our plans. I think they want to keep their mother to themselves but even more so the business. They don't want a new husband getting any part of it if Anna should die first."

The following Sunday the entire family on both sides gathered in Lena's dining room to share dinner and discuss the wedding arrangements. Karlo spoke for both Anna and himself when he said, "We want a Catholic service with just family and close friends present. We're not going to run off and elope as if our love is some sordid affair. We want it recognized for what it is—a love of souls yearning for affection and companionship in later life. And we want your blessing."

Martin glanced at Filip whom he thought should do the honors. But since he had not made a move in that direction, as one of the men of the house, Martin raised his glass and offered a toast. "Karlo and Anna, may you have many years of happiness and may the joining of our two families only increase your joy."

Within the month, the two families were gathered together again along with close friends at the Chapel of Notre Dame on Main Street. The bride, a tall, thin woman with nearly white hair, wore a full-length dress of beige silk and covered her head with a wide-brimmed hat trimmed with flowers and feathers. The groom wore a dark suit with a single white rose in his lapel. The service was a full Mass conducted by the monsignor of St. Patrick's. A day that started out foggy turned to sun as the crowd left the chapel for the reception at Lena and Martin's house. When they arrived, a champagne lunch was awaiting them along with a three-tiered wedding cake decorated with sugar roses.

Martin had met Anna's sons, Dimitri and Victor, a few years before and had served them at his restaurant many times. They were a pair of bookends—both tall, thin, and dark-haired with steely-blue eyes that could cut to the quick. Now he tried to develop more of a friendship with them since they were family. But they remained aloof and only gave curt answers to his questions. Martin realized that this union of Karlo's had not been made in heaven.

After sljivovica had finished off the celebration, Karlo and Anna left by train for a honeymoon in San Francisco. Neither of them had spent much time in the city, especially in recent years, so they looked forward to being there. Martin contacted Stan, his friend who was head chef at the Fairmont, to let him know Karlo and Anna would be staying at the hotel and asked him to give them the royal treatment. The pair returned home, looking like a pair of lovebirds still enjoying the springtime of their lives.

Karlo had barely been back a day when he confronted Martin. "I no longer can devote all my time to fish mongering. Anna is lonely during the day and wants me to keep her company in more ways than one." A sly smile crossed Karlo's lips. "We need to make the most of the time we have left. But I can still work a few mornings a week which will give Anna time to get ready for my return."

Martin was not happy that he was going to lose the best fishmonger he had ever had or probably would ever have again. But he couldn't complain since Karlo had moved out of the house, giving his family both space and peace. "All right, I understand. We will work out a schedule that suits you. I certainly don't want to lose you entirely. You have been a real asset to the store, and you have a lot to teach your understudy."

Despite Prohibition, the twenties were roaring as wealth continued to increase in every sector of the economy. Apple prices were up as demand increased, raising bank accounts of every apple farmer in the valley. Martin's restaurant and grocery store benefitted from the good fortune and tables were filled every night while shopping carts were filled every day. Martin could not believe his luck when he counted receipts at the end of the month.

Meantime, the children were all thriving on the good fortune. Clara was turning into a real beauty with long, blond locks and an hourglass figure. The boys, Frankie, Marty, and Tom Paul, were showing signs of promise as their bodies grew strong and fit. While Frankie's was tall and slim, both Marty and Tom Paul were built with sturdy, muscled bodies. The boys even displayed an interest in books, but it was math and science they preferred. All their teachers had praise for them when Lena attended their school conferences. Their futures looked bright, almost assured.

CHAPTER 36

What had been a dream turned into a nightmare on October 24, 1929 when the stock market crashed, bringing the country to its knees. While stockbrokers in New York City jumped out of skyscraper windows, apple farmers huddled to discuss how to stem the crisis. Martin worried his businesses might go under during this challenging financial time, especially the restaurant to which he had given his heart and soul. He continued to struggle making ends meet for a couple of years, but finally he had to have a serious talk with Lena.

"I'm afraid we might lose everything if we don't do something fast. The restaurant is nearly empty day after day and housewives are extremely frugal at the grocery store. There are few choices left to us."

"Oh, Martin, I know how heavy your burden is. I've been worried sick but didn't want you to know. Clara is twenty now, a young woman who should be thinking of marriage and a family. But who can plan a future in times like this?"

"She could get a job and Frankie could work, too, after school. That would help our situation."

"Maybe I should go to work. Clara is old enough to run the household. If I have to earn a living in a packing shed, it won't matter much since my youth is behind me. But I don't want Clara to become a workwoman with rough hands and fractured nails. No man worth his salt would look at her if she ends up like that."

"If you are willing to work in a packing plant, I will talk with Karlo. Maybe Anna's sons can find you a job."

Martin looked at Lena and saw tears bubbling up in her eyes until they overflowed and sent her into a full-blown crying fit. Instead of hugging her, he hung his head low, feeling like a failure. Lena had held up her end of the bargain, keeping a nice home, raising good children, and always being a loving, supportive partner to him. But had he kept up his end of the bargain? He was rarely home until late at night for the express reason of earning a living. But now, he couldn't even do that with the situation the country was in. Lena was now going to have to help earn a living, too. No wonder so many New Yorkers jumped out of windows—they just couldn't face themselves nor their wives.

Karlo was adamantly against Lena working as Martin suggested. He refused to ask his sons-in-law if they could offer her a job. "You just have to do more, Martin. You are the man in the family. And don't forget you are living in my house rent-free. What would happen if you had to pay a mortgage, too?"

That was a low blow and Martin felt its power rivet through his body and also his mind. Karlo knew the money he was saving on rent was being sent back to the old country to help his family. "If you won't help us, I'll go to someone else. We have friends in this town that are sometimes better than family."

A silence lay between them while they both reflected on their words and the situation. "I'll see what I can do," said Karlo. "But I still don't like the idea that Lena has to go to work in that environment with Chinks, Mexicans, and low-class women. She'll never be the same again."

The next week Lena reported to Dimitri at the packing shed to begin her job. "I am going to train you to be an inspector and sorter. That's an important job and requires awareness and dedication."

"What exactly will I be doing?"

"You will be sorting the apples by grade and type, while separating out the ones not fit for selling."

"I thought I would be packing apples."

"That's done after the grader passes them on. The packer must work quickly, wrapping each apple in paper and placing it in a crate, a job requiring skill but not judgment. You're much better than that."

"I understand and am ready to start my job now."

"You will notice it's chilly in the plant. That's because we need to keep the temperature cold so the apples stay crisp. Remember to dress for the cold when you come. But in case you forget to wear a sweater or coat, I have some extras in the closet that you can borrow for the day."

Dmitri stood up and motioned for Lena to follow him to the shed. She immediately felt the chilled air when she entered, shivering. Dimitri noticed Lena wrapping her arms around herself and went to the closet to retrieve a sweater to keep her warm. Then he introduced her to Rose who was going to teach her everything she needed to know about inspecting apples.

Lena looked around the room and recognized several of the women who were the wives of apple farmers. It turned out that there were different classes of women working in the packing sheds—some farmers' wives and daughters, some townswomen needing work, and some immigrant women of various races. Dimitri assigned Lena to work in an area with the farmers' wives and daughters. Then Rose began to show Lena how to sort the apples and remove culls. The best thing about the job was that Lena could visit with the other women while she worked. Not only did it make the work go faster, but she passed the time in a pleasant way, even making new friends whom she might never have met otherwise.

When payday came at the end of the week, Lena felt a new source of pride at receiving money for the work she had done. It was a major step forward for women when they won the vote in 1920. But it was a huge step for this one woman when she realized she could receive pay for a job well done just like a man. Lena put the money in her purse and went home with a sense of self-esteem she had never felt before. *I like working much better than I realized.*

Meantime, Clara managed the household work and even took in sewing on the side. Frankie got a job at Filip's apple farm while Marty got a paper route. Tom Paul was still a bit too young to work but helped Marty fold and deliver papers and make collections at the end of the month. When Tom Paul was old enough, he would get his own paper route to help the family, too.

Martin had heard that more than a quarter of wage-earning workers in America had no job and now Oakies were heading to California in droves in search of farm work. They started in the southern part of the Central Valley and followed the harvest northward just like Martin had done after the earthquake—only they traveled with their entire family along, which was causing a housing shortage. Squatter camps were set up as temporary living quarters, but even so the million or more migrants put a strain on the communities they inhabited.

From time to time, an unkempt man dressed in tattered clothes would enter the Dalmatian Coast Cafe, looking for a handout. Martin knew what it was like to be without food from his experience living in Croatia. He would take pity on the man who probably had a family to feed and was depending on what he could bring home. But Martin did not want these men hanging around the restaurant during the dinner hour so he would tell them to come back after closing time. Then he would hand them a bag of leftovers and always tried to include a loaf of bread, the staff of life, which had supported the lives of the poor through many troubled times. President Hoover's promise of a chicken in every pot had failed to materialize, leaving the pot empty.

The farmers did not like Martin feeding the Oakies and sent Filip to tell him so. "Martin, I've been chosen to give you the message to stop feeding the hungry."

"What? Am I not to follow what our Lord asks of us?"

"I know you sympathize with these people and I do, too. But we no longer have work for them so we want them to move on. As long as they can get some bread, they'll continue hanging on."

"Tell your farmer friends that if they want me to stop, they need to come and shoo the hungry away themselves. I won't turn them away when I have food they could eat, which would just end up getting tossed in the garbage."

"Is that your final word then?"

"It is." Then he thought about it a moment. "Tell them if they are ever hard on their luck and need some bread, they are always welcome to come by for a hand out, too."

Filip knew it was better to hold his tongue. He shook Martin's hand and left.

CHAPTER 37

In 1932, the country elected a new president, Franklin Delano Roosevelt, who promised a New Deal, telling Americans that "the only thing we have to fear is fear itself." He initiated a number of public works projects, providing jobs for the unemployed. He also put an end to Prohibition, an act Martin especially appreciated. He could hardly wait to tell Officer Soldati to go to hell the next time he came around with his envelope. Paying protection money had never sat well with him.

Soon after President Roosevelt took the Office of President in 1933, another world leader was beginning his rise. The worldwide economic collapse triggered by the stock market crash gave communism and Nazism a chance to spread across Europe thus setting the stage for Adolph Hitler to gain a foothold in the German government as chancellor and eventually Fuhrer of the German Third Reich after the death of Paul von Hindenburg in 1934.

Croatians, whose favorite pastime was discussing politics, gathered for lunch at the Dalmatian Coast Cafe and lingered so Martin could join them. From watching the Austrian regime up close, they could read the hidden agenda in Hitler's moves and were worried about the future of their relatives left behind in the old country.

Karlo started things off addressing Martin who always seemed in the know. "What do you think of this guy Hitler?

"He has had a very curious rise to power which makes me suspicious," said Martin, as he lit a cigarette.

"Me, too," said Michael. "And don't forget he's Austrian. Living in Vienna he had a chance to observe the Habsburgs up-close and learn from them."

"Why are you so suspicious of him?" Filip asked.

"Well, his background is sketchy," Michael said. "He comes out of the Great War with a rank equivalent to our private first class—certainly nothing to brag about. He served mostly as a runner carrying messages back and forth, which was so dangerous only a crazy person would want to do it. Then somehow he gets involved with the Workers Party and forms the Nazi Party, becoming president of it. And then he ends up in jail for treason. But miraculously he was able to keep reinventing himself."

"I'll tell you how," said Karlo. "The depression, unemployment, starvation, chaos. People were looking for a savior and he seemed to have all the answers."

"That's right. And he actually did a few things to make life better," said Martin. He paused to take a drag of his cigarette. "Then he ran for president and lost to Hindenburg who must have believed in keeping enemies closer so he appointed Hitler chancellor. The people certainly knew what they were doing when they rejected Hitler. But the eighty-five-year-old president was probably in his dotage, so he didn't understand the consequences."

"Well," said Michael, "the people should have risen up when he combined chancellor and president into the one role of Fuhrer. He set himself up as a dictator."

"When he disregarded the Versailles Treaty someone should have corrected him," Henrik said.

"Everyone knew the Versailles Treaty was no good, no way to keep the peace," Michael said. "But when other countries learned of the military buildup, they should have sounded a worldwide alarm."

"France, especially, should have been the one since they are the most vulnerable. But Russia, too, was no friend of Germany. It makes me wonder how good its spy network really is," said Karlo.

"Most of you have either never lived in Europe or have been away for a long time. But Michael and I remember how it was," said Martin. "Relationships are very complicated and each country is trying to jockey for the best position."

"That's right," said Michael. "But we should be very watchful."

"I agree with Michael," said Martin. "Watch for now. Action will come later. But I predict this Hitler guy is up to no good." And he ground his cigarette butt forcefully into an ashtray.

Everyone left, shaking their heads, not knowing what was about to happen to the world.

Chapter 38

Clara had been dating a young man named Peter Kalinich during the past year. He was the son of an apple farmer and was following in his father's footsteps. Clara's Uncle Henrik had introduced them since his farm was nearby the Kalinich's. One Sunday Peter had been invited to dinner with the family. But before the meal was served, he asked to speak with Martin privately. "You are aware that Clara and I have been courting," Peter said, his blue eyes fixed and sincere. Martin nodded, urging him to continue while taking his measure. Peter was a well-built young man, tall with broad shoulders. Martin liked the strength his bearing displayed. "I have grown very fond of Clara; in fact, I am in love with her, and I think she feels the same way about me." Martin remained silent, knowing what was coming next. Taking a deep breath, Peter said, "I would like to ask your permission for her hand in marriage."

Now it was Martin's turn to speak. "Have you spoken to Clara about your feelings?"

"Yes, she knows my intentions are honorable."

"And how will your support her and future children?"

"Apples raised me and my siblings, proving their worth. I will continue to farm."

"And where will you live?"

"There is a small house on our property that my father will let me have."

"It sounds as if you are depending on your father for everything. A married man has to be able to stand on his own two feet."

"You are right about that. I have money saved to buy my own farm, and when I find the right piece of land, I will seal the deal. But our love cannot wait so I have made intermediate arrangements."

"Peter, I like you very much and would welcome you as a son-in-law. I just want to make sure you're prepared for all the responsibilities marriage brings."

"Don't worry about me. I am more than equal to the task. My father has set a good example for me."

"That he certainly has. Well, Peter, you have my blessing. A wedding will give our families something to look forward to with hope for the future." Martin took a step toward Peter and shook his hand. "Clara will make you a good wife. She, too, has had a good example to follow."

That evening as Martin and Lena were settling into bed, Lena said, "I guess we're lucky we only have one girl, one wedding. But I don't know what's going to happen to the boys since they won't have much to offer a prospective bride."

"You're right…one wedding is all we can afford, if that." But he was thinking that boys were not going to be such good luck the way the world was heading…war seemed a foregone conclusion, but he wouldn't mention it to Lena, at least not tonight, when she had a little happiness over Clara's engagement. He kissed Lena good night before turning off the light.

Now in the darkness, Martin's thoughts and fears were beginning to confront him. This guy Hitler is up to no good. But maybe he'll confine his ambitions to Europe. Although he knew that would not be the case from his experience with the Great War. England would come to the defense of France, and then we would be drawn into the conflict, like it or not. *My American dream is always out of reach. In fact, it could turn into a nightmare.*

Martin noticed Lena was restless in the bed. They both need to relieve their stress. He turned toward Lena and began caressing her and she responded with caresses of her own. Before long they had both reached ecstasy, trying to control their moans so as not to disturb the children. As was his habit and Lena's preference, Martin let the passion ease and then brought on their climaxes a second time. The way he felt tonight, he could go for a third time, but he wasn't sure Lena was ready for it. But the bad thoughts had not been banished. He asked Lena if she was ready for more. With her permission and willingness, Martin rode the wave of his passion a third time, quite a feat for a man his age, until he finally exhausted himself to sleep. Lena gave him a kiss goodnight and snuggled up close before sleep took hold of her, too.

Within the year, Clara and Peter were married at St. Patrick's Church, guests filling the church, including an entourage of family and friends from San Francisco. Afterward, Clara moved into the cottage on Peter's ranch but continued to take care of the family home so Lena could work and bring in a few wages.

Chapter 39

The news from Europe was foreboding. Tensions continued to rise as major developments evolved. In 1936, Germany and Italy signed a treaty to form the Rome-Berlin Axis. And Germany and Japan signed a pact against the Soviet Union and the international communist movement. In mid-1937 Japan crossed the East China Sea to invade China, a move historians would designate as the start of World War II in the Pacific.

A few days later, Ken Nakamura stopped into the Dalmatian Coast Cafe for lunch, which he did several days a week. Since the cafe was located near Watsonville's Japantown, the restaurant was patronized by many Japanese who appreciated fresh fish and even more, the way Martin prepared it. Today when Ken walked in, Martin noticed he seemed upset and not his usual happy-go-lucky self. Ken had the body of a judo master and, at times, the serene demeanor of a Bodhisattva. Since he had no other customers at the moment, Martin stepped out of the kitchen and approached Ken's table. "How are you today?" he asked with a note of good cheer in his voice.

"Oh, Martin, I am worried. You know Japan is now at war with China. This does not look good for the future."

"Do you have close family members in Japan?"

"It's not my extended family I am concerned about. I am afraid for my family here in America."

"But why? You're all citizens."

"Haven't you noticed we have slanted eyes and yellow skin?"

"But you're American nonetheless. Don't forget this country has the Constitution that protects its citizens."

"I hope you're right. But still I worry. We Japanese think generations ahead, so everything we work toward is long-term, not just the here and now."

"Well, don't think you're the only ones worried about war. We Croatians talk about the events going on in Europe every day and fear for our brethren in the old country. So, I think between Croatians and Japanese, most of our town is caught in a vise. The few Mexicans here are the only ones with no cares. They can just hightail it back across the border until things settle down. Besides they live in the moment, always putting everything off until mañana, you know, tomorrow."

When Martin returned to the kitchen, Liu and Chao scowled at him. "What's the matter with you two?"

"Have you forgotten we're Chinese?" Liu asked. "That bastard's motherland is attacking ours."

"Wait a minute. Regardless of our descent, we are all Americans here. And I don't want you to mistreat any of our customers because of some political problem happening thousands of miles away." Liu and Chao gave each other a look, expressing their distaste for Martin's words. They turned away and refused to look Martin in the eye the rest of the day. Martin understood their body language, but he hoped common sense would restore them to reason.

Chapter 40

In 1938, two major events occurred—one good, one bad. Clara and Peter's first child, a son, was born following two miscarriages, which had caused the families to fear the couple would be childless. Baby Peter was a healthy child of good weight whose sunny disposition brought light into their world, which was receding into darkness. Then in March, Germany annexed Austria, an act known as Anschluss. The day the news broke, Croatians gathered at the Dalmatian Coast Cafe to discuss the situation. "It doesn't look good," Martin said. "Germany is probably gearing up for another war."

"But what does this mean for Croatia?" Karlo asked.

"I don't know. But the Jews are being targeted, and Aryanization is being pursued," said Filip.

"And were does that leave us Slavs?" Karlo said. "We fall below Jews in the pecking order."

"It's out of our hands," said Martin. "Right now, all we can do is stand by and watch."

"And pray and hope," said Karlo. "Never, never underestimate the power of prayer. I'm going to ask for a Mass to be said for our countrymen."

"If necessary," Filip said, "we can get resources to Croatia. A lot of us have the money to do it."

"With prayers and money, Croatians should be able to stand strong," said Martin. But he feared their young Kingdom of Yugoslavia would be vulnerable to the evil powers surrounding them.

Everyone's fears turned to reality on September 1, 1939 when Germany invaded Poland. Two days later, Great Britain and France declared war on Germany while the US remained on the sidelines, watching and speculating about the events to come. Croatians poured into Martin's restaurant for a late lunch and stayed for an impromptu political discussion. "What does this mean for Croatia?" Michael asked.

"What you should be asking is, what does this mean for the US? So far, we're neutral but President Roosevelt will only be able to withstand pressure from Churchill for so long. And then where will that leave us and, most importantly, our sons? Don't forget I served in World War I, if only to protect merchant ships, but I got a taste of war, and it has left a foul flavor in my mouth."

A couple of weeks later, the Soviet Union invaded Poland as well, and less than a year later annexed the Baltic states of Latvia, Ukraine, and Lithuania.

As bad as the situation was, the apple growers conceded it was an opportunity to make money. As long as people need to eat and their own supplies are short, US farmers could meet the demand. And the more the demand, the higher the prices. No one liked to take advantage of war, but that was the reality. And almost overnight, the country emerged from the Depression. Goods and services were needed to fuel the war machine, and America was in the position to provide them.

CHAPTER 41

On Palm Sunday 1941, most of the Croatian community was gathered at Mass to remember Christ's entry into Jerusalem that marks the beginning of Holy Week. Each congregant had held a palm, symbol of peace and redemption, in their hands as they progressed into the church to take their seat. Before the conclusion of the Mass, the priest asked everyone to bow their heads and pray for Croatia. "Just hours ago, it was invaded on all sides by the Axis powers of Germany, Italy, Hungary, and Bulgaria." A communal gasp was let out that reverberated throughout the nave as men grew angry and women wept for their families left behind in a country caught up in a war waged by others. Red and white are the colors for Palm Sunday, symbolizing the blood Christ gave to redeem the world. This symbolism was not lost on Croatians that day, as they linked the colors to the Croatian Coat of Arms set in a chessboard pattern. Martin thought Croatians would be giving blood as pawns in a chess game being played by world powers so evil, they had no respect for humanity.

After Mass, everyone gathered in the reception room for coffee, but even the camaraderie could not take away the somber mood. Michael came up to Martin and said, "Now our immigration to America has really been worth it. Croatians are going to suffer and who knows if they will ever know peace much less prosperity." Martin just nodded and moved his family out the door. He wanted to go home where peace could still be found.

Clara, Peter, and Petie arrived at home just behind them. With a three-year-old running around, Martin guessed he would not have much peace. And he was right. But it was his thoughts that would not give him peace. As he looked at Petie, he thought of his brother and father, both named Peter. His father was now well into his seventies, an old man but one who still lived a full life. An old man deserves to enjoy his old age and the fruits of his labors. It would be a long while before he could do that and would probably die beforehand.

Palm Sunday dinner was a somber occasion as everyone present was alone with their own thoughts, reflecting on the events of the day. When Holy Week arrived, Christ's passion was not something that happened hundreds of years ago, it was a penetrating agony lived to the depths of their souls.

Monday was usually a slow day at the restaurant. But today it was packed to near overflowing with Croatians prepared to discuss world politics. Karlo had contacted the Croatian Fraternal Union in San Francisco to learn about the situation and asked that he be kept apprised. He came prepared today to stir the pot. "Those Nazis bombed Belgrade. Our motherland along with all our relatives, even beloved mothers and fathers, may perish from this earth. Though a lot of us are blond-haired and blue-eyed, they see Slavs when they look at us, and they don't want to have to look at us twice."

The crowd turned to Martin to look for his response. "We have to become politically active, organize, and pressure our representatives to help Croatia. There's not a lot more that we can do from this distance."

A young Croatian in the crowd yelled, "We could send our own army to fight."

That comment fell on deaf ears. Martin spoke up again. "While we organize here, we can wait for our brethren over there to act and then follow their lead."

It didn't take long for Croatians to mount a resistance called The Partisans or the National Liberation Army founded on June 22, 1941, now remembered as Anti-Fascist Struggle Day. The group led by Joseph Broz Tito had two advantages: It was founded on ideology not ethnicity, so it could attract recruits throughout the region. Besides Croatians, units were comprised of Serbs, Slovenes, Italians, Hungarians, Czechs, Jews, Montenegrins, Muslims, and even ethnic Germans living outside Germany. And second, it also had in its ranks Spanish War veterans who had fought a similar war to the one the Croatians now found themselves in. They had the support of the Soviet Union which had instructed them in guerilla warfare and proved to be highly effective over the course of the war due to the rugged terrain that provided good cover. During World War II, they became known as Europe's most effective resistance force.

Through the Croatian Fraternal Union, Watsonville's Croatian community learned about the resistance efforts of the Partisans. They had made several attacks since forming. Meantime, the town's apple farmers were doing their part shipping apples overseas, mostly to England, which was desperate for them. While US ships provided escort, German U-boats occasionally torpedoed the merchant ships, sending its cargo to the bottom of the sea.

CHAPTER 42

On Sunday morning, December 7, 1941, Martin and his family were having breakfast before they departed for Mass. Little did they know that at 9:53 a.m. Pacific time the Japanese had attacked Pearl Harbor. They went onto Mass as if it were an ordinary Sunday, but later they would realize this Sunday had been like no other in their lives or the history of the world.

When the distribution of communion was over, Monsignor sat in his chair to meditate, as usual. What was not usual was that an altar boy delivered a note to the priest. Those congregants deep in prayer or just not paying attention missed Monsignor's face go white while his lips murmured, "God have mercy." Then he sat back in his chair stunned, trying to recover his presence.

During the Concluding Rite, when announcements were often given, Monsignor as shepherd, stood at the podium to inform his flock. "I have just received terrible news of the war. The Japanese bombed Pearl Harbor in Hawaii this morning. There was loss of life and the Pacific Fleet has been crippled."

An uncontrollable outburst of emotion followed as families tried to console each other. The Monsignor quickly turned to prayer, commanding the congregation to join in. This helped focus everyone, stemming the pandemonium that could have occurred. There were a few exchanges of concern between family members and friends before everyone departed to gather around their radios for more details of the sneak attack. With so many Japanese living in town, feelings were mixed about their neighbors. Many people had shared classrooms with Japanese children their age and that experience had led to friendship. Others knew Japanese farmers whom they worked alongside. But others viewed Japanese suspiciously and now they had lived up to their moniker—the *Yellow Peril.*

The next day when Martin entered the restaurant, he was greeted by Liu and Chao who were wearing labels that read, *I am Chinese.* Before Martin could ask the question, Liu volunteered, "We know people think all Asians look alike, so we are making sure they don't confuse us with the Japanese."

Chao added, "Our relatives in San Francisco called last night to tell us what they were doing and suggested we follow along for our own protection."

"That's good thinking. Is Hong wearing one, too?" Martin thought it might be better for business if he did.

Calling December 7, 1941 a date that would live in infamy, President Roosevelt declared war on the Empire of Japan a day later. The Japanese community appeared to lie low for a few days. Then one of the leaders of Watsonville's Japan Society came forward to issue a statement, pledging the Japanese community's loyalty to America.

The next day at the end of the lunch hour, Ken Nakamura appeared in the restaurant, a sheepish look on his face. "Martin, I just want to tell you personally how sorry I am that the Japanese bombed your country. We had no advance knowledge of their plans. My whole community joins in extending condolences and offers to help in any way. Please pass on this message to your family and friends."

Martin motioned for Ken to sit down and he pulled up a chair for himself. "Please don't think we blame you. And this is your country, too, don't forget. You have been a very important part of our community, and we could not get crops harvested without your labor. We will get through this war together and come out the better for it." Although, Martin wondered if this crazy world would ever be the same.

"Thank you for your kind words. I will share them with everyone at our Japan Society meeting tonight."

After Ken left, Martin sat in silence. The image of a thousand Japanese carrying lanterns as they marched in the Apple Annual Parade bubbled up in his memory. How could he ever forget that awesome sight? Later the Japanese entered beautiful patriotic floats in the fourth of July parades, artistically decorated with flowers. And when they learned they were not paying enough taxes for the schools their children attended, due to the Alien Land Law, they donated thousands of cherry trees to the town. They have bent over backwards to become part of our community. People have to be judged by their hearts and minds not by the color of their skin or their ethnicity. There are so many divisions in the Kingdom of Yugoslavia based on ethnicity alone, so he knew what that could do to a people and a country. But the Partisans had been clever and had used ideas not ethnicity as a way to coalesce. Ideas are so powerful. That would make them a potent force.

Nevertheless, fear took hold as rumors spread that a Japanese carrier was lurking off the coast of San Francisco and a blackout ordered. Radar had also picked up enemy planes approaching from out at sea. And Japanese subs launched attacks on American ships up and down the California coast, targeting nine coast towns and lighthouses—among them Monterey Bay.

Within a few days, Ken entered the restaurant looking anxious and upset. Martin had just finished cleaning up the kitchen, so he took off his apron and met Ken half way. "Is something wrong?"

He noticed Ken was on the verge of tears. "Yesterday, the FBI came to Japantown." FBI, Martin thought, this sounds like something out of a spy novel. "They arrested all the Issei (first generation) leadership and put them in jail."

At first, Martin was at a loss for words. Then he said, "I never thought anything like that would happen in this country. In Croatia, yes. But here, never."

"Well, it's true. I just wanted you to know." Their eyes met and held a moment in solidarity until Ken turned and went out the door.

Chapter 43

Since Christmas was coming, Martin thought it would be a kind gesture to prepare some holiday gift baskets for their Japanese neighbors to lift their spirits. He contacted his brothers-in-law who donated apples and offered to contact other farmers who might have excess produce. Martin talked to Hong at the grocery store and they brainstormed items to add to the baskets. "Bread is an absolute necessity." Martin knew there must be close to a thousand people living in Japantown—over a hundred families. He knew it would be impossible to put together a hundred baskets. But he thought with a little sharing, something like the parable of the loaves and fish, a little could go a long way to not only fill stomachs but soothe souls.

The Sunday before Christmas, Martin arranged for his helpers to be at the restaurant to accept donations and put together baskets. The work went quickly and there was more than enough to fill over twenty baskets. At the last minute, a truck arrived and brought in a crate. It was filled with sparkling apple cider—the perfect finishing touch. Once the bottles had been added to the bounty, everyone stood back and admired their festive creations.

Martin knew from Ken that the Japan Society would be meeting later that afternoon for a holiday dinner. He wanted to deliver the baskets there so they would have them for their celebration, and whatever was left over could be taken home. Martin and his helpers loaded up the car trunks and drove to Japantown, which was only a few blocks away at the southern end of Main Street. Martin had driven by many times but had never been through the town and so was quite amazed by what he saw. He said to Liu who was driving with him, "Look at all the shops and services; they have even a church. They are completely self-sufficient."

"I think they got the idea from us. When they first came to Watsonville, they lived in Chinatown located across the river. Then when they began building their own town, they had a good model to follow."

Martin glanced at Liu and saw he had a smug look on his face. He knew Liu was not sorry about the fate that the Japanese had come to.

"Ah, I see they have a grocery store. No wonder they don't shop in mine very often." Next they passed a newspaper office. "I'd like to know what they're reporting about the war. I'm surprised it hasn't been shut down yet."

Finally, Martin found the Japan Society location where Ken was waiting for him, dressed in a kimono. As soon as he pulled up to the curb, Ken called for help and they unloaded the trunks quickly. "We are so grateful for your gifts," Ken said. "At what is a sad time for us, your thoughtfulness makes us feel embraced by your friendship. Whatever happens, we will never forget your kindness." Martin shook his hand and said, "Merry Christmas." As he walked to the car, he noticed Japanese families arriving for their celebration, all dressed in kimonos, even the little children. The women looked very elegant with their hair worn in a chignon style, accented with decorative sticks and flowers. When they took their tiny steps, the kimonos fluttered behind them. It's all very exotic, Martin thought. *I feel as if I'm in another world.*

When he slid into his seat, he glanced over at Liu who was staring out the window. Caught in the act, he turned to face straight ahead but he kept his thoughts to himself. Martin couldn't help but wonder what they were. Was he just intrigued by them or did he have something sinister in mind? *Everywhere it is the same. Instead of looking for the common thread, we look for differences and fight about them.* Then he started the car and headed out of Japantown a different way so he could see more of it. Lots of trees had been planted, and he assumed they were cherries but it was winter so he could not be sure. And then he came upon a second church.

He didn't know much about Japanese beliefs, except for Buddha, but he assumed they must run deep to have built two churches. As they made their way back down Main Street, he wanted to say a prayer for all the people in Japantown. The prayer of St. Francis came to mind…*Make me a channel of your peace…*

When Martin arrived home for Sunday dinner, he found his son-in-law, his three brothers-in-law, and Karlo gathered in the living room in the midst of an emotional discussion. When Martin walked in, an abrupt silence ensued. Then Karlo said to Filip, "Tell him what happened." Martin looked around, taking in the expressions on everyone's faces and drew a deep breath. He had no idea what to expect and wanted to prepare himself for the worst.

"It was just learned that an American tanker was fired upon by a Japanese submarine just off Cypress Point in Monterey Bay. He avoided all eight shots by zigzagging, and the ship was protected by large ocean swells, which prevented the sub from moving in. It was a close call."

The news shocked Martin to his core. He remembered his honeymoon tour of 17-Mile Drive when they stopped at the Lone Cypress, a symbol of strength, endurance, and stability. It had held its ground for at least two hundred years, a silent witness to history. If it could only speak, what stories it might tell.

Karlo, not one to ever lose the humor in a situation, said, "Golfers at Pebble Beach noticed the ship's unusual movement but didn't take their eyes off their balls long enough to realize it was under attack."

"I know about zigzagging," Martin said. "We had to do it during World War I. I guess those golfers weren't navy…probably army…they keep boots on the ground and eyes, too, from what you're telling me."

"This war is too close to home," Josip said. "And my fear is it is going to swallow us up."

"Dinner is served." Lena's voice was a welcome interruption. The men quickly moved into the dining room to share a holiday meal on the last Sunday of Advent.

After grace, Lena said, "What were you men talking about that had you so engrossed in conversation?"

No one rushed in to answer her. Then Karlo, the patriarch, stepped up. "We were discussing the war. You all might as well know there was a sub attack on one of our freighters yesterday near Cypress Point."

The women let out a collective, "Oh no," as they looked around the table to take in the deeper meaning by body language.

"Don't worry," said Henrik. "They missed. Must be bad shots."

His comments added some levity to the conversation. But Martin quickly turned it around again. "We have to be prepared to send sons to war. The draft will start soon, and all my boys will be eligible since they are all single and in their twenties. Remember, I was in my early thirties when I served in World War I and they had no problem taking me. Of course, I volunteered."

Tom Paul said, "I want to volunteer like you did, Papa."

"Me, too," said Marty.

"I didn't have sons to send them off to die on a battlefield," Lena said forcefully.

"It's best to wait to see what happens," Martin said. "Then you will know what your options are."

"All this talk of war is scaring Petie. Me, too," Clara said. "Can we change the subject? How did the basket delivery go?"

Clara had restored a sense of calm to the gathering. Then Martin proceeded to tell everyone about his experience in Japantown. "I have a lot of respect for that community. They work hard and have built quite a town for themselves. Seeing the women dressed in their kimonos transported me to another world. They looked so elegant and exotic. But also humble and kind. Ken and his friends were very grateful for our gesture of friendship and support."

Intrigued, Clara asked, "What was the town like? I've never been there."

Then Martin went on to describe everything he saw while his audience hung on every word, anxious to learn as much as they could about the Japanese who had been living amongst them but had kept a low profile. The memory of the Japanese Tea House in San Francisco came to mind. It had been built by a Japanese man for the International Exposition to let people get a glimpse of his culture they rarely saw. Martin realized by the reaction of his relatives, the same thing had gone on here. The Japanese had lived lives hidden from the rest of us.

A few days later, the family was gathered around the table again for Christmas Eve dinner, smiling, talking, sharing stories. Martin thought, the holidays always brighten our days and the traditions anchor us, even while the tides of change swirl around and try to take us under. No matter if it is Croatia under tyranny, earthquake ravaged San Francisco, or here in California where we wait in fear for war, the traditions of the holidays, along with the intimacy of family sharing them, bring comfort. Martin dipped his spoon into the bakalar en brodo, held it to his lips while he savored the familiar smell, and smiled as he swallowed the dish he had made from an old recipe passed down through the generations.

After dinner, the family gathered around the Christmas tree to open presents and sing carols ending with "Silent Night." The night does become holy as we sing songs to remember the Lord's birth heralding his sacrifice for us. Kisses and hugs ended the celebration as most of the party departed for home. Martin and Lena extended the celebration in the privacy of their bedroom. Even though they were both tired from the long day, they made time for each other and especially for love.

CHAPTER 44

Not long after New Year's, Karlo stormed into the restaurant, looking for Martin. When he came out of the storeroom, Karlo said, "I just got a telephone call from one of my old fishing mates in Santa Cruz. He was all worked up about the latest decree." "Slow down. I can barely understand you. Come, take a seat. I'll have Chao bring us some tea."

"My friend is Italian. His name is Giovanni Fallaci. He said that after January twenty-fifth, the government will not allow anyone of Japanese, German, and even Italian descent west of highway one. Do you have any idea what that means for him and his family? He won't be able to earn a living. His boat and the sea are west of the road."

"I can't believe this is happening. First, the FBI arrests first generation Japanese and imprisons them. Now this action against Germans and Italians."

"Many Italians are farmhands and they work the farms along the coast. That is going to hurt the growers and prices will go up hurting everyone."

"The world is going crazy."

"And do you know what else they are doing? They're putting barbed wire along the coast and in the mountains to keep Japs from invading us."

"Do they really think that is going to stop an army? The Japanese will figure out a way around it."

"Well, Giovanni just wants to be able to feed his family. You know what he asked me? If I could fish for him and he would pay me."

"You…fish again? What did you tell him?"

"I told him I pulled up my anchor and hung up my net years ago. There's no way I can go back to it at my age. It requires too much physical strength and stamina."

"Of course you're right about that. But an idea just occurred to me. Marty always liked fishing and from what I've seen, he has it in his blood. Maybe you could take him out and show him the ropes, then he could take it from there."

"I don't know. If it doesn't work out I would have gotten Giovanni's hopes up."

"I think it would work out, otherwise I wouldn't have suggested it. Besides you would be teaching Marty a skill that he could always depend on. The way the world is going everyone needs a specialized skill to get by."

"Well, I'm going to have to think about it and talk with Anna. I don't do anything without her permission."

"In the meantime, I'll ask Marty about it, but my guess is he will be full steam ahead. Spending a day in an orchard is just not for him."

Before the month was over, Karlo and Marty were aboard Giovanni's boat, *Ave Maria*, with a couple of experienced crew who knew the waters the fish schools favor. Their first week, they pulled in quite a haul and even caught a net full of sardines that were running. Giovanni was pleased with their catch and made arrangements for it to be sold. Of course, Karlo always held back a few for himself which he took by the restaurant for Martin to cook. "On Friday night, I plan to have enough for the whole family to feast on. Be prepared." Martin smiled. He was glad his suggestion was turning out so well. "Your son Marty is a natural fisherman. Soon he'll be able to run the operation all by himself."

As soon as one issue was solved, another reared its ugly head. On February 19, 1942, President Roosevelt signed Executive Order 9066, giving the military commander the power to move all Japanese away from the coast. However, the commander first gave the Japanese an opportunity to do so voluntarily, which was difficult since their bank accounts had been frozen.

When the Watsonville Japantown learned about this option, they met and decided to investigate an apple orchard they heard was for sale in Idaho with the idea that it could sustain them until the war was over. The orchard consisted of several hundred acres and included numerous buildings, a few houses and farm equipment. Ken was among those chosen to scout out the opportunity. While the advance team was away, other members prepared for the move by building wagons and trailers to carry their belongings on the long trek inland.

When Ken returned, he came into the restaurant to talk to Martin, wearing a hangdog look on his face. "The soil was rocky and the trees small. Nothing compared to what the farmers have here."

"So, where does that leave you?"

"We are going to just wait and take our chances. But we have wagons and trailers ready to go in case we need to move quickly."

In early April, when Marty returned from fishing in Santa Cruz, he went directly to his father's restaurant to report the news. "A military regiment has been stationed in Santa Cruz near the lighthouse to protect us from invasion. And it's an all-black unit."

That caught Martin's attention. Later he would learn it was the 54th Coastal Unit that the army had outfitted with World War I uniforms, the only uniforms they could spare for stateside duty. Their work uniforms were made of blue denim so when they wore them with their hobnail shoes, they looked liked prisoners to the townsfolk.

"How are people taking to the military being stationed there?" He assumed they would not like having a large number of black men in town that had only been accustomed to a few—not enough to pose a problem. He remembered the riot in town in the 30s over Filipino men dating white women. The women are always a concern to their men.

"Giovanni told me people are up in arms. They're not used to blacks so they're afraid of them. There are a lot of complaints about the army's decision to station them there. Citizens are trying to keep them out of restaurants and other public places."

"Well, they should just be glad they have protection. If the Japs should invade, those GIs will be worth their weight in gold." But Martin knew prejudice would not be so easily assuaged.

"A military chaplain pretty much told them the same thing and threatened to remove them if they didn't change their ways. Then they saw the light."

"Let's hope that will be the end of it. The last thing we need around here is the Ku Klux Klan making a nightly raid."

"The KKK. I thought they were only in the south."

"In the 20s, a group of masked men made a raid on a bootlegger down in Inglewood. A few years later, the Klan was banned from the state. But sympathies don't die easily."

Chapter 45

On April 27, Martin was walking along Main Street toward his restaurant after picking up some produce at his grocery store. It was a sunny day with a few clouds in the sky, the fog having lifted. He was enjoying the fresh spring air when he was passed by a green army bus headed south and thought it might be going over to Fort Ord. But even at a distance he could see that it was turning into Japantown. Martin hurried along taking quicker, longer steps so he could find out what was going on. When he got to the restaurant, he dropped off the groceries and told Liu, "I'll be back soon. Start lunch without me." In a flash, he was back out the door and almost as quickly had arrived at the entrance to Japantown. He could see luggage and boxes tied with string piled on the sidewalk while an army officer escorted people, even young children, onto the bus. Martin saw Ken helping people with their possessions as he held back tears. After the bus was loaded, Martin made his way to where Ken was standing. "What's happening here?" he asked.

"Oh, Martin, the time has come for us to leave…to relocate. This is the first group to go but within the week all of us will be taken away. We'll be staying at the Salinas Fairgrounds until they can transfer us to an internment camp."

Martin found it hard to absorb what Ken was saying. It just seemed too incredible to him that citizens in the world's greatest democracy would be forced to leave their homes and held in a prison camp for however long it took for the war to end. There was no use fighting it. Now was the time to be practical. "Is there anything I can do to help?"

"Well, we are all worried about our businesses. Some people have found white friends to take them over while they are gone. Would you be able to manage my strawberry farm while I'm away?"

"I'd like to help you but I would need my sons to support me." He also needed to consider the impact his help would have on his own family's livelihood. *I'm in business and, for business to succeed, it depends on the goodwill of the customers. My efforts to help Ken's farm survive could backfire. Then again, could I live with myself if I don't come to his aid?* "When do you have to know?"

"The sooner the better. I would have to have time to show them the operation. But if they have a feel for plants, it shouldn't take long to teach them."

That evening Martin called Frankie and Tom Paul to join him in his den. He wanted to ask them about managing Ken's strawberry farm while he was away. He didn't include Marty since he was already fishing to help out Karlo's friend. Frankie and Tom Paul followed Martin into the room and took a seat, but not before giving each other concerned looks. Martin caught their body language and said, "Don't worry. You're not in trouble. But I do want to ask you a favor."

"Favor," said Frankie. "What kind of favor?"

"Well, I'm sure you both are aware that the Japanese community is being relocated away from the coast. In fact, the first group left today."

Tom Paul's eyes opened wide not quite understanding the implications. "Where are they taking them?"

"For now to the Salinas fairgrounds. Then who knows? Some internment camp that the government is building."

"You said you want a favor from us? What do you need?"

"My friend, Ken Nakamura, has a strawberry farm which will disappear and be worth nothing if it is not worked while he is gone. The plants cannot survive without care. So he needs someone who will manage the farm for him in his absence. Would either of you, or even both of you, be interested in helping him out?"

The two boys glanced at each other again as they considered Martin's request. "Of course, I don't have any experience with strawberries but I've found I've got a knack for farming. I'd be willing to give it a try," said Frankie.

"It has to be more than a try," said Martin. "You would have to make a commitment until Ken returns, which no one knows how long that would be."

"I would need to know more before I make that type of commitment."

"And how about you, Tom Paul?"

"I don't know. Frankie is probably your man."

"Ken wants to show you his operation so you know how to run it. I'd like both of you to come out to his farm with me tomorrow so you can make a decision. This is a way to help our neighbors and to show our solidarity with them."

Early the next morning, Martin and his sons drove out to Ken's farm near San Juan Road. A chilly fog surrounded them as they made their way to the farm office where they found Ken drinking tea. "Good morning," he said. "Your visit is a most welcome surprise, and I hope also an auspicious one."

"Ken, these are my sons Frankie and Tom Paul. They have come to talk to you about the management of your strawberry farm. Keep in mind, they know apple farming but nothing about the fruit you grow."

"Thank you for honoring me with your presence," Ken said with a bow. "Can I offer you a cup of tea? It is green tea with jasmine—a most pleasant way to start the day."

"Perhaps, we can talk over a cup of tea before we take a tour of your farm," Martin said.

Ken put three cups on the table and filled them with tea. Then he motioned the trio to sit down as he joined them. "I don't have a big farm—just enough to provide a living for my family with a little left over to save for a rainy day. So, the farm should not be overwhelming for you to manage. As well, the plants are perennial, meaning they return every year. But the one thing they don't like is a drought. It's important to check the Farmers' Almanac so you know what to expect. So, that is my introduction. Now let's go out and take a look at the strawberry plants up close."

Ken led the way to his pickup truck. "I apologize but I must ask you two boys to ride in the cargo bay." Martin hopped into the cab up front to sit alongside Ken. Once they got out to the main growing area, Ken stopped the truck and got out, motioning to the boys to climb out of the back.

"Well, this is it," Ken said. "My pride and joy." As far as the eye could see, green strawberry plants spread before them with irrigation rows dividing the sections. "I have some very dependable field workers who do most of the caring for the plants and also help with the harvest."

"This is certainly different from apple farming," Frankie said.

"Yes, but it is not necessary to climb great heights to reach the fruit. Although, squatting is imperative. Of course, Japanese are used to squatting." He let out a little laugh. But the joke was somewhat lost on Martin and the boys.

Frankie felt the sun shining down on him and when he looked up into the sky, he saw birds, most likely seagulls, flying overhead. "I like the openness of the field and the exposure to the elements," he said. "This is a much different environment than an apple orchard, which I also love."

Ken smiled. "I can tell you have a feel for the land."

"We named him after St. Francis of Assisi who had a love of nature and all living things, probably even strawberry plants," Martin said.

"Is that so?" Ken said. "Then you have the help of a holy man, which is so powerful. And what about you, Tom Paul, do strawberries interest you?"

"I'm not a natural farmer like my brother. Frankie is your best bet."

"Then Frankie, let's talk some more and I'll introduce you to my foreman who can give you the low down."

"I'd like that. It would be an honor to take care of your farm. Your trust in me will be rewarded."

Ken had not found a caretaker soon enough. Before the week was over, the rest of the Japanese community had been taken away. It depressed Martin to think about what had happened to his friend as well as all the other Japanese. But it was Ken who put a face on the situation. He had a family—a wife and several children. They all had to leave the home they had known to go to some Godforsaken place where they would be held captive until the war was over.

Martin had an overwhelming urge to visit Japantown one more time. As he entered through the gate, he was struck by the stillness of the place. Only a few weeks ago when he came to deliver holiday baskets, there had been a flurry of activity, the sound of voices, children laughing, women bustling about in their kimonos, a town full of life. Now, the abandoned area was a ghost town. Buildings stood empty and belongings left behind lay scattered about. A doll dressed in a kimono lying face down caught his attention. He bent down to pick it up and that's when he saw its cracked face, which must have been crushed in the stampede to leave. He found it hard to believe this had once been thriving community. It couldn't have been more lifeless if a bomb had hit it. A bomb doesn't even have to be used to destroy life.

Yet the cherry trees had blossomed in Japantown and throughout the town of Watsonville, as if to remind everyone of the positive contributions the Japanese had made during their time here. It was almost as if the Japanese had already known their fate when they donated thousands of cherry trees more than a decade ago, those blossoming trees now a sign that spring will come out of darkness. As Martin left, he reverently set the doll down at the base of one of the trees.

CHAPTER 46

With the Japanese gone, farmers all across the state faced a labor shortage. They had depended on the Japanese to tend the fields and harvest the crops. On August 4, the US and Mexico came to an agreement and the Bracero program was born. Mexico would send single men to the US to do the farm work in exchange for room, board, and a fair wage, which they would bring back across the border to their families.

Most of the men assigned to the Pajaro Valley came from the state of Michoacan, also an agricultural area which grew a variety of produce, including strawberries. So, while the workers offered their braceros (arms) in exchange for dollars, they also brought with them a knowledge of specific plants.

The first group to arrive worked in the sugar beet fields. But soon the braceros were needed to harvest apples and strawberries. They had the right touch with apples so they did not get bruised and also knew the right way to pick strawberries to get the most yield from a plant.

Some of the townspeople had noticed the buses bringing Mexicans in to work. Others saw them from a distance working the fields, but their brown bodies were not distinguishable for the Japanese. However, if they had looked closely they would have noticed the men had traded cooley hats for sombreros to keep them shaded from the sun.

For the most part, the braceros kept to themselves, although a few could occasionally be spotted on Main Street. However, when Sunday came around, pick-up trucks brought them from the farms to church, packed body to body in cargo bays. News quickly spread around town that the Mexicans had invaded.

Frankie didn't care what people thought because he immediately realized the braceros value, especially since they could teach him a thing or two. But language was holding him back from learning as much as he could. Sign language helped but he realized he was going to have to learn Spanish if he wanted to be a truly effective manager and live up to the trust Ken had placed in him.

Frankie watched closely as well as listened. More than words, he picked up traits and talents in the men. One man, Hector Lopez, began to emerge as a leader. The other men respected him for his knowledge and hard work and willingness to teach them how to do the job better. A thought occurred to Frankie, *I'm going to have to keep an eye on this guy. He could be worth his weight in gold.*

That night when Martin got home, he arranged to speak to him about the farm operation. "I've noticed one guy who might make a good foreman. What do you think about the idea?"

"It's always good to have someone who can take over in case something happens. And you especially need someone to bridge the gap between you and the Mexican workers. Does he speak any English?"

"Enough for us to understand each other. And I'm also picking up some Spanish words."

"Then he sounds like the guy you should try to develop into your right-hand man."

"La mano derecha."

"You got it. I'm just glad I didn't have to learn Chinese to deal with my crew. But they know to make it in this country you have to speak English."

"The Mexicans don't need to learn the language since they're not living here permanently. That's the difference."

"Let's hope they don't decide to stay. It would just be one more problem."

Chapter 47

In early 1943, Martin got a call from the mayor to attend a meeting at his office the following week. He refused to tip his hand, so Martin had no idea what the meeting was about, only that it was important and had to do with the war effort. *What in the world could he want with me*? At least he scheduled it between mealtimes.

When Martin arrived for the meeting, he was already exhausted from all the talking he had done at the restaurant with several of his patrons. Everyone seemed to be worked up by some aspect of the war. If it wasn't concern that their sons would be drafted into battle or that the town had swapped one brown-skinned race for another, who some thought were lazy and not as bright, then it was fear that the Japanese would attack or that apple shipments would be sunk by U-boats. Now Martin had to sit and listen to more talk about the war with the mayor holding court.

Several men had arrived at the meeting before him and he knew them all. He tipped his hat and then took his seat next to Filip. "Do you have any idea why we've all been called here?"

"Your guess is as good as mine. Let's hope it's worth our time."

Mayor Bill Simpson, a tall man with a full head of gray hair, entered the room right on time dressed in a formal, blue suit fitted closely to his slim figure. Everyone gathered around the conference table rose out of respect, and those nearby extended their arms to shake hands; others nodded their greeting. The mayor didn't waste any time with pleasantries. "I'll get right to the point. The navy wants to take over our airport for its wartime operations. Quite honestly, I don't think we have any choice in the matter. You probably know they've already taken over the Del Monte Hotel for a pre-flight training school."

"What do they plan to use our airport for?" Filip asked.

"Good question. They plan to teach dive-bombing here and deploy pilots to the Pacific theatre. But they also plan to establish an auxiliary airfield so they can send blimps out to patrol our coast."

"So, it sounds as if a decision already has been made," said Martin. 'What do you want from us?"

"I was just about to get around to that. The navy needs a support team here in town. Martin, since you are a navy vet, I thought you would be a perfect fit for the liaison role."

"Liaison? Could you just tell me what you want in plain English?"

"I would like you to serve as the contact between the navy and the town. You know both well from your World War I experience and your businesses, which keep you in close contact with our citizens."

"What all will this involve? I don't have much time to spare but am willing to give what I can."

"My understanding is that this role would have some flexibility. However, if there was an urgent matter you would have to make yourself available immediately."

"I'm in. When do I start?"

"The navy plans to be operational by October but will be getting things ready before then. Also, you need to have a team that you can delegate tasks to when necessary. Do I have any volunteers?"

Filip was the first to raise his hand, and then everyone around the table joined him. Martin knew most of them were trying to win points with the mayor but would bow out first chance they got. "I'd like to recruit Michael Latskovich since I know I can always count on him."

"Well, it looks like you've got a team to assemble. Navy representatives will be here next week to meet you and go over their timeline and requirements. You'll get word as soon as I do."

"One more thing," Martin said, "is this information we discussed here today confidential or should I say top secret? There's a navy saying that loose lips sink ships, so I just want to be sure we have the authority to discuss our latest invasion."

"It would bode well for us to keep in mind the navy saying, at least for now. Soon, it will be quite evident that the navy is invading us as you call it."

"One recommendation, Mayor. The community will need to know what is happening so they don't panic when they see sailors and submarines hanging around town. What we don't need around here is pandemonium."

"Good thought. I'll talk to my press assistant and get something ready. Any other thoughts or questions? Well then, I call this meeting adjourned."

The following week, the mayor called another meeting of the navy support team to meet with key naval officers responsible for the airfield. As Martin expected, the turnout was thin—just Filip, Michael, and himself.

"What happened to the rest of your guys?" Mayor Simpson asked.

"I guess they had second thoughts. But I prefer to work with a small group. That way we'll be more nimble."

Before they could discuss the matter any further, three naval officers arrived. Martin, Filip, and Michael, I'd like to introduce you to Captain Barkley." The Captain, a vital-looking, take-charge type, introduced his colleagues and they all shook hands before sitting down at the table. Martin marveled at the three officers dressed in their crisp blue uniforms, adorned with an assortment of patches and pins. He was becoming nostalgic for the time he served, always surrounded by men in uniform. Although he never made it above Petty Officer Second Class, he was in awe of those who climbed the officer ranks. Barkley was now a captain. *I put money on him making admiral before this war is over.*

"Captain Barkley, this is your meeting so now I turn it over to you to conduct."

"Thank you, Mayor. First of all, I thank you for volunteering to serve in our war effort. You will be an invaluable source of help as we build our infrastructure and conduct our operation. We are currently in the process of negotiating for the land we need to build the airfield and hope to be here by July to start things rolling. Our goal is to have it fully operational by October. As the mayor probably mentioned, we will be teaching dive-bombing and performing coastal patrols. We'll be rotating about twelve hundred men in and out and will have over seventy aircraft here. Watsonville and Moffett Field over the hill in Santa Clara will be the only two naval auxiliary airship fields on the West Coast.

For a moment, no one knew what to say. Then Martin broke the silence. "Is there anything we can do to help between now and then?"

"We will be in touch periodically and keep you informed on a need-to-know basis. At some point, we will have to come up with a plan to introduce the town to the navy. A smooth start will help ensure a smooth operation. Now, before we dismiss, let me show you the plan."

Captain Barkley spread out the map at one end of the table and motioned for Mayor Simpson, Martin, and his team to join him there. "Of course, you'll recognize the current airport, which covers nearly three hundred acres in the north end of Watsonville near Freedom," he said, pointing while keeping his gray eyes fixed. "We plan to purchase an additional thirty-five acres, which you can see rendered on the map. We propose to build support buildings to include an administrative office, fire station, supply building, barracks for our men, and a mess hall as well as a hangar, control tower, and a concrete ramp that will provide a better surface for takeoffs and landings."

Simpson, Martin, Filip, and Michael studied the map carefully. "This is our contribution to the war effort," said Simpson.

"You've got that right," the Captain said. "This town is going to be known as a navy town once we arrive. No small town in the country will do more to help us win the war."

"First our little berg was blessed with fertile soil that put us on the map as the Apple Capital of the World. Now because we had the foresight to build an airport, we'll be going down in the history books and remembered for all time," the mayor said.

"One strategic advantage this town has is that it's a little berg as you called it. San Francisco could be a target of the enemy as well as Monterey and even Santa Cruz because of the lighthouse. But no one would suspect Watsonville of taking on such an important role in the war. I'm only glad we got your Japanese population out of here before they learned of our plan."

The Captain's last remark did not sit well with Martin. He frowned and exchanged glances with Filip and Michael but kept mum. No use revealing his sympathies.

"That's right," the Mayor said. "They're all safely under wraps in Poston, Arizona out in the desert."

"The desert?" Martin said. "I thought they had been sent to one of our camps in California…Manzanar, I think the name is."

"Let me shed some light on the subject," Barkley said as he ran a hand through his short, blond hair. "The government wanted to put its money into an Indian reservation so the investment could be used for the future. Funny thing, though, the tribal council met to discuss the proposal and came out against it."

"Why was that?" Filip asked.

"I heard they didn't want done to others what had been done to them." Of course, since they still don't count for much, the government didn't respect their wishes, Martin pondered. Or maybe they believed the Japanese looked like the Indians and belonged on a reservation. *But better to keep my thoughts to myself.*

"Okay. Enough of a digression. Let's get back to the topic at hand. We hope to have the lease signed in June and then begin the site preparation. October is the operational date we're shooting for."

"The apple and strawberry harvests should be about done at that time, then the town goes dormant," said Filip.

"Exactly our thought. We'll make our move while they're napping."

"No one will be looking out for you. And since most people don't have airplanes, there'll be no reason for them to snoop around the airport. But at some point we're going to have to let the people know something even if it isn't the whole truth," said Martin.

"Once we're operational, our secret will be out anyway. All anyone will have to do is keep their eyes to the skies and they will spot war planes and blimps, which you can't miss even if you are half blind."

Captain Barkley began folding up the map, signaling the meeting was about to come to a close. "This was for your eyes only so do not share it with anyone else. We have to always remember we are at war, and we may not always know who the enemy is."

"You mean there are spies among us," Michael said.

"No doubt. Japanese stand out but Germans and Italians can blend in. We always have to be on guard."

After they left the meeting, Martin, Filip, and Michael stood in a quiet corner of the parking lot to discuss what they heard. "I think one of our duties is to report suspicious characters to the navy."

"How will we be able to know if they're suspicious?" asked Filip.

"If they listen too carefully, ask questions, seem to know too much," said Michael.

"We can't even trust people we've known for a long time. Back in Croatia, anyone could turn traitor with the right incentive."

"That's right," Michael said. "We've got to keep our early training in Croatia always in our minds. It will serve us well."

CHAPTER 48

Martin drove down Main Street on his way back to the restaurant. As he passed the Fox Theatre, he glanced at the marquis to determine if a film was playing that he and Lena would like to see. Sunday matinees were about the only time they had to take in a movie, and this year they had seen one of the best, *Casablanca*, with Humphrey Bogart and Ingrid Bergman. Although, in an effort to escape the war, they preferred a comedy with some romance like *Woman of the Year* with Spencer Tracey and Katherine Hepburn. Even *Dumbo* or *Bambi*, which they viewed with their grandchildren, was preferable to a movie that focused their attention on the war. But the film being advertised and now showing caught his eye. Martin turned around at the next corner and pulled up in front of the theatre so he could get out and read the poster.

The movie's title was *Chetniks. The Fighting Guerillas.* He couldn't believe Hollywood had made a movie featuring Yugoslavians, even though they were behind times with the new fighting guerillas being Tito's Partisans. The poster said the movie was dedicated to the fighting spirit of the Yugoslavian people. That made Martin proud. But it was really the fighting spirit of the Croats, led by Tito, that had that spirit in spades not the Serbians. But most Americans wouldn't know about that. To them, all Yugoslavians were the same—they had no idea about the different cultures and how complicated the relationships were, not to mention the politics.

When Martin arrived at the restaurant, he found Michael waiting for him. "I thought we were all done talking after that meeting we had with the navy."

"I just wanted to mention what I just heard going around town. There's a movie now playing…"

"I know all about it. I just stopped by the theatre to read the movie poster."

"Well, a lot of guys are up in arms about it. They don't like the fact that the Serbian Chetniks are getting all the credit. Mihailović's face was already plastered all over the cover of *Time* magazine last year."

"I couldn't agree more. But this is Hollywood not Washington talking."

"But Hollywood is the propaganda machine. They're making all sorts of war movies to stir up patriotism. They're going to be releasing a movie this month based on *The Moon is Down.*

"Oh, the book by our favorite son. Or should I say favorite brother since it is Steinbeck's sister who lives in Watsonville? So, he's now getting into propaganda writing."

"That's because propaganda works. We need to tell people the truth."

"First, we should see the movie so we can talk from truth. Then we have to get our own propaganda plan together to spread the truth, at least as we see it."

When Martin got home that evening, he told Lena about the movie playing downtown. So they made plans to see it Sunday afternoon. "I will have to prep dinner beforehand or get Clara to cook it, otherwise, we won't have anything to eat when we get home." She gave Clara a call and she was more than willing to help out. When Filip heard about it, he called Henrik and Josip, and they all wanted to go see the movie, too. So, on Sunday they dropped their wives off so they could cook while they had an afternoon at the movies. The sisters didn't mind since they appreciated every opportunity that came their way to share a little gossip and girlish friendship.

When Lena got home she was pleased to see the table was set and the meal almost ready from what her nose told her about the smells in the kitchen. She knew every stage of a pork roast just by sniffing. "I think the roast is about done," she said.

"No, it should have twenty minutes more to go," said Clara. "But I'll check just to satisfy you." When she opened the oven, seasoned air blew into her face, revealing a well-browned piece of meat. She got out the thermometer and inserted it. "It says one hundred sixty degrees...perfect. You were right, mother."

"I just have the experience, that's all. Now, I volunteer to make the gravy." They took the meat out of the pan and placed it on the carving board to rest. But to her dismay, Lena noticed that Clara had not added onions, celery, and carrots to the roasting pan to flavor the drippings for gravy. But she thought it wasn't really that important. Most likely only Martin and she would notice the difference, but to them it would be a big difference.

Once they were seated at the table and were well into the main course, conversation turned to the movie. Filip took the lead. "Martin, what did you think of the movie?"

"On the one hand, it made me feel proud that our brothers abroad are fighting for freedom. They're distinguishing themselves as the best resistance force in Europe. But on the other hand, it reminded me of what some of my nephews are going through. You know most of them are fighting with the Partisans."

"You usually don't talk about the war over in Yugoslavia. This is the first time I've heard about your nephews."

"Well, it's difficult getting news. Just a letter now and then. It usually comes from my sister, Veronika, who either doesn't know much or doesn't want to say. She never did like to pass along bad news."

"Getting back to the movie," said Josip, "what do you think we should do about it?"

"I'm not sure. But before we do anything, we should contact the Slavonic Society in San Francisco. They would know better than we how to handle this sort of thing. But at the very least, we should write a letter to the editor to explain what is really going on over there and who the good guys are. Although, if we keep quiet eventually time will tell."

On Monday after the lunch hour, Michael arrived at the Dalmatian Coast Cafe followed by Filip, Henrik, Josip, and several others. Martin was already waiting for them at a long table that had been made by pushing several of the four tops together. "Sit down," he said, "then we can start." The men all took their places and then turned toward Martin, waiting for him to begin.

"I have spoken to my cousins and in turn they have consulted the leaders of the Slavonic Society. Since the movie is receiving good reviews, even by *The New York Times*, they feel we should take the role of guerilla fighters and only strike when the timing is right. Their strategy is to publicize every success of the Partisans, no matter how trivial, while refraining from criticism of the Chetniks. It will only look like jealousy, then no one will pay attention to us anymore."

"But I still think we need to set the record straight," said Michael. "People don't even know the difference between Serbians and Croatians. When I go about town, friends who don't know better are congratulating me on their success."

"I agree with Michael," Filip said. "We need to do some explaining, even if we refrain from criticism."

"You should write the letter, Martin," said Henrik. "If you mention your nephews who are fighting for the Partisans, people will listen more closely."

"That's right," said Josip. "That will give you authority, and because of your personal connection to the Partisans, you will have their compassion so your words will come across as sincere."

"Then it's settled. Martin will write the letter. We can meet back here on Friday afternoon and have him read it to us before he sends it off to the editor. Do you think you can get the letter written by that time, Martin?"

"I guess I will have to."

Chapter 49

Springtime had arrived and the braceros had returned to the town. Frankie was especially heartened when he saw Hector among them because he wanted to discuss a foreman job with him. But he decided to wait for a couple of weeks until he settled into his work again before approaching him.

One day after work was over, Frankie pulled Hector aside and asked to speak to him a moment. "I can only spare a couple of minutes or else I will miss the bus," Hector said.

"Don't worry about the bus. I can drive you back to your barracks."

Hector looked at Frankie, trying to read his body language. He had no idea why the boss wanted to speak to him and he was worried about it. He could not lose the job his family in Mexico was depending on to support them. Even so, he tried to mask his worry with a façade of confidence.

"Hector," Frankie began, "I have noticed since last season how good you are at your job and with the men as well, always showing them the best and fastest way to pick the strawberries. They have a lot of respect for you."

"I am grateful for your kind words. But I've had a lot of experience in Mexico with strawberries, which some of the men have not had. They need a few lessons so they can be better and make more money. After all, you pay us by the crate not the hour."

Not wanting to get into a labor discussion, Frankie said, "I'll get right to the point." He noticed Hector pull back his shoulders as if bracing himself for bad news. "Relax. I have good news. I'd like to make you a foreman over the braceros."

Hector let out the breath he had been holding. But he still did not understand the meaning of Frankie's words. "Foreman? What would you want me to do?"

"I would like you to spend less time picking and more time managing the men."

"But then I will have less crates and payday will not be good."

"You'd be moving up in management, and a manager receives a salary instead of pay per crate picked."

"Salary? I don't understand how that works. Explain please."

"On payday you would receive a set amount, which will be much more than if you picked strawberries."

"What would this amount be?"

"I will pay twice the money you make for picking alone. You can still work alongside the farmhands, but I want you to help them be more efficient. It will make them happy, too, since they will be able to fill more crates per day."

"I see. This sounds good. Is there anything else to it?"

"We should meet once or twice a week to discuss problems and improvements. That's it."

Frankie extended his arm to shake hands. Hector clasped Frankie's hand in a tight grip, "Deal."

CHAPTER 50

On October 23, 1943 the navy officially invaded Watsonville. Martin was invited to attend the dedication ceremony of the auxiliary airship base and brought all three sons along. The navy had a couple of blimps tethered for visitors to tour as well as several war planes on display—Hellcats, Avengers, Corsairs, Dauntless—all of which made take offs and landings on the new ramp to impress their audience, a few of them catching war fever.

"What do you think about the navy operation?" Martin asked his sons.

Marty was the first to respond. "Sign me up." The glamor of flight, the men in uniform and the excitement of war had all appealed to his young, vital male spirit.

"Me, too," said Tom Paul.

"Now wait a minute. I didn't bring you here for a recruitment campaign. Marty, you're committed to fishing to help Giovanni provide for his family. Going off to war is not something you should be thinking about."

"It's time I do my duty. Being here today is just a reminder that the time has come."

Martin knew he would catch hell from Lena when he got home. She didn't want any of her sons going off to war after what she had experienced with his World War I adventure. But he knew men must be men at times like these and, when duty called, their only recourse was to answer. He had felt it once himself, and he had been more than thirty years old, a time when a man is losing his vitality, and he was a family man besides.

His sons were young and single so there would be nothing holding them back, not even a mother's pleas and tears.

The next week, both Marty and Tom Paul asked to speak with Martin when he got home from work. "Well," Marty said, "I've volunteered for the navy. The ocean has always held a fascination for me. I want to become a submariner. Those submarines we toured were otherworldly. I've spent time on top of the ocean, now I want to learn what's below it."

Martin knew this would be coming. Now he turned his gaze toward Tom Paul. "And what about you?"

"I volunteered, too. But I want to learn how to fly one of those planes we saw last week and become a fighter pilot."

"And what about Frankie? Did he sign up as well?"

"No. You know, Pa, he's a man of the land. He's happiest being outside communing with nature."

"He has certainly lived up to his namesake. But he's nearly thirty so I assume war does not hold the same fascination for him that it does for the two of you. Being young, you have romantic notions. And, of course, war does have some romance to it. But believe me, what you will experience will mostly be a living hell. Even so, we all must do what we can to preserve our freedom."

It wasn't long before both Marty and Tom Paul left to begin their training at Mare Island, the same place Martin did his. Lena bid them a tearful good bye at the train station saying, "Come back to me, you hear." Then she turned to Martin. "You are responsible for this. They are following your example."

Martin thought it better not to reply when Lena was so emotional. They left in silence and after dropping her off at home, he headed for the restaurant, a refuge if there ever was one.

The sight of sailors on the street brought the war close to home. Women had been rolling bandages to support the Red Cross. Now they wanted to do more for the young military men living amongst them. While some of their own sons were serving far away, they could at least do something for these American sons who were at their doorstep.

The mayor's wife had put an idea in his head but not before he had one of his own. Simpson called Martin into his office to brainstorm the problem and solutions. "You know our town has always had a problem with vice—prostitution, gambling, narcotics. Now that the war is on, not only are troops coming over from Ford Ord, but we have over a thousand sailors here supporting these illegal activities day and night. I've heard our nickname is *Sin City.*

"I know all about it. These activities are going on not too far from my restaurant. Of course, men have always liked to play Black Jack or Fan-Tan, which the Chinese run down there by Walker Street. And prostitution's been with us since Biblical times, but I hear it's found a fertile soil here just as the apple trees and strawberries have. I don't know much about drugs, but they certainly should be curbed if not eliminated. So, do you have any suggestions for dealing with these problems? I don't think we can restrict the sailors to base."

"My wife floated an idea by me. She thought we should start a USO, United Service Organization, in town to keep the men occupied. What do you think about that idea?"

"The women do seem to want to do more for the war effort than roll bandages. In fact, Lena's heart goes out to these boys since she has sons in the military as well."

"A USO might improve morale for our women as well as the servicemen. My wife has been moping around, too, since our son left."

"I can talk to Lena about the USO and get back to you on it."

"I have a feeling it will happen one way or the other. Janice is pushing for it and she will take the lead. With all her contacts around town through the Women's Club, church and other organizations, there should be no shortage of women to recruit."

"Don't forget we need young women, too, to attract the young men. My daughter could help with that."

"Then let's get the ball rolling. We've got to nip the town's reputation in the bud."

That night after the restaurant closed, Martin decided to take a drive along Union Street. Sure enough, it was teeming with activity. Servicemen, both army and navy, hustled in and out of establishments making the most of their free time. Mexicans, most likely braceros, lined up waiting their turn at a brothel that appeared to cater to them, a Mexican flag waving at the front the porch amid the strains of a guitar. Martin wondered if by curtailing the so-called "play pens," the town would be setting itself up for an even bigger problem. It reminded him of the riot in the 30s over Filipino men dating the town's white women. Young, red-blooded men were not going to remain monks while living away from their women. And sailors had always been notorious for patronizing brothels whenever they were in port. It was no different here. While the USO may provide a source of recreation, it may have other unintended results, such as wartime romances that leave more than a broken heart behind. There was never a perfect answer.

As he continued down the street, he saw a man he thought he recognized come out of one of the red light houses. No, it couldn't be. But how could he not recognize that tall frame with broad shoulders and slim hips that took long easy strides as he moved. It had to be Frankie. From time to time, Martin thought he'd become a priest. Now that thought was banished. I'll have to talk with Lena about finding him a wife. With less eligible men in town, his best chance is now.

When Martin arrived home, he found Lena in the parlor knitting. "What's this? A new hobby?"

"Don't you know women are knitting for men in uniform, making socks and scarves? It's one way to help the war effort in a very personal way. The thought that my wool creations will help a soldier keep warm uplifts me and keeps my mind from thinking about all the hardships our sons are suffering. And maybe, just maybe, some nice stranger is doing them a kindness, too."

One son did not have to suffer a hardship tonight, quite the contrary. But Martin was not going to mention it to Lena. "Since you want to help soldiers personally, what would you think about starting a USO in town to provide them some recreation?"

"I'm sure they're bored to death in our little town with nothing much to occupy their time. But you should talk with Clara because she would know better than me if this is something that would appeal to the young men."

"Well, the mayor's wife suggested it, so I think we will be moving ahead one way or other."

"You'll have a chance to speak to Clara at Thanksgiving dinner. She and her brood will be here." After a difficult start, once Clara had given birth to Petie, several more followed in rapid succession—two girls and another boy. With two sons at war and another unmarried, Martin was glad to know the next generation had been secured.

CHAPTER 51

The family was gathered around the table for the Thanksgiving feast. They had just finished stuffing themselves with turkey and all the fixins when Martin asked Lena again about the USO. "Let's first start with a Christmas party and see how that goes over, but we'll have to begin planning soon."

"Clara, do you think you could help with the party and get some young women involved?" asked Martin.

"A party certainly beats rolling bandages and knitting scarves. I think my friends will agree and join in."

"The one thing I worry about with a Christmas party is the cookies and pastries. You know I love to bake. Since May when the sugar rationing began, I have barely used my rolling pin. And you'll notice when I bring out the coffee that the desserts are skimpy this year."

Lena got up from her chair to clear the table and Clara assisted her. Then they brought in the coffee service and one pumpkin pie. "We'll have to have just a thin piece since I didn't have the sugar to make another one nor the apple pie, which I prefer." All eyes went to the lonely-looking pie on the table as if wondering how it was going to satisfy all the sweet tooths gathered in the room.

After Lena took her place again, she said, "I've been saving a letter from Marty until we were all together." Then she pulled an envelope out of her pocket and carefully unfolded the letter inside. "Now I'll read."

"Dear Ma, Pa, family and friends,

I wanted to let you know I survived my training but did not make it to submarine school. Apparently, they already had all the men they needed, so I was assigned to a battleship. If they can, the navy assigns you to your state's battleship but since the USS *California* was still being repaired after its shelling and sinking in Pearl Harbor, they assigned me to one named for a neighboring state…the USS *Nevada*. So, by the time you read this I should be in Norfolk, Virginia meeting up with my ship. Apparently, the ship will be doing convoy duty so I'll be following in your footsteps, Pa. And, Ma, you won't have to worry about me seeing any action and ending up battle-scarred. Anyway, military life has been good so far and I've been able to see a bit of the country and soon a bit of the world beyond it. They haven't said anything about leave, so I don't know when I will be able to see you again. But I'll be thinking about you and miss you especially at the holidays. Maybe you could invite one of the local sailors to take my place at the table this year. If I'm lucky, I'll be a guest, too.

With love and best wishes for a Merry Christmas, Marty"

By the time Lena finished reading, tears had begun to roll down her cheeks. "We definitely have to do something for the boys we have here to make their holidays happy. And let's hope others do the same for Marty and Tom Paul."

No sooner had she said his name, then the door swung open and Tom Paul appeared. "I'm back. Did you save the drumstick for me?"

Lena jumped up from her chair and ran to her son, knocking off his sailor's cap she was so excited. Then she helped him out of his navy pea coat and sat him down at the table. "We have plenty of leftovers. I will make up a plate for you."

"What are you doing home?" Martin asked. "Are you on leave?"

"Actually, I've been assigned to the Navy Auxiliary Air Station. I'm going to learn dive-bombing."

"So, I assume you already earned your wings."

"That I have. Flying is an experience like no other, and I took to it like a duck to water or rather a bird to air."

"How long do you think you'll be here?"

"A month or more. It just depends."

"Depends on what?" said Lena, as she placed a plate full of turkey and fixins in front of him.

"It depends on the war strategy and what battles are coming up in the Pacific. That's where the pilots head to from here. Maybe I'll get lucky and get stationed in Honolulu."

"Now wouldn't that be nice…you and the hula girls," said Lena. Tom Paul blushed. He had been thinking the same thing.

"I'm glad you'll be here for the holidays. We're going to put on a party for the servicemen, and you'll be a good source for what sort of party they'd like to have."

"Food, drink, girls. That's all you need to have to satisfy us servicemen."

Clara gave her mother a disgusted look. Martin caught it and said, "Now, we have to keep it above board, especially with the mayor's wife involved." Tom Paul frowned and went back to eating his dinner.

Chapter 52

Martin was in his restaurant on December 4, preparing for Saturday night dinner, when Michael threw the door wide open being the first in with the news. "Radio Free Yugoslavia is announcing that Tito has formed a provisional government."

"Oh, my God. Our prayers have been answered."

"Tito and those Partisans are something else, real fierce fighters. They freed Bosnia fighting a German army more than twice their size and better equipped."

"We have Churchill to thank for that. He decided to put his money on Tito and it's paid off."

"He recognized that the Partisans kept the Germans from advancing to North Africa, which helped the British there."

The door opened again and Filip, Henrik, and Josip entered followed by Karlo and a group of men, some known to Martin, others not. "We're all here to celebrate," said Filip.

"Well, sit down. I'll bring out the sljivovica." As he turned back toward the kitchen, Liu and Chao were carrying trays filled with glasses and a couple of bottles of the plum liquor. When Martin saw everyone had a glass in hand, he raised his. "Death to all Fascists! Liberty to the people!" Then in unison, they all slugged the liquor, thinking of their homeland.

"That toast was the best one you could have made," said Michael. "After those Nazis bombed Belgrade and the country surrendered, that slogan appeared in the square giving voice to the resistance. And no sooner had the people made the decision to fight than their leader Tito appeared."

"And now he needs to liberate the rest of the country. My ancestral home, Dubrovnik, is not yet free."

"Tito is on the move so it will happen in time," said Karlo. "I'm going to contact the Slavonic Society in San Francisco to find out if there are ways we can help. They should know something."

That evening the restaurant remained packed with Croatians wanting to gather to share in their homeland's victory. While Martin shared in the joy, he couldn't keep thoughts of his sons out of his mind. He knew Marty was going to serve on a convoy ship but that also had its hazards. Besides the mission could change depending on the winds of war. And then there was Tom Paul, who would probably see action. The end of the war still was not in sight. He hoped that his sons could survive.

The USO Christmas Party was set for the Sunday before Christmas when servicemen had a few free hours available. Janice Simpson, the mayor's wife, had put all of her energy into making it a success. For a portly woman in her mid-fifties, Janice still radiated energy, her bleached blond hair and heavy makeup providing the façade of youth. She had recruited all of her friends in town, not a small number, to help decorate and cater the event. Because of the concern that the church hall at St. Patrick's would not be able to accommodate all the sailors at once, they had issued invitations in two-hour blocks beginning at 2:00 p.m. until midnight.

Martin volunteered to cater most of the food and knew just how to stretch the rations to ensure enough to go around. The women, most of whom were excellent bakers, had signed up to make as many cookies, cakes, and pastries as their sugar rations would allow, which wasn't nearly enough. Lena was especially distraught over the situation. She approached Martin with her concern. "We just have to get more sugar, that's all. Whatever it takes."

Martin knew just what it would take. Sugar along with other rationed items was available on the black market. He often had to resort to that to fill his car with gas. While goods could be had through the black market, they didn't come cheap. "How much sugar do you think you need?"

"I'll get back to you once I make a calculation."

"Then I'll see what I can do." He didn't want to mention the black market to Lena and get her upset nor the price that would be charged for this sparse commodity.

"Thank you, Martin. These boys deserve a wonderful Christmas party, maybe the last one some of them will ever have."

The day of the event finally arrived, and Janice Simpson was pleased her vision had been achieved. Sailors poured into the hall at their appointed time, smiles on their faces, ready to take part in the festivities. Clara had arranged for young women to be there so the men had the fairer sex to dance with or even just talk to. Girls had a way of transporting military men away from their concerns of war. Near the end of each segment of the party, Martin stood on the bandstand to lead a few carols, ending in a crowd favorite, "Silent Night."

That year Christmas Eve was on Friday, so Martin kept the restaurant open to serve people who had nowhere else to go or just wanted a good fish dinner cooked by an expert chef. However, he closed an hour earlier so he could get home and have the traditional dinner with his family. When he arrived, he could smell the bakalar en brodo simmering on the stove. Lena and Clara made the dinner, since he was not able to do so. Tonight as they took their seats around the table, Marty's place was filled by a stranger, a sailor whom Tom Paul had befriended. "Everybody, I'd like to introduce you to George Markovich. He's a Croatian, too, from San Pedro." George had a Slav's high cheekbones that set off his limpid blue eyes and gave his face an attractive look. He wore a crew cut that made his blond hair almost disappear it was so light in color.

Martin knew there was a large Croatian community in San Pedro, many of them fishermen. “What does your family do?” he asked.

“My father is a fisherman. He grew up on the Adriatic so when he arrived in this country, he found a job doing what he had skills for. He provides a good living for our family.”

“San Pedro is not far from here. Why are you not with your own family tonight?”

“We only have a few hours leave…not enough to get down to Southern California. This is a big state, you know.”

“Well, I’m glad you are able to join us tonight. Lena is especially happy because she wanted to entertain a serviceman since Marty is away.”

“Yes,” Lena said, “it is my hope that Marty is having a nice Christmas Eve dinner in Norfolk, Virginia with a kind, southern family.”

“If so, I doubt he’ll be eating bakalar en brodo tonight.”

“More likely shrimp and grits,” Martin said. “Southerners love their grits.”

“Maybe we should be eating grits, too. Lord knows we’ll need grit to get through this war.”

CHAPTER 53

On January 11, FDR gave his State of the Union speech as a fireside chat from the Diplomatic Room in the White House. He had come down with the flu after attending conferences in Cairo and Tehran with Churchill, Stalin, and Chiang Kai-shek so opted not to go to Congress to deliver his message. Since it was a Tuesday, Martin closed the restaurant for dinner, knowing that most people, like himself, would be listening to the radio message. FDR talked about establishing a lasting peace, which the last war did not, and improving the standard of living for all Americans. But while FDR talked about peace, he also said there was still a long, tough road to go to Berlin and Tokyo, and he cautioned against complacency and overconfidence that the war was already won.

A few days later when Frankie received a draft notice, Martin's instincts told him the big push was coming. Now they were reaching up to twenty-nine-year-olds and all three of his sons would be in it.

Frankie stopped in the restaurant between meal times to show his father the paperwork. It made him wonder how many older men were being drafted. It would certainly be telling if they were taking forty-five-year-olds, too, the upper age limit for conscription. "I was hoping they wouldn't get you. You're not made for war. But I knew things were heating up with FDR being carted off to Cairo and Tehran to have conferences with the other three of the Big Four. And then there was the State of the Union fireside chat when FDR tipped his hand a bit over the difficulties still ahead." Or was he thinking of the upcoming election, trying to lay the groundwork for a fourth term. He was a known manipulator…a chess player. Well, Croatians, too, had learned chess from some of the best players on the planet. They can certainly read chess boards and know the moves coming up.

"Just the same, I have to do my duty. But my concern now is about Ken's strawberry farm."

"Do you have a plan in mind? After what FDR said in his Thanksgiving Day speech about food production in our country being the greatest ever, we need to keep up the good work to help the Allies."

"You know I made Hector foremen of the braceros. Ken had a foreman, too, but he's gone off to war. The only person I have to turn to is you."

"Me? How would I be able to manage my businesses if I took over supervising the farm? Besides, I know nothing about strawberries."

"Do you have a better suggestion? Ken is depending on us so that he has a livelihood to come back to when and if the day ever comes that he's released from the internment camp."

"Give me some time to think about it. By next week I should have figured something out."

Between meal hours, Martin met Frankie at Ken's farm. Unfortunately, since it was winter there wasn't much to see except barren fields. Nevertheless, they walked the fields by way of the irrigation ditches, and Frankie explained the operation while Martin tried his best to visualize it. "I'm not really a farmer, so I don't think I will do much good. You're going to have to ask your uncles if they know someone who could help out."

"Once Hector returns with the braceros everything will run smoothly. He knows what the strawberries need and how to direct the men."

"But what if Hector doesn't return? You have to have a backup plan with someone here who can make sure the farm runs properly."

"Maybe I could get word to Hector that we need him sooner than usual. I think he has relatives who live in town."

The following week Frankie had to report to Camp Pendleton for training before reaching Hector. Now it was up to Martin to figure out a solution to the problem. Through the grapevine he located Hector's relatives and asked them to get in touch with him. A week later, Hector appeared in the restaurant.

"Good timing," Martin said. "We're about to serve lunch. Have a seat and I'll send Chao over to take your order. The meal is on the house."

"Gracias. I am hungry and I have heard from Frankie that you are a great cook. So it will be both an honor and a pleasure to try one of your dishes."

"If you like seafood, then the risotto is the thing to get."

"That would suit me very well. Gracias."

From time to time, Martin looked up from his post in the kitchen to survey the restaurant. He thought Hector looked uncomfortable eating amongst the town's people, most of whom were farmers who employed people like him. But the farmers didn't even seem to notice Hector's presence as they concentrated on their food and drink.

Once the restaurant cleared out, Martin joined Hector at the table. "So, you probably know Frankie has been called up. No telling when he will return. But the farm needs someone to manage it when the season arrives and Frankie told me you're the man to do it."

"I have been making sure the men get the work done so I can continue to do that. But I am sure Frankie had other tasks that also need attention."

"I have talked to my brothers-in-law who are apple farmers, and they mentioned a few items such as ordering supplies, arranging for a crop duster, and so on. They gave me the name of a strawberry farmer to talk to about that, but I haven't had a chance to do it yet. But would you be willing to take on some other jobs?"

"Such as?"

"Such as keeping track of supplies and equipment. That would take a load off."

"I might be. What is it worth to you?"

"Of course, you will receive more pay. How much will depend on the tasks you take on and how well you do them."

"You don't have to worry about me. I do good work. Now I've got to get going to catch my ride back. But I'll try to return ahead of the rest of the braceros." Martin wondered how he managed to get back and forth across the border so easily but asked no questions. He assumed the Mexicans had their ways as most people who live at their level of society do, remembering how people in his homeland skirted the rules to eke out a life. Martin extended his arm and they shook hands. On his way out the door, Hector turned toward Martin. "Your seafood risotto is the best." Then he hustled away.

Chapter 54

That Sunday, Tom Paul showed up for dinner as he did most weeks. Even at his young age he realized time was short. After the family took their place at the table and said grace, especially for Marty and Frankie as well as all the other servicemen, he announced, "George left for the Pacific yesterday with a squadron."

Looks went around the table, not knowing how to read this bit of news. But Martin could see fear on everyone's faces, especially Lena's. "This must mean they have completed their training. The Pacific was always going to be their destination." But even as he said those words to soothe worries, he knew better. All the signs were there and he knew exactly how to read them. FDR had started his fireside chat, talking about peace and future prosperity and ended it with those points as well. But buried in the middle was the bad news—perils ahead.

Clara helped break the tension. "They are probably off to Hawaii for some R&R."

Lena forced a smile. "Wouldn't that be nice. It almost makes you want to be a pilot."

All eyes turned to Tom Paul whose smug smile was a clue to the pride he felt in being a navy flyer. "They were all piloting Hellcats. That's the plane that is designed to beat the Zero Jap's fly. At altitudes it's faster and a better climber. And what a diver it is. They say it even does better at carrier landings than the Corsair."

"Is that what you're flying, too?" Lena asked timidly.

"Yes. But you don't have to worry. It's safer because it has a protective windshield and armor around the gas tank. I've heard it can even make it back to base after taking a few hits." Lena gave a visible shiver that caught everyone's attention. But she said no more.

"You know I still cannot believe we are talking about flying machines, airplanes, that are capable of such astounding feats. When I came to this country, cars were just coming into being, although a German named Benz built the first one in 1885. Then in 1903, we heard about the Wright brothers test flight that lasted a few seconds. No one could have anticipated then what airplanes would become. But we caught a glimpse of the possibilities when Charles Lindberg made his transatlantic flight in 1927. He received a hero's welcome when he landed in Paris and was awarded the Congressional Medal of Honor. And now, as unbelievable as it might seem, my son is not only flying one of these incredible machines but is training to do battle in it."

"I certainly hope to see action. And as long as I'm in the pilot's seat of a Hellcat, I will have nothing to fear. It's the Japs who should be shaking in their boots."

A few weeks later, Martin and Lena gathered at the Watsonville Naval Airship Station to see Tom Paul and his squadron off. It was a clear day in February with scant traces of clouds in the sky, a good day for flying. When Lena spotted Tom Paul, she started screaming his name. He turned and caught sight of his mother whom he had not expected to come to see him off. The last time he had been with her, she had given him such an emotional farewell that he thought that would be the last time he'd set eyes on her until he returned from war.

But there she was, standing next to his father, screaming and waving her arms. Tom Paul went toward the crowd standing behind the guard rope to give his mother once last kiss. He was wearing a flight suit and cap with aviator goggles resting on the top of his head. "Take care of yourself," Lena said as she hugged him, "and come back to me. You're still my baby." They kissed each other on both cheeks then Tom Paul shook his father's hand and left to rejoin his squadron, but not before flashing a smile, displaying his dimples.

They stood and watched as a dozen Hellcats took off over the Pacific where one day soon they would do battle with the enemy. From what Martin had learned, they would be based in Honolulu, just as Clara had predicted. Finally, when all twelve aircraft had departed and they could no longer see any sign of them, Martin took Lena by the hand and led her away.

"Now all three of our boys are in the war. It will only be by sheer luck if they all make it home."

Martin did not answer, although he had been thinking the same thing. Best not to add to her anxiety.

When they got home, Lena checked the mailbox and found a letter from Frankie. As soon as she got into the kitchen, she tore the envelope open, anxious for any word from her son. But all Frankie said was that he finished his training and was heading to the east coast to deploy from there. She collapsed into a chair, not knowing what to make of the news. One son heading west, another heading east—it was all too much for one day. She wondered about Marty and whether he was still based in Norfolk. It had been a while since she had heard from him, so things could have changed. Martin appeared while she was still lost in her thoughts so she showed him the letter. Lena tried to interpret his body language as he read it but couldn't. He had kept a good poker face. "Well," she said when he had finished, "what do you make of it?"

Martin sat down in the chair next to her and took her hand in his. "Lena, you have to understand we are at war. The president even said there are perils ahead. It appears our sons are heading right for them. Everything points to major battles in the coming months in both the Pacific and Atlantic. Prayers are needed more than ever."

A couple of weeks later, they finally heard from Marty. The key line in his letter was that the *Nevada* was no longer on convoy duty. "What does it mean, Martin?"

"It means that resources are being marshaled."

"Is that all our sons are…resources? FDR promised not to send our sons into any foreign wars. He said they were training to keep war away from our shores, to protect our country. And we believed him. I don't think I can ever trust him again."

"Lena, listen to me. The world has changed since he made those promises. Not even he, the president of this great nation, could foresee the threat the Axis powers would pose to our freedom. We have to trust that he will do what is best for us and the world."

"All I care about is our sons."

"But what kind of lives would they have if evil overtakes the world? We left our homeland because of the oppression. If these powers win, their lives would be a living hell."

CHAPTER 55

In early April, Hector returned, stopping by the restaurant to let Martin know. Martin was relieved to see him since he had to question how dependable migrant workers were—especially those south of the border. But Hector had now proven himself responsible. "We should go over to the farm office and start making plans for the season and check on the growth the plants have on them," said Martin.

"I will see you at the farm. I want to look around so we can make the most of our meeting." Then he turned around and walked out. Martin thought he seemed rather abrupt but was glad he was getting down to business. He certainly hoped Hector would pull through because, if he didn't, there would be more on his shoulders.

At the break between meal hours, Martin headed for the strawberry farm. When he arrived, he spotted Hector in the field inspecting the plants. After the fog had lifted, the gentle sunshine warmed the day in the mild way strawberries like before disappearing into a chilly night that helped the fruit thrive. The soil was moist but not wet, so Martin walked through the irrigation rows to where Hector was standing. "What do you think about the crop this year?"

"I haven't been here this early in the season before so it is difficult to compare strawberry to strawberry. But back in Mexico where I live, I have observed many strawberry fields at this stage. I think this looks pretty good…normal."

"By May, most of the field workers should be here. Until then, do you think you need a couple of hands to help you?"

"Probably so. But let's go into the office and talk. I started a list of things we need to do. Since you want me to take over inventory and equipment, I've already done an inspection."

Martin was impressed. Frankie had been right. Hector was a leader—not only of people but process. He was taking a real liking to Hector who was a self-made man like himself. Some people just have it in them to be successful even without an education, although that certainly helps.

When they got to the office, Hector laid out his list…in Spanish. Although he spoke English, he did not read or write it well.

"This is Greek to me," said Martin.

"What? It's Spanish. But I will translate." Hector detailed the supplies they would need right away as well as parts to repair machinery." Then he said, "I have to go." Go where? Martin wondered. What could be so important he had to hurry off? Hector always seemed to have other pressing matters. Martin would have liked to ask what they were but would wait to find out. His mind could only contain so many questions at once.

With the war on, food prices had gone up and shortages had occurred. He had to constantly rework his menu in the restaurant to ensure supplies and a profit, no matter how small. He knew Americans were called on to sacrifice, although FDR preferred to call it a privilege, but he still had to make a living for his family and pay wages to his employees. While the Victory Gardens helped individual families, it hurt his business at the grocery store. People were able to grow most of the fruits and vegetables for their needs. Although in Watsonville, it wasn't as crucial since produce was readily at hand. Even so, once families realized the benefit of growing their own, it helped them stretch what little funds they had for rationed goods such as sugar, butter, milk, cheese, eggs, coffee, and canned goods.

When Martin got home that evening he found Lena busy in the kitchen. "I'm canning," she said. "Take a look at my new pressure cooker.

It's the thing to have to do it right. After I clean the asparagus, I will put it in the pot to cook it quickly."

"Is that asparagus from my garden?"

"Yes, I thought it would be better than store bought."

Martin took pride in his little garden which he had long before Victory Gardens became fashionable. He preferred his vegetables fresh not canned, so he was not happy Lena had taken some of his prized asparagus for her latest domestic venture. "Next time, just come by the store and I'll give you some. Since it doesn't have to travel, it's almost as good." But not quite.

Martin was in the bedroom changing out of his work clothes when he heard a loud hiss followed by a boom. And then Lena screamed. He ran as quickly as he could back to the kitchen. By the time he arrived, Lean was in tears, pointing at the ceiling. Apparently, the pressure cooker had exploded and shot its contents upward. The white ceiling was littered with particles of green asparagus, some still nearly whole, clinging with one end while the other dangled, threatening to drop. "I'll go get a ladder. You get out the mop and pail. If we don't clean this mess up right away, we'll have green specks peering down at us forever."

After the long day he had had, this was the last thing Martin wanted to do when he got home. Once they started cleaning, they discovered that the pressure cooker had spread it contents all over the kitchen—cupboards, counters, floor. It took forever to clean and finally when they had finished, they both fell into bed exhausted.

CHAPTER 56

Marty had just crossed the Atlantic on the USS *Nevada*, which was serving as a convoy for shipments to Northern Ireland. He was expecting the usual break before heading back to Norfolk, Virginia where they'd meet another freighter to convoy back again. That had pretty much been his life the past few weeks and he expected it to continue on that course the rest of the war. But the ship's engines were not turned off nor was it tied up to the dock. Instead, it started to head out to sea again. This was not normal and as he looked around at the other deck hands he could tell that they, too, were wondering what was up.

It wasn't long before the captain announced that they would be heading for the coast of England. "Our orders have changed," he said. "This battleship is going to war." At that word, everyone let out a gasp. Marty still did not know what all this meant. But he had heard rumors that a cross-channel attack plan had been in the works.

When they arrived in Portsmouth, an armada of battleships, cruisers, and destroyers was assembled—most flying the US or British flags. As far as the eye could see, camps were set up along the shoreline and military men were milling around. This must be the staging area for the big battle, Marty thought. *I wonder what our role will be.* As he was pondering all this, the captain's voice boomed from the microphone. "Tenders are being readied. All ashore that's going ashore. Curfew is two hundred hours."

At that announcement, men began to scurry, Marty among them. After several days at sea fighting the storms and swells, he was ready for a respite on terra firma. He hustled down to the bowels of the ship where he would be able to board one of the small boats. This time he was in luck, being near the head of the crowd. He grabbed a place on one of the plank seats right before they shoved off. As the oarsmen rowed through the ships anchored bow to stern, Marty was awestruck by the immense show of naval power. Even his imagination could never have conjured up such a scene that overwhelmed him with pure awe.

Once on shore, Marty and his buddies fought their way through the throng of sailors and soldiers; not surprisingly most of them were American or British, but occasionally an Australian, Canadian, Norwegian, Greek, or other nationality was among them. "Gentleman," Marty said, "while you may know Portsmouth as the home of the British Navy in earlier times, it was known as the best naval port in the world, at least according to my father. And not to mention it was the birthplace of Charles Dickens. I only hope his home was not among the many that got bombed by the Nazis."

Nobody seemed to pay much attention to what Marty had to say as they were on the hunt for a pub but could not avoid the devastation that the blitz had left behind—homes demolished, leaving families without a roof over their heads. This was Marty's first glimpse of the effects of war, and it made an impression. He now realized he was in the midst of a holocaust that was about to explode, leaving even more devastation in its wake. He should have been afraid. But instead of fear, he felt a rising current of courage from somewhere deep inside him. He had fighting in his blood and he was ready. *Bring it on.*

At last the group came upon a pub that looked like there might be room for them. Marty led the way, holding the door for the men to enter the Golden Hind. Right away he spotted a board advertising pub grub—shepherd's pie, fish and chips, bangers and mash, and something strange called toad-in-the-hole. The fish and chips featuring fresh cod appealed to his seafood-loving senses. After they had all ordered a round of drinks and found a table large enough to hold them, a waitress appeared ready to take food orders.

"First, I have to ask a question," said Marty. "What in the world is toad-in-the-hole? It sounds disgusting." The waitress, a middle-aged matron with a red face and round, robust body, let out a laugh, which allowed the rest of the group to follow suit without being offensive.

"I grant you, it is a silly name but sausages baked in batter is a mighty tasty dish and very satisfying as well." That mystery settled, they all began to put in their orders with Marty's fish and chips the first request. The waitress wasted no time getting their food to the table. But there had not been one taker brave enough to try toad-in-the-hole. It didn't take long for the men to consume their meals. The waitress, noting it was time to clear the plates, appeared again. "I'd like to recommend our Knickerbocker Glory for dessert," she said. By the look of their faces she could tell they had no idea what that was so she volunteered. "It's an ice cream parfait interspersed with fruit, topped with meringue and a wafer. I'll even splash a bit of Drambuie on it, if that will suit you."

Marty took a survey of the faces. "We'll have that Knickerbocker treat all around with that liqueur you mentioned." Once they all had the tall parfait glasses in front of them, they dug their spoons into the ice cream dessert. But it was the Drambuie that tantalized their taste buds. Marty just had to ask what it was. "It's made with scotch whiskey, honey, herbs and spices and hails from the Isle of Skye. That's in Scotland, in case you don't know your geography. The story goes that it was Prince Charles who gave the recipe to Captain John MacKinnon in gratitude for sanctuary after the Battle of Culloden in 1746."

Marty took another spoonful of the Drambuie-laced ice cream and smiled. "I'd like a shot of Drambuie straight up."

As he was sipping the liqueur, Marty inventoried the room filled with sailors and soldiers. When his eyes fell on a corner table, he did a double take. The soldier sitting there looked familiar, but he would have to get a closer look to see if it was whom he thought it might be. He rose from his seat and made his way around the tables through the crowded room. When he got to the corner table, he and the soldier locked eyes and then moments later they were embracing. It was Frankie—the last person he expected to run into. He thought Frankie would be kept closer to home and maybe end up in the Pacific. But here he was among the infantry, preparing for D-Day.

Frankie, too, was surprised to see Marty under the circumstances. "What is your assignment here?" he asked.

"I serve on the battleship *Nevada* but we haven't been told our assignment yet. What about you?"

"Well, the Fourth Infantry I'm part of is going to have to take the beaches. And then there is a hill to climb before we can get onto the road and start making our way to Cherbourg. We're practicing near Devon, a place called Slapton Sands, that's supposed to have terrain similar to the one on the other side of the channel."

"That sounds as if it is going to be a bit of a difficult task."

"Well, tomorrow will be my first chance to tell if I'm up to it. We'll be doing a training session there in the morning."

They could have talked the rest of the night, trying to catch up on where they left off, not knowing if they'd ever see each other again. But it was getting close to time for departure so Marty knew he had to get going. "Let's meet here again in a couple of days. I'd like to hear how you do at climbing practice."

"I'll try to make it. I've got to walk a couple of miles to get here, at least. We army guys are spread nearly ten miles down the beach."

As Marty road back across the harbor, he noticed the moon shining its light on the sea, reflecting every ship anchored there, waiting for orders. Waiting and wondering—that was all he or any of them could do right now. But soon enough they would all know and go and do their duty.

CHAPTER 57

On the morning of April 28, Frankie set out with thousands of other soldiers aboard tank landing ships for Slapton Sands at Devon. A small war ship led convoy with a destroyer picking up the rear. As the convoy neared their destination, German e-boats spotted them and opened fire, sinking two and setting others on fire. The men were not prepared for this. And one of the ships that was supposed to protect them had turned back to Portsmouth for repairs. Frankie had been able to scramble into a life raft but many of the men had not been so lucky and were left to chance in the frigid waters, not knowing how to use their life vests or having their heads held down by their backpacks until they drowned.

From the safety of the raft, Frankie tried to pull as many of the men onto it as he could. But the swells worked against him and before he was able to rescue even a few, hypothermia had turned their bodies to flotsam and jetsam. Frankie's raft finally made it to shore where the crew debarked until they could be picked up and returned to camp.

No one seemed to understand how the e-boats had avoided Allied patrol lines and why the escort ships had not been able to protect them. Frankie had never seen such a gruesome scene. All he remembered now were the bodies...bodies floating all around him. . .bodies of American soldiers. . .bodies of men just like him. If this was what practice was like, could war be any worse?

As bad as the incident had been—over seven hundred killed—what was far worse was the command from superiors to keep it to themselves. They were ordered not to talk about it. But what he had seen and experienced was eating Frankie alive. He had to get it out somehow if he were to be effective going forward. He thought about going to the gothic, red brick Catholic church he had spotted in Portsmouth that reminded him of St. Patrick's back home. But any priest he would find to talk to at the Cathedral of St. John the Evangelist would probably be tied in with community leaders and he would be outed for having disobeyed a direct order. No...he couldn't go there to talk with a priest.

So, instead, Frankie went for a walk along the beach. In nature he always found solace and answers as well. Before long, he found he had a walking companion—a shaggy mutt with big, oversized pointed ears—the better to listen to you, he thought. Frankie made his way to the beach and sat down, gazing out to sea. The mutt sat down, too, nuzzling up next to him.

As Frankie petted him, he felt some of his stress disappearing. And then just like his patron St. Francis, he began to let out his heart to this animal friend who could not betray him. "*What I have witnessed no man should ever have to witness. But I fear the war has worse scenes to show me. I am not a warrior. I do not want to take life...any life.* But the evil that is taking over the earth has to be eradicated if life is to flourish as God has meant it to."

Frankie looked at his friend and wondered why animals were able to live as nature intended untouched by evil. They had no duplicity in them. But man was a different story. He who was capable of such goodness also had seeds of evil in him that could sprout under the right conditions. The world can be a complicated mess. Frankie had already seen enough of it and just wanted to get back home to the simple life he had left behind. Although deep down he knew that that simple life could be swept away if freedom did not prevail. This cause was a just cause even though at times its methods were flawed.

When Frankie left the beach to walk back to camp, his animal friend was still at his side. But the next time he turned to look down at him, he was gone. Frankie had not heard him run off so it was a mystery. He was gone almost as quickly as he had appeared. And when he thought more about it, the mutt had not been like an average dog. He didn't bark and sniff and scratch himself. Maybe he was just an apparition or could he have been an animal spirit come to his aid. He guessed he would never really know the truth. But the one thing he did know for sure was that the outpouring of his grief had freed his tormented soul from the claws of Operation Tiger.

A couple of days later, Frankie went back to town to meet up with Marty at the Golden Hind. As soon as he walked in, he spotted him at the bar surrounded by his mates. "Let's grab a table so we can talk," said Frankie as he gave Marty a brotherly hug.

"Go find one and I'll join you after chugging this down."

Frankie had secured a corner table again which made it easier to talk. When Marty sat down the first thing he said was, "We got our orders. The captain called us all on the deck this morning to tell us that we'll be providing support for our forces at Utah beach. We're going to be a flagship for Rear Admiral Morton Deyo."

"Then I'm glad to know you'll have my back. My regiment, the eighth, will be landing on Utah beach."

"That's right. I'll have you're back and much, much more while you're scrambling to climb those hills. So, how did climbing practice go?"

Frankie shrugged his shoulders. He did not want to lie and could not tell the truth.

"Is that all you have to say about it? I'd like to know how long it's going to take to get up over those hills."

"We didn't get a chance to climb."

"Why not? The weather looked perfect for it."

"We just didn't that's all."

Marty just stared at Frankie's face, but he couldn't make out what the hidden message was. "All right then. When do you try to go for it again?"

"Later this week. A new date has not yet been set. Now why don't we order something to eat. Let's get the waitress over here. I might even be brave enough to try toad-in-the-hole."

CHAPTER 58

Although Marty and Frankie had planned to meet up again they never did. Each assumed the other had training exercises for D-Day which had been set for June 5, the first of three possible days that week when both tides and moonlight would be right. But when the Allied Commanders received a bad weather forecast for June 5, they moved D-Day to June 6.

Operation Overlord began in the wee hours of June 6 with an aerial landing of soldiers. The armada of ships had moved into position with the first Allied troops, Regiment 8 of the 4th Infantry, landing first on Utah beach. Frankie swam to shore, weighed down by heavy packs but adrenaline gave him the power to overcome them. Once on the beach, surrounded by soldiers, he took a few breaths while a battleship bombarded German positions. He assumed it was Marty's ship, the *Nevada*, and that thought helped bolster him just knowing his brother had his back.

Frankie's next challenge was to crawl across the beach until he reached the cliffs. A couple of shots from above flew over his head but must have struck one of his troops since he could hear someone crying like a banshee. And then he heard another one. And then he spotted a bullet blow a fellow soldier's brains out just ahead of him. He tried not to look as he went by but it was difficult to avoid seeing the carnage; even worse was the smell… the smell of death, odiferous and overwhelming.

Once he reached the cliffs, he took a break to rebuild his energy for the greatest challenge—a climb over one hundred feet high. Nothing this day was going to be easy or ever forgotten. Frankie was already spent, but he knew he had to move on. Some men were already halfway up the cliff. That was reassuring and meant that if they could do it, he could do it, too. So he started out…gaining a handhold and foothold and moving one step at a time, hand then foot. He remembered his father saying that's how to accomplish a task…one step at a time. Just keep moving forward and you'll get there. So slowly, carefully, he inched his way up, trying to find secure holds along the way. Someone down the line grabbed a hold that broke away, hurling his body back down to the beach. Frankie wondered if he survived and, if he did, were any bones broken. There were so many obstacles to overcome it was a wonder that any men were left to accomplish the mission. But they had had a near perfect landing on the beach, encountering little opposition. Finally, after what seemed like an eternity, Frankie made it to the top and scrambled for cover.

After making it all this way, the last thing he wanted to happen was to end up with a bullet in his back. He took a couple of deep breaths and then pulled out a pack of Camels. A cigarette was what he needed right now. Just one inhale of nicotine revived him and the rest soothed his nerves. Now it was time to meet up with his regiment and push on to Cherbourg—the port was essential for the battle in Western Europe.

The 4th Infantry reached Cherbourg on June 18 and fought until the Germans surrendered at the end of the month. The USS *Nevada* had followed the infantry forces to Cherbourg where it again provided support. Frankie heard the guns of a battleship blasting overhead and knew his brother was protecting him again. But he knew Marty and he would soon have to part ways. The 4th Infantry was heading inland where no boat could follow. Frankie wondered where the *Nevada* would be heading next.

Chapter 59

In the Pacific, Tom Paul was preparing for the Battle of the Philippine Sea. Hellcats were going to be tested along with their pilots. The training they received in Watsonville and elsewhere was going to determine the success of their mission. Tom Paul brought his Hellcat in for a landing on the aircraft carrier where it would be taken out to sea to meet the enemy. Tom Paul found himself in an upbeat mood looking forward to an encounter with Zeros. He had heard so much about the superiority of the Hellcat that he wanted to witness it for himself, from the pilot's seat where there would be no doubt about the plane's ability to perform under the severe conditions of war.

When they reached the Marianna Islands, Commander Spruance ordered Hellcats into the air to cover the fleet. Tom Paul was among those who took flight. Radar picked up a swarm of enemy aircraft approaching, and Spruance sent up three hundred planes to join Tom Paul and the other pilots. Once Tom Paul spotted the Jap Zeros, his adrenaline started pumping, and he felt all his senses keenly alert as if he had a heightened awareness and ability. "*Now I'll see what you can do,*" Tom Paul said aloud to his Hellcat. Using all the techniques he had learned at training school, along with the superior design features of the Grumman plane, Tom Paul was able to take the enemy on over and over again and emerge successful, always ready to fight anew.

The Japs also sent up more planes, most of them picked off by Yankee flyboys but a few got through and got off some shots at the aircraft carriers. However, Hellcats defended their turf and Zeros dropped from the sky. When the battle was over, the Japs had lost two-thirds of their planes and without planes the aircraft carriers were useless. In total, the Japanese lost 243 planes to America's twenty-nine. It had been a real ace maker day, and Tom Paul had emerged as one of them.

But now the threat was not the Japs but the cloak of night covering the aircraft carriers. Without light, it would be almost impossible to land. As Tom Paul flew back, he made his peace with life and felt ready to accept his fate. He would leave this world knowing he had done his duty and that he had helped turn the course of this war. He would die a warrior's death, having given every fiber of his being to a just cause. But it was almost as if acceptance of his fate had changed its course.

As he emerged from cloud cover he could see light. Never before had he realized the power of light—his mood instantly changed into hope. It was against the rules for aircraft carriers to light themselves for fear the enemy would be able to spot the target. But the Commander had ordered them lighted anyway so the Hellcats and their pilots could make it home. Tom Paul wanted to do a cheer…to jump up and down…to dance and sing. His heart was filled with blessing and gratitude for the chance to live another day.

Tom Paul was able to bring his Hellcat in for a near perfect landing. When he emerged from the cockpit, the ground crew let out a cheer but it didn't last long, because they had so many returning planes to guide in. Unfortunately, not every plane made a successful landing. Some crash-landed on the deck, some ended up in the ocean, and others ran out of gas before they were even in range. But rescue crews had most of the survivors picked up by the next day.

There was a lot of celebrating after that victory. One veteran airman called it a turkey shoot and the name stuck since it fit. Anyone who had ever been to a turkey shoot knew that they didn't shoot back. Forever after, the battle would be known as the Great Marianas Turkey Shoot, a pivotal battle in the war.

The Battle of the Philippine Sea was the greatest carrier battle of World War II. Along with damaging or sinking some ships, it dismantled Japan's air power for the rest of the war. The Hellcat had proven its superiority.

Martin's position as town liaison for the naval station kept him in the loop. Even before the newspapers could report the results of a Pacific naval battle, the officers at the naval station had the details. "Our Hellcats showed their stuff the other day," Commander Barkley said to Martin. "They shot down so many Zeros that the Japs won't be able to recover until long after the war's over."

Martin did not know what battle he was talking about but his mind was on Tom Paul. "How did our guys do?"

"Our losses were nothing compared to theirs."

"That's good. You must have trained them well."

"Not only that but those Hellcats outperformed the Zeros just as we thought they would. No amount of training can make up for lousy equipment."

"Where was the battle so I can pass on the word of our success?"

"In the Philippines Sea. But they're calling it The Great Marianas Turkey Shoot. That name couldn't be more descriptive. Those Japs barely got a shot off."

"Good. That may mean my son survived."

"No doubt he did. He was one of my best pilots. The turkey shoot probably made him an ace. It only takes about five hits to qualify and a good number of pilots must've, considering the number of Zeros shot down."

"Knowing Tom Paul, he shot his share." But Martin was thinking that no amount of honor was worth it if you were dead. He could only hope and pray that Tom Paul made it through.

A few weeks later, Michael burst through the restaurant doors between meal hours. "Did you hear?"

"Since I don't know what you're talking about I probably didn't. So don't leave me in suspense."

"The Chetniks have rescued a couple hundred of our airmen that had been shot down in the Balkans and held prisoner. It's all over the news. They're looking like God-damned heroes." By the end of the year over four hundred pilots would be rescued.

"Well, they're getting all the publicity because they didn't do anything until now and could deliver them in a big group. Tito and his partisans have been rescuing our airmen all along and sending them home. They didn't have to rot in a stinking prison awaiting rescue."

"Somehow we've got to get that angle of the story out."

"It will come out eventually. No use tooting our own horn. Besides what the Chetniks are doing finally is a good thing."

"Yeah, as usual you're right." Michael thought a minute and then asked, "Any word from your sons?"

"Not in a while. You know both fronts are pretty active right now. But as they say no news, is good news."

CHAPTER 60

After taking Cherbourg, the 4th Infantry marched over two hundred miles before reaching the outskirts of Paris. On August 25, the French 2nd armored division led by General LeClerc approached the City of Lights from the north while the 4th Infantry approached from the south. At Midnight as the first liberators set foot in the city, the bells of Notre Dame rang out, and soon every church in Paris joined in a carol of the bells. They encountered very little resistance as they swept the city free, German soldiers fleeing or surrendering, not fighting.

The French people greeted their liberating heroes with flowers, wine, and kisses, returned in kind. And they were honored with a parade down the Champs-Élysées. As Frankie passed under the Arc de Triomphe, he blessed himself knowing his footsteps fell on the Tomb of the Unknown Soldier from World War I. Frankie had heard about Paris all his life, and now he was finally here. But he never expected to make such a dramatic entrance into Paris.

This moment would remain in his memory forever. He later learned that Hitler had ordered Paris destroyed rather than captured and that explosives had been laid throughout the city. But the German General Choltitz disobeyed orders because he did not want to be forever known as the *Destroyer of Paris.* Besides, by then he thought Hitler was crazy.

A Mass at Notre Dame was followed by a party that lasted for days. Ernest Hemingway, who was imbedded as a war correspondent in the 4th, served as a sort of tour guide. After liberating the bar at The Ritz, which he proclaimed to have done, the celebrating kicked into high gear. Author and 4th Infantryman JD Salinger took part as well. And even the celebrated writers later admitted, truth is often stranger than fiction.

No sooner had Frankie entered Paris, then he left it, heading toward Belgium to follow German forces. They encountered them in the Battle of the Hurtgen Forest and then again in the Ardennes Forest in what became known as the Battle of the Bulge. The bulge was created by 250,000 German troops and hundreds of tanks spread over a sixty-mile area. It was December by the time the 4th Infantry reached the snow-covered battlefield. Temperatures were frigid and supplies were running low, but more so for the Germans than the Allies. Nevertheless, they fought one of the longest battles of World War II with casualties high and injuries higher.

Frankie had never witnessed such gruesome sights. Men were dying right and left. Limbs blown off, guts exploded, faces shattered, eyeballs oozing goo. He had to put invisible blinders on to keep on fighting. At one point in the battle, a German had Frankie in his sights but was blown away by another GI before he even had a chance to react. Frankie glanced over at his savior and was surprised to see a black man. When they finally reached a resting place, Frankie found himself surrounded by black soldiers who he later learned were part of the 333rd and 969th Field Artillery Battalions. Even though the army was not yet integrated, the high command, desperate and under pressure, sent black soldiers to the front to help fight the Battle of the Bulge. Frankie was grateful that they did. He knew he wouldn't have made it through without one of them, Jethro Jeremiah Jackson, a mighty warrior blacker than the Ace of Spades.

CHAPTER 61

In late October, Croatians began pouring into Martin's restaurant to celebrate—Dubrovnik had been liberated from the Nazis—Belgrade, too, but since it was Serbian they didn't much care about it. But a free Dubrovnik was something to cheer about. Since 1941, it had been occupied by Italians first and then in 1943 by Germans. Michael shouted to Martin, "Aren't those Partisans something?"

"They certainly are," he said as he put up a sign on the door that read, *Closed for Private Party.* Liu and Chao knew what was expected and were already getting the sljivovica out.

Martin held up his glass, "To the Partisans and freedom. May our brothers in Croatia finally know the freedom we know here in America." Then everyone put their glasses to their lips and slugged the liquor in one gulp. "Another round," Martin called out. And the glasses were filled again. Then another toast followed by another round until the sljivovica had been exhausted. The revelers stumbled out of the restaurant, not knowing how they managed to get home.

They all made another appearance on Sunday for a proper celebration at the Slavonic Society. Every Dalmatian in town turned up for the occasion, featuring a buffet of Croatian favorites and plenty of sljivovica to last into the wee hours of the night. At one point, men were taking to the stage to offer toasts or insights into the war in the Balkans. Martin used the opportunity to share what he knew about the war in the Pacific. "I just want to share that our forces won a decisive victory in the Battle of the Leyte Gulf. Many of you, like me, may have sons who fought in that battle. Well, let me tell you those Hellcats, some of which we dispatched to the Pacific from our own little airport, did a hell of a job on the Jap war fleet—taking out over thirty ships. So now, without both ships and planes, not to mention pilots, they are seriously lacking in resources to sustain them in battle. It will only be a matter of time until we have won the war." In his Christmas message, President Roosevelt echoed the same sentiment. "'The tide of battle has turned, slowly but inexorably, against those who sought to destroy civilization.'"

CHAPTER 62

After Cherbourg, Marty and the *Nevada* had gone to Southern France to support the Allies there in Operation Dragoon. Then they were ordered to head back across the Atlantic for an overhaul and refitting to have guns replaced. Next the *Nevada* sailed out of the Norfolk Navy Yard with its new assignment—the Pacific theatre…Pearl Harbor. After passing through the Panama Canal and making a pit stop in California, the *Nevada* crossed the familiar Pacific territory arriving at Pearl Harbor where it tied up at Quay Fox 8—the same one the ship had been at when the Japanese launched their attack three years before. Marty hoped this was an auspicious sign. And it certainly proved to be.

Marty headed for the nearest watering hole as soon as they got leave—Smith's Union Bar in the red light district. As he entered the long narrow room with a bar on one side, tables on the other, he heard the sounds of ukuleles being strummed, offering up traditional Hawaiian melodies. Once he got the bartender's attention, he asked for the best island beer they had and was handed a Kona Longboard. He took his first quaff as he scanned the room and couldn't believe his eyes when he spotted Tom Paul holding court at the other end of the bar. At first Tom Paul didn't recognize him, since Marty was sporting the beard of a seaman, but when he did, he gave Marty the biggest bear hug he ever would have again in his life.

"What are you doing in this joint?" Tom Paul asked. "All the *Nevada* crew hang out at Shanghai Bill's."

"I just ducked into the first drinking hole I saw. Now that I'm clued in, I'll try that one next. But, hey, let's grab a table," said Marty. "We've a lot of catching up to do." Fortunately, they caught a break between the ukulele set and karaoke. Once they were seated and had ordered something to eat, Marty went on to tell Tom Paul about all his exploits and especially his encounter with Frankie in Portsmouth during the D-Day preparations.

"Where do you think Frankie is now?" Tom Paul asked.

"Somewhere in Europe. I only hope he got to participate in the Liberation of Paris. He deserved that bit of pleasure after what he had to do during Operation Neptune on Utah Beach."

"Are you telling me that Frankie was one of the GIs that had to make the beach landing and climb those cliffs while Germans tried to pick them off."

"I know it's hard to believe that our Frankie, the peace lover, had to shoot his way all the way to Cherbourg, but it's the truth. I don't think he'll ever be the same again. Even from the *Nevada*, I could see some of what those soldiers were going through and it was ugly beyond sin."

"I guess we're lucky we don't have to witness the gruesome scenes of war up close."

"Of course, it's nothing like Frankie is having to go through, but we have had some carnage to deal with as well, and it ain't for the faint of heart. Now tell me what you've been doing out here in the Pacific."

"Well," Tom Paul said as he sat up as straight as he could, "I'm a flying ace, meaning I've shot down a lot of Japs."

"Well, I'll be. I still think of you as my kid brother. And now you're some kind of war hero."

"Not hero. Just a good shot from a Hellcat. That plane is something else. Our Hellcats took out most of the Zeros in the Marianas. They don't have much left to fly."

"Are you sure of that?"

"It all became quite apparent how desperate they were when we went back to take the Philippines at Leyte Gulf. Instead of staying in the air to fight us Hellcats, they sent their planes directly at the ships like bombs. They call them Kamikazes—translation, divine wind. Of course, the pilots sacrifice themselves, but they're doing it in a last ditch effort to save their country."

"I never imagined the Japs would resort to using their Zeros like that. It seems inhumane if not crazy."

"But it is effective. They took out the carrier *St. Lo*. It sunk in less than an hour. Overall they downed over thirty ships. I never saw anything like it. Not only did they use Zeros but specially-designed planes that were carried toward their target by bombers."

"It sounds like you've experienced a lot of the naval battles in your short time in the Pacific."

"Yeah, they're calling the Battle of Leyte Gulf one of the biggest naval battles ever, certainly of the war. We destroyed most of the Jap's surface fleet so now without both planes and ships they should be about ready to surrender."

"I don't know about that. They're a proud race. Don't you remember the way most of them were back home? They don't give up easily. My guess is that they'll fight to the bitter end."

"For all our sakes, I hope not."

In attempt to divert the conversation from war, Marty said, "What have you heard from home?"

"Either they're not writing or letters are not getting through. And I have to admit, I haven't had the motivation to write them either. Mom is not going to want to hear all about me being shot at and shooting back. She couldn't care less if I've made ace."

"I know. She just wants her baby to stay safe and come back to her in one piece."

"I'll either end this war in one piece or be blown to smithereens."

"Let's not give tongue nor thought to that. Anyway, I'm only going to be around Honolulu for a couple of days and then we're shipping out again."

"Oh, yeah? Where to?"

"Ulithi Atoll. It's in the Caroline Islands."

"I know all about it. It's a major naval staging area. Guess we're gearing up for another battle."

"Who knows? They don't tell us sailors much. We're on a need-to-know basis."

Tom Paul let out a loud belly laugh. "We all are. Sometimes I don't even think the commanders know much too far in advance."

CHAPTER 63

Back at the *Nevada*, Marty and his mates loaded ammunition and then set sail under full power. Marty had not been at Pearl Harbor when the Japs struck so he could only imagine what the *Nevada* and its crew had struggled through to get underway that day only three years ago, the only battleship that did. It brought tears to his eyes, thinking about that day, knowing that the *Nevada*'s ability to maneuver had given hope despite taking a torpedo in its port side earning its nickname, *Cheer Up Ship.*

As it moved out into the harbor, it was pelted by several bombs and then ordered to beach itself so it wouldn't block the channel. It must have been a sorry sight for sailors to witness their ship going under. Even sorrier to have to carry off dead and wounded mates. Most gruesome of all was encountering body parts of crew who had minutes ago been robust seamen but now not even recognizable.

As the *Nevada* moved along the channel, some crew members pointed to the spot the *Nevada* had been laid down. But like the Phoenix, it was raised from the ashes and sent off to the Puget Sound Navy Yard under its own power to be refitted. When President Roosevelt visited the Navy Yard, it was there to bear witness to the day that will live in infamy. As a former Secretary of the Navy, Roosevelt had a special connection to ships and their crews.

There can be no doubt that the battle-scarred *Nevada* had been an inspiration that would help carry him through war time, a reminder that our country is strong, and though scarred, would come out a survivor as well as a victor. The USS *Nevada* was one of the few battleships that would fight key battles on both fronts. Marty knew he was having the experience of a lifetime aboard a vessel that would go down in history.

After they got through the channel, the seas grew rough as blustery winds blew, but the *Nevada* plowed through to its destination. After making their way through the Mugal Channel, they anchored in a lagoon near an island named Mogmog. But as Marty and his crew were later to find out—don't judge an island by its name. The island was a bit of paradise with its crystal blue waters, white-sand beaches, and palm trees, fronds waving gently in the wind.

Once there, they had unrestricted liberty and there were plenty of diversions to occupy their time. The navy had built a bandstand, which gave sailors with even a bare amount of talent a venue to entertain the troops. Some guys put together a band, others brought out their guitar and some just got on stage and harmonized. Then there was a large arena where various acts took to the stage to entertain as well as plenty of drink stands around so no one ever had to do without a beer for too long. Marty found an ongoing poker game that he was able to last in until dawn when he lost most of his pay.

But just as it seemed too good to be true, it was. The island was crawling with one of the largest populations of coconut crabs whose leg span of three feet was only surpassed by its pincers, the strength of steel. One chop was all it took for a crab to break open a coconut. It made one wonder what they could do to a man's skull.

It didn't take the men long to decide that giant crabs would make good target practice. As it turned out, they provided the makings for the biggest crab boil this side of the Maryland shore.

The navy knew how to do crab boils with Annapolis being located on the Chesapeake Bay, the center of the crab-eating culture. So, they assembled as many big pots as they could find, filled them with water, and set them over a fire built in the sand. When the crabs started cooking, the smell reminded Marty of the San Francisco Wharf where a Dungeness crab cocktail was the order of the day.

Just as the feast was about ready to be served up, an aircraft carrier pulled into the lagoon. Marty happened to be nearby when Tom Paul made his appearance, scrambling up the shore from a tender.

"Ahoy there, mate. Welcome ashore," Marty said as he offered a helping hand to his brother.

"Somehow I knew we'd meet up here."

"This reminds me of the D-Day shakedown when we had hundreds of ships and thousands of military men gathered before battle. But now instead of Frankie, it's you I'm going to be hanging out with."

Tom Paul gave Marty a big hug. "What's that I smell?" The aroma of crab was filling the air, overpowering every other odor in the vicinity including body odor, which was ever-present.

"It's crab…giant coconut crab. This island is crawling with the monsters. But as you can see from the long food lines, it's a hit especially with naval officers who were weaned on crab at Annapolis."

"The admirals seem to be the first in line. I thought officers were supposed to let their men eat first."

"That's the rule but in this case I think they're food tasters. If they keel over their men will know not to partake. But the natives consider the coconut crabs a delicacy and claim it has aphrodisiac powers. When crab is served up, the young women go into hiding while the old wives parade around in their hula skirts."

"Let's get in line," said Tom Paul, "before they run out. I want to find out if what they say is true."

While they dined at long tables covered with paper, hammered at the shells with volcanic rocks, and picked out the meat with their fingers, guys around them discussed the finer points of crustaceans since some had a lot of experience with them. A young naval lieutenant across the table from them said, "The blue crabs in Maryland are the best. And when they begin molting their shell in spring, you can eat them whole. That's how I like them—especially the legs which remind me of French fries."

An army sergeant down the line said, "We got golden crab in the Aleutians. It has a bit of a sweet taste that was quite pleasing. But the red king crab are supposed to be the best. They're big suckers…bigger than the ones here…and fishing for them is a real killer. By that I mean, men lose their lives on a regular basis trying to wrangle those monsters onto the boat. They've got a six-foot leg span."

"If you want to hear something really scary that will give you nightmares," said an airman next to Tom Paul, "I've heard crabs in Japan have a thirteen-foot leg span. Imagine what they could do to a man."

"That's right," said Tom Paul. "Maybe all we have to do is capture them and set them lose in Tokyo until the Japs are terrorized enough to surrender."

On that note, Marty stood up and Tom Paul followed. They cleared their plates, throwing the shells in the garbage. "Now let's see what we can scare up," said Tom Paul. "I'm starting to feel the effects of the crab." He turned his head toward Marty and they grinned at each other as if to say maybe this will be their lucky night.

Christmas Eve arrived with all the servicemen in good spirits. They took shifts attending church services in the hastily built chapel that could only accommodate five hundred—had it not been for the holiday that certainly would have been sufficient seating. Christmas dinner had to be served in shifts as well but even had fresh bread and an assortment of pies on the menu that were baked on one of the navy's distilling ships anchored in the lagoon. But the real treat was ice cream, which crews churned out daily at a rate of five hundred gallons a shift. Today they had a special eggnog flavor in honor of the festivities. When Marty took his first spoonful, he whispered to Tom Paul. "It's spiked." Apparently most of the other servicemen noticed the same thing and were going back for seconds, even thirds.

Marty and Tom Paul had been lucky to draw seats for President Roosevelt's Christmas message. The theatre held 1,200, and then there would be standing room for a few hundred more. Radios had also been set up around the camp to listen in. As well, ships' radios would be tuned in full blast.

President Roosevelt opened his fireside chat by saying, "It is not easy to say 'Merry Christmas' to you, my fellow Americans, in this time of destructive war." Then he went onto say, "The Christmas spirit lives tonight in the bitter cold of the front lines in Europe and in the heat of the jungles and swamps of Burma and the Pacific islands."

Marty and Tom Paul looked at each other and then Tom Paul whispered in Marty's ear. "If our fellow Americans knew we were stuffing ourselves on pies and ice cream, they would trade places with us in a split second."

Near the end, Roosevelt said the words the servicemen were anxiously waiting to hear. "On this Christmas day, we cannot yet say when our victory will come. Our enemies still fight fanatically. They still have reserves of men and military power. But, they themselves know that they and their evil works are doomed." At the end of the speech, the crowd let out a cheer. Even though they could tell the president was being cautious, he was also expressing optimism that the war would be won by the Allies, even if the end point was not yet known.

After Marty and Tom Paul left, they reflected on the words of "the bitter cold of the front lines of Europe" and wondered where Frankie would be found on this holy night, Europe already shrouded in darkness awaiting the dawn of Christmas Day.

The good times came to an end on February 10 when the USS *Nevada* set course with other war ships for Iwo Jima, which had airfields the Allies needed. It took six days to reach the island, and then the invasion began with guns blasting for two days before the marines made their assault on the beaches. Unfortunately, the bombardment had done little to prepare the way since the Japanese were so well fortified. Despite heavy losses and a formidable enemy, one week later on February 23, a few marines raised the American flag on a hill for all to see, more importantly, providing inspiration to the fighting men and all Americans who saw the photo on the front page of their home town newspapers. It took a total of thirty-six days to take the island but the mission was accomplished. By March 11, the *Nevada* was back at Ulithi Atoll for a little R&R.

CHAPTER 64

The Battle of the Bulge ended at the end of January with the Allies victorious despite heavy casualties. This surprise attack by the Nazis set Allied plans for the invasion of Germany back several weeks. When the fighting finally ended, Frankie was spent—he didn't think he had any energy left. But he was no longer an individual—he was part of a unit, and the unit's collective spirit took hold, moving him and the others along. While the Battle of the Bulge had been a harrowing experience, it also showed him what he was made of. He'd always been a calm, peaceful person. Some had mistaken that for weakness. But on the battlefield, he had been tested and his true character had revealed itself. He could fight and when he had a reason to, fight fiercely. The calm that he usually displayed turned out to be quiet courage that could be sustained. After dodging so many bullets and other near misses, Frankie felt invincible, as if he were under some divine protection—that nothing could take his life.

There was very little rest for the 4th Infantry, which had to move on across Europe and invade Germany. After crossing the Rhine, the 4th marched through Bavaria until they hit Frankfurt. From there they followed the Main River until they reached the outskirts of Wurzburg, a city renowned for its Baroque architecture. On March 16 the British bombed the city, destroying ninety percent of it in a bare seventeen minutes and setting off a firestorm.

On April 3, Frankie and the 4th Infantry moved into Wurzburg to secure it but found not much more than rubble and ashes. The magnificent Baroque castle, Wurzburg Residence, was left in ruins. As Frankie and his unit moved through the debris, their movement triggered an avalanche of bricks—some hit soldiers, others hit the ground, but one large brick caught Frankie, crushing his left leg. It took four soldiers to free him, and when they did his lower leg bones appeared to be shattered. His buddy, Jethro Jeremiah Jackson, the same one who'd saved him at the Battle of the Bulge, quickly tied a tourniquet above the knee to stem the bleeding. Then with the help of others, Jethro slung Frankie onto his back to carry him out where medics could treat him.

Before the bombing, Wurzburg had forty hospitals. Now they had to find just one for Frankie. They spotted a building still standing high on a hill with Red Cross flags waving overhead. Not knowing where else to go, the medics transported Frankie to what turned out to be Luitpold Hospital, a highly respected medical clinic. The medics were relieved to have found the place because they knew Frankie's leg had to be amputated.

CHAPTER 65

The Battle of Okinawa was scheduled for April 1. Marty and the *Nevada* moved out a few days before that to wait in Nagagusuku Bay about ten miles off the coast. Even before the battle began, they were being threatened by Kamikazes. After holding them off for a few days, one finally made it through crashing into the front deck leaving sixty casualties in its wake. For the next several days, the *Nevada*'s guns let loose on the beaches and other military targets. Then unexpectedly, the enemy fired a barrage of bullets at the *Nevada*, again damaging the main deck and inflicting casualties.

The *Nevada* answered with a hail of gunfire that shut the enemy down completely. That bought some time to slip into Kerama Retto for repairs. What was a dark time was made even darker when they learned that President Roosevelt had died on April 12. Just like Moses, Marty thought, he leads us through the desert but doesn't get to see the Promised Land.

The *Nevada* returned to battle, clearing sea lanes of mines and bombarding the shoreline. One day as it went about its business, the radio picked up a broadcast from Tokyo Rose, which was a familiar program broadcasting a mix of entertainment and propaganda. While they listened they heard her say, "We know you're out there, *Nevada*." The sailors all wondered how she knew. After that, the crew felt uneasy as if someone was watching them.

While the battle continued, the *Nevada* was sent back to Pearl Harbor for permanent repairs on April 20. For Marty and his crewmates, it was a chance for liberty and pleasure. But it was hard to really relax with a fight underway and Tom Paul in the mix. The news of Hitler's suicide, followed by Germany's surrender a week later on May 7, uplifted everyone's spirits.

CHAPTER 66

No one's spirits were lifted more than the delegates of fifty nations attending the San Francisco Conference to write the United Nations charter. The head of the US delegation, Secretary of State Edward Stettinius, took up residence in the penthouse of the Fairmont Hotel that was the site of behind-the-scene negotiations. As well, a number of other delegations made the Fairmont their headquarters.

Stan Dukich, the Fairmont's head chef, was finding himself overwhelmed by the eating habits of the delegates, who seemed to have no pattern and often required an adherence to special dietary requirements. *If this were only going to be a week or so, I could handle it,* he thought. But it appeared the conference would go on for weeks. There was only one thing he could do—call in recruits.

Martin's phone rang one evening soon after he got home. It was already ten o'clock at night—not a time to pass on good news so he made sure he answered the call rather than Lena. To his surprise, it was Stan Dukich on the other end of the line. "Is there anything wrong, Stan, or is this just the time chefs have to talk to each other?"

"If there is anything wrong, it is in a good way. You probably know there is an important world conference being held here to form a United Nations. Well, the US delegation is staying in the hotel along with a few others, including Yugoslavia, so I am up to my ears in it. We are having trouble keeping up with the demand. I'm calling you because I need your help."

"You know I'm always willing to help in any way I can. What do you need from me?"

"I need you in my kitchen cooking and helping to manage the operation."

"I see. If this were only going to be for a day or two, I could leave my restaurant to my sous chef, Liu. But I cannot do that long -term and make a living."

"I wouldn't expect you to. I know your restaurant is closed on Sundays but we still have plenty of mouths to feed in the hotel."

"Sunday…I could probably help you out then."

"You wouldn't have to get here early. These people stay up late on Saturday nights talking and, of course, drinking except for the Arabs who are Muslim so don't imbibe. I've heard the Secretary of State has cornered the market on Scotch."

"Perhaps, I should come up one weekday to view your operation so I know what to expect. A big hotel kitchen is very different from my little one at the café. I may not be up to the task quite frankly."

"You are more than up to the task. We don't turn out dishes en masse. We do them to order which means a chef, like you, will be able to use your skill to create a palate-pleasing dish—something these finicky diplomats require."

"Your offer intrigues me. It will not only be an opportunity to help out an old friend but witness history in action."

"Don't get too many romantic ideas. Cooking over a hot stove secluded in a hotel kitchen does not give a chef much chance to witness anything except for tempers flaring amongst the staff and the regular kitchen disaster."

"You are not doing a good job selling me on this opportunity. But I'll come up on Wednesday to learn more."

Martin got up early so he could take a leisurely drive along the coast where he knew he would get spectacular views of the Pacific since the day had dawned fog free. But instead of enjoying the beauty of the sea, he was thinking about his two sons still fighting battles in the Pacific. How could such a beautiful ocean be the venue for such horrific acts? As much as he tried, he could not banish thoughts of war from his mind.

Finally, when he entered the Fairmont Hotel, his mind shifted as he took in the scene of so many different types of people milling around the lobby. There were people of every color from the fairest blond to the blackest black, and dressed in every way from Africans in colorful Dashiki shirts to Arabs in flowing robes with daggers adorned in jewels tucked in their belts. Martin had never seen such a display of humanity. He scanned the lobby to try to pick out the Yugoslavians in the group, but failing to do so, found his way to the kitchen.

Stan spotted him as soon as he entered through the double swinging doors. "Martin, it is so good to see you," Stan said as he shook his hand. "Well, this is it…the place I call home most of the time but better known as the Fairmont Hotel kitchen."

"It certainly is impressive. Why don't I hang up my coat and put on my chef's jacket then you can give me a tour."

Stan smiled. "See, I knew you'd be right for this. You're already starting to give orders."

"Don't be so sure yet. But I have to say, I'm feeling inspired just being in this kitchen with so many gadgets, stoves, and refrigerators."

"Let me tell you, the city is really rolling out the red carpet for the delegates. After years of blackouts, we are a city of light."

"In more ways than one I'd say. Just like Paris is known as the City of Light both literally and figuratively, San Francisco is leading the second era of Enlightenment."

"You can say that again. We've had to recruit every citizen we can to help with tours, serve the free buffet at the Opera House, take tickets at the theatre that is showing Hollywood movies for those with a pass. It is incredible to witness. This town has roared back to life, playing an epic role in history. And you're going to be part of that history, too. We all are." Martin was beaming, having been lit up by Stan's words.

After the tour of the kitchen, Stan took Martin into his office to discuss matters further. But before they started, Martin said, "I didn't notice any Yugoslavs in the lobby. Where are they hiding out?"

"They probably had too much sljivovica last night is my guess. But if you really want to meet some of them, you can take up their room order."

"I'd like that. It might be my only opportunity to step out of the kitchen."

"Let me tell my sous chef that you will be going along." Stan left Martin a minute to pass along these instructions and then returned, saying, "It will be about ten minutes until all the food is ready. That should give us time to go over preliminaries."

It wasn't long before Martin was called to accompany the room service attendants to the Yugoslavian delegation room. As soon as the door opened, Martin recognized a compatriot. "Good morning," he said in Croatian.

The man looked at him indignantly. "I understand Croatian but I am Serbian, in case you can't tell the difference."

Martin could feel his face turning red. "I apologize. Welcome to America." The man's face began to thaw.

"If you want to speak with a Croatian, he's in the room next door." But Martin didn't think it would be polite to disturb him.

"Excuse me for my manners. I'm Martin Petrovich. I left home at the turn of the century and haven't been back since. So, I'm curious about how things are now?"

"Well, you should be happy because your fellow Croatian, Tito, is running the country. But the war took a toll on us, just like everywhere else in the world."

"I wish you luck in your diplomatic mission."

"We will need it. With fifty nations all trying to weigh in, the writing of the charter won't be easy."

Martin nodded agreement. And noticing that the room service crew had finished setting up the table, he took his leave. He only wished he could be a fly on the wall who could listen in on private conversations and keep an eye on those secret meetings he knew would be happening. Politics never changed.

Martin continued to show up at the Fairmont on Sundays and occasionally during the week when Stan was desperate for another hand in the kitchen. Whenever he got a chance, he would stop by to visit Uncle Anton, Aunt Mirna and his cousins, and their families. Anton was getting up in age—past eighty—but still cooking at his restaurant. The demands of the conference were taking a toll but he took pride in serving the Yugoslavian delegation, which frequently rented out his whole restaurant for an evening. Marko was thriving in his engineering business and one of his son's had joined him in a junior position. Vlad, had his own family, too, but the children were grown and out of the house. He still ran the grocery store with Katarina who had never let go of the torch she carried for her deceased husband Paul. Her only child Pauli had grown into a man and, after graduating from college, went to work at the grocery store, always a faithful son.

Martin was glad that the conference had given him a chance to reconnect with his family, but it made him realize more than ever how time had moved on. When he first came to San Francisco, he was a young man. Now it was his cousins' children who were the younger generation, anxious to take over and move ahead with their own ideas, casting the past behind.

Of course, that was what the San Francisco Conference was attempting to do, too—move ahead into a new era. Martin thought it curious that the war wasn't even over, yet all these countries were taking part in rebuilding the world as if peace were already a done deal. Marty and Tom Paul were out there in the Pacific, probably fighting the Battle of Okinawa that was still waging. No one expected Japan to win, but as the war went on, Japan fought harder to the point of sending out its native sons to sacrifice themselves as human bombs. But what if Japan won that battle and continued to fight even harder maybe with a weapon not yet known to the world? Then all of this debating and negotiating would have been for naught.

CHAPTER 67

On June 25, President Truman made a grand entrance into town by taking the Golden Gate Bridge over the San Francisco Bay, which connects the strait with the Pacific Ocean, the symbolism of which may have been lost on most Americans but in the mind of their leader was significant, foreshadowing the end of war. Truman proceeded to drive through the streets in a Lincoln convertible while waving to the crowd, a half million strong, supportive of their new president. The people had raised Truman's spirits, but even more so the unanimous vote on the UN charter that the delegates had given. Once he arrived at the Fairmont Hotel with flags of every delegation posted at the entrance, Truman took up a position in the Red Room where he greeted delegates and thanked them for their participation in the creation of a United Nations.

After a lot of hand shaking and back slapping, Truman moved on to the penthouse suite where he was hosting a dinner for the other three of the Big Four—England, Russia, and China. Not only had they succeeded in winning the World War, at least in Europe, but they had also designed peace for the world through their vision and leadership, especially that of Franklin Delano Roosevelt, whose spirit was still a guiding force.

Stan had gotten notice that President Truman would be holding a dinner in the penthouse only a week ahead of time and wanted Martin there to help. "It's almost at an end but the biggest event for us is yet to come. Drop everything and head up here…your country calls."

"If you put it that way, I'll be there in the morning."

Stan never thought the two months of working round the clock would culminate in a presidential dinner requiring every last ounce of stamina his body held in reserve. But he had to get a menu together and procure the ingredients, which in these times of rationing would not be easy. Then they would need a couple of days to prep at the very least.

Once Martin arrived, they went over the menu the president's aide suggested. "It appears he has simple tastes," said Stan. "Nothing that is going to require difficult execution—fresh ingredients simply prepared."

"He grew up on a farm. And he probably knows we have some of the best produce around. He understands that good ingredients only need to be enhanced with a light touch—that it's almost a sin to disguise them."

"I hear a French chef, Fernand Point, is leading the way in this new philosophy of cuisine. His restaurant, La Pyramide, near Lyon is considered the best in France."

"Then maybe I'm wrong about the farm. Truman may have dined at La Pyramide or gotten the taste of it from a chef trained under Point. But I notice he wants beef for the main course."

"He's from Kansas City famous for its stock yards. Anyway, with these suggestions, we should be able to put together a menu that will please the president. And since he is going local, procurement should not be too much of a problem."

"Here's some items we should work into the menu—Dungeness crab, artichokes, avocados, strawberries, apples, and abalone."

"Sounds good to me. We may have to get a little creative to give the diners the full range of tastes."

"Such as…"

"A crab cocktail served in an avocado half with a green apple garnish."

"Now I know why you're the head chef at the Fairmont, and I'm just a cook at a cafe in a little berg no one's ever heard of."

Once the guests had taken their seats at the table and the champagne was poured, Truman stood up to offer a toast. "As they say, a vice president is just a heartbeat away from the presidency. When I learned that big heart of his had ceased to beat and I had ascended to the highest office in the land, I called myself a simple man overwhelmed by the prospect of filling a giant's shoes. But I have to say, I have found my own shoes fit just fine. And tonight I stand before you, sharing in our success of a United Nations that will build a better world for generations to come.

Now I'd like to introduce the Monsignor of Mission San Francisco de Assisi, which was founded a few days before the Declaration of Independence gave birth to our nation in 1776. Father O'Brien, please come forward and lead us in grace."

A tall, thin priest dressed in the hooded brown robe of a Franciscan, tied with a rope and wearing sandals, came forward. "Thank you Mr. President," he said. "Like you, I am a simple man, a follower of one who led a simple life that led him to God. It is an honor to serve as the pastor of Mission San Francisco de Assisi, which has the distinction of being the oldest intact building in the city and, consequently, the longest witness to its history. It is also known as Mission Dolores because it is nearby the Creek of Sorrows. So, it seems oceans of sorrows have brought you to this city. But just like the mission that survived because it had four-foot-thick adobe walls, the four Allied countries have survived and saved the world. Four is a very powerful number, as you may know. It symbolizes both stability and all earthly things. And in Hebrew four letters spell the most important word in the universe...*God*."

After the champagne was finished, a Sauvignon Blanc from nearby Napa Valley was poured to accompany the Dungeness crab cocktail prepared just the way Stan had described it. Martin was supervising the serving in the dining room while Stan kept the courses on track in the kitchen. Truman smiled with pleasure when a generous portion of prime rib was placed in front of him accompanied by a twice-baked potato elegantly wrapped in foil and asparagus lightly napped with hollandaise. A salad topped with marinated artichoke hearts followed as a palate cleanser. Dessert featured a meringue filled with chocolate mousse, garnished with fresh strawberries.

While coffee was being served, Martin hustled downstairs to let Stan know how well the dinner was going and to bring in the tea service. When he got back to the dining room and rolled in the cart, eyes opened wide. "Tea…three ways," Martin announced. In the center of the cart sat a big, ornate silver samovar surrounded by three boxes containing favorite teas of three out of four Allied nations.

Truman looked up. "Why only three?"

"Sir, the coffee that was served first was the nod to America."

"Of course, we're not a nation of tea drinkers."

"And why is that, may I ask?" said the English diplomat.

"Because we work long hours and need to stay awake. That's why we could build so many machines so quickly and so well for the war. You don't get a performance like that taking time out for tea." The diplomat pressed his lips together so he could refrain from speaking his mind.

On June 26 the United Nations Charter was signed by the fifty nations in attendance. China was given the honor of signing first since it was the first nation attacked by the Axis powers. In his address during the final session, Truman said, "Between the victory in Europe and the final victory, in this most destructive of all wars, you have won a victory against war itself. With this Charter the world can begin to look forward to the time when all worthy human beings may be permitted to live decently as free people."

Less than a month later, the USS *Indianapolis* left San Francisco on a secret mission, carrying a load of uranium, half the world's supply, to construct the first atomic bomb.

Chapter 68

After a brief respite in Honolulu, the *Nevada* was sent to the Marshall Islands to take care of a situation there and then went on to the Marianas to refuel and resupply when they received orders to return to Okinawa. But before they could get there, the battle ended on June 22. Okinawa was the last major battle fought in the Pacific during World War II.

The *Nevada* returned to Pearl Harbor where it received new orders for operations in the East China Sea. It participated in a raid in Yangtze Estuary and came within range of Japanese home islands but did not fire upon them. After a brief stint in Tokyo Bay, it returned to Pearl Harbor.

As soon as Marty got liberty, he headed for Smith's Union Bar where he hoped to run into Tom Paul or at least find someone who knew his whereabouts. But when he walked in and scanned the small barroom, he found neither hide nor hair of Tom Paul and didn't spot any airmen. So, he departed for Shanghai Bill's where he would find the company of his crew. On the walk there, his thoughts were about his brother and whether he had managed to survive or had been blown to smithereens. Even though he was trying to keep his thoughts under control, they were running wild with nightmare scenarios. He needed a drink…and now.

As Marty stepped up to the bar to order a Kona Longboard, which he had acquired a taste for, he noticed a group of airmen to his right whooping it up. After the bartender handed him the beer, he moved toward the group to investigate further. And there in the center telling tales was Tom Paul. He was so engrossed in storytelling that he didn't notice his new listener until he finished. But then it was reunion time with hugs and cheers and calls for a round for the house. "You know what Pa would want us to do?" Marty said. Tom Paul just gave him a vacant look. "He'd want us to get a bottle of sljivovica to share until the last drop was drank."

"Then let's do it. Bartender, a bottle of sljivovica." The bartender shook his head. Not only didn't he stock any, he had never heard of it either. A native who cleared tables in the bar overheard their request and came up to them. "I know where I can get some." So, Tom Paul slipped the guy a couple of bills to purchase a bottle. When he returned with it, Marty and Tom Paul found a table, brought a couple of glasses over, and started to share war stories.

"I missed out on a lot of the battle at Okinawa," Marty said. "We had to take the ship back for repairs on April 20. I wish we could have seen it through, but those kamikazes did us in."

"Yeah. I know. They broke enough through our lines to sink thirty ships and damage who knows how many more. I heard we lost a few thousand sailors because of them."

"But at least we got their big, powerful battleship *Yamato.* It barely lasted a week and was supposed to beach itself and defend the island with those humungous guns it carried. Those Jap admirals must have been pretty angry when we deep sixed it."

"So now what?"

"I guess we have to wait and see what the commanders and the new guy in the White House decide."

CHAPTER 69

Frankie returned to Watsonville soon after the Battle of Okinawa had been won by the Allies. He was in Germany when he learned of their surrender, which helped make his sacrifice worthwhile. His left leg had been amputated below the knee, but with the aid of a prosthetic device, he was learning how to walk under his own power. The *Register-Pajaronian* had done a front-page article on him, making him out a war hero. He had in fact earned a Bronze Star as well as a Purple Heart for injuries sustained. But the public was most impressed with his Normandy invasion and Battle of the Bulge survival.

They displayed an oversized picture of Frankie in his military uniform, which set him apart from most of the other men in town. Friends and neighbors lined up to pay their respects. Lena was especially glad for the callers who helped cheer Frankie up and lifted the gloom hanging over them. Ever since the telegram arrived notifying them of Frankie's injuries, she and Martin had slipped into depression. For so long, they had tried to keep their spirits up, but once they got the tragic news about Frankie, they gave in to their emotions and let dark thoughts take over their minds. Frankie, too, arrived from Europe in a depressed state so unlike his former nature. He had seen too much war and the final toll had come as a shock after surviving the worst of it. But it gladdened his heart to be home and see so many familiar, friendly faces. He needed those faces to replace the faces of the enemy he was having such a difficult time erasing from his memory.

One day Martin came home very upbeat for a change. "Guess what," he said to Lena and Frankie." The Slavonic Society wants to throw a reception in your honor, Frankie. What do you say to that?"

"I don't know. They already had that article in the paper. That's enough recognition for just doing my duty."

"Frankie, our friends and relatives want to do something nice for you to show their gratitude. It's not just for you alone. You're a symbol to them of every military man fighting for our liberty."

"I understand. I guess it's my duty to attend."

A couple of weeks later, Frankie walked into the society's hall on Main Street, attired in his 4th Infantry Army uniform with bronze star and purple heart displayed prominently on his chest. The young women present flocked to Frankie as if he were some sort of Hollywood star. They had all read the newspaper account of his war record and were in awe. Just standing near him was such a thrill that they didn't mind he had little to say. But there was one girl in the crowd whom he noticed and remembered meeting years ago, Ivana Rosandich, the daughter of a prosperous apple famer. He imagined she was in her early twenties now and suspected the only reason she was still unmarried was the lack of eligible men.

Ivana always knew what she wanted and usually got it. So, when she set her sights on Frankie, she didn't wait for him to make the first move. When the dinner bell sounded, she went right up to Frankie and said, "It would be my pleasure if you would join me for dinner." Taken aback, Frankie stammered, "I would be delighted."

Lena noticed that Frankie was sitting with the Rosandich family instead of his own. At first she felt hurt by the snub but when she saw him laughing with the Rosandich daughter, Ivana, she realized a blessing had been bestowed. After that Frankie started courting Ivana and love began to bloom.

Chapter 70

On January 2, 1945 Executive Order 9066 was rescinded because the Supreme Court ruled Japanese could not be detained without cause. Soon thereafter, Japanese began leaving the prison camps with $25 dollars in their pocket and a train ticket home. They began returning to Watsonville by early August, Ken Nakamura and his family among them. They had so looked forward to being welcomed by the thousands of cherry trees they had left behind. But not even one was standing vigil—they seemed to have vanished from the earth.

Once Ken got his family settled at the Buddhist Temple turned hostel, the first place he headed for was his strawberry farm. His first glimpse of the fields brimming with red berry plants left him breathless. He knelt down and scooped up some of the rich soil into his hands, held it up to his nose, and took in the fragrance of it bursting with richness so different from the arid, sandy soil of the desert where he had spent the last three years of his life.

Ken was pleased to see his farm flourishing with plenty of field workers tending the plants. He did not know what to expect when he returned home having heard so many stories of Japanese losing their businesses and having to start over from scratch. As he watched the operation from a distance, a familiar figure emerged heading directly for him. It was Martin. Ken could barely contain his excitement at seeing him and ran up to greet him. Martin was already extending his arm, "Welcome home, my friend." *I don't think he'll ever know how much calling me friend means to me*, Ken thought. Then Martin gave Ken a hug, which completely took him aback since Japanese are much more reserved. But he had to admit it felt good to be embraced so warmly.

"The farm looks good," Ken said.

"Yes, we tried our best to keep it going for you. Unfortunately, Frankie couldn't manage it until you returned because he got drafted." Ken nodded, not knowing whether he should ask about Martin's sons or not. Fortunately, Martin continued, "We got lucky that Hector was able to manage the farm because I couldn't be here as much time as it needed."

"Hector?" Ken said.

"Hector is one of the braceros up from Mexico. But he manages to come and go on his own schedule. Don't ask me how. I don't ask any questions. But come along and I'll introduce you."

They found Hector in the office, making a list of supplies. He looked up when the pair walked in. "Hector, I want to introduce you to Ken Nakamura whose farm you have been managing. He just returned home."

Hector stood up and approached Ken, extending his hand in friendship. After they pressed the flesh, Ken said, "I am so appreciative of everything you have done to keep the business alive for me and my family. We owe you a debt of gratitude."

"Of course, I have been paid for my work. But from where I come from, Michoacan, we have a motto, which my parents pounded into me from birth. "We have inherited freedom; we bequeath social justice."

"I don't quite understand."

"It means it is my responsibility to ensure fairness prevails. You and your people have been mistreated by the US government not unlike other races including us Mexicans. And even though I cannot help all of you, I can help one. So, you have given me an opportunity to practice social justice, which is a value where I come from."

"Hector, you and I have been taught many of the same values, even though we come from very different parts of the world," said Martin. "Now that the Japanese are returning, we have an even greater opportunity to practice social justice. And I am certainly going to do everything I can to help the Japanese community recover."

"This is a very good welcome home, more than I could have ever expected. Knowing I have your support means so much. I am going to pass your kind words onto others so they know that here they also have friends."

Martin had extended an invitation to Ken for lunch at his restaurant. He was pleased when Ken walked through the door the next day and went up to greet him. "Thank you for coming, friend."

Ken said, "Every time you call me friend I feel so honored. I tried to time my arrival so most, if not all, of your patrons would be gone. I didn't want to cause any problems by my presence."

Martin did not respond but only looked into Ken's face that was very different from the one he had known before the war. He knew Ken may never be the same again but he hoped for the best. "Sit down, please. I will bring a menu over and you can have whatever you like on the house."

"No need for a menu. Just bring me a platter of your exquisite seafood risotto. And maybe some fried squid as an appetizer if it would not be too much trouble."

"Excuse me a moment while I get things underway in the kitchen. I want to do the cooking for you myself." *It is one way to nurture you.*

The fried squid kept Ken occupied until the seafood risotto arrived at the table. Then Martin sat down to join him with a plate of seafood risotto for himself. At first they just sat in silence as they concentrated on their lunch. Then Ken just had to express what was in his heart. "We were devastated when we didn't see the cherry trees upon our return."

"I'm sorry but there are still three left."

"Three?"

"I know it's not many out of the thousands that had been here." Martin did not want to give voice to the fate that had rid the town of the beautiful trees, a gift from the Japanese community many years before the war broke out.

"Three is very auspicious. Whenever we arrange flowers we use three stems. The long one represents heaven, the medium one man, and the short one earth. My community will be overjoyed knowing three still stand. Where can we find them?"

"Two are at the elementary school on Palm Avenue and the other at the high school."

Martin could see Ken becoming emotional so he changed the subject, although he should have thought better of the topic. "I heard you ended up in Arizona. That surprised me since there were camps in California."

"We were even more surprised than you were. Poston was the most miserable place imaginable. A real hell on earth. It was hot and dusty in the summer. Then in the winter, cold winds blew through the camp even through the walls of our flimsy houses made of tarpaper. Even worse was when torrential rains poured down making a muddy quagmire out of the place. Add to that the fact that they divided our town community amongst the three camps that made up Poston. We called them Roasten, Toasten, and Dustin."

Ken let out a little laugh and then continued. "There was one bright spot, though. A famous Japanese American artist voluntarily appeared wanting to create an arts program for us. His name is Isamu Noguchi and he is best known for his sculptures. In fact, he was doing sculptures for Hollywood stars before he showed up and completed one of Ginger Rogers while he was there. You see, once he set foot in Poston, authorities did not want him to leave. So we had an artist among us longer than expected."

"That was fortunate. So arts programs must have helped pass the time."

"Not really. The US government put Poston on Indian land and in their wisdom they used us as free labor to develop it."

"But I thought Del Webb built the camp? That's what we heard anyway."

"If you say so but I have no knowledge of him. He probably built the barracks and camp buildings. But we Japanese did the hard, back-breaking work of building schools out of adobe bricks, constructing irrigation systems, and doing experimental farming, all under the hot desert sun. The government saw us as free labor. They had seventeen thousand mouths to feed during the war, and they wanted us to earn our keep."

"Oh, Ken. I never knew about this. Of course, I knew they sent you to a relocation camp, but I didn't know they forced you to do work that should have been done by government contractors. It just wasn't right."

"Of course it wasn't but what could we do about it? Write our congressman? Funny thing, at the train station an old Indian came up to me and said the tribe didn't think the government had treated us well but they had no power to change it."

"That's what it's about, isn't it?" said Martin. "Power."

CHAPTER 71

On the morning of August 7, Martin opened the door to retrieve his newspaper as the coffee percolated. He always liked to browse through the paper while having a cup of coffee and sometimes even a cigarette before moving on with his day. He poured himself a cup when it was ready, unfolded the paper and prepared to sit down to have some leisure time to himself. But as soon as he unfolded the *San Francisco Chronicle*, the headline popped out at him like a slap in the face:

"Japan Hit By Atom Bomb"

"Mightiest Weapon in History"

"Tokyo Admits Heavy Damage"

Oh, my God. He could no longer sit down. He scanned the front page article while standing. Then he gathered his things and made a beeline for the door. First, he went by the Buddhist Temple but there was no sign of activity there and Martin did not want to disturb them. Next, he went to the strawberry farm to determine if Ken was there. He ran into Hector but Ken had not yet shown up for the day. Martin left frustrated. He wanted to express his heartfelt condolences to Ken, and through him, the entire Japanese community. Instead, he went to the restaurant where he encountered Liu and Chao.

"Did you hear about the bombing of Hiroshima?"

"We know all about it," said Liu. "News travels fast through our Chinese network."

"Oh…and what is your network reporting may I ask?"

"Only that Tokyo has not responded."

"And why is that?"

"Your guess is as good as mine. Maybe they don't know what just hit them."

Martin noticed Liu and Chao exchange smug smiles. There was certainly no love lost between Chinese and Japanese even if they were both Asians. Martin didn't understand their hatred. But then he corrected himself. *We have the same thing between Croatian and Serbians. Most people can't tell us apart either but we hate each other.* He remembered his encounter with the Serbian diplomat. Some things defy understanding.

Martin continued to make trips to Ken's farm whenever he had a break in his day but he was never there. It was almost like he vanished into thin air. Then on August 9 another, bigger bomb was dropped on Nagasaki. Truman had warned Tokyo that there would be a "rain of ruin" if they did not surrender and he was true to his word. Perhaps, after years of dealing with the complicated mind of Roosevelt, the Japanese did not realize that Truman was an altogether different sort—a straight shooter who called a spade a spade.

Ken continued to elude Martin until after Japan surrendered on August 15. The next morning, Martin went to the farm and found Ken in the office, his face full of sorrow and shame. Martin said, "I have been looking for you for days. I wanted to express my condolences on what the atom bombs did to your ancestral homeland."

"Martin, my family and our community have been in seclusion praying to our ancestors for the relief of our relatives back home. My parents came to this country from Hiroshima, as did other families in our Japantown so we still have many relatives left behind. So far, we have heard nothing and are afraid for them."

"And what about Nagasaki? Do your people have family there, too?"

"Japan is a small island. We have friends and family all over."

"It is a terrible thing that happened. But at least we now have peace."

"Peace on paper, yes. But in our hearts...in our soul? That is why we have been praying...to restore our souls."

"I know it is difficult but we have to put the past behind us and move on."

"Of course, we want that, too. When I returned home, with Poston behind me, I thought the worst had already occurred. But then the bombs were dropped on my homeland, bombs so powerful they killed one hundred thousand people at once and injured many, many, more. I've heard ninety percent of the city of Hiroshima was destroyed. It is so mindboggling that I still cannot comprehend it.

CHAPTER 72

Marty and Tom Paul had been waiting around Honolulu to see what direction the war in the Pacific would take next. They were now fully rested and ready to take on a new fight. They got their answer on August 6 when they saw headlines from newspapers lying around the mess hall. *The New York Times* read:

"First Atomic Bomb Dropped on Japan"

"Missile Is Equal to 20,000 Tons of TNT"

"Truman Warms Foe of Rain of Ruin"

And *The Washington Post* had this three-line headline running from border to border:

"Single Atomic Bomb Rocks Japanese Army Base"

"With Mightier Force Than 20,000 Tons of TNT"

"To Open New Era of Power for Benefit of Man"

"So," Marty said to Tom Paul, "I guess this is how it ends." Tom Paul was speechless.

Marty and Tom Paul were not relieved from duty until the armistice was signed on September 2 aboard the USS *Missouri*. Most people assumed the ship was chosen for the honor since it was named after Truman's home state. His daughter, Margaret, had sponsored it. While the *Missouri* was the last battleship commissioned by the navy, it had seen action in both Iwo Jima and Okinawa, more than earning the honor.

High-ranking officials of all Allied nations took part in the ceremony. The Japanese diplomatic delegation arrived dressed in top hats, tails, and white gloves, accompanied by military officers in uniform, for what to them was a somber even shameful occasion. Two hundred and fifty warships of Allied nations lay at anchor in Tokyo Bay while the event took place, a visible symbol to the losing nation that they still had strength in numbers.

Shortly after the peace was established, Tom Paul and Marty jumped a transit for home. When they returned, they quickly learned that a war of sorts was still going on in their hometown as well as the entire Monterey Bay over the Japanese who were returning to their coastal communities. The Chamber of Commerce did a survey of its members, and most answered that they not only did not want to employ Japanese but they felt their presence would be harmful. A Monterey Bay Council on Japanese Relations was formed to decide how to handle the Japanese problem. Mass public meetings were planned to discuss how to discourage Japanese from returning to the coast and, of those who did, how to best supervise their activities.

A letter to the editor from enlisted men at Camp McQuaid, an army base on the outskirts of Watsonville that was home to a California National Guard unit, called out the Chamber of Commerce for its position of discrimination and bigotry, citing businesses with signs that read, *All Japs Back to Japan*. They reminded the community that many Nisei fought bravely for this country, some making the ultimate sacrifice.

Then in the wee hours of September 24, someone or some group, sent a flare toward the Buddhist Temple, setting fire to a nearby shrub. The temple was crowded with returnees, many women and children, and among them a few servicemen and Gold Star mothers who had lost Nisei sons in the war. When the police arrived, they found a group of Japanese working to put out the blaze, but the suspects left no trail. Authorities made it clear that violence would not be tolerated.

As a response, several members of the professional community in town reached out to help the Japanese transition back into a normal life, among them a prominent doctor, a lawyer, and an educator. But, of course, after war, nothing is ever normal again.

When Marty and Tom Paul walked in the door, Lena and Martin could hardly believe their eyes. Lena jumped out of her seat and ran toward them, not knowing which one to hug first. Martin just stood up and waited for Lena's hysterics to abate and then gave each of his sons a hug and handshake. "You both look well. The war must have gone easy on you." Marty and Tom Paul looked at each other and said in unison, "Wait until you hear our war stories to decide."

But even more telling than their own war stories, Marty and Tom Paul wanted to know about Frankie. "Is Frankie back yet?" asked Marty. "We parted at Cherbourg and I haven't seen him since."

Martin said, "He's home. He's been home awhile."

Then Lena chimed in. "It won't be long until his wedding."

"Wedding," said Tom Paul. "Who's the lucky girl?"

"Ivana Rosandich. You remember her. Very pretty blonde. Her father is an apple farmer."

"So, where is the groom so we can congratulate him?"

Just then, the door opened and Marty and Tom Paul heard the familiar stomp across the kitchen floor. They were afraid to turn and lay their eyes on Frankie for fear of what else they might see. But they had no choice. Marty was the first one to make the move. And when he saw Frankie's smiling face, all in one piece, he felt a wave of relief wash over him. "Frankie," he said, "it's good to see you again. I've missed you since we parted in Portsmouth, but as I told you, I had your back in both Normandy and Cherbourg." Then he stepped in closer to give Frankie a hug. When they parted, he could not help casting his eyes downward for a glimpse of his war injury. Even though Frankie was wearing long pants he could tell he had lost a leg.

"You can probably tell there is something different about me. The Germans gave me a new left leg and it's working pretty well. Thank God for German ingenuity."

Tom Paul was hugging Frankie now. Somehow he felt it unfair that Frankie had had to go head-to-head with the enemy while he was insulated in a Hellcat that he loved to fly. Certainly, it was always a fight between life and death—never anything in between. But he had emerged relatively unscathed in both body and soul. Even Marty had more battle scars than he did, although they were invisible to the naked eye.

"Well, it's past dinnertime but you are probably hungry. Come sit down in the kitchen and I'll make you a sandwich to tide you over until breakfast," said Lena.

"Don't worry about us," said Marty. "When we stopped at Mare Island, we got a chance to grab some grub before flying down here."

"What about you Tom Paul?"

"I'm fine, Ma. But I think Marty and I could use a shot of sljivovica."

"Of course," said Martin. "Let me go get a bottle. Lena, please get out the crystal glasses. The boys deserve the best."

CHAPTER 73

On Sunday, the family went to church together to give thanks that they had all survived the war. Then they went home to gather around the dining room table for a feast that Lena and Martin had jointly prepared. A roast leg of lamb seasoned with rosemary and garlic and surrounded by a variety of fresh, seasonal vegetables was the centerpiece of the feast. The meal was accompanied by mint pesto. Lamb was always a favorite around the Petrovich household. The boys took seconds with Tom Paul stashing away a third. As they waited for dessert to arrive, Clara asked Frankie if he and Ivana had set a date for their wedding. "We wanted to wait until Marty and Tom Paul returned home. But now we will set a date soon. One thing I learned from the war, don't count on tomorrow."

"Well, I certainly agree with you there," said Marty. "That's why I want to meet Ivana as soon as possible. I'm surprised she's not here today."

"I had a discussion with Ma and Pa about that, but we thought her first meeting with you shouldn't be the first time you had a chance to talk with the family about your experiences."

"I agree with that," said Tom Paul. "But let's invite her for next Sunday. Maybe by then you will have set the date."

Lena carried out an apple tart while Clara put out the coffee service. After dessert, Martin brought out the sljivovica and offered a toast. "To God and to freedom. May both reign forever." After they finished their first glass, Martin said, "Now, boys, follow me into the den." After they entered, he closed the door and said, "We need to talk."

Clara and Peter took that as their cue to depart with the kids, leaving Lena with a sink full of dishes to address. They would keep her busy while Martin discussed the war and the future with his sons.

"Now, that we are alone among warriors, we can really talk," said Martin. "Here. Let me fill up your glasses." He went around the room to fill them and then check the remaining contents of the bottle. "Don't worry," he said, "there is more where this came from. Why don't we first start by taking turns sharing our experiences in the war. Who wants to start?"

Marty began by recounting the various battles he and his shipmates on the *Nevada* had been in. "My one disappointment was we were not able to stay in the Battle of Okinawa to the end. But those kamikazes saw to it that we were too damaged to make the finish line."

Next Tom Paul took a turn. "It was a thrill to fight in a Hellcat. That machine was built for doing battle. But it tore me apart when I witnessed my wingman hit and going up in flames while I was too helpless to do anything but fly on."

Now all eyes were on Frankie. "Pa has heard some of what I've gone through so I'd like to spare him a repeat. But there is nothing more inhumane than hand-to-hand combat. In order to do it, you have to become a machine without a heart or soul. But I did it. I made it through Normandy and the Battle of the Bulge. After dodging so many bullets and bombs, who would ever have imagined I'd lose a leg to a rock while securing a building. But better that than my life."

When Frankie finished, there were several moments of silence. Then Martin said, "Everyone paid a price for the war. Some more than others. But now it's time to move on and talk about the future. Frankie, as you know, has plans to get married. And he's going into the apple business with his soon-to-be father-in-law. Have either of you given any thought yet to what you'd like to do?"

"I just want to fly," said Tom Paul. "Maybe I could become a commercial pilot and fly one of those big jets."

"What about you, Marty?"

"I might want to take advantage of the GI bill and go to college. That's what some of my mates are doing. Maybe I'll study engineering like Marko and build ships."

"You know, ship building could be in your genes. Relatives back home in Croatia are ship builders. Tom Paul, what do you think about going to college? Education is the way to prosperity."

"I will have to look into it. Maybe I'd study aeronautical engineering, which would be good for a pilot to know."

"Your plans are very sound. Frankie, you, too, could go to college and study agriculture."

"At my age, I think I've missed out. And, besides, I can learn all I need to know about apple farming from the best apple farmers in the world right here at home."

"As for me, the navy is still here but will be winding its operations up in the next few months. The Japanese community will need support for its future and I'd like to do whatever I can to help."

CHAPTER 74

By October, most of the Japanese who'd planned to return to Watsonville had but it was not the same number that had been living in Japantown prior to the war. This left the community broken as it struggled to repair itself. The reality of what they returned to was a shock—leased land had been lost, property destroyed, even farms that had been put in the hands of caretakers had suffered neglect after initial crops had been harvested.

Martin stopped by the strawberry farm on a regular basis to visit with Ken and bolster his spirits. But instead he listened to Ken's tale of woe. And he was learning more about his Poston experience. A low point happened early on when a guard beat a Japanese prisoner suspected of being an informer. That resulted in more beatings and a camp-wide strike and work stoppage. After a period of negotiations, the camp settled down as internees learned to accept their situation.

Today when Martin arrived, he found Ken in the office with one of his sons who was wearing a Boy Scout uniform. This took Martin by surprise. "Did you join the local Boy Scout troop?" he asked.

Before he could answer, Ken spoke up, "Martin, this is my son, Bill." The boy bowed and when he stood up, extended his arm to shake Martin's hand.

"Actually," Ken explained, "Bill joined the Boy Scout troop at Poston. But we were familiar with scouting since it had been in Japan for many years, although it was suspended during the war years, I understand. Bill likes to wear his uniform around to show his patriotism for America."

"I see," said Martin. "We had scouting in Yugoslavia, too, but I wasn't a member. What did you do in your scout troop, Bill?"

"We learned a lot of outdoor skills and worked on merit badges. We even got to have a couple of jamborees with nearby troops. That was a really good time—so many boys just having fun together."

Martin raised his eyebrows. He was surprised they had Boy Scout troops in internment camps and even more surprised that they let American boys inside to interact with them. "I'm glad you have a few good memories of your time away."

"Now I want to join a troop here if I can find one." At that, Ken motioned for Bill to leave the office so he and Martin could speak privately.

"Have you tried to find a troop for him here?" Martin asked. "It might help his transition back."

Ken let out a sigh. "We are treading lightly until we gain a better foothold. We don't want our children feeling rejection. It's enough that we adults feel rejected."

"Well, if there is anything I can do to help, please let me know." Martin wanted to ask Ken about his relatives in Hiroshima but was afraid that would open up more wounds that were still very fresh and raw.

Chapter 75

In November, the navy pulled up its last stakes and left town, leaving its buildings behind which the town eyed for a new school. Martin was on hand for a departure ceremony, during which the navy thanked the town for its hospitality and cooperation. Captain Barkley said, "I especially want to recognize Mayor Simpson and Martin Petrovich, town liaison, for all their support of our efforts. You contributed to the success of our mission here and our victory in war." A wave of pride welled up in Martin, knowing that his own son got his dive-bomb training at this facility and that training had enabled him to become an ace and, more importantly, saved his life. Martin was overwhelmed by the sheer immensity of his feelings and could not hold back the tears. *I guess this is finally the release of all the emotions I suppressed during wartime.*

The following Friday night, the Captain invited Mayor Simpson, Martin, and his committee, made up of just Michael and Filip, and their wives for an evening of dinner and dancing at the Naval Post Graduate School in Monterey. He and Lena had not been there since their honeymoon when it was known as the Del Monte Hotel. But once they were inside, it felt much the same and brought back memories. They walked down the hallway to the Trident Bar where the group was supposed to meet up. Trident, Martin mused—what an appropriate name. The weapon of Poseidon that legend tells us he used to control the sea. My father always offered a prayer to the Greek god before he set sail and for the most part, he used the Trident to keep the seas calm. I guess the navy prays to Poseidon, too.

As Martin and Lena entered the room, he heard his name called and looked in the direction of one of the large tables in the corner. The Captain and Mayor Simpson along with their wives were already seated, engaged in conversation, and when Martin and Lena arrived they welcomed them warmly. After Filip and Michael arrived with their wives, the group headed for the dining room where a table for ten was awaiting them under a Spanish-style chandelier aglow with candlelight. After they took their seats, the Captain proudly announced, "I asked you here on a Friday night because the navy flies in king crab from Alaska as a special treat." A smile crossed Martin's lips and he had trouble suppressing a laugh. "What's the matter? Do you have something against crab?"

"No, not at all, Captain. But I just heard tales from my two boys about a big crab feast they had at Ulithi Atoll."

"Was it on an island called Mogmog?"

"That it was. Apparently the island was crawling with the creatures so big and strong they could crack coconuts with their pincers."

"Those stories of a crab feast on Mogmog found their way around the world, gaining mythic proportions. They're the stuff of legend now. Your boys were lucky to take part."

"Anyway, they got a lesson in the various varieties of crab and learned that Alaskan king crab is the best, if not the hardest to catch."

"That's why Friday nights are so special here. But there are a lot of other good items on the buffet as well if you don't fancy crab. And by the way, you can drop the Captain. I got my star."

So, he is now a rear admiral. There is nothing like war for advancement.

Chapter 76

A flurry of activity heralded the beginning of December. Not only had the holidays arrived but Frankie and Ivana had set the date for their wedding for the Saturday after Christmas, December 29. Martin was happy they had chosen a date his restaurant would be closed so he could use all its resources to cater the reception. While it would be easier on Lena not having a reception in their home, Martin was not familiar with the Rosandich's home so he was going to have to make a special visit to learn about the venue.

This Christmas was an especially meaningful one for the family as they all gathered together to celebrate. Martin felt especially blessed that all of his children were with him, even though a few were bruised, none were broken. Ivana had chosen to spend Christmas Eve with Frankie's family, and she brought a note of good cheer that could have been overshadowed by melancholy.

As they dined on traditional fare, Frankie spoke up. "Guess who I got a Christmas card from?" He waited out a moment of silence before revealing the answer. "My nurse, Greta, at Luitpold Hospital in Wurzburg."

"That's nice," said Lena. "You should reply to let her know how you're doing and that you're getting married."

"I'll send her a wedding picture. She'll like that. But I want to tell you what she said. They're going to rebuild Wurzburg just like it was. To me, that is just incredible. Only a few building remained by the time

I got there, but from what I saw that baroque architecture is extremely intricate. It's going to be difficult."

"They must have a plan in mind. Germans don't leave anything to chance. My guess is that they have some of the original workmen around who can help."

"That's just it—they don't. Most of their men are either dead or maimed and not up to the task. It's the women who are going to do it."

"Women," said Tom Paul, as if he had not heard correctly.

"That's right…women."

"Well, I'll believe it when I see it," said Marty.

"Don't discount them," said Frankie. "They have building and engineering in their blood. I was amazed at how fast San Francisco was rebuilt—twenty thousand buildings in three years."

"That was new construction, built by men," said Marty. "They're going to try to replicate historic buildings. Not easily done."

"You're already talking like an engineer," said Martin. "No doubt you're meant to be one."

When New Year's Day dawned, Martin was a happy man. Frankie's wedding had been a more joyous celebration than he could have ever imagined and since Ivana's father had no sons, only sons-in-law, Frankie not only gained a father-in-law on his wedding day but a business partner. Martin knew Frankie would prove himself to be up to the task with his work ethic and love of all things nature. It would take a while to get the other two sons settled, but he knew they were on their way, too, and besides they were now men who had to forge their own futures.

When the restaurant reopened after the holidays, Martin got ambushed by Liu and Chao. "The time has finally come to start our own restaurant so we must leave."

Martin began to stammer. "Leave. I don't know what I'll be able to do without you. Is there anything I can do to change your minds?"

"You have trained us so well, and for that we are grateful, but as you know it has always been our dream to own our own restaurant...be in business for ourselves."

"Yes, I know. But as the years went by I thought you'd given up on that."

"Before, the opportunity wasn't right. But now, prosperity is in the air and we want to grab some of it."

"What about Hong? Is he going to join you?"

"You will have to talk to him yourself. We cannot speak for him."

That response gave Martin a bit of relief. At least if Hong was staying at the grocery store he would not have that business to worry about, too. "You once said you would have replacements for me. Is that still the case?"

"We so sorry. We have asked around but things are good in San Francisco and no one wants to come down here where there is no Chinatown."

"I see. So, how much notice are you giving?"

"If two weeks is customary, we will give you that."

"Thank you. And Happy New Year."

"Oh, it is not New Year's for us yet. Chinese New Year starts on February second, which will be our grand opening. It will be Year of Dog, a good time to seize opportunities."

Martin had been blindsided by Liu and Chao and now needed to brainstorm a solution, even if it was only temporary. Then it hit him...I have two sons at home with nothing to do. Until they go to college, they could work for me and learn a thing or two. He thought about this solution all day as he cooked in the restaurant. That's what was good about cooking—he could meditate at the same time and often get an answer, frequently the right one.

When Martin got home that night, Marty and Tom Paul were hanging around in the living room watching television. "Do you have a moment," he asked. They both looked in his direction and nodded before turning back to their TV show. "Then let's go into the den where we can talk without distractions."

"This show will be over in ten minutes. Can't it wait until then?" said Tom Paul.

"I guess it will have to. I'll be waiting for you."

When they finally made an appearance, Tom Paul lay on the sofa while Marty sank down into an overstuffed club chair. "I'm glad you made yourselves comfortable," Martin said. "Now we can begin. I'll get right to the point. Liu and Chao gave their notice today. In two weeks they'll be gone and I'll be without helpers."

Tom Paul suddenly sat up at the news. "What does it mean for the restaurant? They've been with you for years?"

"It means I have to find replacements and quickly. They told me years ago that they would find their own but apparently there is so much work available elsewhere that they haven't been able to find anyone. And, I suspect, they are keeping those they do find for themselves. They'll be opening their own restaurant."

"So, are you looking for some leads from us?" Marty asked.

"Not leads. But cooperation. I need the two of you to help me out." Marty and Tom Paul looked at each other and then gave full attention to their father.

"You know I plan to go to college. That will mean I will be moving away," said Marty.

"Same for me," said Tom Paul.

"I know all that and I don't expect you to work at the restaurant forever. Just to help bridge the gap. I need time to find the right replacements. Now that the holidays are over, the restaurant will be slow. It shouldn't be too difficult for you to learn what to do."

"We owe it to you to give it a try," Marty said. Then he looked at Tom Paul, hoping he would second the motion.

"Count me in," said Tom Paul. "It's about time I learned how to cook."

"On that note, let's get out the sljivovica."

Before Liu and Chao left to start their own business, Martin had them show Marty and Tom Paul the ropes. He noticed that Tom Paul with his outgoing charm was a natural fit for waiter. That left Marty as the sous chef. But he had developed skill at cleaning fish when he crewed on the *Ave Maria* out of Santa Cruz harbor. So Martin felt he had the initial skills he needed in the kitchen.

On Saturday night, things went so well that Martin was able to sneak out early to catch the tail end of the opening of the Lotus Blossom Cafe. He had not heard what they planned to name the cafe, but when he saw the sign something in him stirred. He had heard that name before—it was echoing from somewhere deep in his past but he couldn't put his finger on it.

When Martin walked through the door, the room was still filled with customers who were now sipping tea and opening fortune cookies. The scene was somehow familiar to him but he could not remember when he had come upon it. Liu spotted Martin right away and came over to welcome him. "You honor us with your presence on this most important first night of our business."

"I wouldn't miss it for the world. Now, I am a bit curious about the name for your restaurant." At that moment, Chao interrupted to shake Martin's hand.

"You taught us well as you can see from the happy customers before you."

"You helped ensure my success so I am glad I helped to ensure yours. But I have one tip. Get insurance. If there is a disaster, you'll be able to recover more quickly. Insurance is the only reason I was able to start the Dalmatian Coast Cafe. Otherwise, I might still be picking apples."

"We know all about insurance. Our relatives in Chinatown clued us in and a cousin sold us a policy. Like you, they learned from the earthquake what can happen when disaster strikes. And fires, especially, are not unknown to us. With all the frying Chinese cooking requires, a grease fire is always waiting in the wings."

"So, since you already know about insurance, I will have to come up with a new piece of advice. Anyway, about the name."

"Oh, yes," said Liu. The lotus flower is very auspicious to Chinese. It is a symbol of enlightenment. While it grows in the muddy depths of a pond, the flower that rises above it is white, pure."

"I see," said Martin even though he did not.

"Let me explain more," said Chao. "The muddy water is the life we lead on earth. Once we see the light and achieve spiritual understanding, we rise above the cares of the world, even material riches."

"Thank you for enlightening me. I will reflect on what you said."

"Please sit down and be our guest," said Liu. "I will bring you some of our best dishes for you to sample."

On his drive home, Martin kept rolling the word lotus around in his mind. *Lotus, lotus, lotus. Where have I heard that word before?* Then it struck him…in Chinatown…at tea with Nevenka. Had he come full circle now? All these years have gone by and he had not thought of the Lotus Blossom Tea Room. At the time, he had no interest in the meaning of the name…his only interest was Nevenka. But now his life was beginning to make sense. He had been living in muddy waters for a long time, and finally he had risen above them and gained wisdom, a gift more valuable than all the riches in the world.

Martin continued to visit Ken at his farm on a regular visit. In fact, they had established a regular habit of tea on Tuesday afternoons when they both had less work to do. "How are you doing with your sons helping out?"

"It's going better than expected. But they are only a short-term solution. Both will be going to college in the fall and leaving home."

Hector had walked into the office just as Martin was explaining his dilemma to Ken. When Martin left, Hector was waiting for him. "I was not eavesdropping, but I heard you are looking for restaurant help."

"That's right. I need someone to wait tables and someone to help me in the kitchen."

"I have the ones you need."

"Is that so? Do they have green cards?"

"Of course. I will send them to you tomorrow."

Martin watched as Hector walked toward the fields. He still had not figured him out. But if he had workers available, and no doubt he did, he would try them out. *I wonder if they speak English?* He had forgotten to ask.

The next day, Juan and Carlos were waiting for him at the door. Juan spoke passable English, but with Carlos a lot of sign language was needed to compensate for lack of words. "Juan, I want you to wait tables. Let me explain the menu to you so you can make recommendations to the customers. And Carlos, come with me." He followed the command with a few motions and Carlos understood. *I'm back in muddy waters, Martin thought, but maybe I'm going to learn something new.*

CHAPTER 77

In early September 1946, Martin noticed a letter to the editor in the *Register-Pajaronian* by Dr. Rosen, the same doctor that had treated Lena for tuberculosis. Dr. Rosen wrote about an article that had appeared in a magazine called *The New Yorker*, a publication unfamiliar to him. Dr. Rosen said the only article in the August 31 issue was one entitled "Hiroshima" by John Hersey. He briefly went on to describe the horrific injuries people sustained, all civilians, even women and children, from the atomic bomb which had been dropped on that city.

By telling stories of individuals, John Hersey put a face on the impact war had on human life. He encouraged people to read the article so they would know what the Japanese had experienced in graphic detail, many of whom had relatives in our community. He said he had personally purchased numerous copies that would be available at the Watsonville Library to check out.

The next day, Martin went by the library to get a copy. Before he had a chance to read it, Dr. Rosen called and asked to meet with him about an important community matter. They scheduled a time on Sunday afternoon. When Dr. Rosen showed up at Martin's house, he was accompanied by the superintendent of schools, Dr. MacKenzie, and a prominent local attorney, Mr. Murphy. Lena answered the door and welcomed the group. "Martin is in the living room expecting you. I will bring coffee and tea in a minute."

The trio proceeded to the living room where they greeted Martin warmly. Martin had no idea why they wanted to meet with him and kept his reserve. After everyone had a chance to sip some coffee or tea and eat some of Lena's kolache, Dr. Rosen introduced the purpose. "Martin," he said, "we have an election for mayor coming up in town and Mayor Simpson has just announced he will not be seeking reelection. We are looking for a candidate who can unite our community so we can heal and move forward."

"I agree there are a lot of strong feelings out there that have not been resolved by the armistice."

"That's right," said MacKenzie. "For the sake of the children especially, all of the children, we need to come together in peace and friendship."

"Did you read *The New Yorker* article on Hiroshima?" Dr. Rosen asked.

"I've only read a few pages so far and I don't know if I can read more. Knowing Japanese as I do, it is heart-wrenching to learn what really happened to them and their city."

"That's why we are here to talk to you. You have friends in the Japanese community and therefore, have compassion for them. They trust you more than most round eyes."

"Please don't call me round eyes. We are all just human beings trying to do our best."

"You just put into words what is at core the most important—our shared humanity," said Dr. Rosen, his dark eyes full of kindness and compassion.

"Okay. Before we start down some philosophical tangent, I want to bring us back to our purpose. Martin, you have lived and worked here for most of your life. You have developed relationships with all sectors of our community. We want you to be a candidate for mayor because you have the ability to unite us," said Murphy.

"Me?" Martin said. "I would have to think about it."

"Well, you can't take too long to ponder because the election is coming up. So far, there is only one candidate, Patrick Fitzgerald. I don't have to tell you he's an Irishman and a tough one at that—one of the black Irish, descendants of Spanish sailors who got moored on the Island. He was fashioned from the worst of both heritages. And from what he is spewing around town, he will be both divisive and destructive."

"I know Patrick. He comes into my restaurant for lunch once in a while. He's a real street fighter and will pull no punches to win."

"Glad you are already aware of what we'll be up against," said Dr. Rosen.

"You're right. He would be no good for the town or for anybody who lives here," said Martin.

"Then does that mean you're in?" said Dr. MacKenzie.

"I still need to think it over and talk with my family about it. When do you need an answer?"

"By Wednesday," said Dr. Rosen. "I will come by your restaurant after lunchtime."

When the men left, Martin went to his liquor cabinet, poured a glass of sljivovica, and sank into his armchair. His thoughts had been running wild but the sljivovica helped to clarify them. *Maybe this is what everything in my life has been leading up to, what I have been preparing for. Perhaps, God is singling me out for this task. If so, I will have the right power behind me to succeed.*

That night at dinner, Clara and her family as well as Frankie and Ivana, who was now with child, joined them. Marty and Tom Paul had left for college, both choosing to follow Marko to Stanford, which was now becoming known as the Harvard of the West. After dinner, Martin asked Frankie and Peter to join him in the den. Once the door was closed and everyone had a glass of sljivovica in their hand, Martin broached the subject of the election, more specifically, his candidacy. "What would you think if I ran for mayor?" He saw his audience had been made speechless by the question, so he waited a minute for someone to recover.

"I guess I should speak first," said Frankie. "But before I offer an opinion, I would like to know what brought you to this idea?"

"Three prominent men from town were here earlier today and approached me with the proposition. They want someone in the mayor's seat who can unite the town. They thought I might be the person to do it."

"You certainly could," said Peter. "And you would be much better than that other guy, Fitzgerald."

"I think you realize these men are right when they say we need to unite. The war is over but the wounds are lingering. If we don't apply the right medicine, they'll continue to fester and infect us. That won't be good for anybody. Dr. MacKenzie is especially concerned about the children, as we should all be. We don't want them growing up in an atmosphere of hate, suspicion, and resentment."

"You would be the person who could unite the town if anyone could," said Frankie. "Have you spoken to Ma about it yet?"

"Not yet. I wanted to have a decision before I did. If my decision was no, then I wouldn't have to risk her opinion."

"You never know. She might just fancy the thought of being the mayor's wife. It would give her life a new focus."

That evening after his children left, Martin stayed up reading the Hiroshima article. Not only did it sicken him but he felt tears welling up ready to spill down his cheeks. The Japanese have been through enough. Now we have to reach out in friendship.

When Wednesday arrived, Martin was waiting for Dr. Rosen with a pot of coffee and cookies on the table. "I read all the way through the Hiroshima article," he said. "I don't ever think I'll be able to get those tragic mental images out of my head."

"I certainly hope no one does. While that bomb ended the war and saved thousands of American lives, we humans should never again perpetrate such horror on our world."

"I'm glad you came across this article. People in this town especially need to read it."

"I didn't just come across it. I'm a subscriber to *The New Yorker*. Many years ago when I was a young medical student I did an internship in New York City at Mount Sinai hospital. The magazine was always laying around on a table in our lounge. That's how I got exposed to it and became a life-long reader."

Martin took a sip of coffee. "Well, your team and the article gave me a lot to think about these past few days, and I have decided to accept your confidence in me to run for mayor."

"That is the best news I've heard in a long time. And I know Mayor Simpson will be pleased when he learns of it. He's one of your fans and will be behind you all the way."

Then how can I lose?

CHAPTER 78

The first person Martin wanted to tell about his decision to run was Ken. He found him, as usual, in the farm office sipping green tea. He looked up with a smile when he saw Martin enter. "Please sit down and make yourself comfortable. I will get you a cup of tea."

Once they were settled, Martin began, "I have been asked to run for mayor and wanted your thoughts on my candidacy."

"Of all the people I can think of, you would be the best for the job. You have lived here a long time and know so many people. Your roots run deep—a sign that you have learned wisdom from longevity."

"Thank you for your kind words. I would like to get the support of the Japanese community who I hope to represent well so they can reestablish themselves and flourish here. Do you think there would be an opportunity to speak with your group?"

"Certainly. I will arrange something. But your timing is very auspicious. We just heard from a leader of the Japanese American Citizens League and how important it is to become politically active. He instructed those of us who are eligible to register to vote and then make the effort to cast a ballot on Election Day. He said that is one way to wield power in this country."

"He is right about that. When you don't participate in the political process you have no voice, no power."

"So, I will arrange a time for you to speak to us soon."

"Thank you. I also wanted to mention an article I read about Hiroshima."

"If it is the one in *The New Yorker,* that has been circulated around to us but it has been difficult to read it since it is so personal to many of us. So many people killed and injured in the most horrific ways. The land destroyed. They say it will take seventy-five years until plants will grow there again. We Japanese live so close to nature that when nature is harmed, we feel the pain."

"I noticed that one of the people in the article has the last name of Nakamura just like you."

"Yes, she is a cousin to me of some sort. While my parents immigrated here, hers stayed behind. And look at the difference in our fates. Even though we were interred and many have lost everything, we are still whole and the land is fertile. We have an opportunity to start again. But I have been really lucky because you took such good care of my farm that I had an immediate livelihood to rely on when I got back. For that, I will be eternally grateful."

"It was the least I could do. Hector said it best. It was one way to right an injustice or words to that effect."

Hector was waiting for Martin when he left the farm office. "I hear you plan to run for mayor."

Word certainly goes around town quickly. Or maybe Hector had his ear to the ground. "Yes, I have been asked to be a candidate by a committee of prominent citizens and have accepted the challenge."

"I think you would make a very good mayor. You certainly have a good understanding of everything that goes on around here. I would like to help you win."

Martin was taken aback by Hector's offer. "Of course, I appreciate any help I can get. Do you have something specific in mind?"

"I would like to introduce you to my community of Mexicans. That would be a start."

"Certainly, I would like to meet your friends and relatives but if they are not allowed to vote, they cannot help me win."

"They can vote. They just need to get the paperwork done."

"Are you aware only citizens can vote?"

"Certainly. Do you think we are all wetbacks here? Many of us were anchor babies before the government even coined the term."

"So, you are a citizen?"

"That's right. And also a citizen of Mexico. I have what is called dual citizenship."

No wonder he can go back and forth across the border so easily. "That being the case, I would be very grateful to meet members of your community. But until then, please focus on paperwork."

"This Sunday after the Spanish evening Mass, will be a good time. Many of them will be there."

"Do they speak English? Because I don't speak Spanish." *Although I am learning since Juan and Carlos are not dual lingo.*

"It will not be a problem because I will be there and can translate." Martin wondered how he would know if the translation was correct. He did not yet know whether Hector could be trusted.

CHAPTER 79

Martin easily won the election, even though his opponent cited voter fraud. Fitzgerald's poll watchers had reported that an unexpected number of Japanese and Mexicans had shown up at the polls to cast their vote, most arriving near the end of the day when it would be too late to challenge them in person. So, Martin took office Wednesday, November 6 under a cloud of suspicion.

The nursery rhyme came back to him—"Wednesday's child is full of woe"—that's how he felt about the task before him. But then he remembered he was elected on Tuesday—"a child full of grace"—and he reminded himself that God was with him—why else would he have put these nursery rhyme thoughts in his mind?

The first group Martin met with was what he referred to as his tripartite commission—Dr. Rosen, Dr. MacKenzie, and Mr. Murphy. He felt this brain trust would know best how to approach his term in office.

"As I told you when we first met, I think you need to unite the community. That has to be the first priority. Everything will fall in place from there," said Dr. Rosen.

"You are going to have to direct a public relations campaign. To do that, it often helps to have a slogan to rally around," said Dr. MacKenzie. Martin nodded, trying to absorb his language.

"Do you have a suggestion?" Mr. Murphy asked.

"I have been playing around with some words. Diversity and unity need to be incorporated into the slogan," said Dr. MacKenzie. "Maybe something like 'Diversity is good; unity is better.'"

"That doesn't quite work for me," said Dr. Rosen. "What about 'strength in diversity'?"

"And to follow that," said Mr. Murphy, "'unity in cooperation.'"

Martin mulled the slogan over in his mind. *Strength in diversity. Unity in Cooperation.* "I like it. It is simple yet powerful."

"I have often found in speaking to my patients that the simpler I speak, the better they understand, and the more likely they are to take action to get the desired results."

"So, what you are saying is that you have proven these words already," said Martin.

"In a manner of speaking, yes."

"So now that we have a slogan, we need to put a campaign together," said Mr. Murphy. "And I know just the person to do it."

"Who is that, may I ask?" said Dr. MacKenzie.

"My wife, of course. She was in advertising when I met her. She worked for one of the biggest firms in San Francisco—J. Walter Thompson."

"Well then, she's hired," said Dr. MacKenzie. "Let's bring her in for a meeting."

"Just give me a little time. I may have to apply a little pressure."

If he applies it in the right place, there should be no problem convincing her. Martin chuckled to himself.

Mrs. Murphy eagerly accepted the opportunity to create a public relations plan for the town. After years of drudgery raising children and doing housework, she was ready to do almost anything that would offer her an escape. But she knew it would take time for the slogan to work its way into the minds and hearts of the townsfolk. The approach required subtlety and finesse. By choosing opportunities strategically, the battle for the hearts and minds would be won.

Meantime, Martin knew that the most important thing the returning Japanese community needed was work—a way to earn a livelihood. The Bracero program was still in effect and would be extended until 1964. But labor was always a concern to farmers who needed to get crops harvested at the right time and in the right way. Martin made a point of talking with farmers, individually at first, to explain the importance of getting people back to work. Although he met with some resistance, most had had a great respect for the Japanese before the war and the work ethic they embraced. Once he had made most of the rounds of individual farmers, he reached out to some of the farm groups so he could make a more formal presentation. By that time, many of them would have heard, seen, or read about the new town slogan. God created the world with words. Even Christ is called the Word made flesh. There is a power in words—a power to create, a power to turn dreams into reality.

The letter Dr. Rosen had written to the editor about the Hiroshima article had gotten a lot of attention and had begun to turn whatever hate had existed for the Japanese into compassion. When townsfolk learned that Japanese living in Watsonville, such as Ken Nakamura, had relatives who had experienced the atomic bomb, they were touched even more deeply because the Japanese held little resentment. Most people in Hiroshima blamed the bombing on the war, something that was not unexpected even though the impact of *Little Boy* was not even imaginable in their worst nightmares. But while nightmares were soon over upon awakening, the effects of the atom bomb would be visible for decades, some people forever condemned to live with its after-effects.

In the spring, Ken burst into the restaurant full of joy. "A miracle has occurred," he said. Martin just stared at him, not knowing what he was talking about. "I just got a letter from a relative in Hiroshima. A flower bloomed. It's a miracle. They said it would take seventy-five years for the soil to be fertile again, but a flower has made its appearance in numerous places giving hope to all the survivors."

"That is wonderful…amazing news. What type of flower is it?"

"An oleander, in the color red. This has a lot of symbolism for us. It represents the heart chakra which is love, just as red, too, symbolizes love. But it also helps us grieve and reach peace—to leave the past behind and focus on what is before us. The oleander brought those messages to us and we need to act upon them." When Martin heard Ken words, he knew there was hope for a future in true friendship, especially because within a year after the bombing, Hiroshima dedicated itself to peace.

Chapter 80

The next few years were busy ones for Martin as he tried to juggle the restaurant and grocery store with the duties of mayor. You always have to have one up in the air if you want to juggle. There is no way to have hands on all three at once. So, more and more he was delegating to Hong who was already an expert in grocery store management. And as he paid him well, always giving him annual increases, he had earned his loyalty.

But as the forties drew to a close the world was growing restless again especially in Asia, and war broke out in Korea between the North and South. "Of course," Martin said to Frankie who had stopped by the restaurant, "the big powers are again taking sides."

"Who's on what side?"

"China and the Soviet Union are backing the north in its aggressive move to invade the south. And the US is taking the side of the south. We like to stick up for the underdog."

"Well, I've done my duty. And I'm glad my two sons are too young to go to war. I wouldn't wish that on anybody."

"It seems we can never get along in the world. Once World War II ended, the Cold War began. For a while the Soviets put up a blockade so West Berlin couldn't get goods from the East. Now they're meddling in Korea. And let me tell you, people here in town are so frightened by the prospects of being bombed by the Russians that some of them have built bomb shelters and stocked them with enough goods to last several years."

"Bomb shelters, now that is a new one on me. I'm just going to take my chances."

"Enough about war now. Tell me, how is the apple business going?"

"It couldn't be much better. And we're always learning new methods to improve the crops and yield. Did I tell you I'm thinking of purchasing some land to start my own farm?"

"No you didn't. But I think it is about time to be your own man. You don't want to kowtow to your father-in-law much longer."

"It's actually worked out pretty well for me. Ivana's father is a good guy and quite the teacher. I've learned a lot from him, but I've also added a lot to his knowledge.

That night as soon as Martin walked in the door, the telephone rang. It could be Marty or Tom Paul wanting me to wire them money. The cost of school involved a lot more than tuition. He lifted the receiver and before he could even get out a greeting, the voice at the other end said, "Martin, is that you?"

"It's me all right. Who are you?"

"Stan Dukich. It's been such a long time since we've talked that you don't recognize my voice any longer."

"Exchanging Christmas cards is not enough of a reminder. But I am sure you didn't call at this hour for no reason. I only hope you don't have bad news."

"I hope you will consider it good news. We have a chance to work together again."

"I bet I can guess—the Japanese Peace Conference that San Francisco is hosting in September."

"You certainly have your finger on the pulse of the world. The Fairmont will be playing host to President Truman and his entourage, so you know what that means."

"I certainly do. What kind of a timeframe are we talking about?"

"Truman arrives on September fourth. I think the conference will be over soon after that."

"The last one, as you may recall, took months. What makes you think this one will be any shorter?"

"That's what I've been told. It will only last a few days but during that time we have to put on the dog."

"I have a big problem. Last time I had a couple of Chinese helpers I could really depend on. But they left to start their own restaurant. Now I rely on Mexicans. Even after several years, they still don't speak English well and take their time getting orders out. I'd have to close my restaurant for the week."

"I wouldn't want you to lose a lot of money, but I really need your help. Hopefully, this will be the last conference of this sort until after I retire."

"Retire…is it coming to that?"

"Like you, I'm edging toward seventy, the Biblical four score and ten. And, quite frankly, the general manager is trying to push me out. Surely you understand there are new ways of cooking, fads that are in demand. I'm too steeped in tradition."

"I get the picture and will be there somehow. You can count on me."

"I knew I could. That's why I called. Do you want to come up on Sunday to refresh yourself?"

"That would be a good idea. "

When Lena learned that Martin was going up to San Francisco on Sunday, she invited herself along. "It's been a while since I've been to the city, and it will give me a chance to visit with some friends and relatives… catch up on all the news. Besides, in September it's delightful there."

By the time they got on the road, the fog had lifted and they had a clear view of the Pacific as they drove along the coast. Martin dropped Lena off at the Adriatic Coast Cafe where she was planning to meet Katarina for lunch. Pauli had a corner table ready for her as soon as she walked in and offered her a glass of Prosecco. "It's fresh and fruity as well as perfectly balanced." Lena was thrilled with such a gracious offer of hospitality.

"You have learned so well, Pauli. Your grandfather, Anton, won a lot of faithful customers with his warmth and generous spirit." Pauli smiled in appreciation of the compliment. And before he could reply, Katarina walked in, pecked Lena and Pauli on the cheek, and took a seat.

Meanwhile, Martin headed to the kitchen in the Fairmont where Stan stood ready to greet him. "As you will notice, we have replaced all our appliances. During the war years we tried to make do, but since then money has been good and manufacturers have created ovens, stoves, and refrigerators that were once only a dream. Come. I'll show you."

Martin was impressed. He hadn't replaced anything at the Dalmatian Coast Cafe since he went into business. Now he realized he was behind the times. Although in a town like Watsonville, there wasn't much pressure from competition so he was in no hurry to spend the money. There was something in the word *mañana*...why do today what you can put off into the future...a future that may never come.

"Martin, I just got the word that Truman will be holding a big luncheon on September fourth, the day he arrives. So, I will probably need you up here on Sunday so we can prep."

"You are giving me another opportunity to witness history in the making. I'll do whatever you need."

When Martin got home, he realized he had only a few weeks to figure out a solution to his problem. Of course, the easy one would be to close the restaurant. But not only would he lose business and make no money but he might also lose his helpers since he couldn't afford to pay them to take a siesta. The other solution would be more difficult—find someone to run the restaurant while he was gone. Here he had only one choice—Liu and Chao.

Sunday after church, he took Lena to the Lotus Blossom Cafe for a dim sum brunch, which she had never had before. Liu and Chao were keeping the restaurant open on Sundays since they could make the most of hungry customers while the other restaurants took a break. Instead, they closed on Mondays, which were generally slow in the restaurant business.

Liu waved to the pair from the kitchen while Chao showed them to a table. "Dim sum is the thing to order," he said.

"That's what we came to have. Bring us the best assortment you offer."

After brunch, Martin and Lena lingered over their green tea, waiting for the other patrons to depart. Once they were the last table, both Liu and Chao sat down to join them. "It is an honor to have served you today. But my intuition tells me you are here for more than lunch," said Liu.

"You seem to be able to read the tea leaves," Martin said. "I need to ask a favor."

"So ask, we're listening."

"As you may know from your Chinese network, San Francisco is going to host the Japanese Peace Conference in early September. I have again been asked by my friend Stan to help out at the Fairmont Hotel, but that would mean closing my restaurant which I cannot afford to do. Would you be able to help me out?"

"Of course, Monday is no problem since we are closed but the other days…wait…I have an idea. Please excuse Chao and I while we discuss it privately first."

Martin wondered why he could not just say his idea out loud, but he wasn't going to question Liu's ways—he'd known Chinese long enough to realize they had a different approach to life.

When Liu and Chao returned to the table, Liu said, "We have come to a solution. Let's do a swap. I will cook for you and one of your helpers will wait tables for us. How does that sound?"

"It's a great idea. Now I just need to convince Juan or Carlos to make the exchange."

"Tell them that order taking is much easier in our restaurant. We just use numbers. Language will not be a barrier."

"That should convince them. Thank you."

Chapter 81

Saturday night was slow in the Dalmatian Coast Cafe, so Martin was able to get home early and get on the road at the crack of dawn the next day. As he drove through San Francisco, he already saw signs of life as taxi cabs prowled about looking for fares. Stan was waiting for Martin in the kitchen when he arrived. "Glad you got here early. That will give us a head start."

"Anything going on yet with the conference? I noticed the city has already come alive."

"Well, as usual there are already some issues."

"Of course, it wouldn't be politics if there weren't any."

"I heard the Yugoslavians declined the invitation."

"Oh no. I was looking forward to meeting some of them. What was their reason?"

"I don't know but I suspect it's because Russia is not happy with the treaty."

"Now I understand. They don't want to be caught between a rock and a hard place."

"You're probably right about that. Then China wasn't invited because they didn't know which government should receive the invitation."

"That's absurd. They were one of the Big Four during the war. What about the Koreans?"

"I heard they had to uninvite South Korea since it's got a war on with the North."

"This world is something else. I thought I was getting away from all the politics when I left the old country. But there seems to be even more here and on a much bigger scale."

"Well, the United States is the leader of the world, so it plays on a very big stage. You have to expect the stakes to be big as well—a lot bigger than in Croatia, I mean Yugoslavia. I believe that's what we're calling it again."

"Well, even in my little town, we have our share of politics. I am hoping that this peace treaty will help settle things between the races there. The Japanese are still not back to where they were before the war. As mayor, it really wears on me, and I also have some good Japanese friends whose pain I can feel."

"Enough politics for now. I'm sure we'll be saturated with it before the week is over. Let's go into my office and start working on a menu for Truman's luncheon."

Martin and Stan walked through the kitchen to the small office at the back. After they were both seated, Martin said, "As I recall from last time, President Truman has simple tastes and favors beef."

"You have a good memory." "Not so good. Do you have a copy of the last menu to refresh me?"

When they were done putting the menu together along with the grocery list, Stan said, "So, how is everything with the family?"

"Lena is well. She keeps occupied with the grandchildren—Clara's four and Frankie's two boys. And both Marty and Tom Paul graduated from Stanford with engineering degrees."

"Oh, yeah? I'm impressed. What are they doing now?"

"Marty is at Mare Island learning how to design ships. He has the sea in his blood and also shipbuilding. Did I ever tell you relatives back home are shipbuilders?"

"No, you didn't. But it certainly helps. So, what about Tom Paul?

"He loves flying, so once he earned his diploma, he went right to the airlines to apply for a pilot's job. Pan Am hired him and he's based here in San Francisco."

"So, your family is migrating back to the city.

"Not all. Don't forget both Clara and Frankie still live in Watsonville and, being in the apple business, they are tied to the land."

"Tied to the land. That's how I feel sometimes when I think about Yugoslavia. Do you ever feel that way?"

"Much more so now that I'm older. When I was young I was too busy to think about it."

"Would you ever want to go back, even just for a visit?"

"I don't know. That might be tempting fate."

The Japanese Peace Treaty was signed by most countries in attendance on September 8. Russia refused to sign and its satellites—Czechoslovakia and Poland—followed suit. "Now, it has been confirmed why Yugoslavia didn't attend," said Martin.

"You were certainly right when you said they didn't want to be sandwiched between the two big powers. It will be interesting, though, to see Tito's next move."

"Tito was probably weaned on chess. He won't be able to outmaneuver the Russians at that game but the Americans are not chess players. I'm not sure what game they play, but they're certainly good at it."

"When you hold all the cards or chess pieces, there's no reason to play. You can just forge ahead doing what the hell you want."

"I guess that's the kind of country we're living in now. We don't need to wonder what move our poor pawn of a country is going to make and if it will be captured by the tricky rook."

"That's right. America is so big it can name the game and choose the rules."

CHAPTER 82

When Martin got back to Watsonville, he stopped by the restaurant since it was still open. He was unprepared for what he found. Liu was in the foulest mood he'd ever seen him in and he and Carlos were not speaking. "What's wrong?"

"If you can guess, I don't need to tell you," Liu said. "I should have created a new menu for the week with numbers."

"I understand. Communication has been a problem, has it?"

"If someone orders sand dabs, it comes to the kitchen as seafood risotto. If they order seafood risotto, the order reads bakalar en brodo. If…

"Okay, okay. I get the picture. The week did not go well in other words. Did it go any better at the Lotus Blossom Cafe?"

"Of course it did. Order by number works."

"Maybe I'll have to take a cue from you and redo my menu the Chinese way."

"You will thank me for the idea."

Martin glanced over in Carlos's direction. He had a smile on his face as he greeted customers and moved in an easygoing way. When he put in the order, he waited for Liu to look up and then gave him a smile as well. Liu appeared soothed. Peace does begin with a smile, he thought, just as Mother Theresa always says.

Martin made a visit to Ken to tell him that the Japanese Peace Treaty had been signed, officially ending the war. "I thought the day would never come," he said. "It's been six years since the atom bombs were dropped on Hiroshima and Nagasaki."

"Well, when you have most of the world's countries involved in the settlement, it takes time."

"And what about Russia? Did she sign the treaty?"

"Not yet." Ken's face dropped as a look of concern washed over it. "Don't worry," said Martin. "No one wants another war." Ken just nodded.

"I had a letter from my cousin in Hiroshima. They are moving ahead to build a peace park in the center of town where the bomb struck. And do you want to know about a real coincidence?"

"Yes, tell me."

"Remember the artist I told you about who came to Poston to start an arts program for us. His name is Isamu Noguchi and he is a sculptor. He is creating two bridges. The West Peace Bridge will have a sunset as symbol of the past. The Peace Bridge will have a sunrise as symbol of the future."

"That is amazing. Through him and Poston, you and the entire Japanese community will be connected to the peace park."

"That is what we have been thinking, too. We Japanese believe in the connection to our family and ancestors."

CHAPTER 83

The year 1953 was momentous. Dwight Eisenhower was inaugurated president, the Korean War ended, and a European, Edmund Hillary, and an Asian, Tenzing Norgay, reached the top of the world—the summit of Mt. Everest. How symbolic. Even more symbolic were Hillary's words. "Life's a bit like mountaineering—never look down." Martin thought that was a lot like what the Bible cautioned about looking back and moving ahead. It's what the Peace Bridge reflects in its design—the setting sun is already behind you, keep an eye on the rising sun.

Ken came into the restaurant on Christmas Eve to wish Martin a Merry Christmas. "Guess what? My cousin invited me to the Peace Park Memorial Ceremony which takes place on August 6, the anniversary of the bombing. They have been holding it every year since 1947, but now that the Peace Park is complete, the event will be very special."

"I hope you're going. It should not be missed."

"Unfortunately, I do not have the money for airfare. My cousin will offer hospitality but I won't be able to get there."

"Just hang on a minute. You will be going. We just need to figure out a way to pay for a ticket."

"Do you really think there is a way to accomplish this?"

"There is always a way." Martin began to brainstorm. Donors could be approached. A fundraiser could be held. And Tom Paul...he has flight benefits...maybe he could get a free ticket. "My mind is already working overtime, trying to come up with a solution. And I think I have a few good ones. Start packing your bags."

"Oh, Martin, this would mean so much to me and my family."

"You will be representing our town. It will give us something to rally around."

Martin knew Tom Paul had the day off so rather than wait to talk to him at home on Christmas Eve, he called him during his break in customers.

"Pa, is everything all right? You usually don't call this time of day. If you're making sure I'm coming tonight, I wouldn't miss out on one of our Christmas Eve dinners for anything."

"Yes, all is fine but something important has come up and I need your help."

"I'm listening…shoot."

"Do you remember my friend Ken Nakamura?"

"Vaguely."

"Well, it doesn't matter if you do or not. He came by a few minutes ago and told me his cousin in Hiroshima invited him to the Peace Park ceremony."

"That's good. But why are you calling me about this?"

"He can't afford the airfare. I thought you might be able to help."

"You know my benefits are only for myself and close family members."

"Correct. But, perhaps, you could approach the right person at the airline and tell them Ken's story. Remember, it would be an opportunity for some very good publicity. Businesses are always looking for a way to promote themselves."

"You're right. In fact, I know a gal who works in the public relations department. She might have some good ideas or at least be able to point me in the right direction."

"Now you're thinking."

That evening when he got home, Martin made a few more calls. He had not wanted to mention to Tom Paul his other thoughts for obtaining a ticket. If he did, he knew he would risk Tom Paul procrastinating. There wasn't much time so he had to act fast. "Dr. Rosen, I'm sorry to call so late but I have an important matter to discuss with you."

"I am always glad to hear from our mayor. What is it about?" Then Martin went onto explain Ken's situation. There was a long pause on Dr. Rosen's end before he spoke again. Martin was worried that he had made a mistake in contacting him. "You probably know that I am a Jew. The Jews suffered horrible atrocities during the war. We have tried to turn our suffering into compassion even for our enemies." Martin didn't respond; he just listened. "The Japanese living in Hiroshima also suffered terrible atrocities. Most of those injured were civilians, even women and children. I would consider it a privilege to help Ken take part in the Peace Park ceremony. By doing so, it would connect my heart to their suffering."

Martin was momentarily speechless. "Thank you for your help."

"Not only will I write a check, but I will reach out to my friends with deep pockets and ask them to help, too. We will get the money for Ken. You have my word."

When Martin hung up the phone, he leaned against the wall for a few moments reflecting on his conversation. Certainly, he had struck a note in Dr. Rosen…one that played on his heartstrings. Almost anything is possible when people are moved to compassion.

CHAPTER 84

At the beginning of August, Martin drove Ken and his wife, Ami, to San Francisco International Airport to meet Tom Paul for the flight. Martin had collected so much money that both Nakamuras were able to afford the trip. The evening before, the Japanese community had a special bon voyage party for the Nakamuras at the Buddhist Temple. Everyone wanted to participate in the occasion as much as possible. When people learned they could put messages in lanterns that they would send down the river to the dead, everyone wanted to write one. But since only two people were going, only two messages were selected. However, everyone had an opportunity to make a paper crane for the children's monument, dedicated to children who had been victims of the bomb.

Both Ken and Ami were dressed in western clothes for traveling but they had packed their kimonos for the ceremony and other traditions they expected to take part in. It was going to be a long journey but Ken and Ami were looking forward to it. They planned to fly to Toyo and spend a few days taking in the sights in the capital city—the Imperial Palace, Senso-ji Temple, and Kabuki-za Theatre in the Ginza district. From there, they would take a train to Hiroshima.

When the flight was announced, Martin took out something from his pocket and said, "This is a statue of the patron saint of Dubrovnik, St Blaise. He is a healer not only of man but plants and minerals, too. It is my prayer that he can help Hiroshima heal."

At first Ken did not know what to say. "I have not heard of this saint before but I thank you for your thoughtfulness. What should I do with him?"

"Find a little niche. It could be a hollow in a tree or some obscure corner in a building. For us, he is a powerful saint, our heavenly protector. He warned the city of a Venetian attack many centuries ago but he is also a healer we look to whenever illness presents itself."

"This is certainly a very special gift. In some ways it will connect your ancestral homeland with mine. A powerful force." That's exactly what Martin had been thinking as well.

The Nakamuras waited for their turn in line patiently until they were given the go ahead by the attendant to move through the loading ramp into the plane. Martin waited by the big picture windows until the Pan Am plane with the Nakamuras aboard took off under Tom Paul's command. He had never been on a plane so he had no idea what the feeling of flight was like but it seemed awesome, almost magical the way the jet lifted so effortlessly into the sky. Before departing, he quietly said a prayer for travel mercies.

Two weeks later, Martin was at the gate waiting to greet the Nakamuras on their return. He was surprised to see them wearing kimonos. "Please excuse us for not wearing western attire but we had no time to change before we boarded our return flight."

"No need to apologize. It's good for people to see how proud you are of your heritage. The world needs to move forward and you are helping us do just that. So, how was the trip?"

"It was so amazing. I met cousins I didn't even know I had. But it was sad, too, to hear how they suffered during the war, especially after the atom bomb struck. Some of my relatives will never be the same. The skin on their bodies melted from the heat of the bomb. And one woman lost a side of her face. It is not easy to go on with life like that, but she is doing it, and so is everyone else there. To Ami and me, they were an inspiration."

"I cried when I saw the monument dedicated to the children victims with a statue of Sedako Saski on top holding a crane," said Ami.

"What is the meaning of the crane?" asked Martin.

"The story goes that Sedako, who was dying of leukemia, wanted to make a thousand paper cranes so her wish to live would be granted. But she fell short and her family and friends finished making them for her with the wish changed to peace. That is why people all over the world still make paper cranes…for peace," Ami said.

"You are leaving out the words on the plaque," said Ken. "It reads: 'This is our city. This is our prayer. Peace on Earth.'"

"That is such a beautiful sentiment," said Martin. "Let's sit down and talk while we wait."

"During the ceremony, at the exact time the bomb struck on August 6 at 8:15 a.m., temple bells rang out and a moment of silence was observed. After the peace declaration, doves were released into the air to fly over the Peace Park and the city of Hiroshima."

"Did you get to walk on the bridges Noguchi created?"

"Yes, and they were beautiful. They lead to the Fountain of Prayer dedicated to those who died crying 'water, water.'"

"And when we came back to the river at night to release the lanterns bearing wishes for peace, we were awestruck by the sight of so many lanterns, as if on parade, passing the Atomic Bomb Dome for review," said Ami.

Immediately, the image of a thousand Japanese carrying lanterns in the town parade so many years ago came to Martin's mind. No one who witnessed it ever forgot that sight. Now he wondered, if instead of a blessing, it had been an omen.

"And another thing we learned," said Ami, "Hiroshima has a sister city in Belgium…Ypres. Unfortunately, they are sisters in sorrow. They both share the legacy of chemical weapons in war. Ypres has a ceremony every evening to honor those who died."

"Oh, I almost forgot about the statue of your saint," said Ken. "I found a niche just as you recommended in one of the Chinese Umbrella trees that had been badly injured by the bomb, so much so that everyone thought they were dead. But they had a big surprise in store the following spring when they began to bud as if to say *life overcomes death.*"

"That makes me very happy. Those trees are a living reminder of what our faith also teaches...death will be triumphed by life."

CHAPTER 85

In 1960 a Catholic was on the ballot for President. Many thought a Catholic couldn't get elected to the highest office in the land and others feared the influence the Pope would have on him. Of course, John F. Kennedy was partly formed by his faith. And as Martin and Lena discussed the campaign, they were overjoyed they had a candidate who shared their deep belief in God and the power of prayer. When Kennedy won the election, Martin thought the future had finally arrived and he looked forward to it.

But not long after Kennedy took office, Lena developed a cough that led to a lung infection. "Are you wearing St. Blaise's medal?"

"No, I stopped wearing it years ago after I was clear of tuberculosis. But I think I put it in my jewelry box for safe keeping."

"Well, let's find it and put it on. It's you who needs safe keeping."

When Lena returned from the office visit to Dr. Rosen, the son who had taken over his father's practice, she had bad news. "Martin, let's go into the living room. I want to tell you what the doctor said."

After they had taken seats on the sofa so they could sit side by side, Lena took Martin's hand in hers, "He said the tuberculosis has returned. Remember, years ago his father told us that it could and now it has."

Martin put his arm around Lena and hugged her close. "You beat it once, you can beat it again. You need fresh air and good nutrition."

"I don't think it will be that easy this time. I was younger and stronger then. Dr. Rosen said the disease is already quite advanced."

"What about the sanatorium near San Francisco? Ari something?

"Arequipa. It closed a few years ago."

"So what does the doctor recommend you do?"

"There's a drug called streptomycin that's been effective for some people."

"And if it's not?"

"They are also experimenting with a combination of drugs to keep the patient from developing drug resistance."

"So, what is the plan?"

"Dr. Rosen is ordering the medication. Then I have to go to his office for an injection."

Martin and Lena sat on the sofa for quite awhile and hugged each other. Silence is better than words sometimes. They were embraced by the stillness as if God held them in his hands.

Lena went to get injections on a regular basis but she only seemed to be getting weaker. They always knew that the tuberculosis could return and now it had made its appearance just when they were ready to reap life's rewards. They had been through so much together—children, world wars, the depression, business challenges and worries. Finally, it seemed that life had been set on an even keel—that the seas promised smooth sailing ahead. But that was not to be.

Lena took a turn for the worst in August and by September she was gone, Martin's heart leaving with her. They had reached their 50th wedding anniversary which they celebrated the previous year with a family party and weekend at the Fairmont Hotel in San Francisco. But even as they celebrated, they both knew the end was drawing near. Four score and ten. That's what the Bible says. And they both had exceeded it. They had been blessed and the blessing would continue throughout the generations to follow. That's how life unfolds. Death is not something to fear…our faith tells us it is our reward at the end of a life well lived.

The Mass took place at St. Patrick's Church where they had belonged as long as anyone could remember and where their children were baptized, confirmed and married. The monsignor presided and since he knew Lena personally he had some very meaningful words that were a comfort to Martin. Frankie read the eulogy on behalf of the family. And afterwards, a friend of the family sang "Ave Maria"—Lena's favorite song, a musical version of the Hail Mary prayer.

Their three sons and three grandsons served as pallbearers. The hearse led the way to Our Lady Help of Christian Church on the outskirts of town where the cemetery was located. Martin and Lena had purchased a vault years ago and that's where her mother and father were already entombed. There was a short graveside service before the casket was slid into its place. The plaque contained both their names but only Lena's side had been completed with her date of death. Martin thought how odd it felt to be looking at his own marker as if trying to guess the date that would be written there. It's written somewhere in that big book of His. *But I hope it is still a ways off. There's still more I want to do in life.*

Martin went back to work at the restaurant the following week. His old friend, Michael, stopped in for a late lunch and stayed on to visit, hoping to cheer up Martin. But, of course, politics was never far from their thoughts. "What did you think of that wall going up in Berlin last month?"

"Stalin may have been an ally of sorts during the war but he has turned out to be a tyrant with his people and anyone else he has the ability to control."

"I hope this isn't a precursor of things to come in Yugoslavia."

"Tito was smart not to align himself with Russia, even though he's become a dictator himself."

"The people will never be better off until they have the ability to rule themselves." "Freedom…that's what it's all about. Speaking of freedom, I am now free to do what I want."

"Oh, and what is it you want to do?"

"My sister has invited me to visit and I'm thinking about going. Tom Paul can probably get me a cheap ticket."

"If you're going to go, best go soon before anything else happens."

"I couldn't possibly go until after the holidays. Clara would never forgive me if I missed Christmas with the family."

"It's good to have something to look forward to. I once heard monsignor say that a person needs three things in life—something to do, someone to love, and something to look forward to."

"Ken told me a similar thing. Ikigai—a purpose in life."

"As long as you have a purpose, your life will be satisfying. And as long as I've known you, you've had a purpose…some sort of goal. Now in your twilight years, it should be no different. God's gift of length of years should not be squandered. Wisdom should never be wasted."

CHAPTER 86

On December 10, the Croatian community gathered to celebrate their countryman, Ivo Andric, winner of the Nobel Prize in Literature. Even though Andric considered himself Serbian, he was born to Croatian parents so there was no doubt that he was one of theirs. Michael spotted Martin and made a beeline for him. "Can you believe this? Croatians are now on the map. I thought they'd choose a writer like John Steinbeck instead. Certainly our neighbors were hoping for that, but the Nobel Prize Committee in its wisdom chose Andric."

"*Grapes of Wrath* was a masterful work with an ending that left me utterly stunned. But Andric wrote some interesting books about Bosnia and the various ethnic groups there—Serbs, Croatians and Muslims. You are right about the committee having wisdom; those Swedes promote world peace and understanding by choosing writers whose works speak to the human condition and highlight cultures that are often overlooked."

"He was a diplomat so he really understood things. Once he said, 'If people would know how little brain is ruling the world, they would die of fear.'"

"That's a true Croatian speaking. You don't have to be a diplomat to figure that out, but only watch what's going on and share your findings with others."

"The Croatian pastime."

"You know, I read that Andric wrote a poem in his youth promoting Croatian-Serb unity. He often talked about bridges. About how differences amongst people could be bridged to better understanding. But he also believed that bridges, and here I can't help but think of the Golden Gate, are more valuable than any other structure man builds because they belong to everyone. His book, *The Bridge on the Drina*, is a living example in that it bridges the east to the west. He believed that bridges are more durable than buildings and only serve what is good."

"That's his diplomatic voice talking."

"Yes, I'm sure he also meant that when bridges are built between people, they stand up better than any policies, treaties, or anything else heads of state can conjure up."

"All I can say is, when I read his books, I'm glad I left Yugoslavia when I did."

"But we didn't escape everything what with two World Wars to contend with and the Depression. And let's not forget the earthquake that quashed all my dreams."

"Martin, you are made of a tough breed, one who perseveres until the end with the resilience to create new dreams until they're realized."

"Ah, the program is starting. I don't know what they can say that we haven't already spoken of between us."

"Only that it's one thing to read a book and quite another to live the story."

"And the families we left behind are still living that story but through history and blood we are connected to it."

"Let's sit down and listen. It looks like bottles of sljivovica are open and waiting."

CHAPTER 87

Sometimes Martin liked to listen to the radio when he prepped before opening his restaurant. As he was at his chopping block, he heard the announcer say that Tony Bennett was debuting a new song. Martin liked Tony Bennett so he turned an ear to listen.

When Tony sang out the opening line, Martin thought that's what happened to me after the earthquake; *I left my heart in San Francisco.* And again, remembering his engagement to Lena, he had lost his heart twice in that city. But it you changed the lyrics from cable cars to ramparts climb halfway to the stars, the song could be about Dubrovnik instead. That's when he realized he had really left his heart in the Old Town, a walled city that had stood for centuries and would probably remain until the end of time. He must go back before his own time runs out. Nowhere is the sun more golden than on the Adriatic Sea.

So, he picked up the phone to call Tom Paul. "I'm going to take you up on your offer to fly me to Dubrovnik."

The family said their good byes to Martin on Palm Sunday, toasting him and wishing him bon voyage. The next day Martin paid visits to a few friends, Michael in particular, to say so long. He stopped in his restaurant to see the Croatian he had elevated from sous chef to chef and give him some last minute advice. But Martin could see that Ivan already knew what to do and would take good care of the restaurant until he got back.

Then he could decide whether he wanted to keep it or sell it. But right now was not a time to make that type of business decision.

So, Martin had tied up all the loose ends he needed to before leaving for Croatia. He planned to be gone a few months and certainly be home for Christmas. But you never really know how things will work out… how fate intervenes.

Chapter 88

On Tuesday, Frankie drove Martin to the airport where they were met by Tom Paul, looking every bit the pilot in his captain's uniform. He was an impressive sight. A sight that gave Martin confidence he knew how to fly the plane and would get him to Rome in one piece. Since Pan Am didn't fly to Dubrovnik, they would use another airline for the last leg of the trip. And not knowing who was at the controls would give Martin peace of mind. With Tom Paul, thoughts always entered his mind about how much of a screw up he had been at times growing up. Even his war record did little to erase those early impressions. An anonymous pilot was like a machine you could trust to always do the right thing.

When it was near boarding time, Tom Paul led Martin onto the plane and guided him to his seat. He introduced him to the stewardesses and asked them to look after him on the flight since this was his maiden voyage by air.

The flight stopped in New York to pick up more passengers but there was no time to get off the plane. Then it flew nonstop to Rome where they would spend Easter. Martin waited for all the passengers to leave before getting out of his seat, per Tom Paul's instructions. It was actually a lot easier for him that way since he didn't have to fight the crowds and could take his time. At his age, he was in no hurry. When he reached the cockpit, Tom Paul was waiting for him. "How was your first flight?"

"Much better than that boat ride I took across the Atlantic years ago. The turbulence we experienced was nothing compared to an ocean's fury. I still can't get over how fast one can travel from one continent to the other these days. When I came to America, I was amazed there were trains."

"You've certainly witnessed a lot of changes in your lifetime."

"You can say that again."

Once they got their luggage they checked into a small hotel near the Vatican and settled down for a nap. When they awoke it was time for dinner. "Let's find a restaurant and check out some sights on the way," said Tom Paul. And he knew exactly where he wanted to go since Rome was a regular stop for him.

After a dinner on the Piazza Navona where Bernini's *Fountain of the Four Rivers* presides, they headed back to their hotel for the night.

CHAPTER 89

On Easter Sunday, they got up early, ate breakfast and headed to St. Peter's Basilica for Mass. The crowd had already begun to assemble but it moved slowly together as if it were a single creature until it got through the doors and disbursed, each person taking his place in a pew, awestruck by the Basilica's grandeur. The Mass was a glorious one with so many celebrants on the altar and so much incense filling the air that the devoted felt transported into a heavenly realm. After Mass was finished, Martin said, "I want to take a look around as long as we're here. I'm interested in seeing more of Bernini's work. That *Fountain of the Four Rivers* captivated me. I can't imagine what he did in here."

"The brochure states that he created the Baldachin, the canopy that sits over the high altar and St. Peter's tomb."

"Let's start heading up front so we can see it." They were taken with the intricacy of the design and marveled at how anyone could have created it out of bronze. "Only God could have inspired that," Martin said. As he stood underneath and looked up, the image of the Holy Spirit met his eye and for a fraction of a second he felt overwhelmed by its power.

"Over to the left above the exit door is one of Bernini's last works entitled, *Monument to Alexander VII.* It depicts the four virtues that the pope practiced: charity, truth, justice and prudence."

Martin looked closely at each element of the sculpture. Death was lurking there, too, with an hourglass marking the sands of time. When he got to Charity holding a baby to her breast, his mind connected the image to the one Steinbeck had depicted at the end of his novel *Grapes of Wrath. I never quite understood the ending until now. And no one was ever quite able to explain it to me.* In Christianity, charity and justice are connected—themes in Steinbeck's novel. And now that odd smile on Rose of Sharon's face made sense—truth—the divine truth that charity is the highest virtue in life. She had reached perfection, become a rose of Sharon. No wonder Steinbeck had given her that unusual name. Martin was momentarily stunned. The divine truth had been revealed to him as well and it did not come in a whisper, more like a wallop. *Oh, my God.*

CHAPTER 90

Now Martin and Tom Paul were on the last leg of their journey, sitting together as they flew across the Adriatic Sea to Dubrovnik. Martin looked down to glimpse the sea he loved but they were so high up he couldn't get much of an impression. They made a near perfect landing at Cilipi Airport, claimed their luggage, and picked up the rental car. The first thing that struck Martin was the stands of Italian Cypress that grow in the Eastern Mediterranean and are rarely seen elsewhere. Rising high toward the sky, they are a symbol of immortality. And to become immortal, Martin reflected, one needs to become perfect.

The road to old town Dubrovnik was a coastal one set high on cliffs that provided a panoramic view of the Adriatic. "I have to admit, this is the most scenic route I've ever taken between an airport and town."

"And the best one you ever will take, too." The ride into town took little more than half an hour. "The first thing I want to do even before I greet the relatives is to walk the ramparts."

"Alright, I'll drop you off in front of the gate and find a parking space." Martin headed for a bench, nearby the Yugoslavian flag proudly waving its red, white and blue stripes in the wind. In the center, a single red star stood out, a symbol of Communism, the five points representing the five fingers of a worker's hand. He was reminded of what was happening with farmhands in Pajaro Valley through Cesar Chavez's efforts. From what he knew, workers were no better off under Communism but maybe some hope for them lay with Chavez.

When Tom Paul returned, he found Martin sitting in the square nearby the Pile Gate. Then they headed over the drawbridge into the walled city through the centuries old gate. Martin looked up as he entered, "That's St. Blaise still presiding over the city and protecting it." Then they passed through the inner gate that opened to the Stradun, the main pedestrian thoroughfare in the city. From here the town stretches out nearly a thousand feet along the limestone walkway, showcasing historic buildings, shops and monuments.

As soon as they passed through the inner gate, they found stairs leading to the ramparts. But they also found a booth to purchase an entrance ticket. "I can't believe we have to buy a ticket. Even though they're Communist they're taking on some capitalist ways."

Tom Paul offered his arm to his father and they took the steps slowly, resting along the way. The walls are 80 feet high so it took awhile to reach the top. "Let's turn left and head in the direction of the Adriatic." The walk toward the sea didn't take long. "This is where I used to come when I was a young boy to watch for merchant ships. The view hasn't changed a bit. There are some things man can change but some will remain forever as they are. Nature holds the trump card."

"I don't know why you ever left this place. It's so beautiful here."

"Opportunity...a chance to have a better life...to help relatives back home. Yugoslavia was dominated by the Habsburg Regime back them. The people had nothing. Now they've got a dictator and communism. They're not much better off. It's only the charity of relatives that have left and made good that have kept them going."

"It's good that you were able to help your family."

"People from town who come to visit here leave with only the clothes on their back. They leave everything they brought with them for the relatives.

"The brochure says it's a mile and a half around the town on the ramparts. Are you up to it?"

"My sisters' home is only a little further down so let's walk until we get nearby then take the closest stairs. Let me see if I can remember the way to get there. Veronika and Zara are living in my boyhood home. I believe this is where to turn. Again, little has changed."

Finally, they reached their destination and rang the bell. Veronika and Zara had been waiting for them to arrive. When they opened the door, the first thing they did was give Martin and Tom Paul kisses on both cheeks. Martin took one look at them and thought, they have changed. When he left they were young girls with the first blush of womanhood. Now they were old ladies, both plump with gray hair and wrinkled faces. They wore dirndl skirts with puffed sleeve blouses and sturdy black leather shoes, tied with laces. There was nothing fashionable about them and probably never had been.

"Please come in and make yourself at home," Veronika said. When Martin stepped in and took a look around he saw that his boyhood home was much the same--a couple of leather chairs, a sofa with doilies on the arms, a fire in the hearth. "Please sit down and we will have tea and visit. We have so many years to catch up on."

Once everyone had their tea and had taken a selection of baked goods, Martin asked, "How are things in Yugoslavia these days?"

"The war was difficult but with Tito we now have stability, even though there is little money to go around."

"What about the people? Now that you're unified as one country of the South Slavs has that helped relationships?"

"Martin, these differences have been going on for generations and they're likely to continue for many more. In fact, a Serb opened a grocery store nearby. It is the closest one to us. But we prefer to walk further and buy from a Croatian. And Serbs do the same. That's just the way it is," Zara said.

After tea was finished, the women went into the kitchen to prepare dinner. Veronika called out, "We are having a big feast in your honor tonight and the whole family is coming. And tomorrow, if you're up to it, my son will take you out fishing for sardines and anchovies. It will be a full moon so conditions should be perfect."

Martin and Tom Paul glanced at each other. "That's how I got my start with my father," Martin said. "I guess I've come full circle."

Tom Paul was waiting for a chance to check out the town and saw his opportunity. "I'll go get the luggage and be back as soon as I can."

Now Martin was left alone in the living room. He could almost see his father sitting in his favorite chair, a glass of rakija in one hand, a cigarette in the other, his mother sitting nearby on the sofa with her embroidery. The family Bible was still resting in its place of honor on the coffee table, a focal point in the room. Martin stood up to retrieve it. He remembered that every family Bible had a place to record family events such as births, deaths and marriages. It served as a history of a family.

He turned to the middle pages where the entries began going back to his grandparents. When he got to his own family he saw the entries for his parents' births, marriages, children's births and deaths. Now looking at the dates his parents died brought tears to his eyes. They made it through World War II while living in fear and suffering the effects of old age. That day at the port, he had known he would never see them again and his mother knew it, too, her tears ones only an anguished mother can shed. Martin blessed himself as he murmured a prayer for them both.

Then turning the pages, he found the entries for his brothers' and sisters' families as well as his own. *They had not forgotten me.* Even with all the time and space between us, our blood always kept us bound. The image of Bernini's monument of the four virtues suddenly popped into Martin's mind. *Not until charity becomes stronger than blood will the world ever change.*

Author Bio

Barbara Anne King is the author of *The California Immigrant*, the first book in her Monterey Bay series, featuring multicultural stories told from the heart.

Barbara was born and raised in Watsonville, California, set on the magnificent Monterey Bay. After graduating college, armed with a political science degree, she headed east for a job on Capitol Hill. But while she may have left California, it never left her and she remains a *California Girl.*

Now she lives in a New York City suburb with her husband in the place they've called home for over 25 years. After raising three children, she's reinvented herself as an author so she can share her stories with readers wherever she finds them.

www.barbaraanneking.com

author@barbaraanneking.com

Acknowledgments

I would like to thank the following organizations for providing valuable information, either oline or through exhibits, that served the story and helped bring it to life.

Croatian Fraternal Union

D-Day Museum

Densho

Japanese American Citizens League

Naval History and Heritage Command, USS *Nevada*

Noguchi Museum

Santa Cruz JACL Collection, Mas Hashimoto Interviews

Slavonic Mutual Benevolent Society of San Francisco

Smithsonian Exhibit on Japanese Internment

UCSC University Library Regional History Project on Apple Farming in Watsonville, Interview with Ray Travers

Watsonville Public Library, Japanese Histories

Watsonville Memories that Linger, Volumes 1 & 2, Betty Lewis

Yale University Exhibit on Japanese Internment at Beineke Library

Book Club Questions

- Martin was an immigrant. What makes it difficult to be an immigrant? Are there differences between then and now?
- Most of us started as immigrants. What it your family's story?
- Pearl Harbor changed everything for people in the town of Watsonville. It triggered our entrance into the war. Do you think we would have entered otherwise? Or too late? How did things change for other people? People in your own family?
- Do you think it was right to inter Japanese? Do you think people should be judged individually rather than as a group?
- How do you think people should have treated Japanese upon their return?
- Power is mentioned several times in the book. What does it mean to be powerful or powerless? How can an individual in society exert power?
- Martin came from the country with a lot of racial divides. Why do people not get along? Can they ever make peace with each other? How?
- The cover has a picture of the Golden Gate Bridge. How does the theme of bridges fit the story and our own lives?
- What did Martin mean by charity? Do you agree that if charity became stronger than blood the world would find peace?
- What are the themes in the book?
- What are the major takeaways?

Note: Please feel free to contact me if you would like me to participate in your book club discussion and we'll find a way.

37497475R00234

Made in the USA
Middletown, DE
02 March 2019